Lillian E. Dash

ALSO BY SAM TOPEROFF

Jimmy Dean Prepares
Queen of Desire

Lillian & Dash

A Novel

Sam Toperoff

OTHER PRESS
NEW YORK

Original lyrics to "I Don't Stand a Ghost of a Chance with You" (page 327) by Ned Washington and Bing Crosby, music composed by Victor Young, 1932.

Production Editor: Yvonne E. Cárdenas
Text Designer: Jennifer Daddio/Bookmark Design & Media, Inc.
This book was set in 11.25 Goudy Old Style by
Alpha Design & Composition of Pittsfield, NH.

1 3 5 7 9 10 8 6 4 2

Library of Congress Cataloging-in-Publication Data

Toperoff, Sam, 1933–
Lillian & Dash : a novel / Sam Toperoff.
p. cm.
ISBN 978-1-59051-568-6 (trade pbk.) —ISBN 978-1-59051-569-3 (ebook)
1. Hellman, Lillian, 1905-1984—Fiction.   2. Dramatists, American—20th century—Fiction.   3. Hammett, Dashiell, 1894-1961—Fiction.
4. Authors, American—20th century—Fiction.   5. Motion picture industry—Fiction.   6. Blacklisting of entertainers—United States—Fiction.   7. Blacklisting of authors—United States—Fiction.
8. Hollywood (Los Angeles, Calif.)—Fiction.   I. Title.
PS3570.O6L55 2012
813'.54—dc22
2012017137

To Tracy Kidder,

at the beginning and later.

Lillian & Dash

.1.

Meeting

MANY YEARS LATER, here's how Dashiell Hammett re-membered it:

The Brown Derby restaurant, not that second-rate sequel on North Vine, but the original on Wilshire, the Sunday before Thanksgiving, the year of our Lord nineteen hundred and thirty. Darryl F. Zanuck was throwing the party because even after the Crash, Warner Bros. was having a better than good year. Hell, if you were out of work, what better place to hide than in a movie house?

He had just bought the rights to *The Maltese Falcon* and told me he had lots of other interesting scripts he wanted to develop with me. *With* me. He'd think up the stories, I'd de-velop the stories, he'd write the checks. And you wonder why they call the guy a genius? A boy genius at that. He looked about eighteen.

You couldn't name a Warner star who wasn't out that night. Cagney? Right up there next to George Arliss. Eddie

Robinson? Holding forth like a professor between Fay Wray and Myrna Loy. Dolores Costello? Paul Muni? Sidney Blackmer? Lila Lee? Yes, yes, yes, and yes. They were all up there at a long, flowered table with Boy Zanuck and his Missus. Writers, directors, cameras, sound and lighting guys, the entire brave ensemble of acting folk, the musicians, office personnel, invited guests (read as anyone who could attract publicity and some shirkers like me), we were scattered like salt and pepper at tables all around the room.

They put me between Eugene Pallette and Joe E. Brown. I knew them only from their movies but wasn't the least bit surprised by the fact that their screen personas were pretty much who these guys really were, wonderfully flawed and irreverent masks of humanity. Naturally, all they talked about at first was themselves. That was to be expected. When they finally—at long last—got around to asking me what I'd been in, I told them I hadn't been in anything. A writer, Pallette guessed. Brown asked was I a real writer or did I only write for the movies? Just for the hell of it I said, Was there a difference? Only about twenty grand a script, he said. Well, then, I guess I write for the movies. Good man, and they both slapped my back.

Then, just for the moment, Brown got serious about writing, and said no one ever gave a shit about words before talkies but now one good word was worth a thousand pictures, and that was why the money had gotten so good. And no one appreciated the fact more than Mr. Zanuck up there, who, did I know, started out as a writer himself. Hell, he used to pull out scripts like they were taffy.

Did I know that Zanuck wrote almost every Rin Tin Tin movie there ever was? Brown said this with the utmost respect, in spite of the fact that this "writing" was for movies before sound and starred a German shepherd. My god, was I ever going to love Hollywood. I said, Here's to the *mot juste* whether human or canine, and Brown and I touched empty glasses.

Every table had pitchers of water and glasses of every possible shape—wine, highball, martini, shot—waiting to be filled with alcoholic beverages of every sort. The Derby couldn't serve booze officially, of course, so everyone who imbibed—and that was everyone who breathed—was required to bring his own, usually in a flask. America was still like that in 1930 and I was completely comfortable with it, even pleased by the gangster business it created. At least there would be no raid tonight—this was, after all, a Zanuck affair. Pallette didn't want to be left out of the toast to literature; so he reached under the table, pulled out a small pail, and filled our glasses with a greenish gin. We three clicked glasses and downed our booze. Surprisingly good stuff actually. It was going to be one of those nights.

The word *starlet* hadn't been invented back then, but they were there in the delightful flesh even if the word didn't yet serve. Pallette saw me eyeing a redhead two tables away. He whispered, Sweet meat indeed. I alluded to the well-built young man with her. Brown laughed and said, Warner pansy. The studio just hooks them up for publicity photos. Pallette asked me if I saw anything else in the room I liked, a silly question, but implying he hoped to have the redhead for himself. I looked around and said, Nope, she's the only one here for me tonight. It wasn't until I broke a grin that he smacked me on the back again. This here is my kind of guy, he announced to the noisy room.

I was a much better drinker in those days, by which I mean I could drink a lot more and not get as drunk. Back in the army I drank plenty with the guys and there would even be an occasional brawl. I'd seen guys almost kill one another. Me, I'd just try to pin someone down so he couldn't hurt me or anybody else. Even back then, the good cop.

In spite of Pallette's friendly request, in spite of the fact that we were drinking his very good gin, I still had my eye on the redhead. It didn't seem to me as though I'd have any great problem edging him out unless of course there was to be some sort of fiduciary exchange. I doubt I'd be able to win a bidding war, or might not even want to. But I think we're supposed to be talking about Lillian here, aren't we?

As I recall, Mike Curtiz, the director, was just about to begin a speech of gratefulness to and introduction of Mr. Zanuck when I realized it was the perfect time to stand, walk toward the redhead's table, and touch her bare shoulder as I brushed her chair on the way to the men's room. I downed my green gin and rose. As I got close, a small woman blocked my path. We stutter-stepped for a while. Lillian of course.

I have to trust my pathetically broken memory here. I remember being struck by the fact that she wore a suit, a mustard-colored suit, and a small cloche hat with feathers. I recall thinking how out of place—this was a major Hollywood soiree and here was a gal dressed for a New York literary luncheon. But I liked her face immediately. Nature had created it. As unforgiving as Mount Rushmore, as beautiful as the Rockies. She hooked my arm, walked along with me, and quoted my line from, I think, "The Girl with the Silver Eyes." Something like, *"You beast!" she spat, and then her smile grew gentle again* . . . I have to admit, it struck me as pretty funny. She camped in front of the men's room, looked absolutely helpless, and waited for my line, which of course I'd forgotten but which I've learned from her over the years was supposed to have been, *"You're beautiful as hell!" I shouted crazily into her face, and flung her against the door.* Instead I think I said something about how surprising it was to run into Bette Davis on my way to the men's room.

She told me how disappointed she was that I couldn't remember my own lines. What kind of writer was I anyway?

One who got paid by the word, I said.

Some would call that a description of a hack, she said.

Acerbic wench, I said.

I am not a bitch.

I didn't say bitch; I said wench.

Okay, that one I'll buy, she said.

Who can resist such charm? I suspected even then that talking to a very, very smart woman in Hollywood was going to be as rare as finding an honest man there. Lillian had lots of both, smart and honest.

She came real close then, ran her hand under my jacket, up my stomach to my chest and whispered, You are not going home with that redhead. No, no, no, no. You will be going home with me. So which of us is going to tell my husband?

As it turned out, neither of us told Arthur. She simply arranged to have a cab waiting for us when the party began to break up. I didn't know her name until she had taken our clothes off.

TOWARD THE END OF HER LIFE, long after Hammett had died, Lillian Hellman remembered their first meeting like this:

The occasion? Something about Zanuck and Thanksgiving and all of us being cringingly grateful to the brothers Warner all rolled into one. I'm not sure where exactly. If you forced me to guess, gun to my head, as Dash used to say, I'd venture the Coconut Grove. Is that correct? Now I'm not so sure. Is it important? Anyway.

At first I swear I thought he was Gary Cooper. Honestly. It couldn't be, of course, because Cooper was at Paramount in those days. Our table was pretty far away from the action, that I do remember. I never forget where they put me. And I remember saying to Arthur, That's not Gary Cooper? He said, No, it's Dashiell Hammett. I said, Jesus Christ, he's beautiful. Arthur probably knew what was coming even before I did. He made believe he didn't care. Rather, he made believe he didn't care as much as he really did care. It hurt him less that way, I suppose.

I don't remember his sitting up on the dais. Couldn't have been, he had just signed with Warners, but he was up there pretty prominently, after all he was Hammett. As writers you could argue Hemingway and Fitzgerald. For me Hammett clearly had the better of them both. By a mile. And just look at him. Tall, graceful, self-contained, talented, not Jewish, everything I really liked in a man. I had no intention of letting him get away. To be perfectly honest, I was hoping I could get him to read one of my scripts and then maybe . . . You know what ambitious girls are like in Hollywood. I was young—twenty-four—although surely not a girl. And God was I ambitious. Like now, like ever. Good thing for American letters, our meeting, don't you think?

I studied him for a long while. He drank from a shallow glass but only a little more than moderately. Conversed a bit but mostly he was casing the joint, as the Op would say, for potential female suspects was my guess. Going home alone was not in his plans. From time to time a girl would go up to flatter him, flash the goods, ask him to dance. He'd demur. Girls, the guy who invented the ultimate tough guy, the loner dick, is never taking to the dance floor! Banter and wit, yes. Dancing, no. I watched this ritual, observed his every move, his stillness. He looked into his liquor before he drank it. He threw his head back and smiled at the ceiling when a thought pleased him or when a companion said something he liked. He rarely smiled fully with his lips. His eyes registered pleasure. Mostly, though, he tried hard to accommodate himself to being there by holding his greater self apart.

There was, near the toilets at the Grove—if it was the Grove—as I remember, a very comfortable and very private smoking area. The sofas and seats were plush, the foliage papier-mâché, the soft lighting perfect. The setting of choice as far as I was concerned. A moment before he downed his drink and pulled his chair back, I left my table without excuse or apology. Arthur's eyes were on me, I knew.

There on the sofa—mauve it was, and glad I'd worn the flowered gown—I displayed a lot of leg—I've always had good legs—and propped the rest of me up to best advantage. He didn't show for a while, probably chatting his way here, although it did occur to me he may already have arranged to leave early with some Kewpie doll. Gloves were de rigueur as accessories then, and I slapped them on my knees in time to the Latin music from the ballroom.

I swear I saw a backlit halo on him when he came toward me. This was some beautiful man. If I were writing the scene, it would read like this:

"Please sit down, Mr. Hammett."

"Have we met?"

"That's what's happening right now. Sit down, I have a small bone to pick with you."

"God. Only a small bone? I'm disappointed. And you would be?" He spoke slowly with a faint drawl.

I adjusted my own drawl to his. "Names aren't important. But what I've got to say might be. I'm a really smart woman and a very close reader who hasn't the foggiest idea what the fucking plot of *Red Harvest* is all about . . . that's what's important."

Hammett sat down. If you've ever read that miscarriage or seen the movie they finally made of it at Paramount, you'll know how preposterous the plot is, especially when the goddamned narrator—the Continental Op—cannot even remember if he killed Dinah Brand with an ice pick. I put my hand on Hammett's knee: "Imagine. Your main character doesn't even know if he's a murderer! Come on."

"The poor man was hopped up. Ever tried gin and laudanum?"

"Every morning with my Corn Flakes. And then you expect us to believe his fingerprints got on the ice pick because he touched it by mistake. Mistake! He's the goddamned detective! That's an even worse 'come on' . . . And has anyone ever totaled up all the murders in that book? I gave up after thirty-five. What the hell are you writing, medieval revenges?"

"That's exactly what pulp is, my dear. You give 'em gore and then you give 'em a lot more gore."

"I can do without the patronizing, my dear. I shouldn't have to remind you, you're the same guy who wrote a hundred lines this good: *Play with murder enough and it gets you one of two ways. It makes you sick or you get to like it.* So I ask you, Why does that same writer settle for crapola?"

"Oh. Now I get it. You want to reform me. Save me from myself. Make me into a *literary* gent."

"You are a literary gent who thinks he has to be so damned tough all the time he's afraid to open his fists."

"Sweetheart, the world already has too many literary gents and too much *litter-a-toor*. Maybe some other time you can tell me what else is wrong with the story. And what did you say your name was?"

"Dinah Brand, and don't you dare touch that ice pick."

"No, tell me."

"Another thing I don't get is, you create this incredibly interesting and sexy woman and your Op not only doesn't shtup her, he never even thinks about shtupping her. And I'm really worried that the same thing might be happening right now."

"Stoop?"

"Not 'stoop,' you dope. *Shtup*. 'She *Shtups* to Conquer.' It's Yiddish, but that's not the point."

Eventually Hammett learned lots of Yiddish, but that night we sat in the lounge and talked and drank and talked some more until everyone had left and they finally threw us out. All exit stage left. We went to his place, I think, a real dump as I recall.

EVEN THOUGH HAMMETT was twelve years older with hair already flecked with gray, the two were compatible and easy with each other from the get-go. Both were children of the South—Hammett from rural Maryland, Lillian from an Alabama and Louisiana childhood before moving ▓▓▓h—and their ease with the gentle accents of their youth allowed them to blend comfortably, even when they were teasing each other. Especially when they were teasing each other.

Lillian did not work at Warner Bros. She had just started a job in the script department at Paramount as a reader, but her husband, Arthur Kober, who had published some stories in the *New Yorker,* had already done some script work for Zanuck. A *New Yorker* writer had a cachet with a man like Zanuck. Jack Warner, on the other hand, wouldn't know the *New Yorker* from the *New Republic.*

Arthur Kober was Lillian's entrée that night. Although Hammett had indeed sold the rights to *The Maltese Falcon* to Zanuck, he had not yet been paid, and he had not as yet become a studio writer under contract. That was likely to happen soon, which was why he had been invited to the party.

The most important thing that happened at the Brown Derby that night was that Lillian Hellman met Dashiell Hammett and they would know one another, sometimes for better, sometimes for worse, for thirty years. The undisputed star of the evening, however, was Darryl F. Zanuck. Yes, he was the genius behind the incredible financial success of the Rin Tin Tin movies. And, yes, young Zanuck had played a major part in *The Jazz Singer*'s astounding success. He spent a good deal of his time at Warners urging the brothers to commit completely to sound. But they did not see the future for sound quite as clearly as he did. They did not—or would not—acknowledge that spoken words required very good writers, that movie music now demanded very good lyricists and composers. How many times had Zanuck told Jack Warner about scrimping on talent, "You get what you pay for." And how many times had Jack Warner said, "When they need the work, they'll give you their best for peanuts."

Darryl Zanuck never thought that way. Even while at Warners, he busted the budget repeatedly to get the best talent. He considered himself a connoisseur who could spot true talent anywhere and determine exactly how best to employ it. In his first years at Warners, he had Cole Porter and Oscar Hammerstein contribute some wonderful tunes to some very creaky musicals. In short, the Warner brothers were satisfied to make the silents talk. Zanuck intended to make them cry and laugh and shout and sing.

Zanuck knew his relationship with the brothers, especially with Jack, couldn't last, and although he was supervisor of production at twenty-seven, he had his eyes on bigger things, perhaps at Paramount, perhaps at a brand-new studio he planned to start himself. So all those "guest" invitations his secretary sent out to all sorts of talented people—Hammett and Arthur Kober, to name just two—were bread cast upon the water that would bring Zanuck some very talented people when he made his move.

The *Falcon* wasn't the first script Hammett had sold to a studio. *Red Harvest*, his first novel, was bought by Paramount the year before, early in 1929. The deal was made before the Crash, his first big movie money, more money than he had ever seen before. But even a year and a half later, when times were bad, Zanuck had made a good offer for the *Falcon*; whatever was happening elsewhere in America, there always seemed to be plenty of cash in Hollywood.

Scriptwriting beat writing for the pulps and their penny a word by a long shot. Even Paramount paid ten times as much for the rights to *Red Harvest* as Alfred Knopf had paid him to invent and write the novel itself. Money, which had long been his primary need, became in Hollywood Hammett's primary want.

The Maltese Falcon had been published by Knopf in February 1930, nine months before Zanuck's party. Most of the writers in the room—even if they wouldn't admit it—had read at least parts of it and most of these were secretly jealous of his talent. Hammett knew it was good, the best work he had done so far, almost better than he believed he could ever do, so he thought he had simply gotten lucky with it. A good time, he also believed, to cash in on his luck.

The actual meeting that evening in the Brown Derby occurred as follows. Lillian Hellman approached Dashiell Hammett's table. She adjusted the single strap on her red gown, leaned in over Frank Fay's shoulder, and whispered into Hammett's ear, *"Mr. Spade, oh Mr. Spade, they tell me that you don't mind a reasonable amount of trouble."* The breathy words were warm on his ear, the pauses perfect, the girl pretended to be frightened but still playfully sexual.

Hammett didn't look up but took her chin with firm fingers that climbed up Lillian's cheeks. His frown was severe, his voice rough. *"Tell me, Miss O'Shaughnessy—if that's your name—just how much trouble is a reasonable amount?"* Lillian believed him to be the most beautiful man she'd ever seen. Hammett could not get over her sexual force and presence.

Two Ideas

LILLIAN HELLMAN HAD A UNIQUE, paradoxical, and artistically rich childhood. She was a daughter of the deep Deep South, having spent her earliest years with her grandmother's wealthy family in Demopolis, Alabama. But her girlhood years were spent in her aunts'—her father's sisters'—boardinghouse in New Orleans. The contrast in those experiences limned her consciousness. Her formal as well as her political education happened mostly in New York's Upper West Side during those times of year when her father and mother came north. Growing up Jewish in those various worlds helped give context and texture to Lillian's creativity. She also chose to be strong.

As the result of such a mishmash of diverse cultural influences, Lillian's ear for all sorts of speech rhythms and dialects was superb and helped her tremendously as a dramatist. Her reputation in Hollywood and New York as a raconteur preceded her reputation as a playwright. Of all the voices she could deliver on demand she especially excelled in that help-less female pout and whine of the Southern belle. She per-formed a flawless Scarlett O'Hara years before there ever was a Scarlett O'Hara. Just for the hell of it, from time to time, and after a drink or two, she occasionally mixed in some Yid-dish when studio big shots were her audience. She also did a grumpy Upper West Side Jewish matron to perfection.

Too often, when they were out with friends, Hammett insisted she tell her Captain Beauregard story. She would demur twice, he would insist twice, she'd comply. The per-formance became somewhat famous in Hollywood.

Lilly told the story in a warm, cooing voice dripping with syrupy Southern innocence: Louis Ferdinand Beaure-gard, an aristocratic gentleman and captain in the Confed-erate Army, was madly in love with one of Lilly's great-great Alabama aunts, Miss Amanda Sweets Stonefeld. Fictitious of course. Captain Beauregard had family background but not much wealth. Even worse, he had the slightest harelip that Miss Amanda could neither abide nor take her eyes off when she was with him. If he asked her to accompany him on a stroll to the edge of the woods, she'd say the sun was too hot or the road too muddy. Her constant refusals reduced the captain to a love-sick puppy. At last he told her his regiment was being sent north to engage the Yankees, so wouldn't she please consent to walk with him to the ga-zebo in the garden. He had something of great importance to ask her.

At this point Lilly's act put even the coyest Scarlett to shame. Fluttering her lashes and fanning a hand before her cheeks, she said breathlessly, "'My word, I do declare, Captain Beauregard, it is simply much too humid for me to take a single step outside today. Perhaps another time would be a bit more more pro-pi-tious, suh.'"

Hammett, who retained a natural drawl, provided the baritone voice here, his only line in the scene: "'But I may not live to see you again, Miss Amanda.'"

Now Lilly really laid it on—the breath, the accent, the flutter: "'Then, my poor dear boy, I'd suggest you kill as many of those bad old Yankees as you possibly can before you die because you'll never get to fuck little ole me as long as you live.'" Lilly fanned her face furiously at the punch line. Hammett slapped the table and guffawed every time.

The bitter punch line pretty much revealed Lilly's true attitude about love, an attitude that was formed in her own Southern childhood.

Isaac Marx fled Germany in 1844, nearly twenty years before the American Civil War, and landed quite by chance in the unlikely town of Demopolis, Alabama, a German-Jewish peddler in a most bizarre American setting. Quite remarkably, he became the town's richest citizen. His sons eventually owned the Demopolis bank. After Reconstruction the Marx family became a formidable Alabama dynasty. Isaac's daughter Sophie married a respectable man named Newhouse, primarily because this is what an Isaac Marx daughter was supposed to do. Marrying for love in those circumstances was a preposterous, naive impulse. But for some inexplicable reason Sophie's own daughter—Lillian's mother, Julia Newhouse—yielded to that mad impulse.

Not only was Max Hellman a mere New Orleans shoe salesman, he was a Jew of a class now intolerable to the newly patrician Alabama family that had put Isaac's peddler years so far behind them they had ceased to exist. The worst offender was Sophie, Lillian's grandmother, who after her daughter Julia's marriage to Max Hellman never ceased disparaging him in Julia's and Lillian's presence. The black-sheep Hellmans along with their daughter were dismissed, and not in any sweet Southern style either, but driven away harshly and with malice. Lillian's portrayal of the Hubbard family in two of her most successful plays, *The Little Foxes* and *Another Part of the Forest*, historical family dramas set in the South, was her retribution. Lilly called them angry comedies.

The families in these plays are ruled by raw ambition, greed, jealousy, and deceit, all against an absurdly romantic background of the lost aristocratic dream of the Confederacy. This was the world and a social value system Lillian took in at the dinner table as the girl who grew up with the Newhouses, né Marxes, in Demopolis.

Lillian especially loved Max's sisters, Jenny and Hannah Hellman, who ran the New Orleans boardinghouse where the family lived for long periods of time when Max's business wasn't going well and where Lilly learned throughout her girlhood how the world actually worked for most people. From her mother she got strength of character and independence; from her father even more strength of character, brains, and wit. By all accounts Lillian loved her shoe salesman father enormously, even though she inherited his looks and not those of her exquisite mother. And from her time with the Marx family she derived an absolute disgust of Southern hypocrisy.

In all of Hellman's plays love comes at a terrible cost. It is most often a form of cruelty, at best a phantom never fully seen and never embraced as anything real or viable. Young lovers may see it vaguely, but when they reach for it they come away with nothing. Disappointment is the important life lesson love has to teach the young in Hellman.

I COULDN'T BELIEVE he'd never had French toast for breakfast, but he hadn't. My Aunt Jenny made the best French toast in the world when I was a girl and let me in on the secret, a pinch of cinnamon in the batter and sweet butter well browned in a cast-iron pan. Even though I didn't have the stale bread, I made French toast for him one morning and he loved it. And that would have been what the morning was remembered for if he hadn't looked up from his book and said, "Did you know the word *Lesbian* had nothing to do with sexual panky-hanky until only about a hundred years ago?"

He thought stupidities like *panky-hanky* were funny, but no, I didn't know that. "So what did it mean?"

"Anything pertaining to the Isle of Lesbos, mostly the wine."

Hammett often began important talks with "Did you know that . . ." This was to be an important talk.

Who but Hammett would have come across and then spent days reading up on the Drumsheugh trial, a now-forgotten but way-back-when notorious court case that took place in Edinburgh more than two hundred years ago? I was at the stove and did not turn around. It seemed to him that Drumsheugh might be just the subject I was looking for to turn into a drama.

"Gumshoe, you say?"

"Yep, Drumsheugh. It'll take you exactly where you want to go."

In a fashionable quarter of Edinburgh, if there could be imagined such a place, two young women—Jane Pirie and Marianne Woods—opened a small, selective school for teenage girls of the town's elite families, the Drumsheugh Gardens School. The new school had just begun to establish itself as the proper place for a proper education in proper Scotland when one fine day, quite unannounced, carriages began arriving at the door with orders to take the girls away. To take them home immediately and without any explanation to the flabbergasted Mistresses Pirie and Woods.

What had happened, in Hammett's retelling, was this: One of the students, a particularly unhappy girl, told her influential grandmother, Dame Cumming Gordon, of seeing the two headmistresses engaging in acts of sexual intimacy in their bedroom, not once but repeatedly. Dame Cumming Gordon contacted other parents immediately. Word spread like a virus or as only a vicious sexual rumor can. In two days' time the two young women were ruined professionally and personally. Their only public recourse was to sue Dame Cumming Gordon for defamation of character. The long trial, whose testimony was reported in newspapers throughout the British Isles and was as lurid and juicy as any scandalmonger could possibly have hoped, was decided in Dame Cumming Gordon's favor by a judicial vote of four to three. That wasn't the end of it.

The mistresses appealed the verdict and after a second extended trial won a reversal, forcing Dame Cumming Gordon to pursue the case all the way to the House of Lords, where in 1819, ten years after the alleged misconduct—it was officially termed "illicit carnal knowledge"—the court finally ruled in favor of Miss Pirie and Miss Woods. They were awarded their ten-thousand-pound claim, which yielded them each about one thousand pounds after legal costs. Now the two were ruined financially as well as professionally. There's no doubt that they loved one another, whether or not they actually made love. The two separated. Each then sought and achieved anonymity in her own fashion.

"What happened to the young women," Hammett said, "is now called a Scotch verdict. You win but you lose."

"Like Arbuckle," I said.

"Different case of Scotch."

Hammett didn't do any more selling. He didn't have to. The Drumsheugh case really did have everything I was looking for. Forbidden sex, or at least the public threat of it to polite society, class conflict, the power of a childish lie—if it was a lie—people's more-than-willing complicity in the ruin of others. The heart of the matter offered an exploration of love and attraction. Can a really deep friendship, a love in fact, always stay within the bounds society has established? And if it doesn't? What does that mean? I could handle all that dramatically and still leave the question—Did they or didn't they?—unresolved. Of course I'd want to make the story contemporary, move it to Boston or Philadelphia, but Jesus, what a temptation to put it in Demopolis, Alabama, and make Dame Gordon my Grandma Sophie.

Hammett's last word on the subject that morning was to the effect that even when they're queers, women get screwed. Weren't the British public schools always rife with homosexual tutors, almost proudly so? Some repressed faggot canes a kid to within an inch of his life and Eton has once again upheld the high standards on which the Empire was built, but let two women slip out of their panties in the dormitories and all hell breaks loose.

If they slipped out of their panties, I corrected.

I immediately began outlining the play, first in my head and then on paper. When Hammett saw the first decent draft of *The Children's Hour* five weeks later, he said it was worse than bad because it was half good. I cried and made the mistake of letting him see me do it.

LILLIAN, THANK GOD, wasn't at all like me in that respect. She never said, *Dash, you're really writing shit.* We both knew I was writing shit when I was writing at all. Studio work those days meant presenting story ideas, stuff I didn't even have to put on paper. I could walk into a story conference cold and come up with at least six impressive—not necessarily good—ideas right on the spot. That was my true Hollywood talent and it paid all the bills and more so but didn't impress her in the least. Lilly loved me most when I would go away for a week and come back with pages for her to read. That hadn't happened for a while.

One night she hid behind her newspaper, a sure sign something was up. She made *mmm* sounds, *tsk-tsks* I was meant to respond to. I refused to take the bait, so she was forced to say, "Speaking of Arbuckle, it says here they're looking back into the trial transcripts to see if maybe there's a way to get his kids some money. Civil suit against the prosecutor. Didn't you work on that case?"

"Nothing big. I just went around collecting affidavits for the defense. I did actually speak with Arbuckle a couple of times. I liked him. I liked him a great deal, as a matter of fact. Can't think of anyone in Hollywood who ever got screwed worse. But I'm not going to write about it, if that's what you're thinking."

Lillian put down the paper. "You've got notes on the case. I've seen them, Dash. Isn't it time to set things right?"

Actually it wasn't time to set things right, not even close to time. In fact, it might never be time because in the world there was no "setting things right." The Hays Office still called the tune as to what could and could not be produced in Hollywood, and the Arbuckle case all but created the Hays Office, made the Legion of Decency crowd seem legit. Why take them on if you didn't have to?

Truth is, no one in movies was larger or funnier than Roscoe "Fatty" Arbuckle in '27. Hollywood's first million-dollar-a-year star. I was back working for Pinkerton that year. The fat man apparently forced himself upon one Virginia Rappe in room 1220 of San Francisco's St. Francis Hotel, which was, given the times, no irreparable indiscretion. Problem was that the following day, or maybe the day after, I don't recall, Virginia Rappe died in the hospital of peritonitis caused by a ruptured bladder.

Arbuckle was indicted first for murder, a charge which was then brought down to manslaughter. He was tried three times—two mistrials and finally an acquittal. But he was really convicted in the papers by the publisher, William Randolph Hearst, who kept a national frenzy alive with a flow of lurid details for a year, almost none of which were true. Rumor and innuendo not only sold newspapers but ultimately, if repeated and exaggerated, became accepted as truth because most people wanted it to be the truth. So now, even all these years later, people believe Fatty Arbuckle killed Virginia Rappe by cramming a Coca-Cola bottle up her vagina and then crushing her with his three-hundred-pound corpus. That did not happen. But rumor is a tar baby; and the uglier the rumors are, the longer they survive. The big lie always sold papers.

Fatty Arbuckle's sexual "liaison" with Virginia Rappe was tawdry but financially consensual. Miss Rappe was in terrible health when she made her way up that elevator to room 1220. Doctors I interviewed confirmed that she'd had a very recent abortion and a fairly long history of bladder problems. Any form of sexual activity, they swore in their affidavits, could easily have induced the hemorrhaging that caused her death.

The only potential defense witness on Rappe's behalf was her friend Bambina Delmont, a woman with a long record of racketeering, fraud, and extortion. Bambina—she was not beautiful but the name alone speaks volumes—never took the stand. Matthew Brady—no, not the photographer, the San Francisco D.A.—pulled every prosecutorial dirty trick in the book to get his celebrity conviction. There is no doubt that Arbuckle's kids ought to sue his ass from here to Sacramento.

I attended the final trial. The jury deliberated about six minutes, declared him innocent, and issued an exceedingly rare statement of apology for any injustice done to the defendant. No one I spoke to had ever heard anything like it in a courtroom. The apology didn't matter. All was lost for Arbuckle and he knew it. Keaton gave him some work afterward but Arbuckle could never be funny again.

"Scotch verdict. Or worse, Hearst verdict," Lilly said.

"So why in the world would I want to write about that?"

"For the same reason you gave me the Drumsheugh idea."

"We're only allowed just one great idea per family." Lilly loved that I called us family.

"If you won't write about that, then why not write about us?" Said grumpily, almost as a throwaway.

That was her gift to me that day. Exactly what I was looking for, right in front of me all along yet something I'd never have seen in a million years. Ex-detective, private eye, marries a clever, wisecracking doll who travels in a smart, glamorous social world living the high life. They're careless, they drink—before and after repeal—they're eccentric and funny and chic and irreverent and Jesus Christ . . . they solve murders together. Exactly the sort of idea that might hit me walking from the parking lot to a story conference—but it never did and never would—a flighty antidetective detective story, a flip on every dark private eye cliché ever invented, full of sarcasm and puns and irony and wit and bad jokes. And sex. The more I thought about it, the more I liked the fun and the challenge of it, something I thought I could still pull off. All I'd have to do is write about the two of us and throw in a murder or three.

I showed Lilly a three-page outline of *The Thin Man*—modestly named after myself—two weeks later.

She said, as Nora would, "Darling, your character's not tipsy enough and I'm not clever enough, but it is a start."

Later she said, "Let him always seem to be just a little inebriated, even when he's not drinking, roguishly off balance and carefree. After all, he's happy as hell to be living on her money, happy not having ever to be a working stiff again. And his wife loves the hell out of the guy—his looks, his brains—and she always keeps him from going too far over the line. It's moderately funny already. He's a very sharp detective when he wants to be. She's an amateur but not so bad either. It's going to work. Take it directly to Mayer, no middlemen. Then maybe, afterward, the Arbuckle story."

I was shaking my head. "Before the *Thin Man* screenplay, the novel. For Knopf."

Lilly thought the names were wrong. I had Gilbert and Jillian. She thought the same first initials were important and that there ought to be a paired rhythm to the names. They also had to suggest different class backgrounds. We worked that out on a tablecloth at the Trocadero later that night. She suggested Nino for him. I told her there were no Nino private eyes. So I became Nick. And for Lillian, Nora. Our waiter was named Charles. Nick and Nora Charles it was.

The little dog Asta didn't get added until Lillian came back from a visit to New York with a description of a woman she saw in Bendel's who had the smartest little pooch she'd ever seen.

These were good times for us. We fought, not so much with each other as over ideas. Ideas were like sex, an excitement, a frustration, a disappointment, a thrill. As long as ideas interested us we could share our lives, and there was then no reason to think ideas would ever stop. I knew better, of course, but Lillian Hellman was overwhelming, a rare young woman who could make you believe the limitations the world placed upon you, and those we placed upon ourselves, might be suspended indefinitely. And in those working days for us they were.

LOVE IS HARDLY EVER MENTIONED in Hammett's novels, appropriately so because the Hammett world is such bleak terrain populated only by wanters, needers and takers, victims and victimizers. Love in Hammett is desperate and financial. When the word is employed, it is not love at all but a transaction, a useful sexual trade between a woman who has something to sell—information usually—that the detective, either the Op or Sam Spade, happens to need. The barter is rarely consummated on the page because there's a limit to what magazines will allow, but mostly because love in his dark world is such a bad deal. Dashiell Hammett, the detective story writer, does not believe in love.

In 1918, when he was a member of the U.S. Army Ambulance Corps at Fort Meade, Maryland—his only contribution to the war effort was turning over an army vehicle—Hammett contracted tuberculosis as a result of the great influenza epidemic of that year and was hospitalized. Eighteen months after discharge he picked up his Pinkerton career in the Northwest. His TB flared up again quite seriously and Hammett was admitted to the infectious diseases ward at Cushman Institute, a U.S. Public Health Service hospital in Tacoma, Washington. One of his nurses was twenty-three-year-old Josephine Dolan, a prairie girl from Montana.

Josephine Dolan was very beautiful. He was swept away by her movie-star looks; she was taken by the tall, gentle, well-mannered boy from Maryland, a distant place she could barely imagine. The encounter had all the elements of tragic romance—youth, beauty, disease, random chance, courage, war—indeed all the elements of a great love story. She called herself Jose and pronounced it "Joe's."

The two really could not have helped but fall in love. They were married in a Catholic church in San Francisco's Chinatown in July 1921. A first child, Mary Jane, was born in October. The Hammetts were a family briefly in San Francisco. Hammett's health remained poor. A second daughter, Josephine, was born five years later, by which time Jose and the girls were living back in Montana. Hammett supported his wife and his daughters from a distance thereafter. Love may have produced a family, but there wasn't enough of it to sustain a family. Hammett convinced himself then that love, like good health, was rare and most of all a matter of luck.

When they met that first night at Zanuck's party at the Brown Derby in 1930, neither Dash nor Lilly was a great believer in love or marriage, which is why biographers are befuddled by their long, inconstantly constant relationship. None of those biographers understood the rare power of their love. When the word is mentioned at all, it is defined in ways that torture it, that make it to be not love at all but some sort of grotesque love monster. That bond, however it is presented and whatever it is called, endured for three decades, contorted, stretched, and strained but unbroken by distance, professional jealousy, countless flings and more serious affairs by each, pathetic need, insult, drink, recrimination, and disappointment.

Hammett once told a would-be biographer, "Beware biographers, young man, they eat lives whole and spit out all the wrong details. Samuel Johnson himself once told me that before he died." No wonder, then, so many biographers don't understand what love is or make so much of the fact that Lillian Hellman was not a pretty woman. It is reason enough to dismiss anything else they might have to say about her and the relationship. The implication is that a good-looking guy like Hammett would only seduce or be seduced by beauty. This was Hollywood, for Christ's sake; everyone was beautiful. Almost no one was remarkable.

You wonder if these biographers know anything about seduction. Do they know anything about attraction or why people fall in love to begin with? Could they so easily overlook how remarkable this Hellman girl, Mrs. Arthur Kober, must have been? Or how preternaturally perceptive Hammett was in finding her attractive, and then incomparably interesting, for all those years? Of course, the very premise is incorrect to begin with, for Lillian Hellman was indeed beautiful. All originals are beautiful. Unoriginals do not know this simple fact, which is why the judgments of biographers in matters biographical cannot be trusted.

A more interesting question about looks is this—did Lillian consider herself homely? Likely she did. Hammett's affection and admiration for who she was and what she meant to him must have made her less self-conscious about her looks. It might even have confirmed in her the unique beauty he perceived.

LILLY, BECAUSE SHE WAS YOUNGER and less accomplished in the world's eyes when they met, saw Dash as the brilliant and successful writer she desired to be. She had felt the same way years earlier when she first met Arthur Kober in New York, but now the ante had been raised. Hammett immediately saw a first-rate creative mind, a very well-read and independent thinker, a woman who told her husband to take a hike so that she could fuck the more successful Dashiell Hammett. That word, by the way, was not in his personal lexicon when they met and he never got to be comfortable with it. Lilly teased him about such selective scrupulousness since she so loved the power of profanity in social situations. Once while at Louis Mayer's house Dash told a story in which he said "effing." She broke in with "You mean to say 'fucking,' don't you, darling?" and added, à la Mae West, while playing with his belt buckle, "S'matter, big boy, my Anglo-Saxon botherin' you?" Ruined his story but he loved it.

They stayed more or less together for a whole mishmash of reasons. Let the mishmash fall away and you have something very simple really. It was the sudden satisfaction of Hammett upon seeing Lillian enter a room. Or Lilly listening to Hammett on the phone with a director. It was the vaulting thrill of a wink or a shared sarcasm, the intimacy of a true smile. It was there when Hammett would say after a bad writing day, "I hate myself," and Hellman would counter, "Don't be so hard on yourself. I hate you more."

.3.

Missings

I WAS WITH the Pinkerton Detective Agency before the war—that would be "the war to end all wars," 1918, in case you missed it—and for a while again afterward, at least while my postwar health held up. To the extent that my detective stories have the real smack of truth to them, it is owing to my training and work with Pinkerton. Probably the best job I ever had, even though the company has a shameful reputation and history, doing a lot more strikebreaking and union head-busting than real detective work.

Was I proud of myself working for a company like that? Hell no. Did I like having a job and did I like the job I had? Damn right. My starting assignments were tailing wayward husbands, which was lousy because mostly you just sat in a car or on a bench eyeing a doorway till all hours in all kinds of weather, waiting for them—the *subjects*, we called them in our reports—to be done with their necessaries. Or sitting behind a newspaper in a hotel lobby. Naturally I liked the lobby better because I got to be warm, could talk to a few people and maybe get a drink or two. I got to know house dicks all over the country, a far more interesting fraternity than you'd ever guess from the movies, where they're pretty much all drunks and dopes. I can vouch for the fact they're not dopes.

I never had to break into a room with a flash camera; that was for sleazebags, and Pinkerton didn't work that way. The courts back then generally accepted an accurately written Pinkerton report of a so-called illicit liaison as sufficient to prove a spouse's infidelity. It's worth mentioning that I enriched my vocabulary and improved my spelling while writing up those reports. Imagine me, a simple country boy—*liaisons*. More often than you'd think, said spouse was a good-looking young Missus with a substantial amount to lose. So I got to see the power of the irrational at work in a lot of second-rate hotels. Only three times in my years on the job did the fallout from one of these situations become violent and only once result in a homicide—a rich old man who first forgave his wayward young Missus and then poisoned her two months later.

SHADOWING PEOPLE IS an art form, and I was an artist. Each person has a unique way of moving, of holding head and shoulders, torso, either slightly forward or back, bobbing and swaying distinctively. Inevitably you're bound to lose your guy for brief moments but you pick him up again not so much by the color of his clothes but much more by how he moves. I ought to mention that the company gave us what we called a shadow allowance, a few extra bucks to buy a different hat or jacket so we wouldn't stand out on shadow jobs. I liked that, the extra money, I mean.

In those days we were "Ops," Operatives, a better-sounding term than dicks, which meant back then exactly what it means today. When I finally wrote about an Op for *Black Mask*, I couldn't call him the Pinkerton Op, so he became my Continental Op. The Continental Detective Agency was modeled in every way on Pinkerton and I had my first popular detective.

I didn't really have many missing person cases—*missings* was our shorthand—maybe four or five, and frankly I didn't solve any of them, but the best jobs by far were the missings. Not the ones where foul play was suspected—those people probably were dead—but cases where someone just took it into his head to up and disappear. These were the most interesting cases for me, especially when a guy just wanted to drop off the face of the earth or get out of his own life and become someone else. Ever since I was a kid I always tried to imagine what it would feel like to be someone else. I still do. I think everybody does in some way or other. I don't think I lacked the daring, it was just that everything in my life would become too damned messy.

From time to time, whenever I'd run into old Ops, we'd naturally and automatically drift back to talking about old cases. Rather, *they'd* talk about old cases. That wasn't my style. I wanted to write about them—that's how I made my money when my health went bad and I couldn't work for Pinkerton. A good Op and a good writer always learns more when he listens. You'd think it was murder or kidnapping cases, or even the gaudy embezzlements the guys wanted to talk about. It wasn't. What most other Ops wanted to talk about were the missings. I think deep down most of the guys envied someone who could step out of one life and try another one on for size. Actually I just got a pang of envy writing that last sentence.

After I married Josephine and had the kids, and given my lousy health, there was no possible way I could do the Pinkerton job and hold the family together, which finally was okay with both of us as long as I could make enough money to keep them safe and, as the man says, free from want. Something else was happening to me too. Ops deal with crimes of one kind or another—some pretty terrible—and the darkest sort of cynicism comes with the territory, and cynicism eats families. So eventually I worked alone in San Francisco. Jose and the girls moved out to Montana. I might have missed a check to them occasionally, but Jose will tell you I took care of them well enough, even during the times when my health went bad and I couldn't work.

Unlike my old man who went off on toots that lasted months and never came back with any cash for us, until thankfully he hardly ever came back at all. I learned about missing persons early. How do I feel about him now? I feel nothing. Absolutely nothing. And a hundred sessions with Dr. Freud won't change that because nothing is exactly what the bastard deserves from me.

I remember that I had left Pinkerton by then. It was late '28. I'm in Frisco working on the *Falcon*. I'm typing away nonstop at the Post Street apartment, twelve, fourteen hours at a clip. The story is pouring out of me. Even though I had a detailed plot outline—a good one, really tight—the story kept wanting to run away from me because the characters were so strong they each wanted to take it in their own direction. It was getting stretched way out of shape. The characters all started out as variations on the same grifters I'd known when I was an Op, but once they got on the paper the greedy bastards wanted lives of their own, wanted to say things that even the real grifters wouldn't say.

Whenever I fell asleep, there they were, Gutman and Cairo and Iva, and especially Brigid O'Shaughnessy, telling me what they wanted me to know, whom I ought to trust and not trust. In Brigid's case, of course, it was nobody but herself. I didn't get many good nights' sleep. Didn't matter; personal turbulence was good for the book. I was trying not to drink, first not at all and then not too much, which made things harder—and easier.

The *Falcon* was the last of my three-book deal with Alfred Knopf in New York. I'd missed the last payment to Jose, who wrote just the week before to say she needed some money for the girls. Never for herself, and I'm sure that was true. I intended to mail out the first big chunk of the book, six chapters, about eighty pages, tomorrow morning first thing and ask Knopf for an advance. There's a natural break in the action right there, end of Chapter Six. The story was going to pick up again in Chapter Seven with Brigid in Spade's apartment—which is also on Post Street, why not?—where the two are waiting for Joel Cairo to show up. My plan was a dinner out and then an all-nighter with Brigid and Cairo exchanging lies.

I bought a *Racing Form* on the corner and made for Tait's. Wednesday, the goulash was the special. Who's sitting at my regular table but Buddy Krinsky, an old-timer from Pinkerton. No one else at the agency called me Samuel, my given name, but Krinsky. He saw it once on my license. I wasn't sure I wanted him to spot me. He bellowed, "Samuel, come join me, my friend."

Krinsky assumed I was still an Op, had no idea I had quit to become a writer. I let that go. He told me about a missing he was just wrapping up: "Damnedest thing in all my years, Samuel. Damnedest one ever. " He assumed I would say, "Tell me about it," and he did. Krinsky was one hell of a talker.

When I got back to my Underwood I typed Krinsky's story pretty much verbatim, I didn't want to miss any details. Krinsky didn't want to tell me his missing's name, which I thought was a pretty professional thing to do. He said, "Let's just call him Flitcraft," which is what I did when I got back to the apartment. I don't know when I decided to use the Flitcraft story in *Falcon*, but if I didn't intend to use it, why couldn't I wait to get back and start typing?

I can't say I absolutely understood the Flitcraft story myself, certainly not what it meant as a general description of the human psyche. I think I might have typed it to try to understand it better. Because Krinsky and I had both been trained to be respectful of facts, and I knew him to be a loudmouth but a damned good Op, the Flitcraft story probably only means what the facts tell us it means. In the detective business you soon learn that meaning is nothing more than what people do, what they want, what they need, and how they go about trying to get it.

Rule number one in detective fiction: *Thou Shall Not Stop the Plot*. For any reason. Ever. So then what made me want to begin Chapter Seven with the Flitcraft story and bring everything to a dead halt? And why in the world do I have Spade—my own Samuel—tell the Flitcraft story to Brigid as though it were a case he worked on himself when it has nothing to do with the Falcon? Why? You tell me. Lillian says I put it there precisely because I realized that was where it didn't belong, and that's why she loved it. Who knows, maybe I thought the plot needed the squeal of brakes to build suspense. A couple of times that night I almost pulled it out but decided finally that's what editors are for.

Here is what Krinsky told me: "A man named Flitcraft had left his real-estate office in Tacoma to go to luncheon one day and never returned. As best I could make out, his wife and he were supposed to be on the best of terms. He had two children, boys, one five and the other three. He owned a house in a Tacoma suburb, a new Packard, and the rest of the appurtenances of successful American living. There was nothing, absolutely nothing, to suggest that he had more than fifty or sixty bucks in his immediate possession at the time of his going. His habits for months past could be accounted for too thoroughly to justify any suspicion of secret vices, or even another woman in his life . . ."

Krinsky said Flitcraft's wife wanted Pinkerton to find her husband, bring him home, and make him pay for what he had done to their family. Krinsky was the company's missings specialist in the Northwest so he began by picking up the usual loose ends. The guy didn't gamble. The dealership was still making money for the family. Even a good-looking secretary didn't lead anywhere. Nothing led to Flitcraft's whereabouts. It was one thing to type out Krinsky's story, quite another to have Spade take up the tale and tell it to Brigid as his own.

I had Spade pick up Flitcraft's trail after someone spotted a man in Spokane who had won a car race in a vintage Packard. His description matched Flitcraft to a T. Years had lapsed since Flitcraft's disappearance when Spade finally caught up with his man and discovered that he had indeed changed his name, owned a successful business, and was married with a baby boy. Flitcraft, when Spade discovers him, didn't feel a great deal of guilt; after all, he had left his Tacoma family well provided for and felt that what he had done was perfectly reasonable under some very bizarre circumstances.

Five years earlier in Tacoma Flitcraft was walking past an office building that was being put up—just the superstructure. A beam fell eight or ten stories down and struck the sidewalk alongside him and then toppled over. Now even Brigid, who was only interested in matters that affected her well-being, became a bit more attentive. At that point I went back to my Krinsky notes and read: "He felt that somebody had taken the lid off of life and let him look at the works. And that scared the bejesus out of the man." He realized that the good father-citizen-husband could be wiped out between office and restaurant by the accident of a falling beam. He knew then that men died haphazardly like that, and lived only while blind chance spared them. Chance ruled everything. So why were we kidding ourselves?

After the beam fell and missed, Flitcraft chose to live a random, uncommitted life of chance. But a few years later up in Spokane when there were no more falling beams in his life, he pretty much becomes his old Flitcraft self again, a stable, predictable, solid citizen. This idea Spade particularly enjoys and he tells Brigid, "That's the part of it I always liked. He adjusted himself to beams falling, and then no more of them fell, and he adjusted himself to them not falling." If you want to know our species in a nutshell, there you have it.

Rarely do I falter or allow myself to be taken in by my own rare good writing. "Somebody had taken the lid off of life and let him look at the works." Jesus, that's an epitaph. Does it even matter whether that was Krinsky or me? My whole life up to the *Falcon*—up to Lillian—was nothing but dealing with "the works" under the lid, so much so that I thought that "works" were all life had to offer. Not complaining, no, not at all. Some people don't even know life has "lids" and "works" and couldn't even give a damn about the difference. Samuel Spade, however, is not one of them. Nor am I. Lillian, of course, makes metaphysical poetry out of Flitcraft, but then again she functions on an entirely different plane of existence than I do.

Even though we're both Samuels, Spade is not quite Hammett, nor vice versa. I have to remind myself of that in certain situations. It made sense to me then that Spade wanted to hear himself tell Brigid something she couldn't possibly understand. And I certainly knew better than to allow myself to wax philosophical in a thriller and stop things cold. But that's what I did, so I wrote a note to Alfred telling him to knock the story out if he didn't think it worked. He left it in. Thank God, John Huston, when he made the movie, got rid of the damned thing.

WHICH VERSION OF IT is he dishing up now? The old Buddy Krinsky bullshit or the truth as he invents it on the run? I hope you're smart enough to figure out why he made up that Krinsky cover story out of whole cloth. I called him on it the moment I saw it in an *Esquire* interview.

I was in New York when I read it and phoned the apartment in L.A. He was there but wouldn't pick up. I left a message three places at the studio for him to call me, which he did, three days later. God only knows how he filled those days. He swore he was crashing on a *Thin Man* script. Not possible, but I allowed myself to believe him. It didn't matter at that point for me, my concern was the unadulterated crap he was telling people about the Flitcraft section. When he finally phoned back, I said, Why are you doing this? There is no Krinsky. You know there is no Krinsky and I know there is no Krinsky. He said, Lill, I swear to you there is. I said, I called Pinkerton. There is no Krinsky. There never was a Krinsky. Long pause. He said, I do not appreciate the people I care about not believing me. He was seething. And you never would have called Pinkerton.

I told him he was right, that I hadn't actually called Pinkerton. I told him I wanted to but finally didn't. I loved him too much.

I've desired many men over the years for a variety of reasons but mostly for the short term. Dash was for a lifetime, unfortunately *his* lifetime. He was still unusually handsome until well into his ruin, but even ruined he was beautiful. I was the only one of his women to have known him fully because we worked so closely for so long.

Once, I remember, he read a book about sixteenth-century glassblowing in Bohemia—he collected esoterica like Lincoln pennies—and after we made love he talked so teasingly about how Cranberry glass was blown that we made love again. The Bohemians made many kinds of glass; *cranberry*, though, became our code word for sex. If we were at a bar and I asked for a little cranberry juice in my gin, Dash knew I had expectations for the evening. So, no, I wouldn't have called Pinkerton about Krinsky; I didn't have to. I knew.

Ask yourself this question. Why would a writer, a fiction writer, invent a story attributing some of his very best work to some crude working stiff who does not even exist?

What you had with Dash was, on the one hand, someone who accumulated knowledge like a coin collector but refused to ever show anyone his collection. And on the other hand, someone who absolutely humiliated himself in public with asinine pranks and fall-down drunkenness. Not to mention his insulting faithlessness. It took me a long while to see these were uncorrectable parts of the essential man. Extract them and there was no Dashiell Hammett left. Damn it.

And, really, how could I help him when, let's face it, back then I was often something of a drunk myself. But never, I don't believe, out of shame.

I'd always felt—and I told him this too often—that he suffered from a Goldilocks complex, couldn't or wouldn't find the bed or the chair or the porridge that was just right. The novels and screenplays were too easy for him—that's why they were pulps or bad movies. When I wanted to get him angry with himself, I used to pout and say, "Oh, I'm so sorry. I know you won't forgive me. I—I'm sorry, sorry, sorry." Except I used to say "sowwy."

Trust me, there was no fucking Buddy Krinsky. Flitcraft is pure Hammett, perhaps for the only time on paper. It's Hammett lying next to me, his head on a pillow, smoking a Fatima, sharing a true, intimate thought. It's great thinking and writing and in *Falcon* it's two and a half pages. But, oh, how I do love it.

Naturally, afterward, that craziness in him had to find a way to disclaim the good work, to disinherit it, invent another source, and then castigate anyone who saw how very good and important it was. That's the essence of Hammett, the man with all his quills out. Too bristly and dangerous to approach. Too tough and inconstant to allow himself to be admired.

Here's what you really have to know about people like Dash—and there's only Dash, not people "like" him—who grow up piss-poor and unloved. They're ashamed. Ashamed of what they come from, of who they are, and if they happen to be successful, ashamed of their talent and accomplishments. I do not suffer from those particular deprivations—there are others we can talk about later—but if you spent any serious time with Dash you couldn't miss the symptoms of profound shame. No one else was ever allowed to spend any serious time with Dash but me. So you just have to take my word for it. The Flitcraft story is brilliant and it's all Hammett.

.4.

Hatred

IT WASN'T THE FIRST TIME he'd humiliated her, or the second, or the fifth. This time, though, it was of longer duration and at a greater distance—she in New York, he in Hollywood; behind her back, it seemed to her. And more people appeared to know about it than ever before, making the sheer quantity of humiliation greater than it ever had been.

It took her the better part of three days to cover the United States, first by train and then by plane. Lilly had much time to cosy up to the humiliation, so quite naturally its effects ran deeper. Which bothered her more, she wondered, that he couldn't keep his dick in his pants for two weeks or that so many people she disliked intensely now knew that the man she loved couldn't—or wouldn't—keep his dick in his pants? Lilly didn't even need an hour to figure that one out. She'd been made into a laughingstock. The taste on her tongue was gall.

If Hammett wanted to fuck around, fine. No, not fine, but given the bastard's track record, certainly not unexpected. What was exasperating, truly maddening, about this one was that he'd done it so publicly it was obviously meant to be deliberate. It was one thing, she explained to herself, to care about her as sincerely as she knew he did and still not be able to quell his need to be with other women, as pitiful as that need was. It was quite another to undo her just as she was poised for a great personal success. She tried to convince herself on the journey westward that, at least until she confronted him, she might be able to accept that Hammett loved her still but was simply bad Hammett being bad Hammett, boys'll be boys . . . or some such bullshit.

Hadn't she, after all, once gone to bed with men, a fairly wide variety of them, simply because the experience promised to be interesting and possibly more than that? Perhaps she wasn't so different from him after all. She told herself this while avoiding the most important difference: she had flirted to the very brink of bedding but actually slept with no one—and certainly not her husband—since the night she met Dashiell Hammett. Sentimental as it may have sounded for the Hollywood of the early thirties, Lillian Hellman had finally chosen to be faithful.

Throughout the trip west she grudged and ruminated and found herself swinging back and forth emotionally—and strategically too, because she didn't want to lose him over this. Her fury always triggered the same question: Why should it be different for him? Why did she feel as though this time something had broken within her that could not be repaired? And why for Christ's sake couldn't she even breathe right? She wanted to pummel him, scream obscenities at him, beat him down, and then kick him until she herself, exhausted, collapsed.

He really did not love her.

No sooner had she allowed herself to think the thought than she conjured up moments of Hammett's kindness, his encouraging notes about her writing, his surprise gifts—a first edition *Père Goriot*, a jeweled nightingale hatpin, imported New Orleans gumbo—his affectionate nicknames—Lillushka, Lillia, Lilletta—the tenderness he displayed in bed when he knew she needed attention. He loved her of course. Of course. But, no, clearly their fidelities were not equivalent. If that were so, Lilly concluded it could not be love.

She'd heard the statement uttered as truth her entire life. Men were just different. Constitutionally. She'd heard it first at the Demopolis dinner table even when the pseudo-aristocratic Marxes and Newhouses and the far more plebeian Hellmans thought she was too young to understand. Even then it was all too clear that the banter about uncles and cousins who visited those "certain ladies" was perceived one way by the gents at the table and very differently by the ladies. It was something men did, a need they had, this one should understand. The women, of course, knew what was their business and what was not their business and opted to look askance, a small price to pay for their privileges and protection. Yes, Lillian understood the subtleties at an early age. She was merely young, she wasn't stupid.

New Orleans life in the Hellman sisters' boardinghouse significantly furthered her sexual education. Her aunts often joked quite openly about who was visiting whom after the lights went out. But that was unnecessary. From her room on the fourth floor, Lillian could hear and discern the treads of different gentlemen calling on Amanda Sweet—this time the name is not fictional—next door in 421. Sometimes three different treads on the same night. Prepubescent Lillian thrilled to the ghostly sounds, the repressed squeals, the moans, the occasional growl, that came through her flocked wall.

She enjoyed seeing the participants at breakfast the next morning playing their public parts. Invariably Miss Amanda was the first one up, sitting proudly by the bay window, sipping coffee, teasing a croissant, perusing the *Picayune*, ready with a welcoming "Maw-nin'" for all who entered. The gentlemen, some of whom came in with their wives and children, more or less acknowledged their breakfast companion with polite smiles. Really, what else could they do given Amanda's charming civility? The women were even more guarded, perhaps only because Amanda was so darkly beautiful, perhaps because she was so completely free to be herself—and dangerous to them if only for that reason. Lilly appreciated Amanda's breakfast room performances.

The Hellman aunts—neither of whom was ever to marry—were of two minds where Miss Sweet was concerned. Aunt Jenny wanted the woman spoken to and her activities in the house curtailed; well, spoken to at least. Aunt Hannah cherished and protected Amanda as an older sister would, deeply appreciative of a strong, self-made woman who made her way proudly in a man's world with what she called "admire-able a-plum." Aunt Hannah, Sophronia, the maid, and through them, Lillian, those three were the only ones in the house who knew Miss Sweet owned a short row of buildings down on Bourbon Street. "Beat the hypocritical bastards at their own game" is how Hannah Hellman put it over some late-night cognac, which Lilly was allowed to sip. Beating the bastards at their own game made perfect sense to Lillian too, even when she was twelve.

Lillian had been in New York for those two weeks trying to beat the bastards at their own game. Rehearsals finally over, *The Children's Hour* was working its way to Broadway for its premiere. Everyone who had read it knew it could be a hit. Word spread quickly, expectations grew—good things—but now Lillian felt more pressed than ever to deliver something special on opening night. She was polishing dialogue, even rewriting some very delicate scenes between the schoolmistresses—indeed, Drumsheugh and the nineteenth century had been left far behind—working with the director, the actors, trying to get the damned thing absolutely perfect. She was working so bleeding hard she honestly didn't know if she was now making the play better or worse.

Hammett knew how important this was to her. Damn him. He was the one who told her to give it a month, to bring it from Boston to New Haven and then to Broadway and to make absolutely sure the story always stayed exactly the story she wanted to tell the way she wanted to tell it. His idea from the outset, from the Drumsheugh history to pushing her through half a dozen killing revisions, and now it was to become completely hers, the great success on Broadway, *her* success. His part, he told her before she left, was long done; this time, the glory was all for her. The bastard. He knew the play was still in New Haven. She'd left her notes with the director. How could he do this to her? Just now, just when . . . It had to be deliberate.

Just before she married Arthur Kober, actually in the cab on the way to the temple, her mother Julia said, while facing away from her, with an ironic tone Lilly rarely heard from her, "They say Jewish men are different. Maybe, I'm not so sure. Friday nights, then the *Shabbos*, maybe it's only harder for them to find the time to squeeze it in." They both laughed.

Sitting alone in the darkness of Pan Am Flight 82, Chicago to Los Angeles, Lilly laughed again at the thought. What was all this crap she was telling herself about men? How did she allow herself to get so off track? This wasn't about men. Or Jewish men. This was about Hammett. About his willingness—his desire—to hurt her.

Her stomach ached. That was where she'd always been vulnerable, even as a girl. Now she recalled something Hammett once told her about fistfights. Hammett's Continental Op, when he gets into it with the bad guys, tries to punch at the body. "That's where the real damage gets done, and it doesn't even show," the Op explains to a naive client. Hammett told Lilly that was true and also you didn't hurt your hands on bone. Lilly touched her own stomach tenderly. That's where the damage is and it doesn't even show. She was very angry again.

Every rag with a Hollywood gossip column had a story on his escapades and featured some variation on "When the cat's away . . ." Hedda Hopper, who despised Lillian for calling her "Greta" continually at one of Jack Warner's croquet parties, gave the item daily play and provided more details than anyone else. "What famed studio Boswell has been making the round of all the night spots with a different exotic China doll or three on his arm now that his once-true-love is back East scripting her new drama? She'd better put a private eye on the case fast. Unlike our antisocial Greta who 'Vants to be alone,' this is one guy who apparently can't ever get enough pleasant company. Piece of advice: 3,000 miles is a very long way to stretch fidelity, if it was ever there to begin with."

Lilly didn't need the gossip mill to tell her something had gone terribly wrong. None of her calls to Hammett had been answered, not to their place, not to his place, not to the studio. She left messages for him everywhere, none of which got returned.

There was a day or two when she thought it best just to throw herself into her work, leave the matter unresolved until she got back. What she didn't know would hurt her less than any detailed truths. And she could rewrite whatever imaginary scenarios were required to suit her needs. Her friend Laura Karp changed her thinking over the phone with these sentences: "Lilly. He's not like I've ever seen him before. He's gone way over the line. These girls are trash. Street whores. He's in a stupor every night. He's debasing himself. It's disgusting." She almost made it seem as though Hammett were the victim. It took a sleepless night and lots of pills for Lilly to confirm that she was the sole object of his wickedness.

Hellman was still needed for the polishing of *The Children's Hour*, so she left New Haven thinking she could get to L.A., see Hammett, set things right, or at least as right as she could, and still return to New York in time to clean up the play and enjoy her triumph. She doubted the "set things right" part.

Flight 82 was over Albuquerque in the hour before sunrise. The stewardess brought her black coffee and a sympathetic smile, which surprisingly Lillian accepted. At bottom the wounding had less to do with love than with loyalty. No, it was simpler than that. It was about being untrue. Lilly liked the way that sounded as dialogue. She may have been disloyal to Kober. She was never untrue to him. She had not lied to him about anything. She had not been deceitful. Hammett was false, disloyal, untrustworthy, all those things, but mostly untrue to her, the selfish bastard. That everyone who mattered in their professional world knew, that she was either to be pitied or mocked—she preferred mocked—took the situation to humiliating depths. She begged the stewardess for a bit of Scotch for her coffee. The stewardess winked.

The Thin Man had been released by M-G-M just before Lillian left Hollywood for New York. Hammett had not wanted to attend the premiere, claiming an absolutely unnecessary visit to Jose and the kids in Montana that very week. The timing didn't feel right to Lilly. When he made her promise not to see it without him, it began to smell bad too.

It wouldn't be fair to say she helped him with his script as much as he did with hers, but she did provide Nick Charles with some of his best lines. Hollywood writers used to play this game, Lillian called it Hayzing, the object of which was to see how many off-color puns and double entendres a writer could slip past the studio censors and the Hays Office crowd. The studio censors were tougher simply because it was cheaper for the studio to catch the fixes before Hays bounced them back. The studio censors were also just plain smarter. The reigning king of Hayzing was Ben Hecht, with Charlie MacArthur a close second. Lillian in her brief Hollywood career was closing fast on the leaders.

She and Hammett sat at their regular table at Barney's Beanery with the rough *Thin Man* script and tried to slip in as much iniquity as possible. So, for example, there's Nickie at the bar, high as usual, with two chorus girls. Lilly wrote in the margin:

FIRST GIRL: Oh, Mr. Charles, you're so much fun,
    but I have to go to bed early tonight. I'm taking
    my lifeguard test in the morning.

NICK: No need, I'll show you my breaststroke and
    you'll be just fine.

NORA (TO GIRL): Just try that, my dear, and not even
    mouth-to-mouth resuscitation will save you.

Hammett's contribution to the same scene struck her as less witty, more mean-spirited.

FIRST GIRL: Oh, Mr. Charles, you're so much fun,
    but I have to go to bed early tonight. I'm taking
    my first golf lesson early in the morning.

NICK: I've got my nine iron right here. I'll be glad
    to show you how to use it. Nora, darling, you
    wouldn't mind coming along as our caddie, would
    you?

Lillian never told him that the nine-iron banter bothered her, that it crossed a line between erotic and obscene, but worse, that it struck her as cruel to Nora. That thought clarified something for her: cruelty was in fact precisely what made the erotic obscene. She understood then her discomfort when Hammett got too rough with her in bed. It wasn't just the force of his smacks; or perhaps it was, even though he stopped when she made it clear that he had hurt her. More, it was what he said, the taunting. He would squeeze her nipples, playfully at first. Then he'd say, *So you like that, do you?* As he got a bit rougher, so did his voice: *And that? How about that!* And then meaner: *Not so much fun now, is it? Is it?* She knew that same line had been crossed—that this was the onset of cruelty. Hammett had that in him. Could a man work all those years in that criminal world, that demimonde, and not become cruel? Or maybe the reverse was true. Maybe he was drawn to that world precisely because its cruelty matched his own. Another thought: the only way Hammett's behavior made any sense was to see him as two men, two personalities.

The problem with reason was that it undermined passion. As her flight approached Los Angeles now, her severest anger had subsided. Understanding had produced that undesirable effect.

Hammett, she reminded herself, had only gone to the eighth grade before his lout of a father pulled him out of school so he could put the boy to work at a man's job at half-a-man's pay. Nevertheless, this was someone who taught himself Latin and Greek, who never met a crossword he couldn't defeat. Who'd read all the classics, could discuss the arts brilliantly when he chose to, had a grasp of European and Asian history, a knowledge of wine and fine cuisine, who could talk baseball or boxing with the best sportswriters in America. Not to mention archaeology and analytical psychol . . . Lillian closed her eyes.

IT IS REALLY VERY HARD to tell people what my father did—for a living, I mean. Unless, of course, they paid people to be drunks back in those days, which I seriously doubt. I'm not trying to be obscure or mysterious here; I honestly do not know. Sometimes he came home wearing overalls, sometimes his Sunday suit, sometimes a lumberjacket and boots. Mostly he didn't come home at all. "On the road" was my mother's explanation. Sometimes she added, "He's doing it for us." I never quite believed her or knew quite what that meant.

When he was home, he hardly ever spoke. And he never talked to any of us. *Us* was Reba, my older sister, and my little brother Dick, and of course my mother. When he did speak it was to tell us what we could not do. "No dolls at table, young lady, if you want to eat here tonight." "Young man, I don't want to hear you sass your mother ever again, or it's out on your ear." Dickie, who looked like my father and carried his name as well, took the brunt of his *could nots*. There was such a sour smell about the man. I'm sure my mom was happier when he was "on the road, doing it for us." We all were.

In the family I was called Sam. I didn't choose to become Dashiell—my middle name—until I left home and decided who I really wanted to be in the world. My mom used to call me Dash sometimes. My father made fun of the name. "When was the last time that slowpoke ever dashed?"

I realize now that maybe he was too defeated a man to sit down and talk, especially to his older son, who he must have known was watching him very carefully all the time. I've always been grateful I never had sons. You might think drink would have loosened his tongue a bit. It did at the gin mill. At home Richard Thomas Hammett was one sullen SOB.

The closest we ever came to a talk was one night when I was probably about nine or ten. I had a bad dream and must have woken myself up. I made some noises I was hoping my mother or sister would hear but no one came. I saw a light on in the kitchen. My father was alone at the table. It would be convenient to say I remember a bottle and glass, but I honestly do not. He may have been crying. He waved me in. I sat on the floor by the kitchen door. He talked. He said he always tried to do the right thing, always, by his family, by his neighbors, by the Lord, even to strangers. Yes, he wanted to go to church more often—we were Catholics—but there were so many days he couldn't, he didn't feel wanted there, felt like a Judas. That's what he said, *a Judas*.

He was talking more to himself. I was just there. But then he did look at me and I sensed he was sending out a warning. It all began with his grandfather, he said, or maybe even earlier than that, this curse on the Hammett men. His own father had passed the warning along to him. Did that mean, I wondered, that his father had heard this same nocturnal talk when he was a boy?

"There is the wolf within us, Sam, and there always has been." He said it and left a pause he seemed reluctant to fill. "We are men. You will be a man. But that is not our only nature. There is the wolf too, lonely, hungry, untamed. It makes us the kind of men we are. Our eyes, they're different from other men's."

That part was true. I could see it was true. Pale eyes, pale, pale eyes. He had them, Grandpa had them, I had them. Kids called me Ghost because of my pale eyes. But the eyes weren't the real issue. They were only the sign of our wolfish natures—restless, solitary, ravenous. Jesus, what a thing to tell a boy.

"When you least expect it," he said, "that's when the wolf comes. In your belly. In your throat. All over your skin." He shivered. He was sobbing again. Try to imagine how hard it was for a boy to understand what this father was saying, how he was acting. Imagine also how the man that boy would eventually become would be shaped—well, maybe not *shaped* but *touched* at least—by his father's madness.

"Wolf? You mean there's a wolf's blood in me, Paw?"

"We attack defenseless things, we Hammetts. Things that mean us no harm." I could see now in the dim light he was crying more deeply now. "We can't let things be peaceful. We have teeth and claws and have to use them. Pity us, Samuel."

He rose, stood me up, took each of my shoulders in his strong hands, and said, "It isn't so terrible after all, boy, as long as you never let anyone see you do this." Papa threw his head back and released a long whispered howl. He was laughing.

He was gone not many days later. I didn't see my father except on and off briefly for a great many years. Eventually I developed a vague sense of what he meant about Hammett men. I would never have come up with wolves myself—every drunk has at least one great metaphor in him—but that's a better understanding than what I did come up with. His poetry was better than mine. I only have a sense of something dark, something dangerous, something other, and there is a compelling desire to free it, precisely because it is shrouded or caged or whatever . . . so why not call it my father's wolfish nature? I'd been the wolf with Jose. I've tried not to be the wolf to my children, but I hurt them simply by staying away. And now Lilly. God help me.

Did I know what I had done? I knew, whatever anyone else may believe, that I had no choice in the matter. I knew I would have to ask her for some consideration but that I would do even that in a wolfish way. Worst of all, I knew I would do something like it again. Wolves don't apologize.

Wolves never apologize.

HELLMAN WAS SOUND ASLEEP when her plane touched down at Mines Field in Los Angeles, so soundly asleep that she was the last passenger into the terminal. Their regular man, a tiny Filipino named Kai Mindao, met her at the gate. He worked for them when they were both in town and kept their place when they were not. She asked him if he knew where Mr. Dash was. He believed Hammett was at the studio. She told him to take her to the Santa Monica apartment as long as he was sure Mr. Hammett was not there. Kai said he'd make sure, but he had driven Mr. Dash to the studio yesterday and he had not seen him return.

"And how was he? Yesterday I mean?"

"Himself, Mrs."

"Which himself?" She tasted her gall again.

"Himself. As always."

Lillian needed time. To sleep. To make some phone calls. To think.

Kai had indeed located him. Hammett was in a bar in Culver City, right across the street from the M-G-M commissary.

Of all possible venues for a showdown, not so bad. Certainly better than breaking into a hotel room. She still didn't know what she would say. She had a better sense of what she would do. Hit him. Try to hurt him if she possibly could; there was a chance if he was drunk enough.

As they approached the bar on La Cienega, Lilly realized she knew the place. She had spent some time there with Hammett when they first met during her days with Kober at Paramount. The familiarity of the bar both calmed her and made her more angry. For some reason the matter of leaving or staying with him never came to mind; all she wanted to do was batter him.

The day was warm, the bar very dark. For her it was like entering a movie at midday. She stood by the door and let her eyes adjust. The clock above the cash register said 1:20. She noticed as she approached from behind that he'd had his hair cut very recently. He was newly shaved too. There was talc on his collar. Sure signs that his toot was recently over. It must have been an incredible drunk.

Once when she was a teenager back in New Orleans, Max took her to the fights on a barge in the harbor. She wore a newsboy cap, a leather jacket, knickers, and she passed too easily for a boy. The fight she saw and still remembered, a coal-black man against a Creole, ended so suddenly she never saw the punch that put the black man down and out. Not many others saw the punch either; men in the crowd booed and shouted "Fix!" Later her father explained to her as he counted his winnings that the knockout blow was no phantom but a short, perfectly placed solar plexus punch.

"Solar plexus, Daddy?"

Boxing historians, of which Max was one, knew the provenance of this particular blow. The huge American heavyweight champion "Gentleman Jim" Corbett lost his title to the slight Brit Bob Fitzsimmons back at the turn of the century when he was hit in the small, particularly vulnerable area—the solar plexus—just below the chest cavity and above the stomach. When perfectly placed, the blow didn't have to be powerful to arrest an opponent's ability to breathe and render him absolutely helpless. Exactly the outcome that would satisfy her this afternoon with Hammett.

That was her ideal retribution. The image of Hammett on his knees, gasping for air, unable to speak, pleased her greatly. The two were, after all, already well beyond words. First a fist, then an openhanded smack, a clawed hand, a kick, and why not a scream—no, a shout—while pummeling him, that at least would tame the rage pulsing through her now.

Lilly had no idea he saw her coming up behind him in the mirror—there are some things a detective never forgets to do. She noticed when she got closer he had only a coffee cup before him on the bar. The drying out had indeed begun, probably it had started just this morning with the haircut and the shave.

She stood directly behind him and now saw him looking at her in the mirror. They said nothing. Did nothing.

"You know, if I had a piece of piano wire, I'd garrote you."

"No, you wouldn't." She'd forgotten how calm his voice could be in very emotional moments. "You'd only *try to* garrote me. I wouldn't let you garrote me."

"So tell me why."

"Because I want to breathe a while longer on this earth."

"No. Why won't you keep your dick in your fucking pants?"

Hammett took a breath and looked with sadness at the bartender. "My business."

"Stand up and turn around."

Hammett smiled. "Sounds like you've got a gun."

"No. I want to hit you."

"Fair enough."

Hammett slid his stool back a bit and rose. The bartender moved away. Hammett turned around slowly and faced Lillian. He was tall and straight and clean. He was not smiling but nodding, seeming to acknowledge her right to some form of retribution, just not garroting.

His jacket was open. She had bought him this tie with a small floral design. His solar plexus, as best she could determine, lay behind the widest point on the gray silk. Hammett's scarred, tubercular lungs lay behind that too. The punch, she knew, had to be sudden, had to be sharp, thrown with all the force she could muster and with all her anger channeled into it.

Lillian exploded at Hammett's chest.

He caught her fist in midair, mere inches from his tie. His pale eyes narrowed: "Not here, Lilly."

He was hurting her wrist. "Humiliation for humiliation."
He pulled her close. "I said, not here."

"I'm going to spit in your eye."

"No, you are not."

Once in Galatoire's in New Orleans a man came over to the table where she was having crayfish gumbo with her father. As the man approached, Max Hellman touched her hand and quietly said, *Don't say a word. Whatever happens, let me take care of this.* The man was large, but so was her father. The man stuck his head low over their food. He called Hellman *Maxie* and said something about *You people . . .* and *Better watch your kosher ass . . .* Max Hellman waited, smiled upward and spit squarely in the man's eye. Since Max had not quite swallowed his gumbo, the sight was disgusting in the extreme. Max then rose quickly and landed the first hard blow before they took the other man away. Galatoire's did not want to lose Max Hellman's patronage.

Lillian Hellman spit squarely in Dashiell Hammett's eye. The amount of phlegm she produced surprised her. Hammett snorted and laughed.

Hammett said to the bartender, "Hey, pal, how about a towel?" And then to Lillian: "You are really something, you are." And then to the bartender again: "She's got a legitimate gripe. We're not married."

Lillian said, "No, we were only lovers."

Movie Business

IT WAS RELATIVELY EARLY for them to be driving home, not yet 1:30 a.m. Hammett claimed he was tired and produced convincing yawns to prove it, which was fine since they were with old friends, Myra Ewbank and Phil Edmunds. The yawning began, Lillian observed, after his first cigar and snifter of cognac. It may even have been partly real; he had after all been up early and locked away writing a *Thin Man* sequel the entire day. After his second cigar and cognac, his weariness became more phony and more honest.

Phil and Myra had a place, a modern, Frank Lloyd Wright-ish home in the hills above and beyond Hollywood. They were married but Myra's credits were always in her own name. They were both writers under contract to M-G-M. Everyone knew Myra as the stronger writer. The couple were known in the business as "fixers," actually as "fixers of last resort." When a once-promising script had gotten mangled beyond recognition by half a dozen failed approaches, Myra or Phil was called in to save the project before it was written off. Of all the staff writers, they were the only ones Louis B. Mayer could always identify correctly by name.

Myra, whom Lillian liked a great deal, once explained the simple secret of her success: go back and find the original script and then the first rewrite and discover exactly where the second version lost its way. Then simply bring it back to what Mayer or the production supervisor, David O. Selznick, liked about it to begin with. Pick up and follow that old trail. Of course, leave some small spaces for the big shots' input as well. Just to make them feel as though they too were important fixers.

Once over lunch at the studio commissary, Myra told Lilly the story of what she had done with *Red-Headed Woman*. The popular novel had been far too racy for Mayer and certainly would have been bounced by the Hays Office. It had gone through seven rewrites and the studio's last option was about to expire, so quite a bit of money had already been invested. The redhead in question was a beautiful but penniless young woman, Lil Andrews, who was willing to do anything—anything? Yes, anything—to improve herself in the world. Seduction of rich old men was her method of choice, and it was used exhaustively in the novel. She was killing old men off with bedsprings. Attached to the original screenplay was a memo recommending Garbo for the lead. A second memo said Garbo was not available, so the script was rewritten twice for Joan Crawford. Crawford still didn't want to touch it. A new director came into the picture and thought Lil Andrews ought to become the innocent victim of these powerful old lechers. So yet another version was written. And on it went for seven rewrites.

Myra found the original script and retyped it—not rewrote it—making one simple script change throughout: Lil Andrews actually loved and truly admired each and every old man she seduced on her way up the social and financial ladder. Myra attached a memo recommending Jean Harlow for the part. And Harlow, with her comic flair, vamped her way through the role. *Red-Headed Woman* was a great success. For her "typing" job, Myra Ewbank received fifteen thousand dollars, her regular fee and a bonus. "Took me all of two weeks. When I got the check," she told Lilly, "I put it into my account that very morning. And when I endorsed it, I also wrote, 'Hooray for Follywood.' Of course I tried to make the *F* look a little like an *H*."

"You've got your own account?"

"Sure. Don't you?"

"Yes, but I'm not married to the guy."

"What has that got to do with the price of babies?"

Lillian raised her glass. "May I ask you something even more personal . . ."

Myra nodded.

"The house, is it in both your names?"

"Actually, it's mine. I bought it myself. Why? Thinking of getting your own place?"

"We're talking. Maybe something in New York."

"Oh no. I'll really miss you two."

"Don't let on to Dash."

That conversation confirmed what Hammett always averred, that Myra was the brains and the talent, Phil the charm and the studio connections. Together they had everything covered that was important professionally with Mayer at M-G-M. Hammett also knew that Phil Edmunds and Lillian had had a bit of a fling back when Arthur Kober got his wife her first job. Lilly knew that Hammett knew about Phil and hoped to see some indication of jealousy reveal itself, but she never did, other than a small disparagement of Phil's talent. She thought he was a decent screenwriter. There were certainly worse. On the other hand, Hammett valued Edmunds as one of the most discreet drinkers at M-G-M and as the source of very reliable studio information.

Although Hammett was yawning, Lillian was the one who should have been exhausted. She had gotten back from New York and the opening of *The Children's Hour* just two days earlier. She had been on the phone continually dealing with new production problems as they arose and requests for interviews and, even worse, well-wishers who wanted tickets and whose conversations with Lilly should have ended after her thankyous but did not. There were some very lavish Hollywood parties planned in her honor, but Hammett thought a quiet evening with Myra and Phil, old friends, would be a more pleasant way of reentering this artificial world. It didn't hurt that Hammett considered Myra the best cook on the West Coast and that she promised to make Stroganoff.

Both Phil and Myra were genuinely happy with Lillian's success. They could not reasonably be jealous because much earlier, when they had read the final drafts of *The Children's Hour*, they knew neither of them could ever have written it. They had chosen for themselves the relative anonymity and excessive pay of screenwriting over the more dangerous literary pursuit Lilly attempted. But word of the play's enormous success had come west instantly, that is to say electronically, and Hellman had become a literary star out here as well.

During the evening Phil kept wanting to know more about the opening, more about the audience reactions, about the performances, more about the reviews, and who said what exactly. Lilly kept insisting she didn't know or couldn't remember. Anyone pan it? Myra asked.

"Of course," Hammett said, "the Hearst flacks went after it like it was *Das Kapital* for lesbians."

"Still," Phil said, "it's an unqualified Broadway success."

Hammett said, "In New York there is no 'unqualified' anything."

"For Christ's sake, Lilly, tell us more about it, everything," Phil said. "You haven't even basked."

Myra, who happened to be in the kitchen, called out, "Don't humor the girl. She's basking in silence. That's the worst kind of basking to have to listen to."

They didn't speak very much as they ate the best Stroganoff in Southern California and drank a good Napa Valley burgundy. The bread and cheese were French, the dessert a baked Alaska. "Jee-sus," Hammett said to the ceiling, "this woman could possibly cuisine her way into heaven . . . Brava, Myra Ewbank."

At dinner there were toasts to Lillian's success, and to future successes, to Myra's wonderful meal, to friendship, and to more good work by all and bigger paychecks. Mostly the after-dinner talk was of the movie business. The transition came when Myra wondered aloud about something Lillian had been thinking for a while: Could there be a way to adapt her play about a possible lesbian affair into a film? "Not while Louie B. draws breath" was Myra's opinion.

"Imagine," said Lilly, "this from the genius who made that little redheaded tramp into a charmer? Turned Emma Bovary into Old Faithful."

Myra said, "Your two ladies truly love one another. And that's a Mayer taboo writ large. Only thing I can think of worse is maybe cannibalism."

Hammett said, "Bite your tongue, Lill."

Phil steered the conversation to the various projects in the works at the studio, not only what he and Myra were working on—he on some *Grand Hotel* dialogue; she on a first draft of *The Barretts of Wimpole Street*—but also about what future projects looked intriguing. "That's how they get us hooked," he said. "You go round and round always thinking there's a bigger, more wonderful brass ring coming on the next turn."

"Sure, the ring shines, but it's never gold. In fact, by the time you grab it, it's usually not even brass. The real attraction is the check that comes when the carousel stops." Hammett wished he hadn't said it. "That's the only gold there is."

"Did you see the numbers on *The Thin Man?*" Phil asked. "In the stratosphere."

"You didn't tell me," Lilly said.

"Didn't know." Dash downed his burgundy.

"Word is," said Myra, "they're going to make at least three more. *The Thin Man Picks His Nose . . . The Thin Man's Fly Is Open . . . The Thin Man Wipes His Arse . . .*"

"When it rains on you two, it really rains on you two."

Dash said, "In the words of the ole Negro spiritual, 'So when we gonna get dat Rolls-Royce car?'"

Lilly could tell that Dash had been told nothing about possible *Thin Man* sequels and that wasn't a good thing. Could they be squeezing him out? By way of changing the subject, she said, "I see the studio optioned Hemingway's short stories. Who's going to get first crack at that?"

Phil: "How about Hemingway his own self?"

"Get out of here. The great man deigning to corrupt his art with a movie? For two bits a pop in crummy theaters? That's not the Papa I've been drinking with." Lilly turned to Dash. "Tell them about the spoon."

"No."

And Dash meant no, so Lillian told how one night at Ratoff's Hemingway was particularly obnoxious and challenged Dash to bend a spoon inside his elbow by flexing his upper and lower arm muscles. "Dash said he didn't do party tricks, nor did he ever fight—present company included— just for the hell of it. But if Hemingway wanted trouble all he'd have to do was lay a hand on him. Then the two of them stared at one another for the longest time. I thought, there's a puffed-up African silverback and a lean, hungry tiger, and it's a stalemate. At the end of it all, Hemingway called out to the crowd to step up and watch how he could bend the spoon."

Hammett raised his empty glass. "Still, you have to tip your hat to the guy. He may not be Dostoyevsky but he has this powerful trick of making cardboard characters speak true. He does it better than any of us. By far."

Edmunds said, "Alas."

Myra said, "Don't be so fucking willing to acknowledge his talent. He's an overblown arrogant shit, fatuous, second-rate, and incredibly derivative. I despise him profoundly and resent his success absolutely."

Myra's outburst drew laughter, even though she had been dead serious. Phil said, "Please, dear, tell us how you really feel about the guy."

Lillian realized anew why she liked Myra Ewbank so much and disliked most other Hollywood women she knew. Not only could Myra outwrite and outthink her husband and most everyone else, she could outcook, outtype, outwit, and in a fairer world, outearn him as well. Lilly could count on two fingers of one hand the other women she knew like that.

Lillian asked Myra if Hemingway were a woman would she still dislike the work as much. "That's my point, Lilly. A woman couldn't get away with half the bullshit Hemingway gets away with, on and off the page. And a woman wouldn't write that crap to begin with."

"But look at our spouses," Lilly said. "They're both writers, both as virile as Turks—I believe I'm correct in surmising—and they don't write that garbage." Of course she was really talking about Hammett, since Phil would write anything Selznick asked him to, a wet-hankie for Bette Davis or a Jack Oakie college romp with fart jokes. And probably there was more he-man, stoical Hemingway in Hammett than she was comfortable with.

Hammett rose and blunted his cigar in a tray. "There you have it—the importance of being Ernest." He knew this was about the time when Lilly usually went up to and then over the line. "C'mon, Miss Broadway, no one here is bending spoons, no one here is beating their chests. Can't you see, they just want to go to sleep."

Lillian didn't stand up. "I want to stay. I want to tell the whole world that was the best damned meal since I had a rhino roast at the foot of Kilimanjaro."

Hammett finished his drink while standing and lifted Lillian's hand.

"Jesus," said Phil, "it's not even one. This isn't like you people."

"Lillian's brain is still on Eastern time."

"It's not."

"One more drink then."

Myra moved everyone to the living room. Phil set cognac snifters on small tables. The couples sat across from one another on matching sofas. Myra turned down the lights and said, "There."

Silence matched the change of mood until Edmunds said, "I didn't want to bring this up earlier." His altered tone matched the new subject. "It would have been unseemly to bring up business before . . . We really did invite you to celebrate Lilly."

Lilly muttered, "Unseemly. Some word."

"It's not business," Myra corrected her husband. "It's politics."

Phil glared at his wife: "Then you do it."

"I'm sorry, I'm sorry."

"We're thinking of trying to organize the writers." He let the words sit there while he looked at each of them. Hammett smiled. Lillian frowned. "It's all preliminary, very preliminary. We're just feeling people out, good idea, bad idea, what? The technical people—electricians, sound and camera guys—seem to be way ahead of us on this. In fact, they want us to be a part of what they're doing . . ."

Myra interrupted: "Word is the studios are getting together to fund a fake writers' union. *Screen Writers Association*, they want to call it. They want to control all the talent at bargain basement prices. If we want a real union, we've got to act, we really can't be screwing around."

"As you can see, my wife gets passionate. But she also happens to be right. We have to figure out what sort of association we want and when we want it."

"Union," Hammett said, stopping Edmunds short, "not association, not organization—union. It's important to call a thing what it is."

"Fine," Phil said. "So you think we need a union. What sort of union should it be? And when should we get it started?"

Hellman said, "Some of us do, some of us don't. The question isn't really about who needs what, it should be about whether all of us would benefit from a union now."

Hammett said quickly, "I find I must disagree somewhat with my esteemed friend from New York. Unions are always about need. The four of us here are fine, aren't we? But you never know what the future holds. No, let me amend that . . . You can be sure as hell that somewhere down the line one of us is going to need some protection. That's a given. So count me in. Ditto for my skeptical young friend here."

Lillian turned and glared at Hammett: "First of all, I'd like to know more. I'd like to know who's doing the organizing. Secondly, I'd like to know who else is in and who's out and why. I'd like to know what to expect from Mayer and the other studios. And finally"—here she stuck a finger into Hammett's stomach—"I'd like to answer for myself."

Myra Ewbank began to outline some of the reasons why a writers' Writers Union was a good idea.

Lilly broke in: "Myra, Myra, I know why we have to protect ourselves, but isn't that what we each do before we sign our contracts?"

Hammett whistled: "Spoken like a woman with a Broadway hit in the oven . . ."

"Don't turn me into the villain here, Comrade."

"I think you've done that pretty well for yourself already."

Everyone felt the tension building. Myra said, "Lilly's right in asking for some more time, more information. At this point we're just asking people how they feel in general."

"And?" Hammett asked.

"There's a great deal of interest . . . and there's a great deal of uncertainty."

"There usually is at this stage. It changes." Hammett rose. "Count me in no matter what." He yawned. He reached down for Lillian, who pulled her arm away.

OUTSIDE, A SOFT, SWEET-SMELLING RAIN had begun to fall. Lillian, who had driven to Myra's house because she knew the way, had the keys and insisted on driving back to Santa Monica.

The wet road wound down toward Burbank over hilly, lightly forested land, twisting ever so slightly, almost no road lighting to guide a driver in the dark. He could sense her anger in the blue silence. The hum of the great Packard engine, accelerating and slowing by turns, was almost musical. The beat of the windshield wipers supplied the tempo. The scratch and flare of the match surprised her when Hammett lit a cigarette.

"Want one?"

"Why not."

He lit hers too. "I should not have answered for you. I have no idea why I did that." She noticed as she always did that he would not say the word *sorry.*

"Yes, you do."

"I do?"

"Sure you do. Because you have no idea where you end and where I begin, that's why."

He was silent, thinking over what she had just said.

There was a traffic light ahead. Hammett knew Lillian had no intention of stopping if the light turned red. It did. She didn't. He glanced to either side of the tree-lined intersection where a motorcycle cop or a police car might have been hiding. He saw none. The wet road glistened in their headlights and the humming silence began to comfort them again.

Hammett may have seen it first, a squirrel darting across the road, stopping suddenly, looking up at them stupefied.

Lillian pulled to the left and hit the brakes. The squirrel ran forward into her path. Lillian turned the steering wheel abruptly to the right and set in motion a long, unnerving skid that ended with the Packard off the road, front forward in a ditch. Amid the high pitch of brakes on wet road, Hammett's sustained grunt, Hellman's nasal squeal, another sound, a barely perceptible *klup* that nevertheless stood out on its own. They knew. The squirrel.

Before he got out of the car, Hammett touched Hellman's arm and said, "Okay?"

She snorted. "I'll live. He won't."

Hammett went back up the road but couldn't find the squirrel. He almost convinced himself she hadn't hit it after all when Lilly called, "Here. It's here."

The squirrel was on the far side of the road, off the surface, on the pebbly shoulder. Literally knocked for a loop, it lay on its side breathing slowly but deeply, its eyes blinking. Lillian was saying "Shit" repeatedly.

The rain had not diminished. Behind them, from the direction they had come, a car with a swirling red light approached.

Hammett knelt down quickly and ended the squirrel with a sudden and efficient crack.

Two cops, the same size exactly, interchangeable it seemed, came out of their car. One carried a flashlight. "Seen you run the light back there, ma'am. Big hurry. Seems to be the trouble?"

Hammett said, "I was having a problem with the accelerator back there, officer. Proof is I couldn't avoid this fellow when he ran into my path."

"No, no, let's not try this. Lady was driving. We both saw her, right, Newt?"

"My wife doesn't drive."

"Sure, sure. Driver's license. Both of you."

Lillian said, "My husband's telling you the truth, officer. I wouldn't even know how to start up a big car like this."

Newt put the flashlight on her face and said, "Doing some celebrating?"

Hammett said, "Some good food with friends, nothing crazy."

Newt put the light on Hammett's wallet: "You two sure you want to stick to your story? Because if you think you got trouble now, you have no idea what's in store when . . ."

His partner, inspecting Hammett's wallet under the flashlight, said, "Pinkerton man? How long?"

"Too long."

Newt said under furrowed brow, "Hey. You're the guy writes the detective stories. I read them all the time. They're good."

"Thank you."

"You know what you're talking about. The other stuff is pretty much just made-up crap. Excuse me, ma'am."

"Why? They are just made-up crap."

"Exactly. Well, well . . ." To his partner: "This is Dashy Hammot."

"Oh."

"Maybe you fellows could call someone, help us get the car out of there?"

"Might be able to help you ourselves. We've still got the hook and the tow rope, right, Newt?"

"If the Missus could get behind the wheel, Mr. Hammot and I could help push."

"You forget, she can't drive."

"What the hell was I thinking?"

The police car tow rope hooked the Packard's bumper and the huge car came out easily. The cops asked for autographs. Hammett said, "You'll want my wife's more. It'll be very valuable some day." They each autographed blank speeding tickets.

"Put down something that says who you are and what we did, like, *To my favorite nonarresting officer*, or something like that."

Lillian wrote, *Thank you for this second chance at freedom!*

Hammett: *To the sweet pleasure of getting away with murder!*

After they all shook hands and began to leave the scene, Hammett took the squirrel's body into the woods.

Hammett was driving now. The rain had intensified. The mood was better than it had been before the Packard struck the squirrel. He looked over to see her sadness.

"It couldn't live on that way."

"It isn't that."

"What then?"

"Everything."

.6.

Junk

"HOW DO YOU EXPLAIN the fact that there are only four people I have ever wanted to sit down and talk with seriously and all four of them happen to be Jews?"

Hellman, who had been scribbling in a leather-bound notebook, didn't quite stop, merely slowed, and said without looking up, "They don't just *happen to be*. But, just out of curiosity, who are the other three?"

"Two of them are dead. Don't know the whereabouts of the third. And the fourth won't return my calls."

She put down her pen: "I'm hooked. Tell me."

"Jew number one. Jesus . . ."

"He doesn't return anyone's call . . . Number two?"

"Karl Marx. Dead."

"Three?"

"Siggy Freud. I doubt he's still in Vienna . . ."

"Actually he is. I spoke to people in New York who are trying to get him out but he's stubborn and won't leave."

"Or gripped by a death wish."

"But why not give him a call? I'm sure he reads *Black Mask*."

"The point is: Do you have any idea how many billions of people have been in the world and how few of them have been Jews? One-hundredth of one percent. So why do they become so damned important?"

"Figure that out and you'll know why everyone hates us so much." She began writing again.

Later that evening Lillian remembered to ask who important Jew number four was.

"L.B."

"Mayer? Why him?"

"I need to find out if I'm going to be working here a while longer."

"You've got a contract."

"He has a legal department."

"It's about what Phil said, isn't it, about the *Thin Man* sequels?"

"I'll know where I stand if I can see his face. He won't return my calls."

Dashiell Hammett, whenever he got into a serious conversation with someone he didn't know well, usually about the time the second drink was being poured, often asked, "So what's your story?" Clearly, every life had a plotline and every plotline developed in interesting ways, at least potentially interesting to Hammett, a brilliant listener and questioner, qualities that had served him so well at Pinkerton. Most people said, "What do you mean, 'What's my story?'" So Hammett usually engaged the bartender instead. Bartenders always got it. Once on a radio program when the interviewer asked him to describe his profession, Hammett said, "I collect life stories."

Here is what he collected on Louis B. Mayer over the years, not from Mayer himself of course, who made it a point to bury the true story and create his own biography, but from people who claimed to have known Mayer along the way: A Russian Jew, probably Meier or Meyer, whose family emigrated from Minsk. Louis took over his father's scrap iron business, a more respectable way of saying he owned junkyards. Then he bought one theater in Haverhill, Massachusetts, which he quickly grew into the largest movie house chain in New England. Lots of guys, Hammett realized, would have stopped there, which was why those guys were not Louis B. Mayer. No one, by the way, ever discovered what the B. stood for.

Mayer leaped from local theater exhibition to national film distribution and motion picture production in Hollywood in no time at all. As its production boss, Mayer built M-G-M into the most financially successful studio in the world, the only one to pay shareholders dividends every year during the Depression. Even Boy Zanuck wasn't able to do that. Louis B. Mayer was all about selling—scrap iron or dreams, the product didn't much matter—and that he did brilliantly. Hammett was honestly impressed by Mayer's story. He'd done in Hollywood what Isaac Marx had done half a century before in Demopolis, Alabama.

What Hammett knew about recent Mayer activities, he admired less. Mayer had been vice-chairman of the California Republican Party, and as a delegate to the 1932 national convention publicly endorsed Hoover for a second term over upstart FDR. Mayer was a man of profits; Republicans were bad for unions, good for profit. So Mayer was a Republican.

Among most of Hammett's colleagues, the writers, directors, studio intellectuals and pseudo-intellectuals, and lefties in general, Louis B. Mayer was a laughingstock and a pain in the ass. Hammett had no problem working for him and being well paid, mostly because he had no pretensions about what product he was making. For him, movie studios cranked out mostly harmless diversions; Mayer and M-G-M did it more successfully—and profitably—than any of the others.

One important detail of the Mayer story that Hammett heard from Irving Thalberg, Mayer's protégé before Mayer fired him for becoming too "artsy-fartsy"—Thalberg's word—revealed all you'd want to know about L.B.'s success: Mayer's first theater back in Haverhill was an old burlesque house, a dingy dump, lice- and rat-ridden. Even a new paint job and a name change to "The Orpheum" couldn't overcome its soiled reputation in the more respectable community. So how did the junkman fill the place up night after night? For his first presentation he chose *From the Manger to the Cross*. There you had it—respectability among the goyim and ticket sales all at once. Mayer's philosophy has never changed or varied: Give 'em what they like and how they like it. Finishing up his tale, Thalberg, a Jew, said to Hammett, "And that, ladies and gentlemen, is one very smart Kike."

Getting a meeting with L.B. was extremely difficult, unless of course you were one of M-G-M's major stars. Creating stars—actresses and actors people liked to look at—along with making uplifting stories—these manufacturing principles were Mayer's great contributions to the movie business. Unless you were Garbo or Harlow, Gable or Crawford, you'd have to stand at the end of a very long line to hear back from Mayer's office. Meeting with L.B. happened when L.B. required a meeting.

Hammett called Mayer's secretary, Elise Weiss, early in the morning. She asked what the meeting would pertain to; he said he'd rather discuss that with Mr. Mayer. Did it relate to a project in which he was presently involved? Hammett gave the same response. Would he wish to discuss it with Mr. Selznick or Mr. Gelb? The same.

There was no return call.

L.B.'s DAUGHTER IRENE was married to David O. Selznick, M-G-M's vice-president for production, Mayer's right hand. Hammett, when he heard news of the marriage, likened the match to betrothing the Infanta of Spain to the Duke of

Burgundy, a marriage made in the best political interests of
Metro. Selznick's role was to keep things rolling. In a different
factory he'd have been in charge of making sure the production line never stopped.

At luncheon in the garden of the Flamingo Restaurant
about a month after *The Children's Hour* opened in New
York, Irene Mayer Selznick came over to Lillian's table to tell
her how much she admired the play, not only for its artistry
but for her courage in taking on such a taboo subject. Lillian
was polite, appreciative, and grateful. This was after all the
boss's daughter, the underboss's wife.

Irene turned the subject to Hammett by inquiring about
his health. Fine, he's fine. Oh, I'm just curious, haven't seen
him around for a while. "When he's busy writing, Irene dear,
even I don't get to see very much of him."

Irene Selznick's eyes locked on Lilly's: "I do hope he's writing well. David would hate to lose him, such a brilliant man."
A warning, the reason Irene came over in the first place.

"Thank you, Irene. We get the message loud and clear.
Dash is drinking a lot less these days."

"I certainly never meant to imply . . ."

Lilly had heard the rumors even back in New York. As
a *Thin Man* script got closer to deadline, Hammett wrote
less and less of it. Fixers had to be hired. They even brought
Phil Edmunds in to help out. Hammett got paid to the very
end, though the final two checks came late. All Lilly said
to Dash about the meeting was, "Saw Selznick's wife today.

I think you've got some fences to mend. Why not sit down with David?"

"My business is with L.B."

"How much longer do your contracts run?"

"As if you didn't know."

Lillian walked into the kitchen and said back, "We don't need them. We can go to New York. You've got your novel. I've got my play. And it's New York, Dash, not this fucking painted desert."

"Speak for yourself, sister. There is no novel. I need this goose to keep laying."

ELISE SHOWED ME IN, indicated where she wanted me to sit, but the large sunlit room was empty. I assured her I'd be fine all by myself. It was important I be standing when the great man strolled in, if the great man strolled in. She was not comfortable leaving me alone in here, and of course she was right to distrust me. I paced the length of the room, kicked the deep pile, looked out the high wall of windows to the back lot. Mayer's desk top was very large, highly polished, and displayed three sets of my contract. I was certainly supposed to see them there. It was possible someone was watching me; just in case that was so, I offered a tourist's wave to a large mirror on the wall.

More than the sheer size and grandeur of the office, adorned with photos of all its stars under golden lettering—MORE STARS THAN HEAVEN—M-G-M, more than the staging and manipulation, more impressive than anything, was Mayer. I reminded myself that this was an estimable man, a self-made man—not admirable, estimable—a Jewish immigrant for whom the promise of the United States of America and corporate profitability had become one and the same. My job here was simple. Show him how I could make the company even more money.

Mayer blew in as though he'd just come a long distance especially to see me. Both his smile and his strong handshake betrayed too much effort. This Republican may have hated FDR but he sure as hell looked like him, the smile, the silvering hair combed straight back, the same rimless glasses. "Been meaning to talk to you for quite a while, Dash." Like so many successful immigrants, he took pains to enunciate clearly and correctly—a bit too much so. Still, you couldn't miss the Eastern European *esh* in his *Dash*, the *ean* in *been*.

"Sit there, there, if you will, away from the desk, so we can be comfortable. I've wanted to have this talk ever since I read your first book. Time we cleared the air."

He hadn't read any of my books. "I feel the same way, Mr. Mayer."

"Tell me, Hammutt, how old are you, forty, forty-five?"

"If those are my choices, I'll take forty."

"Funny. You realize that a man your age, with your accomplishments, shouldn't have to call anyone Mr. What do you and your Lillian call me when you're alone?"

"You wouldn't want to know, sir."

"Clever, very clever. Very smart. 'L.B.' would be fine." Mayer took out some lemon Lifesavers and offered me one while getting to the point: "Did you see the numbers for *The Thin Man?*"

"Actually, I haven't. Been too busy writing plots for possible sequels." I managed to laugh in such a way that what I said might be taken seriously or as a joke.

"Surprising numbers. Yes, of course we'll consider a sequel. The question: Are you really up to it?"

I flexed my arm like Popeye the Sailor, or Hemingway bending a spoon.

"There were some stories, some not-so-good reports about pages coming in late or not at all on the first script." Mayer mimed downing a shot glass. "We can't have that. I can't allow that."

"You've got my word on that, L.B."

"Word's not good enough on something like this, I'm afraid." Mayer smiled to indicate just how serious he was about the matter. "I'm going to offer a new contract. Same money but with penalties if you miss delivery dates. Legal tells me I can do this. A handshake and we're almost done here. So what do you say?"

I could do nothing but offer my hand.

Mayer sat back in his armchair. "Tea? Coffee?"

"Not necessary."

"They tell me you're a very erudite man, no schooling, like me, but very erudite. I admire that. I learned more about human nature trying to get an empty boiler out of a basement and onto a truck than I could have learned at Harvard, believe me. And you, you got your education at Pinkerton's, am I right?"

"More or less."

"Ever do any union busting for them?"

"I was strictly homicides, kidnappings, bank jobs." It wasn't true but it sounded good, even to me.

"Unions, the hell with them, I say. They get any kind of foothold here and we're all in the crap. What do you think of that?" He looked into my eyes.

I knew instinctively not to look away and said, "I think we may disagree on that one, L.B., but then again I don't run a major American corporation. I'm just an ink-stained wretch."

"Baloney. Not what I hear. I hear you're about the smartest guy in this place. And that's a consensus of opinion. You see, I've asked around, heh, heh."

I suspected this silliness was leading someplace serious. I was wrong.

"So let me ask you as an erudite man, Hammutt, what do you think about Shakespeare? For the movies, I mean." Mayer made a sour face as though to indicate the response he expected.

I warmed to the subject quickly. "I'll try to keep this short, L.B.—you're busy—but my view of Shakespeare is just a bit unconventional. I don't see him as the great artistic and philosophical genius upon which all Western literature is based, not the man everyone has to read in order to be considered truly educated. That's not my Shakespeare."

"So tell me your Shakespeare?"

"My Shakespeare is a genius, yes, but a genius of production and presentation because he could tell a story that packed them in his *own* theater, that packed them *all* in—the peasants, the merchants, the aristocrats. A genius of the storytelling business. And what really made him a man for the ages, L.B., was that he had to be successful against the toughest competition, had to sell more tickets than any of his competitors, and he did it by telling better stories, putting on better plays, providing better entertainment. He didn't set out to make *art*; he set out to be a successful showman." I refrained from saying "Like you." "So just find whatever his audiences liked and adapt it for *your* audience and you're in business."

Mayer's face had unknotted when I mentioned Shakespeare's success in selling tickets, but he certainly wasn't completely sold. I couldn't wait to tell Lilly what I thought I had pulled off. She'd absolutely piss herself.

"But it's such gloomy stuff. You kill your father. A black man strangles his wife. This guy is cursed by witches and kills everyone in sight. Who needs it! I want people leaving happy so they know where to come to be happy again."

I snuffled a laugh as I was supposed to. "Of course he knew most people didn't want gloom and doom all the time. That's why he wrote comedies too."

"Yeah, but would they be funny today?"

"With the right actors, the right director. Absolutely."

"You could work on something like this, you could find the time?"

"I'd give my eyeteeth and my molars."

"What would be a good one to start with?"

"A *Midsummer Night's Dream*. Ideal for us . . ."

"That's what David thinks too. This is all his idea. Not mine. I'll have him call you today. I'm still not sold. He didn't like Jews. Doesn't he have this Jewish guy who has pickpockets all over the place and lends out money for a pound of flesh?"

Dickens's Fagin and Shakespeare's Shylock had become a despicable Semite in Mayer's mind. "There are no Jews in *Midsummer Night's Dream*."

"Still. Shakespeare, who needs him?"

Louis B. Mayer stood. The meeting was over.

AFTER THE MEETING Hammett needed some time to sit with a drink and evaluate what had just happened to him. He'd have preferred to do it alone, but lunch with Lilly would have been almost as good since she asked such sharp questions. Neither was about to happen because as he left Mayer's office, Nick Charles, the Thin Man—William Powell himself—was coming out of Selznick's office. "This is impossible," Powell said. "We were just talking about you. I uttered your name not ten seconds ago. My, my, my." The style was inimitable on screen or off. "Unless . . ." He grabbed Hammett's arm. ". . . unless this is a setup and they've got you tailing me."

"Not unless you're planning to jump over to Warners with all our secrets. Even then I'd never jeopardize my only meal ticket."

Powell was now patting Hammett's shoulder: "*Your* meal ticket! Hardly that. Where'd I ever find another character this perfect? No, no, *au contraire*, wouldn't want you killing him off for some ungodly reason."

Hammett spoke and didn't quite hear himself say anything.

"Say, old man, can I buy you a bite? Important. Give me a minute, though. Got some photos to autograph. One's public must be served. Say twenty minutes?" He stepped away.

"I have to say yes first." Powell stopped. "Yes."

"Twenty minutes then." Stardom, Hammett reminded himself, was impossible to comprehend rationally. Look at this guy. A kid from Pittsburgh takes some elocution lessons to correct a lisp, becomes an actor, grows a mustache, and in middle age gets transformed into something akin to a British aristocrat, adored by millions of American housewives who really think he's the cat's pajamas. It's all illusion of course, a simple magic trick in the dark. A movie star appears on the screen and no one can know who is real—Lord William Powell, Nick Charles, or the kid from Pittsburgh who used to lisp.

Tactically this Powell maneuver, this "chance" meeting, was worthy of the Jewish junkman at his best. Powell's implication that *he* was being tailed. His alleged concern about his future as Nick Charles. The setup for lunch. Brilliant stuff.

Powell's table wasn't the most prominent at the Beverly Hills Hotel, but it certainly could receive significant attention from other diners. When the waiter approached, Powell said to Hammett, "Drink? Bit early for me."

"I always tell myself I'm in Bangkok and it's tomorrow night. Just gin, no ice, an olive."

The waiter said, "Dry martini then, sir?"

"No. Don't even disturb the vermouth bottle. Gin, no ice, an olive."

Powell said, "Same here." He waved to people in the room while appearing to come to the point: "Word is pretty strong that there's at least one more *Thin Man* coming to your neighborhood theater. True or false?"

"Something in between."

Still waving: "I heard it was pretty much a done deal."

"Bill, there are no done deals until the deal is done. Rule number one with L.B."

The drinks arrived. Powell touched Hammett's glass: "To crime."

Hammett said, "To criminals."

Powell pointed to his stomach when he ordered his salad. Hammett ordered a steak rare. After a bit more *Thin Man* nonsense, Powell said it was time "for me to come clean." He needed Hammett's professional expertise . . . no, not as a writer, as a private detective. Hammett joked that he'd let his license expire but that his fee was still fifty bucks a day plus expenses.

The matter had to do with a very messy divorce action Powell's wife was pursuing against him. The actor squeezed his cheeks across his nose: "Apparently Carole's got a detective willing to testify I haven't been the most faithful scout in the troop." Carole was Carole Lombard, at Paramount, an even bigger star than Powell. "L.B.'s concerned. So what am I to do with her detectives?"

"You said detective, singular, now it's detectives."

"There are a few." He signaled the waiter for two more drinks. "You realize, Dash, that I'm not admitting to anything here. I'm simply asking you what's the best way to deal with this detective situation, you having been one for so long." Powell couldn't help delivering his lines in the blithe singsong of his screen persona, so it was hard to take the guy and the situation too seriously, especially when everyone in Hollywood knew he'd had an affair—what Lilly called "a shtupping bee"—with Jean Harlow for quite a while. Hammett had only seen Harlow twice and had to catch his breath each time.

"So basically you want my professional advice on the cheap, a steak and a couple of drinks." Powell mimed indignation. Hammett laughed: "Bad joke, forgive me. Well, really there's only one way to go with this, as I see it. Discredit the detectives. What do you know about them? Independent guys for the most part?"

"That's what I've gathered."

"Good. Means they probably hustle for cases. That helps you. Find some of their previous victims, go out and get depositions, tons of them. Pile them on. Guys like this have made a lot of enemies. Find them. And see if they'd be willing to testify, or could be made willing. At the very least you should be able to neutralize their testimony with the judge."

"I guess I'll have to find my own investigator, won't I?"

"Should have already."

Hammett judged this professional advice personally important to Powell but still peripheral to Powell's studio business with him this afternoon; namely, giving L.B. a report on Hammett's trustworthiness and ability to deliver on future *Thin Man* scripts. Powell brought the matter up more directly just as Hammett was about to taste a superb steak prepared perfectly. Because improvising a scenario was what the Hollywood Hammett did best, he said, "I've already started writing the next one."

"What can you tell me about it?"

"For now I'm calling it *The Thin Man Goes Hollywood*."

Powell said, "Hmm." And then again, "Hmm."

"An important producer is murdered in his office. Scripts have been stolen."

Powell was hooked. Hammett made him wait while he chewed his steak. "I want the entire film shot against a real studio backdrop. People love seeing all the behind-the-scenes stuff that goes on at a studio. We feature M-G-M itself, we show some of their biggest stars, we show the way movies are made."

"Interesting. Where does Nick Charles fit in?"

"Nick's a beard." Confusion masked Powell's face. "A beard, someone whose real identity and function are disguised. He and Nora are brought in as a sophisticated new writing team from New York by the head of the studio . . ."

"Someone like L.B.?"

"Someone exactly like L.B. . . . to discover the murderer."

"Who is . . . ?"

"No idea, could be anyone, even the boss himself, but that's the easy part."

Powell held up two fingers to the waiter.

Days to Come

Occasionally, and without knowing exactly why, Hammett stopped working on a *Thin Man* idea and typed a page or two, a memory, a backwoods Maryland reflection, about his mother Anne and his sister Reba. In his most recent memory they are sitting at the rustic kitchen table his father had made years earlier. Slanting light brightens the dark kitchen only a little. It is quiet except for the woodland sounds outside. At the table they are peeling the potatoes they had just dug from the garden. Each had dug the black potatoes with a short hoe and afterward washed them off in the pails outside until the precious water was black with earth. Then they poured the water carefully into the irrigation furrows of the cabbage patch. Reba, just twelve, was a woman already. Dashiell saw the scene perfectly in his mind's eye.

The two women sit facing one another in the kitchen. The sun illuminates their strong hands as they peel carefully yet quickly the small potatoes, not speaking but communicating pleasantly with soft sounds. They save their parings in a blue enamel pot. At the bottom of the page he typed, "These women, who could have been Russian or Balkan or Irish peasants, shared moments that, I realize now, I'd be jealous of my entire life. They lived in a place I could never even visit, only see from an unbearable distance. Since I could never have their moments, which I knew didn't rightfully belong to me, I did not venture back to places where I knew I would not be welcome."

Hammett already had a nice collection of such memories. Showing his little brother Richard how to hook a worm for bait. Seeing Reba kiss the Burnett boy in the woods. His father shooting their mule after it broke down. Learning to drive in a neighbor's Model T. The precious chess set he won in a guess-how-many-beans-in-the-jar contest. His mother butchering the Christmas pig in his father's absence.

Lillian had read most of these pages without letting Hammett know.

He put a new page in the machine and typed:

Darling Lillush,

 I'm down.

 I'm at war with myself again, sweet Muse, as if you didn't know. There is no chance of Victory, unconditional surrender is impossible, and certainly no peace treaty in the offing, just this war of attrition to the death

between myself and myself—my best self and my worst
self, but I'll be damned if I can tell which is which anymore. (I hear you saying aloud, Fuck you, Hammett, yes
you can! Everyone can!) I swear to you I can't.

You're a terrible example to me. You're making a
fortune and still you're a real writer. You have to know
how jealous I am of that. When you tell me I'm better
than you and could easily do the same thing you do even
better, it kills me, because, dear Lilly, I know it just ain't
so. Wouldn't things be easier for me if you accepted that
plain, demonstrable fact and we still somehow managed
to be to each other as we are, maybe even more so!

Anyway, the new Thin Man deal is almost fine. I'm
making a ton swatting ideas over the net like a shuttlecock.
But I've got to tell you, I've come to despise Nick and Nora
Charles, their careless banter, their smug superficialities in
a world where suffering is and always will be the dominant
chord. They are beyond hateful. For me they've become
insufferable—make that intolerable—upper-class villains.
Of course, brilliant and psychologically attuned as you
are, you've already figured out that what I hate in them is
myself. Still, it pays well and doesn't really damage anyone.
This is what I tell myself as I lay my old gray head on the
pillow each night and reach across to where you are not.

About your enticing offer to come to New York, settle
down with you and do litter-a-toor, I must regretfully
decline. Yes, I have heard about all the new electronic

doodads that make it possible to be in two places at the same time, but there are many reasons I'll stay west young man for the time being. I could never win back there. You're the home team and you are just too good.

I have another meeting with the Junkman today. I plan to ask him for the moon but am prepared to accept Ur-anus. You'll know the result before you receive this missive, grace the aforementioned electronic miracle.

For what it's worth, Days to Come is a shimmering piece of work and deserves all the effort you're taking to make it flawless.

Love you, Dash-Dash-Dash

When he finished typing, he was unsure of whether to pull the page and place it in the envelope he had already addressed. He left the letter in the typewriter.

THAT'LL BE HIM. Preternatural, that man. I'm not here. Oh, God help me. I need a drink.

"Hello?"

"So what have you heard?"

"Officially, nothing."

"Unofficially?"

"Nothing. It's a gut thing. I think I know."

"Lilly. Trust me, you don't know. You'll know when you know, not a moment before. When?"

"About three more hours, but I already know."

"Stranger things have happened."

"I walked out middle of the third act."

"So you didn't see if they bought the story or not. I'd be surprised if they didn't."

"You don't understand, *I walked out.* I couldn't stand it. Your fault—you always liked this play way too much."

"Because it's very, very good."

"A play about a labor strike in fucking Ohio? What the hell was I thinking? The play stinks, Dash."

"Doesn't stink."

"Does so."

"*Does not.* It's wonderful. You're wonderful."

"I find I must demur. *You're*—"

"At least you'll have your vast and growing wealth to fall back on. I'll miss you tonight."

"I doubt that very much. You could fly out."

"No, no, New York is a Hellman home game."

That line called for *There are no home games without you.* I said, "Behaving?"

"Drinking or womanizing?"

"Each. Both."

"You'd be proud of me on both counts. How about you? Behaving?"

"Drinking or womanizing?"

"Come home soon."

I said, "I think I am home." Then I graveled my voice like Durante: "I'll give 'em dis, I'll give 'em dat, show dem bastards where I'm at . . ."

LILLIAN HELLMAN HANGS UP THE PHONE SLOWLY, as though to re-create a movie fade. She drinks a second glass of Scotch, throws a mink over her shoulders, and pulls closed the door to room 1212. In the cab she tells the driver, "The Apocalypse, please." He says, "Where?" She says, "Sardi's."

At Sardi's Arthur Kober gave Lillian a soft hug and a kiss on each cheek, French style. Arthur was working as a press agent for Herman Shumlin, the producer of *Days to Come*, and had done a first-rate job. He got the play a tremendous amount of attention in the weeks leading up to the opening. The angle was, *Genius young lady playwright has not one but two hits on Broadway at the same time—unheard-of phenomenon*. The timing didn't quite work out that way. After a run of two years at the Maxine Elliot Theatre, *The Children's Hour* was due to close just before *Days* was scheduled to open. Still, it was *almost* unheard of.

She rarely discussed Arthur with Hammett, but he always remembered her most telling criticism. It was while smoking and drinking in bed right after they had met. Hammett asked Lilly about her sexual preferences with Arthur and immediately wished he hadn't.

"*Preferences*, hah. Arthur is a man afraid. Arthur will always be a man afraid. Afraid to take, even afraid to ask. He apologized even for wanting. He apologized before, during, and after we made love. Even when he wasn't apologizing, he apologized. So how could he be any good to anyone?" Hammett lit a cigarette. Lilly continued: "Of course he was great for my career. He knew everyone. Everyone. So he wasn't a great lover, big deal. Who couldn't live with that?"

"Apparently you couldn't."

Lillian could have been glib and dismissive on the subject of Arthur just then. But even though they had just met, this Hammett was a man she was actually going to try to love, so she chose to explain: "There's a certain kind of Jewish man—you wouldn't know about this—who is so fucking fearful of everything in a world that is not Jewish he doesn't even believe he has a right to breathe its air. He apologizes for his very existence on the planet. For any shadow he casts."

"A for instance."

"For instance, let's say you're invited to lunch by rich old Episcopalians. Your hostess offers you some lemonade. It's hot as hell and you're dying for lemonade. If you're Arthur, you say, 'No thank you, I'm not thirsty,' because you don't even have the right to be thirsty in front of Episcopalians. Don't make waves, don't cause trouble, be very nice and make people like you and maybe they'll think, 'You know, those Kikes might not be such a bad lot after all.'"

Hammett brought his fingers to her nipple. "These Kikes *are* already extremely likable." He pinched.

She smacked his fingers away. "Who can stand someone who can't be a man because he's a Jew? It's crazy."

"Come on, Lilly, there's a history there. It's the way people cope and survive. My old man learned how to be *not* nice, it comes to the same thing."

"No it doesn't. I'm talking about a timidity that threatens the future of an entire race of people."

"I look at Max and I don't see any Arthur in him."

"Thank God for Jews like Max Hellman." She put his hand back on her breast.

Producer and director Shumlin had reserved a large room downstairs at Sardi's. A combo—piano, bass, drums—was playing Gershwin to a large crowd of cast, friends, backers, well-wishers, and disguised ill-wishers. The mood was brave and gay. Not a confident gaiety, not a *We showed those bastards, so let's tear the place up* celebration. Rather an exhausted *We all rowed like hell for the other shore . . . and we made it. Imagine, we actually made it.*

When Lillian entered, the music jumped to "That's Why the Lady Is a Tramp." Applause built to a rumble. There were loud shouts of "Bravo" and "Author." Lilly raised an arm above her head like Jack Dempsey, her face beaming. She was pleasantly surprised and a bit undone by the welcome. These were believers who really had no idea what was coming in just a couple of hours. She picked out the older actors—the "players," as

Hammett called them—and was again touched by the courage of their choice of lives, their Broadway commitment. She remembered Ned Wever, Joe Sweeney, and Don Smith from some failed Hollywood projects and felt a new responsibility to get them more work. The younger ones—Florence Eldridge in particular—caught her eye; they couldn't be happier. Here they were, on Broadway actually living their dreams.

As Lillian passed through the room kissing and being kissed, hugging and being hugged, complimenting and being complimented back, wisecracking and laughing and sipping and smoking and performing beautifully, she began to take heart. This was the world of the theater; this was her dream world too. It had its own atmosphere, its own gravity, its own inhabitants. It was, she realized, populated with people she admired. This was exactly where she wanted to be this night.

She was on her second martini when she finally got to Florence Eldridge, who called her "Miss Hellman."

"Miss Hellman? I'm not the schoolmarm, dear. *Lilly.*"

"I just wanted to tell you, Miss Hellman, what a privilege it was to be allowed to be your 'Julie' and to . . ."

"And I just want to tell you, Miss Eldridge, what a brilliant future you have on the . . ."

It was now impossible to be heard amid the noise in the room, which was growing to a roar, but the two women had indeed said what they had to. The boisterous crowd was overflowing with freeloaders and awash in hubbub.

After one a.m., though, the crowd had thinned considerably, even some of the backers and cast members had left. The musicians were packing. Smoke clouded the ceiling. A few gray heads rested on scattered tables.

Twelve reviewers, one from each of the daily newspapers, the same bunch that had given her ten thumbs up for *The Children's Hour*, would again be calling the tune. The bar would be set higher for this one because the author would be expected to outdo herself, having already proven her bona fides as a Broadway playwright. Also because a second success is more deeply resented than a first.

Four of the reviews mattered more than the others—the *Times*, the *Herald Tribune*, the *Daily News*, the *Mirror*— morning papers that would hit the streets in a matter of hours and set the tone. The *Times* and the *Trib* were most important because some of the people who read their reviews actually bought theater tickets.

The *Mirror* review arrived at Sardi's first, around two-thirty. The kid who ran it over might have read it in the cab but he knew enough to deadpan it as he handed a warm tabloid to Herman Shumlin.

Shumlin opened it to the exact page and began reading aloud: "Blah, blah, blah, ah, here . . . *which opened at the Vanderbilt Theatre* . . . blah, blah, blah . . . *Just to relieve the suspense immediately: No, dear reader, it did not—lightning rarely does—and it certainly did not strike a second time on Broadway last night, even though all the ballyhoo for* Days to Come *promised thunder and lightning. Unfortunately for theatergoers that rare atmospheric phenomenon did not occur on the stage where playwright Lillian Hellman and director Herman Shumlin attempted to repeat the crashing success they created on Broadway two years ago with* The Children's Hour . . ." Shumlin stopped, took off his glasses, and pinched his eyes.

Lillian took the review from him and continued: ". . . *the play's main action—none of which we ever get to see—takes place offstage and attempts to capture the human suffering and strife created during a labor dispute at an Ohio manufacturing plant. Bravely, the highly accomplished cast—let me single out the fine Ned Wever as Henry Elliot and lovely Florence Eldridge as Julie Rodman as just two among an excellent ensemble. No, we cannot blame the actors for this . . ."* Lillian looked up and said, "Thanks from the bottom of my heart to all and each of you. You were the *lightning* tonight."

She went back to the newspaper and found her place: ". . . *accomplished cast struggled mightily to make believable a Midwestern world which Miss Hellman, who is from New Orleans, clearly knows absolutely nothing about.*" Here Lillian raised her eyes and addressed her small audience. She put on a British upper-class accent: "Notice, students, I chose to end that previous sentence with a preposition. I could have said, '. . . about which the author, from New Orleans, knows absolutely nothing,' but that would smack a bit too much of erudition, too much of the *Times*. It would be, in fact, highly literate. So, no, no, no, we must say 'absolutely nothing about.'

Next thing you know I'll be dangling my fucking modifier for everyone to see . . ."

She continued reading with the same strained accent: *"This, of course, is the sort of artificial drama that is produced when the playwright's politics and not her artistry—which we suspect she may possess—determine her narrative and characterization. All the characters in* Days to Come *are moved around like checker pieces, mostly red ones, wooden and circumscribed"—* she read it as *circumsized—"by ideology, unfortunately not their own but Miss Hellman's. This work is yet another example of the political claptrap we are beginning to see too often on Broadway these days. When Odets offers it up, we invest ourselves even if we feel a bit uncomfortable. Miss Hellman, on the other hand, had better quickly return to a world she knows, and that is most assuredly not small-town Ohio.*

"If these are indeed 'The Days to Come,' I'd suggest you sleep through them. That is, as a matter of fact, what I saw a number of audience members doing . . ." Lillian stopped and spoke softly, normally: "There's more, folks, and it's not funny anymore. I let you all down. I'm very sorry." Then she stood and said over her shoulder, "Forgive me if I don't wait around for the rest of them."

As she neared the steps, Ned Wever called out, "We love you to pieces, Lilly."

She was crying when the cold air on Forty-fifth Street struck her face. She didn't remember Arthur being there when she left; she didn't remember him saying goodbye either. Why was she thinking of Kober—spineless, irrelevant Arthur—when the events of the evening were so painful?

Lilly intended to call Hammett from her bed in her hotel room after a long bath, but she fell asleep in the tub. She awoke to Manhattan's thin, spare sunlight. *I'm not dead* was her first thought. *I didn't dream it either,* was her second.

Days to Come played seven performances.

.8.

Working Detective

HAMMETT HAD BEEN AWAKENED from a stupefying sleep that could only have been—he tried to see the clock—a couple of hours. "Dash. It's Myra."

"Myra?" His voice didn't work right.

"Ewbank."

"Of course. Myra."

"I'm really sorry to bother you like this . . ."

"Just tell me." He masked impatience with concern.

"I got a call from Phil. A friend of ours is dead. Phil wonders if you'd come down and look things over." There was a pause on the line, which Hammett heard as a plea.

"Sure. Give me the information."

The essential information came from Myra as this: *Jerry Waxman, mid-fifties. Staying at the Regency Arms, 450 West Figeroa, Apartment 10-B.* Hammett said the information back slowly to Myra Ewbank and she confirmed it. Phil Edmunds would be there waiting for him.

"What day is this?"

"Sunday."

"I'll have to double my expenses." Death had for so long been a commonplace in his life that Hammett did not give it the weight other people did. He sensed Myra's irritation and said, "Sorry."

There were two police cars parked on Figeroa. Hammett put the Packard a block away and walked through the bungalow complex. Day was breaking and warming. He saw Phil Edmunds talking to an older cop in front of 10-B. Hammett caught his eye and shook his head, indicating he did not want to be recognized by or introduced to the policeman. Edmunds nodded and let Hammett walk behind him up to an open door barred by an even older cop. Two men appeared to be moving about inside the darkened apartment. Hammett ambled up to the guard, flipped his wallet, and said, "Hammond, L.A. Times."

"Go chase stray dogs."

"Why? When I have me a homicide scoop right here."

"Homicide? Some guy kicks off getting it off. And not even working too hard at it 'cause she's sitting on top. That's no homicide."

Hammett crossed himself: "Let's hope his eyes were watching God, bless him. Still, of all the ways to go . . ."

"You got that right."

"Body still in there?"

"Gone hours ago"

"That fast? Still, can I get a look around inside?"

The cop's face reflected just how preposterous the request was.

"Who's in charge?"

"Lieutenant Donegan."

Hammett saluted and sauntered around the grounds, eventually making his way to the rear, where access was undeterred. Through the bathroom window he saw clearly into the lighted bedroom, to the rumpled unmade bed, to the night table still illuminated. The table held some books, two drink glasses, an ashtray, fountain pen, eyeglasses, a hairbrush, the normal stuff of a man on an out-of-town stopover. On a second bed, still made, there was a suitcase opened and neatly packed. A lipstick case sat on a wallet near the pillow. The lipstick and the wallet seemed to confirm the cop's tale of a dalliance and a payment.

Hammett had seen enough to tell him something here was not right. A talk with Donegan, if possible; a longer talk with Phil Edmunds on Waxman's background and he might be able to tell where the not right feeling was coming from. And, of course, if he could get to the girl. The French had it right in situations like this. *Cherchez la femme.*

He waited at the front door for Lieutenant Donegan and one of the medical examiners to emerge. He waited quite a while. He smoked and offered one to the cop. "The girl, she's in custody?"

"No reason. No homicide."

"When did soliciting stop being a crime in L.A.?"

"Come on."

"Donegan take her story?"

"Hers and everyone else's."

Lieutenant Donegan then came out of 10-B, a chunky fullback of a man in a brown suit with a matching brown crew cut. Donegan remembered Hammett from a police testimonial dinner and seemed flattered by meeting him again. Hammett remembered the lieutenant.

Donegan extended his hand: ". . . seeing you here. Did you know the guy?"

"Friend of a friend."

"Well. Looks straightforward enough. I've got this Waxman picking up a girl downtown in a cab. The cabdriver checked out. They come back here. They conduct their business. He starts gasping, then kicks off. She's scared shitless and calls the front desk. The desk calls us. We take everyone's story. Everything checks out. Like I said, straightforward."

"The girl. You know her?"

"Why? You think there's something here?"

"No, no, I'm sure it's like you said."

"Yeah, I do know her. Pretty good kid."

"In the old days at Pinkerton, I had dozens of these things. We used to call them 'dicker-tickers.'" He let Donegan smile. "Personally, all I ever cared about was, Did the girl get her money before the geezer checked out?"

"Angel is a true pro. Does all her business right up front."

Hammett extended his hand now. "Thanks, Lieutenant. See you in the funny papers." They were already walking toward their respective cars. "Will there be an autopsy?"

"Doubt it. The examiner thought he saw enough back there."

"The family might want one."

"That's their business, isn't it? He's from back East, right? New York?"

"Think so."

LATER, AT A BREAKFAST SHOP on Flower Street, Hammett asked Phil Edmunds to tell him everything he knew about Jerry Waxman. This is what struck Hammett as important about Phil's report: Jewish guy. Brooklyn. Tough as nails. Vice-president Northeast Electrical Workers Union. Yes, mid-fifties, but in great shape, beat me two sets of tennis yesterday at my place. Single. Dynamic sort of guy. Obsessed . . . labor organizing was his whole life. I knew him back in New York from his organizing electricians on Broadway. He was amazing at what he did . . .

Phil was getting off track. Hammett brought him back: "Myra and I invited him out for a week and set up all sorts of meetings with people who are interested in maybe getting some of the writers organized out here. You remember, what we talked about. He was going to sit down with guys from different studios . . ."

"Which ones?"

"M-G-M, Paramount, Warners, RKO, Universal, all of them. Myra knows the specifics, dates, places, et cetera. Anyway, we wanted him to stay with us at our place. He said he needed to be on his own, he had preparations. I found that apartment for him. I reserved last week and dropped him off last night."

"What time?"

"Early, before eight. He said he had work to do. I believe he did. Those meetings, lots of them, lined up all week. Jerry was a pretty serious guy."

"Did he smoke?"

"Never."

"Would you say he was a vain man?"

"Vain? Yes. Very. Why?"

"Any idea where he might have found that woman? How she got there?"

"None whatsoever, but knowing Jerry as I do something about this is just not right. I feel it. So does Myra."

Hammett lit another cigarette and tapped his coffee cup signaling for a refill. "I don't know how involved you want to get, Phil, but the important thing now is to pressure the medical examiner's office for an autopsy, and do it fast. I have a strong feeling they won't want to do it, so you might have to bring some real pressure to bear with his family . . ."

"An autopsy? You suspect something?"

"I'm in no position to get involved myself but . . ." Even as he said this, Hammett knew he was already involved simply by letting his identity become known to police at what he now believed to be the scene of a murder. "You have to move very quickly because if you wait and the official judgment is *death by natural causes*, you may have to try to prove a negative. So get the jump on it. A reliable, independent autopsy and, almost as important, the girl's statement. You'll probably have to get the newspapers involved. Even if the prosecutor is reluctant, bang the drums loud enough to get a grand jury impaneled. This might get pretty messy. Not to mention costly."

"You think someone may have killed him?"

"A distinct possibility."

"Why would anyone . . . ? For trying to organize? Jesus."

Hammett now got to play the Op or Spade or even Nick Charles, explaining how a "dicker-ticker" could be a murder: "In the ashtray next to the deathbed were two cigarettes, each lying on opposite sides of the tray, whose long ash revealed they had been lighted but neither of them had been smoked, simply allowed to burn themselves away. Even though her lipstick case was prominent, there wasn't lipstick on either cigarette. And then you tell me your man Waxman didn't smoke, well then . . .

"Secondly, if the cash deal between Jerry and Angel had been completed before any sexual activity began, why would his wallet be on the pillow of the other bed rather than on the night table, the bureau, or in his pants pocket? Possible but unlikely. And why was her lipstick case on top of the wallet? How did it get over there? He pays her, puts the wallet down on the far pillow, then she does her lips and puts her lipstick on top of his wallet? Strange.

"Third, and most important, on the bathroom sink, a set of dentures. Jerry's. With a whore in his room, Jerry, vain Jerry, as you tell me, pulls out his teeth and puts them on the bathroom sink? That's the sort of thing a guy like Jerry does when he's alone and thinks he's going to sleep. These things have to be explained because right now none of them add up." Hammett was proud of himself.

Edmunds whistled. "My god, someone killed him. How?"

Hammett didn't explain and pushed his coffee cup away from him. "We need a working photographer right away. Let me call a friend at Pinkerton. This might cost. Are you willing to spring?"

"Whatever it costs. It's the least . . ."

On the way back to the Regency apartments, Edmunds said, "How much? Approximately?"

"Depends on what's needed, how far we have to go with this. It's a Sunday. The pictures should cost no more than fifty or so."

The photographer, a scarecrow in a suit and bow tie, met them at the Regency. He had done lots of Pinkerton work and knew of Hammett through his Continental Op stories in *Black Mask*. In fact, he'd submitted a few stories there himself. One, he told Hammett, got an encouraging, handwritten rejection letter. Hammett clapped him on the shoulder. The cameraman used a Silvestri Flexicam with a large flash, exactly the right equipment for the job at hand. Hammett appreciated a pro.

The door to 10-B was closed now but the old cop, sitting on the steps and smoking as they sauntered up, was still on guard.

Hammett flipped his wallet again: "Hammond. *Times.* Remember?"

"You're still not getting in there."

"There's a news story here. You can't keep us out."

"Don't like it, talk to Donegan."

"How about we just peek in this window right here."

"How about you just get the hell back in your car."

Which is what they did, or appeared to do, making sure the cop saw them make their way to their car out on Figeroa.

A block away they parked, circled around the apartment complex, and made their way to the rear bathroom window of Jerry Waxman's rooms. The bathroom window was left exactly as Hammett remembered it. Hammett peered in the window. "Son of a bitch."

No dentures on the bathroom sink. No towels tossed carelessly on the floor near the shower. Even though the lights were turned off in 10-B now there was enough sunlight coming through the front windows to see that the room had been cleaned up. Hammett looked at his watch; it had been barely an hour. Both beds were now made. There was no suitcase, no wallet, no lipstick. The night table had been stripped clean, only a darkened lamp, no glasses or books or papers, no hairbrush, and certainly no ashtray.

Hammett expelled breath slowly from puffed cheeks. "God damn me."

Phil said, "Why?"

"I screwed this up royally. How did I let them . . ."

He explained to the photographer that just a few wide shots were now needed but be sure the time and date on them could be confirmed. "Thirty bucks for two shots and all your trouble?"

"Not necessary, Mr. H. Just meeting you was good enough for me. But maybe if you'd be kind enough to look at one of my stories . . ."

"We're sorry for the inconvenience." He put the money in the young man's suit jacket. "Phil, give him another ten." Hammett slowly began to walk away.

LATER THAT EVENING at Phil and Myra's, he gave his summary analysis: "The autopsy is only important now if it can get you to a formal inquest that determines the actual cause of death. I'm speaking legally here, so you're going to need a tough, smart lawyer who knows what he's up against and is willing to take these people on. They are very good at what they do, a hell of a lot better than I thought. I'm not wild about our chances now, and . . . and I'm profoundly sorry for falling asleep at the switch."

Phil said, "You said *our* chances. That means you're willing to stand with us on this?"

"I'll do what I can."

For her part, Myra Ewbank was still frozen by the fact that somebody had murdered her friend. Just last night Jerry Waxman was sitting right there in Hammett's chair. She looked out the window and imagined Jerry serving 30–love.

Hammett said, "If you want to proceed with this, call everyone you know in the business, newspapers, radio people. Get the word out everywhere, most especially to his union guys back East."

Myra said, "What do you mean, '*If* we want to proceed'?"

"Phil will explain."

"Does Lilly know about this?"

"No, not yet. Why?"

"She knew Jerry Waxman too."

"Really?"

Sitting in his car, Hammett berated himself. In the old days he'd never have left the crime scene. He didn't have to leave. That was a careless mistake. It was the *why* of his carelessness he searched for while smoking alone in the car.

Deep down, he knew the *why*: He had been reluctant to get completely involved as a participant. He was from the outset not, as he liked to say, *in for a penny, in for a pound*.

He was only *in for a penny*. Working from a distance, he convinced himself he could have it both ways. That was a luxury he could never have had when doing good detective work was his livelihood. And maybe at the heart of *why* was his unwillingness to jeopardize the good M-G-M money he was still making writing movie scripts? The Waxman case would have found its way back to him. That *why* carried the weight of truth.

As he drove home, he was convinced that someone had gotten away with murder. The idea was abhorrent to him. Hammett suspected how it might have been done. He remembered a case up in Frisco. The feet, an injection between the toes, insulin was his best guess. Maybe it still wasn't too late.

His sense of failure was every bit as acute as Lilly's had been with *Days to Come*. In her, failure revealed itself as shame. In him, it came as hatred, not directed at whoever might have murdered Jerry Waxman, but solely at himself.

·9·

Secrets

LILLIAN WAS STAYING at the large, sun-filled corner apartment on Riverside Drive she had leased for two years. She was hoping to entice Hammett to leave California. Of course, she preferred him to leave on his own terms, not be driven out, as looked more likely since he was being squeezed out of *Thin Man* scripts.

The sun arrived in Lillian's place in late afternoon. There was a superb view of the Hudson. A continuous line of small boats, barges, ferries, and large ships passed up, down, and across the river. They helped give her writing hours just the diversion she presently desired. She would write a sentence on a lined sheet in her tight hand, reread it, alter a word or two, perhaps move a phrase forward or back, look out the window, and tell herself she would start the next sentence when that Jersey ferry touched the pier.

It was a writing pace she'd never experienced before. Normally words poured out in such a rush she'd let them spill across the page, at least in first draft. Afterward there was plenty of time to see what she really meant, time to rearrange and reorder. Here at her neat desk alongside the window she felt herself writer, editor, and reader at once, participant and observer simultaneously. She told herself she enjoyed the ease of composing in this fashion. It wasn't true. She was, in fact, writing haltingly, uncertainly, because she didn't fully know what she was talking about.

Hammett was finally coming East. Just for a visit, he made clear. Still, she was hopeful. He'd be in New York on Thursday. She needed him right now. One good evening's talk with him would clarify her problem and give her a choice of solutions. No one knew more about what was actually happening in Spain in the first months of '37 or of the political events of the previous year than Hammett. She had not yet told him about the commitment she'd made to write a documentary film about the Spanish Civil War. She didn't think he would approve, especially if after coming to New York Hammett discovered it was Lillian who had opted to leave. No, surely he would not like that. But wasn't that all the more reason for him to come with her to Spain?

Lilly didn't fully understand why Hammett had agreed to come to New York. True, he didn't have a lot of work in Hollywood at the moment. True, his mishandling of the Waxman murder was a blow to his ego. True, he wanted to talk Alfred Knopf into a good advance on a new novel and thought that if he was based in New York for a while,

Knopf was likely to think him serious and go for the deal. And true, he missed her company, although she certainly wished he would actually declare that to be so. Just once. But she perceived something else, something halting in his voice over the phone that suggested discomfort. She put her pen down and looked out the window for a very long while and watched an ocean liner, probably arrived from Europe, being pulled by tugs up the river and alongside the West Side piers. She missed Hammett terribly.

His plane was due to arrive in Newark at three p.m. American Airlines Flight 111. She was at the terminal building early, unwilling to repress her excitement. He ducked out of the plane, stood for a moment at the top of the ramp and looked around at the people pushing forward below. He stood thin and tall, buttoning his suit jacket on a very cold day; his pewter hair against his tanned face made him look glorious. She saw him first and touched her throat with her hand. Hammett, there. She was like a young girl again with a crush on a movie star.

He carried a leather valise, which he put on the ground when she appeared before him. Seen up close he looked weary, his eyes fatigued, his face lined. It had been a hard trip; he looked very like what he was, a used forty-four-year-old. Hammett embraced her tightly with both arms, raised her off the ground, and rocked her gently back and forth. Neither spoke. Why had there been so few moments like this one between them? They loved one another strongly in each other's presence, especially when they came together after a long absence. It was Hammett who did not want to end the embrace.

Then, abruptly, as though a director had called *Cut*, Lillian pushed away, took up his valise, and, trying to be funny, ushered him through the crowd. "Coming through, folks. Coming through." And when she had sufficient attention: "That's right, God has arrived. We're all saved." Until a great many years later when she became an icon and an old lady, there was always something playful, devilish about Lillian.

In the car she chattered as she drove, throwing around names and places, friends' successes and failures, mostly failures, marital problems and scandals. Hammett did not know all the people involved and did not want to. He was more concerned with how erratically she was driving. Lillian did not stop talking. Just before she entered the tunnel, he touched her arm and said her name in a way that made her understand they were fine. She looked over at him and smiled. He was smiling back in the same way.

Lillian didn't speak again until they were in midtown traffic. "Tough flight?"

He reduced a paragraph to two words. "Very. Always."

"At least now it's legal to get high while you're high."

"Haven't had a drink in about three weeks." About the time Waxman was killed.

"Why didn't you tell me, for Christ's sake?"

"I think I just did."

"Dash. My god, that's—"

"Don't say *wonderful* or I'll puke."

"Open the window quick . . . *wonderful*."

"I've got to be careful. I don't want any of my temperance to rub off on you."

"I do."

Later, in the apartment together, they watched in silence as the winter sun set over Jersey, sending diagonal light into the darkening room. Lights came on along the riverfront on both shores; the gliding boat traffic on the water was illuminated faintly. The two were at ease. He was tired. She was tamed. They drank tea out of beautiful cups. Neither wanted to break the silence until Lilly said softly, "How come?"

He understood. "The Waxman thing. What else?" He had never told her of his carelessness in leaving the crime scene and chose not to tell her now. "Had to get away."

"I sent Phil five hundred. He says the thing is costing a fortune. Where's that all going?"

"The money?"

"No. The case."

"It's not too promising. The bad guys have a lot of clout, financial, political. Until I can be sure, we have to assume he was killed because he was going to try to make Hollywood a union town."

"They would do that?"

Hammett opened his eyes wide: "They wouldn't? I'll get a better handle on things when I go back."

When I go back came as an affront. He just got here. How to keep him here was Lilly's new concern. "I know you are far too manly to admit it, but if these guys are killers and they know you're onto them, isn't there a chance, the slightest little chance, you're in danger?"

"Actually a pretty good chance. But of course they can tail me here too. Probably will."

Lillian said in a voice close to Nora Charles's, "So Nickie, you came back to me because you needed a hideout."

"Some hideout. Who couldn't find me here? No, mostly I came because I needed you, and only you, to tell me that I wasn't a piece of garbage." Dashiell Hammett expelled a breath. He had never made such an admission to her. Another woman, he knew, would want to know why he considered himself garbage. Never Lillian. It was simply out of the question.

A long silence was broken by the sustained wail of a nearby tugboat's horn. When the silence returned, it and the darkness had deepened.

Lillian had been moved by this hard man's defenselessness more than at any time she could remember. She heard herself say the word. *Garbage,* not as a question, just as a word, the sound of it. She reached for his hand. "You? Hammett? Garbage? My god."

It was exceptionally dark outside now, the moon had disappeared into the wintry night, which made the lights of Manhattan and towns across the river seem braver. There was a faint red glow in the far western sky. Snow.

Lilly sat silently pressed against his side. His arm hung loosely about her. After a while Lilly said, "Hungry?"

"Uh-huh."

"Want to go out?"

"Don't feel like other people just yet."

"Eggs okay?"

"Eggs are magnificent."

Lillian made scrambled eggs with buttered muffins and then more eggs and more muffins, which they devoured, stopping from time to time to toast themselves with champagne, which is what they decided to call their ginger ale. After the last toast—a mock pledge of eternal loyalty to one another—they left the dishes in the sink and went to bed arm in arm. They did not make love because it seemed so unnecessary.

Hammett was up before the sun rose. This was his favorite time of day, at least when he was sober. He cleaned the dishes, the cups, the frying pan, so quietly he didn't have to close her door. Then he found his jacket and walked out through the lobby and down the front steps without encountering a soul. There was a bracing chill in the morning air. It hadn't snowed but certainly would.

He had almost forgotten how alive the seasons made a person feel, as did a true neighborhood setting. Hollywood was unreal in almost every respect but its essential artificiality lay in its invariable sunlight. Seasons and their unpredictable weather would, of course, have made location shooting too uncertain and therefore too expensive, so even the sun ended up in the movie business.

Broadway was awake, at least its commerce was. Stores, some pushcarts, newsstands were open, and people of all shapes, sizes, types, and backgrounds were all about and mingling. Hammett bought a *Times* and asked for a pack of Fatimas, which he pronounced "*Fat*-i-mas."

"Here's your '*Fa-tee*-mas.'"

"Duly noted. And could you direct me to a good Jewish deli?"

"There ain't none. But on the corner is the best of the worst."

Dashiell Hammett turned away smiling. How long had it been since he'd smiled this way, appreciatively, pleasurably, and without wearing the mask of satire. This smile made his face feel good. He was the only one smiling in the deli, where numbers were handed out even though no number was required.

When he returned to the apartment, Lilly was awake and in a short kimono. He whistled at her very good legs.

He sliced her bagel, smoothed on the cream cheese and lox and onions. She made the coffee. Lilly waited for what she thought was an appropriate amount of time over breakfast before she touched his *Times* and said, "I have a far better hideout than this place."

He put the paper aside and did a Tallulah: "Who doesn't, dahling."

She had not told him of the meeting she attended a few weeks earlier at Shumlin's office in midtown. "Want me to drop names? Of course you do. Dos Passos, MacLeish, Blitz-stein, Shumlin of course . . ."

"I knew you were seeing someone behind my back, but the Dalton gang, come on, Lilly . . ."

"Martha Gellhorn. She was there too. Hemingway's already gone over to Spain. They want me there. I want you there with me." Hammett said nothing.

The project was Shumlin's brainchild, a film on the war in Spain. Americans knew almost nothing about it. None of the studios, of course, was interested, but Shumlin had raised some of the money already, and the rest was promised. He said the White House supported the project but was, until the film was made, unwilling to let that support become public.

"No surprise," Hammett said, "since they're bending over backward at the moment not to offend our fascist friends anywhere. What's Hemingway in for?"

"Herman said he put up a ton of his own money and raised even more. He wants to narrate it."

"Hemingway will read your words as written? And you believe that?"

"I talked seriously with Martha afterward. I believe they're both sincere. Hemingway is on the right side on this one, Dash."

"And you?"

"I want to write it. I want to make it mean something. But the whole thing is so confusing, I'm in over my head already. I need advice."

Yesterday's Hammett, the Hammett who didn't know how to smile properly, would have said, "What's it pay?" The Hammett in front of her now said, "Lilly. You are a shining piece of work in a tarnished world. Fire away. I'll give you the best advice I've got."

She handed him about twenty handwritten pages, as she had so often done before. She did not have to say, *Tell me what's wrong*, but she did.

Hammett said, "How firm is all this?"

"Firm. I'm going. Interested in cowriting? There's money for us both to go over."

"I'll be the guy in the shadows on this one, if it's all right with you."

"It could be important in our lives. For *us*. We could make a great film together."

Hammett did not say, *Impossible*. He thought, *Wasn't that just the way of the world? Just when you decide to come together, the damn thing flies apart.*

"I'm sailing in two weeks. Come with me, Dash."

"Let me read the pages. We'll talk. Where's a good place?" Lilly had the impression that his feelings had been hurt but didn't know precisely how or why. It was better to address that problem later. Or never.

"There's a desk in the bedroom. Remember, it's just a first pass. I'm concerned about the approach."

He looked heavenward: "Writers. Lord, spare me."

Hammett emerged more than three hours later, which meant he'd read the draft many times. She peered into his face for a sign. She detected puzzlement. As he handed her the pages, she noticed only a line through her title, *Spain Is Waiting*, and in a smaller, cleaner hand, *The Spanish Earth*. She flipped through the pages; it was the only change. A bad sign.

It was wrong conceptually, he told her. Much too much history, much too much politics, too much documentary for a documentary, all in all too puffed up. You're not going to change people's attitudes, he said, unless you first touch their hearts. In a documentary everything starts with the heart. This version didn't even come close, didn't even try to. This is polemics. Be a playwright. It's the human drama that matters, that always matters, that only matters. Capture the drama of people, innocent victims, caught in a world where suddenly bombs are falling out of the sky on them and on their children. How would you folks like that in Pittsburgh or Poughkeepsie? Then maybe a line—but no more than that—about those bombs and the planes dropping them being German and Italian. Nazi and Fascist. This killing is the true face of fascism, this is what totalitarians do to decent people. And we've got to stop them now or there may be an even harsher lesson for us further down the line.

Make your case humanly and a correct understanding of the politics will follow. This draft has the process backward—politics first and not really enough room for the human tragedy, or even worse, the human tragedy is made to seem secondary.

She knew he had it exactly right.

How many times had this happened before? Hammett tells Hellman what is wrong and it is something she sensed already that would not let itself be known to her. "Oh Jesus. Of course."

"About the title. The Spanish soul rises from the land. Their land is who they are. Tell the story of how they will fight for their land, for their very souls, and you will have told your story well."

Hammett wasn't quite done. "Who's directing?"

"Joris Ivens. He's a Dutchman is all I know."

"I know his work. He makes beautiful films." The word was intended pejoratively. "Seems to me you've got too many geniuses involved in this project. Good luck."

"You're the only genius I want involved."

"I've got another *Thin Man* deadline," he lied. Mayer had cut his work to the absolute minimum. "But just be careful that there are no insurmountable problems going into the project. Whatever comes along later, you're equipped to handle."

"What do you mean, *going into the project?*"

"I mean, who'll be driving the bus?"

"Which means?"

"Will Ivens shoot what *your* story demands, or will you have to follow *his camera?* With documentary work in the field, the camera usually calls the tune. Just remember, you're the better storyteller.

Lilly stood up beside him and smoothed his hair until he looked up. She said, "Don't you dare touch me."

"I wouldn't think of it. But I would love a strong glass of cranberry juice."

"Ah, the cranberry juice. I think I left it in the bedroom."

HELLMAN HAD KNOWN from the outset that Hammett was a Marxist—it was part of his attraction—which meant mostly that he understood much personal and political behavior as economically motivated. It probably should have but did not occur to her that he might actually have been a member of the American Communist Party. He was already, but chose never to tell her. She did not know that six months earlier he had volunteered to fight in the Abraham Lincoln Brigade, composed of Americans who supported the Spanish Republicans. He was advised through Party channels—"ordered" would not be too strong a word—that he was considered far more useful to the cause in Hollywood.

Lillian knew none of this partly because he did not want any of it to hurt her. As she had not told him of her commitment to this documentary project and her impending trip to Spain. Ironically, although most of her political enemies assumed she had been a member of the Party, she never was.

Lillian and Dash watched the sun go down yet again. It revealed its splendor only briefly before falling away. The music in the room was Scarlatti. The champagne was still Canada Dry.

"So where to?"

"Beg pardon?"

"Tonight. Celebrate at '21'?"

"Why not? We can always start the Revolution tomorrow morning."

. 10 .

Alone, Perhaps

Before Lillian left they spoke almost exclusively about *The Spanish Earth*. Hammett's main idea—a good one—was to find a representative village somewhere in or near Catalonia and tell the story of the war through the lives of the people there.

"There are fishing villages along the Turia, great for your story if you decide to go that way. Find your village—you'll know it when you see it—tell the story of the war through the lives of the people there."

"Let's find the village together. I think I need you with me. Dash?"

He paid no attention: "Don't lose your point: War comes to a village and everything that was human in a simple, recognizable everyday way is made thoroughly grotesque. A simple *before* and *after* of images will suffice . . . that's what cameras do best. Reenforce it with Hellman words—not too many—*Señor Almadino has not had a delivery of flour for* two weeks . . . so the people on Calle Colón do not have their bread . . . Doctor Vences can no longer treat his patients . . . Yesterday the town's only pharmacy was destroyed in an air raid . . . The planes were Italian, the bombs were German."

"Please come with me, Dash. We'll make our own film."

Her ship was the *Rotterdam*, a fair-sized Dutch liner, amenable but far from splendid, headed for—where else? Rotterdam. Hammett had urged Lilly to travel light, which for her meant an immense steamer trunk and two large suitcases. When the call to leave the ship was given, the two embraced tightly but did not kiss. They held the embrace. Hammett handed her a thick envelope. "Wait half an hour. Promise?"

"Promise."

"I mean it. Promise?"

"Yes, I promise."

Standing on the pier alone, Hammett felt the soft pleasure he always experienced when leaving or being left, an emotional exhalation that presaged a drink at the nearest bar. No one seeing him at that moment would have been impressed, a skinny man with a foolish mustache, tall but now slightly bent, wearing a worn camel hair coat and a fur hat he'd picked up in a secondhand shop on Broadway.

Hammett stood in the freezing damp alongside the river and watched her ship being tugged away. He did not find a bar, or even look for one, but flagged down a cab and returned to the apartment. It was empty now in precisely the way a new page in a typewriter was empty. You filled it, you intended to fill it, or you walked out the door and stayed away. Hammett sat down and rolled a new page into her machine:

My brother Richard—I called him Dickie—was younger than I by four years, which meant that when I was almost nine he was four and a half. Because my father was a danger to the family, I made myself Dickie's protector when our father was home. My good mother and older sister were usually so busy filling the void Papa left, it fell to me quite often after chores, especially on summer days, to be responsible for the care of my little brother.

This was really not such a good idea because I was a very selfish boy and either wanted to be alone or to be playing baseball with my friends. Alone, I loved to read—adventure stories mostly; I could play baseball real well too. Either way I didn't want to be encumbered by having to care for a four-year-old who made either pleasure impossible. Did I resent my role? Indeed. Did I resent Dickie? I did. Sometimes. I loved my brother, as I loved my mother and sister Reba, but it is always hard for me to admit of love, hard even to put the word on the page. Even though we live in the dawning Age of Psychology, do not expect me here to engage in any glib self-analysis as to why. Even the admission of so private a matter as lone would

Oh my, how Dr. Freud would howl—I just misspelled the word love *as* lone! Hammett scoured the page and discovered he had made another typo in his text, so he rolled the page out of the machine, put a clean sheet in its place, and began to retype. The look of a page so mattered to him—even in a working draft—that he allowed himself no more than one mistake per page. And sometimes even that single error bothered him so much he simply had to retype. Lillian knew never to tease him about this idiosyncrasy.

Hammett picked up the story of Dickie at the swimming hole one summer afternoon in Hopewell, Maryland:

You see, at the pond I could be alone and super-
vise Dickie at the same time. We could fish a bit. We
could swim bare-ass, although Dickie could really
only splash around. And then I could read. Miss Gaffer at the library gave me a *Huck Finn* when school
let out, an oversized edition with illustrations. I didn't
know what *abridged* meant but it was written on the
cover and I could sound the word out. I could sound
out and understand almost any word. I was a lot like
Huck that day, sitting on the low pier with my line in
the water hoping to catch something my mom could
cook up tonight. A catfish was our best bet.

Dickie said he wanted to swim, which meant
splash around. I wanted to read, especially after I discovered in that book that Huck wanted to get away

from his own Pap as bad as I wanted my father to get away from me.

The *Rotterdam* had not yet edged into the river, although the gangplank had long been pulled away. The anchor had not yet been fully hoisted. Lillian opened Hammett's envelope as soon as he had left her cabin. Its bulk was caused by brand-new thousand-peseta notes, freshly minted and bound by a rubber band. Tucked in with the bills was an automobile map of Catalonia, with Valencia circled in red at its southern border. Then she pulled out a typed page folded perfectly in thirds. Within its folds was a small photograph. A thin dark man, boyish but undoubtedly a young man, in a white suit with a bow tie, sat on steps before an imposing building, one that was familiar to her. The man was not familiar, but she felt as though she knew him. The building came to her before the man because she had frequented it—the NYU University Library. Turning the photo over, she saw the inscription, in a tiny hand, in English: *Courage, of course. Federico Lorca.*

Lorca. But how?

Federico García Lorca was dead, assassinated one year before in a great Falangist killing and torture spree after the war first broke out. How then this photo? This inscription? She held the photograph up and turned it over and then over again. The ship lurched. She was leaving a safe place where she was Lillian Hellman and everybody knew that. It occurred to her that his letter might explain the extraordinary gift.

Dear dearest Loollia—

You promised to wait half an hour and you did not. So, because you have been a naughty girl I will not tell you how the enclosed photograph and dedication—your deserved gift—came into my hands. Yes, obedience will be a painful lesson for you to learn but believe me, dear girl, it is for your own good.

Now, about the money. These are the largest denomination of Spanish currency presently available, even though each bill is worth only about fifty bucks. Where you are going, however, cash in any denomination will be king, especially for bribes, of which there will certainly be many required, or to help buy your way out of tight squeezes, of which there will also certainly be many. Use the cash judiciously—buy someone decent a can of sardines, peaches, some chicory, a liter of milk. Bargain well. This I don't need to say because I've seen you at work at the farmers' market. Be sure you keep the money in a safe private place. I'd suggest pinned inside your bra where only a handful of men will have access.

(I still have not had a drink since you've left, which might explain why the punctuation in this farewell note is so slipshod.)

*You have chosen to love me—only your enigmatic
God could possibly know why—and so you attribute
qualities to me that I do not possess. I have a talent, it's
true, but it is a small one, an ability to entertain, "a talent
to amuse," as the song goes. Nevertheless, in your absence
I shall endeavor mightily to be the man you think I am,
and if not that at least a writer worthy of your respect.*

*Do your best work there, dear girl, as I shall try to
do mine here. Please stay alive because I want to order
Hamm and Leggs when you get back. Oooof. Socko.
Boffo. No, that's not the right way to go out, is it? This
is. Hammett: I hate myself. Hellman: I hate you more.*

Muchas Mierdas—*Dash*

There was nothing about the Lorca photograph.

I did not notice at first Dickie was no longer with
me. He wasn't splashing around or trying to get his
line into the water from the pier. He wasn't anywhere.
And no, absorbed as I might have been, I would not
have let my little brother drown. I shouted his name
and shouted it again. It echoed. In the summer silence
I heard bird sounds come back, the breeze whipping
the overhanging trees.

Hammett stopped typing and took the pleasure of visual-
izing his memory. Then came the thought—What had he

felt then with his little brother missing? Fear? Worry? Irritation? All three or nothing at all? Hammett couldn't remember, so he did not say.

I left my book face down, marking my page, and,
still calling his name, began to make my way around
the pond. I expected to see him behind every large
tree as I approached, struggling to get the line into
the shallow water, but I was disappointed each time. I
really did begin to worry.

I tacked threats onto my shouts: "Richard, if you
don't answer me, I'll smack you senseless." That's
what my father used to say whenever he threatened.
Now I looked into the dark water more carefully even
though in most places it was so shallow you couldn't
drown even if you wanted to. Not even a four-year-
old. Still . . .

I'd made my way about halfway around. I was on
the Wayland side when I stepped out of the shade
into blinding sunlight. I called out again and saw a
flickering movement come from behind an oak tree
near a horse corral that belonged to the Freeman
Farm. The flickering was my fishing pole appearing
and disappearing behind the trunk of the tree.

I really intended to smack some sense into
Dickie now. As I rounded the tree, I noticed that
my brother held the pole from the bottom as high as

he could—that's what made it wave wildly—trying
to reach a pair of shoes hanging down. When I got
closer, I saw feet in boots and then legs. A man was
hanging from a rope.

I thought it was my father.

I felt neither shock nor sorrow.

The head was cocked severely sidewise where the
noose wrapped its neck.

Dickie stood wide-eyed looking straight up into
the face. Somehow he'd made his way here, spotted
the body, and remained transfixed below. When he
touched the foot lightly with the pole, the entire body
swayed.

I took the pole from him and made him look
away. I turned the body with the pole. It was not my
father. It was Mr. Freeman, not the old Mr. Freeman,
his son. I told Dickie to hurry home and fetch Ma.
Tell her not to worry, nothing is wrong, but she has to
come. Can you say that back to me? He said it back
perfectly. Before he left he said, "Mr. Freeman has to
get cut down, right?"

"Go get Ma."

Hammett looked over and down at the Hudson flowing,
so perfect in shallow sunlight. Why was there no satisfaction
in what he was writing? Who in the world now could care
about him, his brother Richard, or Mr. Freeman's suicide? He

scanned the page in the typewriter. Mere scratch marks and loops, hatchings on a page—none of this meant anything to anyone. He was unable to make it mean anything. He did not have that particular talent. That was Lillian's domain. So why even bother to continue?

I waited in the shade of the pond watching Mr. Freeman's legs for a long time before a police car came down the road. Mama was in it. She had known what to do. She always knew what to do. The policemen got out and circled underneath the body, which was swaying in the breeze.

One policeman stood on top of the car and tried to get a knife up to the rope. Then the other policeman climbed up too. No matter how they pushed or pulled, the body flopped around. It was pretty funny, I have to say, though I knew it was wrong to laugh. So I walked up to them and said if they needed help I could cut Mr. Freeman down. Mama said for me to be quiet and the first cop said he could do everything himself. Except that Mr. Freeman came down with a crash and then slid off the top of the car and got himself stuck in the rear bumper. His eyes stared right at me all the while I walked around him. That's when Mama took me home.

Before going to sleep that night I asked my mother why a man would want to do something like that to himself. Didn't it hurt to get your neck snapped that way? God doesn't want us to do harm to ourselves, she said. Then why does God let it happen, Mama? Because he's busy watching over so many other things, sometimes other things just slip his mind.

Just a few years ago Dickie and I had dinner at a good restaurant in Chicago and I asked him what he remembered about that day. He told me he just picked up the fishing pole and wandered off into the woods around the pond. He peed right in the pond although he knew he shouldn't have. Then he saw a man riding horseback on a large chestnut. He followed the horse but stayed in the woods.

The man rode up alongside the corral fence and, leaning against the tree, stood up on the horse's back and then the fence, a coil of rope in his hand. He smacked his horse with the rope and whistled; the horse bucked and dashed away. Then he moved from fence to lower limb and to higher limbs almost out of sight in the tree. Dickie watched all this silently. He had moved, he estimated, to within thirty feet of the tree, stopped, and then began to edge closer still. He called, "Mister." No response. Then again, "Mister."

Mr. Freeman plummeted down out of the tree. Dickie heard the gasp—he called it a wail and a *crack*—and saw the legs trying to climb back up in the air. He watched silently as the gasping and flailing

ran down and Mr. Freeman finally hung as dead
weight.

I asked my brother if the experience had made his
life any different, deflected it in some knowable way.

Dickie said, "Nope, that's just what happened.
God only knows what it all meant."

Hammett liked to type "End" when he finished a story or
a chapter. It gave him the feeling that something had been
done. He typed "End" and the phone rang.

"It's me. Been trying to get through for days."

He had no idea who *me* was, only that it wasn't Lillian.
"I've been busy."

"Are you sitting down?"

"It's three in the morning." He'd be damned if he'd ask
who *me* was.

"I can't believe he's done it, Dash. The scoundrel." It took
about twenty seconds more to determine *me* was Myra Ewbank and the *scoundrel* was her husband, Phil Edmunds. It
took a while longer for Myra Ewbank to elaborate on what
the scoundrel had done. The scoundrel list included "a
rabbi—who knows what he paid the guy?—who persuaded
the Waxman family to forgo the postmortem because Jewish
tradition would be compromised by an autopsy. Waxman's
sister turns out to be a religious nut who bought the whole
deal and convinced the rest of the family that—"

Hammett said, "Easy, Myra, there's always exhumation."

"Exhume what, his ashes? Phil had Jerry cremated. His old friend, Jerry. His old tennis partner. For whose murder the coroner has found, quote, no reason whatsoever to suspect foul play, unquote. So much for Jewish tradition."

"Hmmm."

"Hmmm, indeed." Myra didn't sound drugged anymore.

"When did all this happen?"

"Weeks ago. I've been busy as hell too. But, yes, it's my fault. I left all the Waxman stuff to him. I just got caught up with everything else that's happened. I should say everything just got caught up with me. I can't believe the things he's done. He put the money that was raised to find out what really happened to Jerry Waxman—some $17,000—into his own personal account. Stole it, Dash. Then three days ago he was named president of the Screen Writers Association, and you know what a phony front organization that is. And they're paying him a fortune. How come you don't know? Don't you get *The Reporter?*"

"Myra, I'm in New York writing."

"Still." She sighed and brought her voice back up. "Then I check and see he's cleaned out our joint account. We were going to do Europe next summer." She was unsteady again. "He's taken the sports car. When I was away on location, he packed his fucking bags and left. Leaving was the only good thing in the whole deal. He's not going to get away with this, is he Dash?"

Sounded like he already had. "That's complicated, Myra. I think the Waxman case is pretty well shot. But let me think about it. As for the money and your wayward husband . . ."

"Ex-husband."

". . . there are still some options. I have to think about it. But do this immediately. Call Peter Carey. He's a lawyer and a private investigator. First-class guy. Mention my name. Give him my number. He owes me, so we should be able to work something out."

"Dash, I'd much rather you . . ."

"Of course you would, dear. I simply can't right now. I'll be on it with Carey. Promise. He'll do everything I would do. And I'll do everything I can from here until Lilly gets back."

"That's when?"

"Your guess . . . Been calling and calling. Can't get through."

"Can he really get away with all this, Dash?"

"Maybe not all of it, Myra."

This scoundrel turned rat was one clever son of a bitch. Phil Edmunds was the kind of guy Hammett really despised, a cunning sneak and a coward who took enormous advantage of people's good opinions and misreadings of his character. He was the same devious prick when he was drinking to Lilly's success and Myra's superb Stroganoff as when he was getting Jerry Waxman cremated to set himself up.

Myra's phone call three nights later was worse. Personally. She'd been drinking. "They canned me," was how she began the conversation. "The best writer in the place—well, debatably anyway—and they just cut me loose. After I . . ."

Hammett whistled into the phone.

"You think this is his doing?"

"Probably so. He's really got some leverage with important people. I'm curious. You've got a contract. How did Mayer deal with it?"

"He didn't. Mayer wouldn't see me. Neither would Selznick. It was Selznick's assistant, Gelb. The little bald bastard. He sat me down like I was a naughty child and said the company couldn't risk keeping anyone whose personal behavior was about to become grist for the gossip mills. That was his phrase, can you believe it, *grist?*" She laughed and repeated *grist*.

"So I asked what *grist* those *mills* found out about me. He said he was uncomfortable talking about specifics. I said comfort was not the point. This was my goddamned career, for God's sake. He said did I ever read my moral turpitude clause? I said, Jesus, you wouldn't do something like that would you? Didn't say a word, just moved things around on his desk. Dash?"

"Ever get him to reveal specifics?"

"I asked, What morals? What turpitudes? He said it was all too tawdry for him to discuss. I said I wasn't going to leave until he did. He says, 'Illicit sexual behavior.' I say,

'Not specific enough.' Dash, he wouldn't even look me in the eye. Just, 'illicit.' Who's the guy? I said. Not with guys. With women. Plural? He still wouldn't look at me. He just nodded. I was steaming. *Name them, you bastard, name them!* He said *they* would if *they* had to. Publicly. So what do I do now, Dash?"

"Nothing for now. Did they offer you a settlement?"

"Nothing great. I mean, I'm not a saint, Dash, but I'm not a piece of shit either."

"You've got your talent to fall back on, Myra. Lots of friends in the business . . ."

"I've already made calls, a dozen of them. No one calls me back. I don't get it."

Hammett got it. It wasn't very complicated. Phil Edmunds told someone important he could make the Waxman thing go away and named his price. It was substantial—all of the above. But he couldn't guarantee his wife wouldn't blow the whistle; they would have to take care of that.

"All I want to do is work."

"And you will, you will. Myra, we'll help you through this." He was speaking for Lillian too. "Remember, I'm three hours later here. Call earlier."

She had already hung up.

Hammett lit a cigarette and lay back on his pillow. Already a strategy was forming, not a winning strategy but something to upset the applecart. Call it an insurgency. There was enough material—photographs of the crime scene, affidavits, alternative theories of the crime—to keep the Waxman murder alive as scandalous gossip in the newspapers for years. The cremation still left things open to interpretation. Books could be written, films made. Hell, it never had to go away completely and eventually something would break, someone would crack. That, too, was human nature. But sometimes human nature took a vacation.

Dashiell Hammett had invented so many complicated murder plots with so many unlikely twists just for the sport of it, he had to remind himself now that normal people had no idea a murder like Waxman's—a political assassination in a sense—often went unpunished. Perhaps *usually* was the better word. Such a crime altered the course of people's lives a bit, but it did not tip the world out of balance and cause events to wobble out of control. In fact, such unpunished crimes changed very little. It only makes us sad when we know the truth.

HEMINGWAY WAS NOT IN PARIS as had been arranged. Lillian took it as a sign that things would not go well for her project—there had been many such signs—and maybe even for the war. He had left a note at her hotel informing her that he was in Madrid because that's where the front was. Martha Gellhorn and Joris Ivens were filming up in the Basque country, where the war was especially brutal. They would all meet in Madrid in one week's time. Filming had already begun, successfully, he claimed. His letter ended, "We need to beat the hell out of these bastards. Your good words will help us do that. Hem."

While in Paris Lilly had written in her notebook, *How do you dress for this goddamned war?* It was not an unimportant consideration. How did you show the participants the respect they deserved? Show them you were neither a naïf nor a dilettante? How should you look so that people could trust you? Certainly a beret, because so many Republicans wore berets. A leather jacket because it indicated a certain military standing, but fleece-lined because it did get pretty cold at night. Dark slacks for mobility and dash, and to break down gender distinctions, with dark athletic shoes for the same reason. Lillian Hellman looked like an experienced war correspondent and she liked the confidence her costume instilled.

Her contact in Paris was a Spaniard named Pascal Rubio, a small dark man from the Spanish government's Office of Diplomatic Relations, whose task it was to get this important American writer to Barcelona, and from there to the front safely and expeditiously. The first part was easy since rail lines from the French border to Barcelona had not been touched. To get her from Barcelona to Madrid alive might be more difficult. Rubio also believed Lillian Hellman to be an American diplomat without portfolio and a personal friend of President Roosevelt. Her direct influence might move the United States to more active support for the Republican cause. Because his English was spotty, he referred to her sometimes as an "Emmissionary."

The Nationalists—a coalition of rightist groups led by insurgent army officers and the fascist Falange party—had indeed pushed the front to the western banks of the Manzanares. Madrid was exposed to their artillery. Republicans and Nationalists were locked in a battle for the superb old city that in all likelihood would determine the outcome of the war. The Nationalists held the skies, thanks to the support of fascist German and Italian aircraft. The Republican army swelled with volunteers from all over the world. In October 1937 the outcome was still in doubt. Lillian was hopeful that there was still time for her efforts to matter as she approached Madrid in a black Ford covered with road dust.

Twice her trip from Barcelona had been canceled, the bombing along the road was so great no driver was willing to attempt it. The Republican army press office, which wanted its story told by Señorita Hellman, could find no one to take so dangerous a trip. Enter Julio Gómez. Gómez agreed to drive the Mees Hellman to Madrid for four thousand pesetas. Lillian reached for Hammett's cash and agreed.

Lillian immediately liked his looks—dark wavy hair, tall for a Spaniard, ever-eager smile—and liked how smartly he'd put all her things in the trunk of his black Ford. The car was

polished and spotlessly clean inside. Gómez declared in excellent English that it was "My car, my own, my contribution
to the cause, Señora Hellman."

"Señorita Hellman." And off they went on a clear morning at a fairly brisk pace.

Although the road from Barcelona was straight as a
string on the map Hammett had given her, it had been
bombed so severely that you'd have to drive double the
350-kilometer distance. It was now a trip of six or seven
hours at best under terrible conditions. They'd gotten off
to a good enough start, but it soon became clear that Julio
Gómez was not Lillian's kind of guy. Not only did he never
stop talking, everything he said about the world and the war
was dead wrong, and everything else was about Julio Gómez
and unlikely to be true. The second category dominated the
first. It would have been amusing if there wasn't so damned
much of it. But he was beautiful to look at, which gave him
another hours' grace.

An hour into their trip, Lillian touched his hand on the
wheel and said, "Shush."

He scowled and said, "That is no word, *shush*."

"How about 'Shut the fuck up' then?"

Planes flew over the nearby main road from time to time;
the shelling of Valencia from offshore could still be heard.
Gómez told of having been a fighter pilot shot down in the
Pyrenees. A bald-faced liar in addition to everything else.
Hours passed slowly in the misery of his company.

Just beyond Valverde, Gómez drove off the road about half a kilometer and into a small plaza in front of the village church. Lillian got out and sipped from the fountain and splashed tepid water on her face, the back of her neck. Gómez climbed atop his Ford and sang some lines from "La Paloma." Women gathered in a few doorways. Were there no men left in this village? Gómez engaged some of them in conversation and eventually he ushered Lillian through a door and down a long blue hallway to a large kitchen.

A straight-backed old woman stood at the head of the table and indicated a place for Lillian to sit on a bench. Against the wall was a middle-aged woman who appeared to be the old woman's daughter. Seated at the table were the daughter's daughters, girls in their twenties, one with two babies. All the faces indicated that they had never seen anyone like Lillian in their lives.

There was cool water and red wine and bread and cheese and beans and, of course, sardines. She tried to eat as little as possible but she was very hungry. Gómez quickly asked for seconds.

Back in the car afterward, Lilly spoke of the marvelous generosity of the Spanish people, the women at least.

Gómez said, "They would have fed us even if you were not so famous."

"I'm not famous."

"To them, you are Charlie Chaplin's sister."

"You didn't . . ."

"As I said, they would have fed you anyway."

It was nightfall when they spotted Madrid in the distance on a high plateau above them. It was lighted periodically by bombs exploding near the city center. There were no airplanes. This was a constant artillery barrage from the Nationalists. "The front is just to the west, so close, within range already of the big cannons," Gómez explained, which was why it was better to try to enter the city from the rear, even though that would take much longer. Gómez was nothing if not prudent, you'd have to give him that. Lillian was frightened when they finally drove into the city.

Gómez pulled his Ford through and around the rubble of devastated neighborhoods, past the skeletons of old homes, and then down alleyways and streets almost untouched by artillery bombardment, but all in all what she could see of Madrid was in very bad shape. Perhaps it was the time of night, but the city had a ghostly quality. It took Julio a very long time to make his way to the villa where Lillian was finally to meet Hemingway and Gellhorn and Ivens.

Hemingway. He brought up such conflicting emotions in her. Jealousy foremost. Superb writer, really. And prolific. But even more successful than superb or prolific justified. Wasn't he exactly what all writers wanted for themselves? She said no and thought yes. Wasn't he what she wanted for Hammett? Again, no was yes.

Eight o'clock was its usual time, and the night's bombardment had just begun. They drove again through the patchwork of destruction quite a distance to the safety of the higher ground north of the city. The large villa stood alone on a cliff just above a chapel. Gómez escorted her to the door and said he'd wait in the car, all night if necessary. If she could remember to bring something for him, dessert, fruit, cheese, anything, he'd be grateful.

Lillian walked unsteadily up a flight of unlighted stairs. She entered a darkened room and saw the silhouettes of Ernest and Martha on the balcony against the red backdrop of the city. They were watching the shelling of Madrid from this safe dark place. Lillian approached and leaned on the railing of the balcony, a bit weak in the knees, watching the flashes and then waiting for the impacts. No one spoke. During a brief lull, they kissed their welcomes, still without speaking.

"You're here," Martha whispered, "thank God."

"Welcome to hell," Hemingway said.

"Pleasure's all mine."

They faced the bombardment as they spoke, more pauses than conversation. Slowly, information emerged and was exchanged. The important thing for Lillian, the only thing, was the footage from Ivens so she could see what she had to write. There was no footage yet, either from Ivens or from Gellhorn. Soon, it would all be here soon.

Ivens was not in Madrid but at the front shooting the fighting ten miles west of the city. The fighting there was vicious, the outcome of the war might hinge on it. If that line were to crack . . . But not to worry, Joris will get her his film. And where was Martha's? Being processed.

Lillian very much wanted to talk about her narration. Didn't Hemingway want to collaborate on it?

"I'd only screw it up. You're the best film writer in the world. Well, at least the best one in Madrid tonight. Hah. Don't think I don't know how lucky we are to have you. You just write it. I'll just say your words, and that will be that." All said distractedly, so fascinated was he by the explosions. It was easy for her not to believe him.

Lillian noticed that the shelling this night was not really random after all. Although there were flashes around the city center, mostly they illuminated a towering building and the surrounding complex of downtown buildings near the bridge that spanned the Manzanares. Fires had started there and begun to spread throughout the area. Distant sirens sounded continually. "It's the central communications building," Martha said. "They've been trying to knock it out for a week. Somehow they can't."

"Look at that," Hemingway said, "just look at it. Hell itself."

"I'd love to turn it back on the bastards."

"Of course, but look at it. Beautiful."

"Not beautiful to me."

Hemingway wasn't listening: "It's sickening, but it's beautiful too, a modern war can be stunning."

"Fuck that romantic bullshit about modern war," Lillian said and turned to go.

Martha followed her to the stairs. "You'll get your film, I promise, Lilly. Be careful. And forgive him, he's not been himself lately."

"Careful, yes. Forgive him, no."

Martha called after her, "We'll be in touch."

LILLIAN WANTED TO SEE last night's devastation to put herself more directly into the war she had to write about. Early as it was, horses pulling carts filled with rubble clomped over the cobblestones. A few cars and trucks rolled by slowly. From one she saw a leg hanging limply. The smell of damp ashes was ever present.

She found the greatest destruction by looking up and across the river. Dark smoke rose from just beyond the dome and spires of the Madrid Cathedral. A soldier would not let her walk across the bridge. She distracted him and ran across. As she approached the smoke, the odor—now it was almost a taste—got stronger. The church was not on fire; everything around it was. She turned the corner and saw all the devastation she could possibly want.

In a hushed quietude, small fires were still being extinguished by firemen. Rubble was being sifted, collected, and piled. The efforts at reordering had yet to make a dent; destruction still held the upper hand. Not all the bodies had been removed. They, too, were being stored like reusable wreckage in the shade of the rectory, covered for the most part, but more coverings were needed. She walked toward the place where bodies were being laid, in some cases with their arms and legs intertwined or grotesquely outstretched as if reaching or striding. These people had been killed so recently and so violently that Lillian was stunned by the life still on their faces. She had the mad thought that she was looking at an accident that could somehow be undone.

One face in particular held her attention. A woman about her age, roughly thirty, lay on a stretcher apart from all the others, placed there, it was explained, because she had not yet been identified. She was, apparently, a visitor to someone unknown in the neighborhood. Though closed, her eyes were unusually large; lidded, they conveyed an expression of peacefulness teased by the irony of her half-smile. One cheek was dimpled. Lillian could not break off her gaze. She was asked to move aside by a man backing in a truck to take away some of the identified victims.

The face had shaken Lilly to numbness. She sat down on the steps of the rectory. Movement around her slowed. She heard no sound. Many years before in New York at dinner Hemingway told of arriving at a battlefield near Udine, and smelling the war dead for the first time and being pleasantly surprised by its sweetness. She smelt death now, beneath the choke of wet, charred wood. There was no sweetness whatsoever. Lilly coughed and almost threw up.

There was no electricity in room 323 so she sat with her notebook perched on the windowsill. She sat down intending to write some narration for a film she hadn't seen but could now imagine. Instead she wrote:

Damn you Hammett, damn you—

I blame you for this of course. (The "this" is my profound confusion, my ravaged emotional state and utter hopelessness, and any damned thing else that's happened to me because of this fucking war!) And why is it all your fault? Because you should be here with me to soften the blows, and you are not. I'm here alone. And you're there alone too, perhaps. When in good conscience—something you've always lacked—you should be here to explain, clarify, translate, illuminate, and just plain make sense out of what I'm seeing and why it's happening to innocent people. I'm blaming you because I certainly can't be expected to blame myself, can I?

You've seen men killed. Probably have even killed some. (Have you?) But I have never seen a corpse, so many corpses, so many people killed so wantonly, par hazard as the French say. It's one thing to believe in the cause, surely, as we believe the Republicans must win and to hate fascism in the marrow of our bones. It's another to see what the war does. The war. The war. The fucking war.

It undermines everything your mind tells you you have to believe because it absolutely must be won. But it is a monster that only wants to feed itself. I'm in a bad way, my dear Dash. If you had come with me, I'd know how to begin to sort out all this crap in my head.

Asshole Hemingway and his poof Gellhorn have no such problems. They are documenting a vision of hell and doing it like art critics hovering over Bosch or better yet a Goya nightmare. For me, it's something I'd rather not have seen. In the newspapers the thing made some sense. Inhaling the stench of it fogs the mind.

Everyone seems to have a horse in this race—Hitler, Mussolini, the pope, the king, Uncle Joe. It's a war by proxy, war as a sport for spectators and gamblers. From a distance that may make some sense. But not when you see the faces of the people, living and dead. The experience is so surreal I need to invite Buñuel and Dalí over for drinks. We'll use corpses as the tables, skeletons for chairs.

Last night I may have seen the future. They asked me to give a speech thanking "our Russian comrades" for their contributions to the cause, La Causa, in case you didn't think I've learned any Spanish. I never got to speak. Each and every pipsqueak who had anything to say about their so-called contribution spoke and spoke and spoke. As the night wore on the tone began to change. Hope and gratefulness became by degrees criticism and then blame. The evening ended in a brawl, and they had to sneak me out a side door. It was the fucking Tower of Babel retold.

Blame. In one form or another I've seen it every-
where here. I don't think the bad guys have it. Pope and
king were always beyond blame, never any surprises, al-
ways infallible and cruel. Didn't you used to say, "Blame
before endgame"? That's what I'm feeling here.

Here is what my really dumb driver said last night,
"The world is fighting here. The Spaniards are dying, all
the Spaniards. My countrymen." And, really, I had noth-
ing to say.

I want to come home. Please be there.

I love you again, Lilly

The Republican press office promised to send the letter in a pouch to its New York consulate and then have it
hand-delivered.

. 11 .

Love Again

S AMUEL D ASHIELL H AMMETT WAS A MAN for whom
the word *unattached* was not a negative thing, for whom the
un- was not a prefix but an integral part of its Teutonic root.
Attached meant a harnessing—meant limitation, restriction,
and unhappiness all rolled into one. Even when it came to
Lillian Florence Hellman.

More often, though, being attached to Lilly meant a
greater sense of "unattachment" to everything else in his life,
and that could become a source of his contentment. This
was, of course, the only way a man alone, an *isolato*, could
love, although such a man did not even think to acknowledge the term. Hammett could not write about the subject of
love, could not even think clearly about love. His detective
heroes—the Op, Sam Spade, the more recent Secret Agent
X-9—were such men, men who could not love or even talk
about it, especially not talk about it.

Nick Charles was most assuredly not the loner. Nick Charles, a bon vivant and raconteur, a schmoozer and bullshitter par excellence, who had too many old pals and drinking buddies from his single days, an irrepressible ladies' man and flirt; but also married and fundamentally loyal to Nora because he loved her. Of course Nickie professed his love in the only way a Hammett lover could—ironically. So when he says, "Of course I'll miss you, dahling. If you go out shopping, my beloved, I won't have anyone to throw darts at," he really means, "Please stay home, sweetheart. I need someone to drink with this afternoon."

In Lillian's absence, Hammett still had not taken a drink. That didn't mean his mind was clear. Actually, drinking produced wonderful clarity until drunkenness kicked in. Sober now, Hammett was woefully confused about something as emotionally charged as his love for Lillian. So he walked the city a great deal and wrote a bit.

The hardest part of writing about his family was thinking about his family, bringing it back in memory. During his walks he tried to see more clearly the true events of his childhood years. He particularly liked to stop at construction sites and watch men working. Their actions gave him a sense that there was a positive counterforce to human impermanence and the physical law of entropy. Even if it wasn't actually so, the illusion gave him pleasure. He liked watching the girders go up and stay up. He particularly liked to walk to Grand Central Terminal and watch passengers going and coming, especially arrivals being greeted by friends and family, something he'd never done.

Hammett bought a new notebook just before Lillian left for Spain in a shop down on Sheridan Square. It was slightly less than full-size and had lined pages. On the spine the word NOTES stood out in embossed gold. He bought a black Waterman fountain pen that had just the right heft to it. Its nib produced a sinewy script that gave him pleasure as he put it on the page.

Here he was, a middle-aged man, a famous writer by any reasonable standard, someone who received tens of thousands of dollars for simply telling a story, and now he was walking around Manhattan scratching observations in a notebook like a kid serving a literary apprenticeship. That realization gave Hammett pleasure. He kept his notes and sketches in the back of his notebook, preserving the front pages for an early memory of his mother. He had accumulated quite a few typed pages of family memories already. He reserved the story about his mother, Anne Bond Dashiell, because he wanted it to inaugurate his notebook.

The *Queen Mary* was due to dock by midmorning, so Hammett rose early even for him. He sat in very pale winter light in the most comfortable chair in the living room, notebook propped on a knee he folded over his leg. Before he began, he realized that the penalty for mistakes in the book would be more severe than a typescript—his page would be forever marred by corrections. He printed TALES and DASHIELL HAMMETT on the title page. Had he already made a mistake? Why in the world had he committed to that title so quickly? He looked at the word TALES and narrowed his lips in a considered smile. He turned the page and imagined a first line. He wrote, *Everyone hates a drunk.* It wasn't at all the sentence he intended to write that morning. He had intended to write, *My mama had a capacity for love of humankind so great it was almost self-defeating and very difficult for the rest of us to live with.*

He wrote on:

Everyone hates a drunk. Even drunks know this. And who in this world wants to be hated? Which is why most drunks often go to great lengths not to look like drunks. The very best way not to look like a drunk is to drink with friends. Usually those "friends" are drunks too. The point at which sociability gives way to drunkenness varies from person to person, of course. In my father, Richard Thomas Hammett, it was the point at which he became mean. It came by degrees, but once it was there, the meanness was a fright to my mother, all us children, and most everyone else. I think I'm the same kind of drunk.

One night—I must have been about eleven—Mama sent me to the Bog Hill to try to get Papa home. It was early, but Mama wanted him home

because we were all supposed to go visit Mama's folks
in Grant Mills next morning, a visit I always looked
forward to because I could spend almost the whole
day by myself in the barn.

I used to carry whatever book I was reading along
with me to the bar so everyone there could see I was
nothing like my father. Could see right away I was not
ever going to be a drunk like him.

I heard shouting before I entered. Sometimes,
when the men saw me come in, the place would go
quiet, not for long and not on the night I remember.
The real shouting was between my father at one
end of the bar and Phil Burroughs at the other end.
Burroughs's nickname was Ball-bustin' Burroughs,
and everyone knew what the name signified and that
Burroughs had truly earned it. Usually they started
out the evening drinking together—two drunks being
sociable. Then they would come to differ over something very minor. That and further drunkenness led
to a fistfight with bruised hands, torn clothes, and
bloody faces.

That particular night my father and Burroughs
were still reasonably sober but shouting wildly at one
another over the general placement of the Mediterranean Sea. Insults reigned: "ignorant fool" and
"jackass" and "dumb bastard." As best I could make
out, Burroughs had sited the Mediterranean correctly

between North Africa and Southern Europe; my father had it between Persia and India. It was not my place to settle the argument. It was my task to get my father out of there and home.

I pushed through the crowd of large men over to my father's side of the bar and the argument. Two men appeared to have backed my father; everyone else correctly supported Burroughs.

I touched my father's large-knuckled hand and told him we had to go home to get ready to leave on our family trip in the early morning.

He said, "Right, Sammy. You're right. Almost forgot." He smiled at me and announced to the crowd, "Big day tomorrow, boys. Visiting the rich relations . . . You all know my Sammy." His body began to unbend itself off the stool. I did not relax.

Burroughs said, "Hold up. You run out of here and never have to admit how wrong as hell you are." The bar quieted.

"Not wrong."

"Wrong as hell."

"Right as rain."

"Let the boy decide."

The crowd agreed that was the fairest way to end the impasse. Smart boy. Educated boy. Burroughs said, "Sammy, do you know for sure where the Mediterranean Sea is?"

No one moved. You could hear a pin drop. I'd be a liar if I said I didn't know what was at stake. I knew perfectly well. And I also knew my options. I could say I didn't know where it was. I could say it touched India. Or I could say where I knew it to be. So I can't claim innocence or ignorance as an excuse. I said nothing at all, which was yet another option, and pulled on my father's arm.

Burroughs approached and touched my shoulder. My father slapped his hand away. Burroughs said, "Well, boy, do you know or don't you?"

"Uh-huh."

"Well, where the hell is it?"

"Between Africa and Europe."

"Not anywhere near India?"

"No, sir."

The hand, my father's large, powerful hand, moved suddenly, not more than six inches, from the end of the bar into my face. It was the back of his hand flush on my nose mostly. I flew backward. I saw sparkles and blackness and then dark blood. I was on the floor of the Bog Hill with men's faces leaning into me, none of which was my father's.

That instinctive movement of my father's hand was invoked and powered by shame and jealousy and guilt. I do not know what makes someone a drunk, but I do know those things are always part of it. Guilt and jealousy and shame. For drunks with money on a higher social rung, like me, add an olive, a touch of vermouth. That's an even sadder personal cocktail.

End

Dash reread his pages and was surprised to discover errors, lots of them, mistakes he'd not have made had he typed. He made all his small corrections neatly in his notebook, but this new carelessness was now something to worry about. Why, he wondered after rereading, when he wrote about his father, did he never really capture the man? God, he really despised Richard Hammett, and it showed.

DASH WAS NOW seven weeks without a drink.

Hammett's bags had been packed for days, for more than two weeks actually. But he knew that if he were not in New York when Lilly returned from Spain he risked losing her . . . *really* did risk losing her. Risked losing this affinity, affection, engagement, caring, stimulation, everything he had with Lillian and with no one else in his life. Why did he not think love when the only word missing was *love*?

Her cable said little and implied much:

DON'T WANT YOU TO SEE ME THIS WAY STOP TAK-
ING QUEEN MARY STOP NY NEXT WEEK STOP SEEKING

SANITY STOP BINDING OF WOUND STOP GREAT LOVE
STOP LILLY

The reunions at Pier 54 were always interesting for him
to watch. He could be part of this one. The day was clear
but cold. Same camel hair coat, same fur cap, Hollywood-
thin pants and slipper shoes. He wore the gloves Lillian had
bought him before she left. Hammett walked down Tenth
Avenue. A wind coming off the river caused his eyes to tear,
his nose to run, his cheeks and chin to tingle with frost.
Something within him was happy. Bars were already open
on just about every corner. He stopped at a coffee shop on
Sixty-third Street.

Why hadn't he tried to find out what time the liner was
due to dock and be certain to be there when Lillian debarked?
Because this was how Dashiell Hammett dealt with matters
emotional, distancing himself with studied nonchalance and
carefully misplaced intention. Chance ruled in these matters, he told himself. He sat in the shop too long and wrote
nothing in his beautiful notebook. He paid for his coffee, left
a big tip, and walked to the river.

The streets were full of taxis and fancy autos. Horns
honked. All sorts of anxious people waved and dodged and
shouted. Porters were already loading steamer trunks and
luggage onto carts and piling them near the curb. Finding
Lillian in this crush would not be easy. He had a built-in
excuse.

Hammett made his way through the long, noisy shed all the way up to the customs fence, where he was stopped by police. Beyond customs he saw a green awning designated PRESS in large yellow letters. Mixed in with cameramen and reporters, some carrying portable microphones, Hammett saw Alfred and Blanche Knopf. Then he spotted Shumlin with Dos Passos and Archie MacLeish, the *Spanish Earth* brain trust.

The newspapers mentioned Lillian's return. In fact, the Hearst papers had kept a "Hellman Watch" while she was in Spain. Diplomacy, they editorialized, was a very delicate and complicated matter best left to a trained corps of professionals. A fair enough criticism, but Hearst didn't let the matter die. In an editorial Hearst himself declared, "Miss Hellman does the cause of neutrality and peace a great disservice by stoking up emotions that can only cause discontent and greater violence. One can only wonder what her true motives can be in trying to embroil Americans in what is and can only be seen as a foreign and thankfully very isolated conflict. Miss Hellman should stick her nose only where it belongs, namely in the wings and dressing rooms of Broadway theatres."

Hammett read that and smiled, recent photos of William Randolph and Adolf Hitler warmly shaking hands in Berlin fresh in his mind.

Hammett saw her first at the landing where the gangway turned sharply for a final descent to the pier. She stood talking to a ship's officer. Other passengers moved around them. Clearly the press was waiting only for her. Lillian listened

intently while the officer pointed and spoke. Hammett didn't
remember her being so small. He waved modestly with no
possibility of her seeing him. When he saw Lilly still speaking quietly, he dropped his arm.

As she came down to the pier, Hammett noticed that
she was not searching the crowd for him, and observed that
there was something vacant about her, as though she had
lost something important and was thinking about where it
might be. He wanted to rush forward to help her find it. She
looked wounded. Lillian never looked wounded.

He watched her come to the landing. Watched as she embraced her friends. Watched as she did not search the crowd
to see if he were there. Watched as she prepared for the rush
of reporters. Watched her begin to speak into a microphone
as he turned and walked away.

Whenever he sensed emotional paralysis, Dashiell Hammett got himself a drink. This Hammett walked past every
bar as he made his way up Ninth Avenue. Although he had
a destination, he made the journey seem like a wandering.

She was already in the apartment beginning to make coffee
when he arrived, chilled to the bone and looking frail. It was
as though he were the one arriving home from the war. They
stood and looked at one another. It hadn't even been a month.
It seemed like forever. Nothing had to be said for a while.

Lilly said, as though reading from a script, "They each
stood there, frozen for a long moment, gazing helplessly at
one another, looking for a sign. The moment was fraught . . ."

"Yes, fraught, heavily fraught, but fraught with what, he wondered quizzically."

"Oh, I dunno, just fraughtfully fraught I imagine." He saw a spark of something in her eyes.

"'I've missed you,' he said, wondering if that wasn't really her line."

"Not so terribly that you weren't there to meet me."

"I was there."

"Really?"

"I just didn't know how to . . . couldn't approach you with all that going on . . ."

"So maybe you could approach me now." Lillian opened her arms slightly waiting to be embraced. Hammett stepped forward, put his arms around her, chin on top of her head, and picked her up. As he squeezed and released three times she expelled air—"nyah . . . nyah . . . nyah." Lillian said, "Don't. No more."

He heard tugboat whistles and car horns. She heard nothing. They stayed together a long while. They said nothing when they separated because they wanted to talk, to tell, but before that there was explaining. Explaining did not qualify as talk.

"The war," is what he said eventually. "It got to you, the war?"

"Incredibly. Take off your coat. It's warm in the kitchen."

"I'm still a bit cold."

"I feel like cooking. What do we have?"

"Not much of anything, I'm afraid. I didn't think."

"So what else is new. Any cheese?"

"Some old cheddar."

"Eggs?"

"Not sure."

"Come on, let's cook. Warm you up."

Hammett stopped her by placing a hand on each shoulder, forcing her to look up at him. "I think I know how to help you."

"I haven't been hit by a car, you know."

"Yes, you have. If I help you, I help myself. Still selfish, you see."

There were eggs he hadn't remembered buying. There was cheese. There was milk and butter and flour and a jar of grape jelly. The oven quickly heated the kitchen and Hammett stood next to her in gray slacks and a knitted sweater, his hair tousled from the fur cap, looking nothing like Gary Cooper anymore but comfortably and domestically handsome. He found the pot and baking dish she requested, measured out exact amounts of flour and milk and butter. Lillian was humming. Occasionally their hands touched. When they did, they stopped and considered each other for a moment. A wonderful thing began to happen then. Lillian asked cooking questions and didn't receive cooking answers.

"Can you find the sifter for the flour?"

"I called you regularly, you know. Called press offices in Barcelona and Madrid. Left tons of messages. Worried sick about you."

"How many eggs are there?"

"I saw you at the ship. On the gangplank. I waved. Thought maybe you wanted to be with your friends."

Her expression said, *You're my friend.* "Do you know how to separate egg whites?" Of course he did; they had made soufflés together before.

"I'm in a bit of trouble myself. You know my inclination is to run and hide. I'm fighting it."

Lillian stopped greasing the baking dish and said, "I'm in trouble too. My inclination is to run and hide. I'm fighting it. Et cetera, et cetera." His hands held eggshells so he pressed her with his elbows. She said, "Put on some really mournful music."

They ate in the kitchen by candlelight because it was the warmest room in the apartment. Alone, together, in warmth on the eighth floor, each felt safe in a dangerous world, closer than they had been in a long while. They ate and drank ginger ale, still their champagne, and shared wounds.

Hammett went first. Given his known involvement with *l'affaire* Waxman by the powers that be at the studios, it was unlikely he'd be signing any lavish contracts with anyone. He recounted Myra's report. He passed along Phil Edmunds's deceptions and larcenies, which led naturally to Myra Ewbank's professional tribulations. Lilly asked lots of questions for which he could supply few satisfying answers. When she wondered why he hadn't gone to L.A. to try to help, he said he put off the trip because it was important to know when you were beat. No, that wasn't it. "I thought I might be needed more here." Still not it. "I wanted to be here more than there." That was a Hammett profession of love.

Hammett left silence.

"Dash, we need each other. More than ever."

He said, "True."

Her explaining began with, "Nothing I wrote about the war is valid. The only thing I got right are the bad guys. It's such a confusing mess, and I was so in over my head all I could think about was that you'd be ashamed of me. I hated you for not being there to help me through it all . . . Deep down, I felt used. I know that's crazy."

"You probably were in an impossible situation."

"And I'm still in it. Herman said he doesn't want me to walk away until we have our film."

"That's crap. Hemingway can write the film in two days."

Then she recounted everything. In detail, at length. The trip to Madrid. The siege of the city. The incredible destruction she saw. Hemingway and Gellhorn. The tangled course of the war. Its hopelessness. "I was scared all the time, Dash, deep-down scared. I failed. I know I failed."

They ended up curled on the couch with Lillian describing her last glimpse of a country in utter despair and she right along with it. He very much wanted a drink. So did she.

It was already tomorrow when they began to talk about what to do tomorrow, and the days after tomorrow. What was comforting was their understanding that they would now go their separate ways together. That was not only what each needed, it was what both wanted. The music now was Mendelssohn and they fell asleep on the couch.

The next morning, coffee was made, the kitchen was clean, bagels and lox had been bought, and Hammett was at the table reading the *Times*. Lillian leaned in the doorway unseen for a while letting her happiness grow. Hammett made believe he didn't see her. Finally he said without looking up, "Just thought of two more Jews I'd like to powwow with."

"Let me guess. Meyer Lansky and Emma Goldman."

"Nope. Neither at this particular time."

"Why not?"

"Lansky would probably kill me . . . and Goldman would get me killed."

Hammett poured her coffee and they tapped cups.

"Thanks. So who then?"

"Baruch Spinoza and the Baron Rothschild."

"Rothschild is easy. You want to learn how to become very rich without working."

"Cor-rec-et."

"Why Spinoza?"

"Because he's come closer than anyone in history to figuring out what love is all about."

That word from his lips made a sudden and stunning impression. She said, "Really."

"Yup."

She made it a point to sound only slightly curious: "And what does my celebrated *Lantsman* have to say about love?"

"Well, back when he was at the top of the philosophy game, he decided to take on the fearful subject, and in the end defined love thus: *I love you because you exist*. It was pure *reductio ad amore*. Nothing more nothing less. And when you think about it, you can't reduce the matter to anything less, or more, than that. But there is some stuff I'd like to ask him." Hammett still hadn't looked fully up at Lillian.

She pushed into his lap. "So why do you have to talk to *him?*"

"Because it says here they found his diaries and it turns out quite a number of ladies shared their existence with the sage."

She stood up. "Some detective you are. You want to find out about love and you track down the wrong Jew."

"And the right Jew would be . . . ?"

"The Jew who wrote *Set me as a seal upon thy heart, Love is stronger than Death*. The Song of Solomon Jew. That's who."

Hammett's laugh gave them both pleasure. He said, "True, rich old Solomon's—what was it?—seven hundred wives and three hundred concubines, or vice versa, would make Spinoza look like a piker."

"Word in the temple is that he loved every single one of them to pieces."

The day was spent reacquainting. And the next and the one after that. They did not answer the telephone, which was hard for Lillian. They went to the movies each day, sometimes twice. They walked along the river when it wasn't too cold. They ate in Chinese restaurants and cooked together. They made love in bed like kids with cooing sounds and tickles because each wanted only to surprise and entertain the other. Thanks to Spinoza they talked about love as a subject, an interesting and desirable one. Hammett did not declare it.

LILLIAN BEGAN ANSWERING THE PHONE because in time that is how the world reenters. She picked up only when her instincts told her it was relatively safe. Her instincts were often good. She turned down all dinner invitations, requests for interviews, and whatever else would have distracted them from their working lives together. There was work now, not work she welcomed, not well-paying work, work to be got through.

After avoiding Shumlin for as long as she reasonably could, Lillian received by messenger a handwritten shooting script from Joris Ivens. Well, perhaps not a true script, more like a log of sequential shots with each shot described briefly, and identified with place and date. So she would attempt to create the narrative of the film without being able to see the film itself, at least for now. A note from Ivens added the caveat that there would of course be changes in his and Hemingway's final version. How significant, he couldn't be sure.

As she began writing narration to images she could only imagine, the loathing that she carried back from Spain re-emerged. Lillian imagined the first dead person she touched—that woman's face—behind the cathedral. She again saw the nightmare vision of hell—Madrid in flames. Felt briefly the fear engendered by a bomb falling from an unseen airplane at night. Slowly, a bit at a time, every event she experienced during her weeks in Spain was transformed into story.

Lillian looked at the first page of Ivens's notes and wrote:

Distant sirens, that is what they hear first. Closer ones next. Then the drone. By now for most people it has become just another way of marking time. Like the noon church bells that peal across the entire country. Like the whistles calling workers to the factories or sending them home. Imagine. Bombs falling from the sky each night, and it has become a commonplace. Collecting the bodies the next morning; that too has become routine. What is not routine, and never will be, is the suffering.

Ivens's note said that footage of the recent bombing of Guernica could be inserted here.

In the beautiful Basque village of Guernica terror came in broad daylight . . . on Monday, market day, when the whole town was gathered in the square, exposed, vulnerable.

Matching word and picture, Hammett reminded her, ought not be done slavishly. Film narrative could be more partial and fragmented than straight storytelling, and even more effective. Word and picture could be moved around quite easily, new material inserted where needed, invented on the spot where necessary. The important elements now for Lillian were authenticity of voice and emotional truth. She convinced herself she finally had both.

HAMMETT BEGAN THE MEMOIR of his mother with the sentence he had intended before Lillian returned home. *My mama had a capacity for love so great it was almost self-defeating and all but impossible for the rest of us to live with.* He gazed at the sentence and read it aloud once for Lillian, who said it sounded beautiful but what did it mean? Hammett then read it to himself a few times and concluded it was an excellent beginning precisely because it begged for elaboration. He also admired its balanced tensions, good and bad qualities perfectly at play. He didn't want to rush the story so he let the sentence stand and began a new paragraph.

My mother Anne was a great beauty. There were
photographs in the house of her as a girl with very
long hair and eyes so kindly and soft you thought
that portion of the photograph might have been out
of focus. She wore a sailor's blouse and a spangled
scarf that somehow created the impression of impermanence, as though she were a casual visitor passing
through. Her soft eyes were pale and inward-looking.
Her hair, highlighted in the photo, was pulled off her
face to show a wide brow. A lovely girl with a soft,
vulnerable beauty.

When I was of an age—about nine or ten—when I
could see my mother as a woman, someone other than
only my mother, I saw a very different beauty. Anne
Dashiell was the most stunning woman I had ever
seen. Unlike her girlish photo, she was bony and strong
and sinewy; her features were regular but elongated,
giving her appearance an imperfect perfection that was
continually surprising. Her hair was always cut very
short and she never wore lipstick or makeup. Her skin
was suntanned and textured—not weathered—and
one side of her face—the left—was heavily dimpled
when she smiled and when she was hurt. Her pale eyes
did not have expressive range. Mostly they belied innocence and curiosity even when she was not innocent
or curious. My mother was strong and shy.

Other members of her family were rooted in their proud American pasts. The Bonds, her mother's family, were of fine English stock. The Dashiells, the father's side, were even prouder and finer and French. So in her family old national rivals had come together and made peace in the New World.

Anne Bond Dashiell was well educated for the time, having attended school until the age of sixteen and then trained as a practical nurse and midwife, a plan she also had for my sister Reba until family fortunes delayed and denied it, but that is indeed quite another story. Mama's folks said I looked most like Mama. I didn't really, they just wanted me to. In truth Reba looked most like Mama.

Late one night—so much happens when people can't sleep—I sat up with her in the kitchen. She always needed something to do with her hands, so we shelled peas. Dickie was asleep. Reba was reading. I didn't know where Papa was. The difference in being alone with Mama late at night was that I was encouraged to talk. I asked her things I truly wanted to know about. With Papa there was never any asking. Only his telling. I asked Mama what she wanted most when she was a girl. She stopped shelling. A look came over her face, a combination of surprise and pleasure. She looked almost like a girl just then.

"Two things, Sammy. I wanted two things. I wanted to fall in love with Prince Charming like in the books I read. Like Cinderella. Like Sleeping Beauty. Swept off my feet, Sammy. 'Cause you're not a girl, you probably won't understand." Mama stopped being Mama just then. She became more like my sister.

"And that was Papa?"

The spell was broken. She picked up a pea pod. "Yes, Sam, I guess that was Papa."

"And the second?"

"What second?"

"You said you wanted two things."

"Oh, yes. To please the Lord Jesus."

Mama was a Catholic and made us be Catholics, but she was a particular kind of Catholic. Papa made fun of her, called her a Jesus Boy Catholic. For him most Catholics were Voodoo Mary Catholics. Many Catholics believed in things that couldn't possibly be true, in visions and miracles. A Jesus Boy Catholic saw Jesus as someone who loved all his children and wanted them to be fed and housed and loved. Mama was a socialist back then without knowing the first thing about politics. She loved people, especially the lost and unwashed, as Jesus had, and as he commanded we all should.

When we lived near town, Mama went to Mass every morning. When we lived in the country, as we

did now, she prayed at table before anyone awoke.
She was visited frequently by Father Boylan, a young
priest who looked quite a bit like the picture of Jesus
hanging in her bedroom. Papa used to tease Mama
about how often Father Boylan visited her. He called
him her Priest Charming. Mama said the father heard
her confession. Papa said he hoped she had nothing
to confess and laughed through his nose.

One morning the sheriff's car pulled up to the
door and Sheriff Haynes asked if we might have seen
a man who escaped from the penitentiary the night
before. Mama said no and asked what the man had
done. Bank robber, the sheriff said.

I asked if he was a desperado.

Only if you own a bank, he said.

Later that day a man in tattered clothes came
to the door and asked for something to eat. It was
him, it had to be, the bank robber himself. Reba and
I were scared as anything, but Mama sat him down
and gave him almost everything she was saving for
Papa's supper. The man looked up from his bowl with
narrowed eyes and scared Reba and me even more.
I didn't know if it was the way he looked, dirty and
with his hair falling down over his face so that he
looked sneaky, or if it was the way he ate, using his
hands and not taking bites but stuffing the food into
his cheeks. Mama didn't treat him at all like a thief or

a criminal. She treated him exactly like a guest, like Father Boylan almost.

When the man was done and it was time for him to go, Mama wrapped some bread and cheese in a towel and gave him a bottle of her juice for him to take away. He never talked and never said thank you. He just ate, looked around with a fearful expression, took the food and left, and I was glad when he did.

Mama said, "Little that we have, we still have more than he does, more than enough to share." That part was true. We all watched as he went around the back of the house and off into the woods behind Papa's shed.

Not long after the convict left, Sheriff Haynes's car pulled up to our house again. Mama made a sign for us to be quiet and went out on the porch to talk to the sheriff. Here is what I heard as best I remember it:

"We've traced the man back down here, Miz Hammett. Keep that door of your place locked good now. No one comes in, y'hear? Suggest you lock those kids of yours up good too."

"You know, Sheriff, I think I saw the man you're looking for. He passed right down the road in front of the house."

"Down the road? Really? Which direction, ma'am?"

"I'm sure he went that way." She indicated the road to Wayland, exactly opposite to the way we had all seen him go. I was about to say something out loud. Reba put her hand to my lips.

The sheriff asked if he was alone. Did he look dangerous? Did he appear armed?

No, no, Mama said. He just looked like a sad man walking down the road. That way.

The sheriff drove off in the direction my mama showed him and that was about the end of it. Except before Papa came home that night I got to ask Mama why she lied to the sheriff. Mama said it was a deception and deception was different from lying.

"Mama, that really can't be so."

Then Mama agreed. "A kind of lying, I guess, Sammy."

"But you tell us never ever to lie. And you lied and Reba even went right along with it too."

"Don't be blaming Reba, Sammy. I was the one who said the lie. Your sister only heard the lie." As she said this, she touched my sister's hair and I remember getting angry, jealous most likely. Reba and Mama were already preparing some bread pudding and greens for dinner.

"So how come I'm not supposed to lie but Reba can lie plenty and you even like her for it?"

She saw that I was very upset and came over to me. She kneeled down so she was looking up into my face. And perhaps she saw herself as a child because she just looked at me without saying anything.

"He was in prison, Mama. He was a bad man who did a bad thing."

"Not everyone in prison is a bad man, Sammy. When you get older you'll see that's true." She kissed me but didn't let go of Reba. "Sometimes, Sammy, you have to make a choice of which sin— telling a lie or sending a poor man back to prison— would have been worse. Sometimes life can get very complicated."

"So how do you know?"

"Jesus always, always shows us what to do."

"I bet Jesus would not have said anything at all."

"Maybe, Sammy, but I thought Jesus might want to give the gentleman a better chance than that."

I never did get the lying and not lying exactly right. Or sins of omission and sins of commission either. I guess that's why I became a fiction writer and a detective story writer at that, since everyone in those stories lies about almost everything to get what he wants.

The next day my father discovered his best tools were all missing from the shed and asked us all if we knew anything about it. None of us said we did.

Such indiscriminate love as my mother possessed for humankind confused and troubled everyone in the family. Except her.

End

LILLIAN AND HAMMETT worked and spoke and cooked and walked and slept and made love sometimes, quietly. Each was happy to be with the other and took pains not to be disruptive. They were unhappy with their work, though, for different reasons. Lillian saw the war and her project as a lost cause but remained unhappily committed to both. She had never before worked in such a strange manner, writing to pictures she hadn't seen about a subject she hadn't taken real control of. It was more a test of character than of talent, a test that would end before long.

Hammett knew he could fill hundreds of pages with family stories, but until he understood the point of his "Tales," they would remain not much more than pages with family stories. He didn't know what he was doing either. But he was learning. At least he wasn't drinking, and the stories had something to do with that.

They each soldiered on until Herman Shumlin obtained a rough cut of Joris Ivens's film. In three days' time, watching it on the living room wall of the apartment, Lillian took her phantom script and gave it life with structural bones and sinew. She only wished it all hadn't come so late.

When she delivered her script to Shumlin, she told him she was through. Hemingway would be disappointed, he said. Hemingway should be disappointed, she said.

When *The Spanish Earth* was released, Ernest Hemingway did indeed narrate it. Most of the narration was Lillian's. President Roosevelt may or may not have seen it. All her liberal friends complimented her on her noble attempt to save the world. Each compliment wounded her because by then Lillian had begun to know what she had not known about Spain. She knew that Hammett knew it as well. He never referred to the film.

The United States, of course, did not enter the war and the Spanish Republican cause went from difficult to hopeless to lost.

Yiddishkeit

THE BEACH AT MALIBU in early evening is a place where some New Yorkers are easily seduced. As part of their new California ritual at the end of a writing day, if it was a writing day, Lillian and Dash sat in adjoining chairs and watched the sun descend to the Pacific. They usually drank red wine. The arms of their chairs often touched. They didn't speak much while the sun approached the water and they only got up to cook dinner when it had disappeared completely. Occasionally they sat and watched until Venus, the white planet, emerged slowly. On those nights they either went without dinner or drove late to Calabasas for seafood.

The beach house at Malibu was not theirs. They were paying guests and that meant not just the utilities but substantial mortgage payments for the three months the new owner was traipsing through Europe with the new love of her life. The new owner, Myra Ewbank, after almost a year with no work and then many months working under another name for minimum, was back in the film-writing business bigger and better than ever before. She was working again as Myra Ewbank for none other than Louis B. Mayer. She was not required to join her ex-husband's phony writers' union and was being given all the studio's most important assignments.

Myra attributed her good fortune to efforts on her behalf by Hammett and Peter Carey, the L.A. attorney, as well the various producers, directors, and actors who once valued her considerable talent. Myra was wrong. One person alone saved Myra Ewbank's career and did it secretly. Lillian Hellman.

Even though there was no way Myra could possibly have known that Lillian was her great benefactor, Lilly deeply resented having to make the mortgage payments on Myra's new Malibu house. She groused about Myra's lack of generosity and stopped only when Hammett said, "Quiet. You are ruining my sunset." If that did not stop her, he reminded her they were renting the house from a woman who had been out of work for over a year and who could not possibly know she owed Lillian her new wealth and livelihood.

Hammett knew he had lost the debate when Lilly said, "Still, seven hundred bucks for old friends. Come on."

Lillian had decided to step in on Myra's behalf the previous year, back when she had to fly out to California to meet with Sam Goldwyn about her next script project.

Hammett knew these movie matters could be done easily over the phone. "I just want to see if I can do something for Myra," Lillian had said.

"Feeling guilty?"

"About what? I didn't kill Waxman."

"Neither did I. And that was low."

"Neither did Myra, but she's the only one paying for it."

Hammett said, "There's not a hell of a lot can be done."

"I'd like to try Mayer face to face."

"Sure, look him straight in the eye and touch the soul which he no longer has because he sold it for junk when he was a kid."

"Read all about it—Louie Meier is a human being."

"Perhaps. But if he's one of the Waxman guys, he can't leave himself exposed, not even a crack. If he dumped someone like Myra in the first place, it was because he couldn't risk having her around anywhere, in any capacity."

"That was then, dear heart. New times call for new arrangements. I think Mayer trusts me."

"Let me be the first to congratulate you. The word *trust* and *L. B. Mayer* have never been used in the same sentence before."

Finally Lillian said, "Professor H., I have nothing but the highest regard for your judgment on the subject of human nature, its depths, its mysteries, its madness, but there is one member of the species I am better qualified to judge than you."

"Namely?"

"Jews."

"ELISE? THIS IS LILLIAN HELLMAN. I'd like to make an appointment to see Mr. Mayer."

"Would it be about a project or potential project?"

"Actually, it's a personal matter, but if it'll help me get to see him, then, yes, it is about a potential project."

Elise knew of Mr. Mayer's abiding interest in Lillian Hellman. She knew of Lillian Hellman's interest in Dashiell Hammett. She knew of Mr. Mayer's dismissal of Hammett the previous year. It was exactly a situation that called for, on the part of the secretary, something like, "I'm sure a meeting can be arranged. Give me time to work it out. Let me call you back." But because she liked *The Children's Hour* so much, Elise responded instinctively: "Tomorrow at ten. Is that suitable?"

"Suitable? I'd say 'wonderful.'"

AS AN ACTOR PREPARES for a role, and as she did in Spain when she wanted to be accepted as a correspondent, Lillian knew it was important to dress appropriately for this M-G-M performance. Mayer, of course, expected to see the

Lillian Hellman he had met a dozen or so times at various affairs around town over the years, a handsome, confident, very talented young woman, witty and slightly flirtatious, but only playfully so. That was not the Lillian he would get at the meeting.

Her role required someone older, back from defeat in Spain, sadly carrying too much of the world's weight on her shoulders. Onstage the actress would have dulled her hair and darkened the skin beneath her eyes. For Louis B. Mayer's office the effect she desired had to be more subtle, more the studied result of appropriate clothing, carriage, and voice. Lillian wore a small gray hat with a half veil, a boxy gray skirt, flat black shoes, and a black button-down sweater over a white linen blouse. Lillian chose this costume with great care before her meeting. She left the sweater open. To the blouse she pinned a cameo brooch. Her theatrical purpose was not only to appear a little older than she was but to suggest, merely suggest, that she was an Old World poor relation come to ask for a favor. It was eighty degrees in Hollywood that morning.

Louis B. Mayer's role was ever the same. He looked up from behind that immense desk and saw someone he did not expect to see. This Lillian Hellman took him by surprise. She sensed an initial advantage.

He rose and said, "Lillian, Lillian," before they embraced. She put her head lightly on his chest and held on to him a little longer than he expected. Nothing was said. Even after they sat facing one another, nothing was said.

"So. You are looking well."

"You're kind."

"You should be living out here, dear. You could use a little color. New York, *feh*. Dark and cold, too hard on people." His *feh* was more than she could have hoped for.

"We've still got the place in Santa Monica."

"'Still got' isn't living in a place. You said *we*. That means you're happy together?"

"*Happy*. That's a word I haven't dusted off for a while."

"It's the entire purpose in life, my dear, to be happy." Louis Mayer fancied himself something of an expert on the subject of happiness. Happiness was what he made for people. Happiness was what he sold. Happiness was his contribution to the world and what he hoped he'd be remembered for. He placed both his hands on top of his head. "So. Elise tells me you've got a project idea."

"Mr. Mayer, that's only partially . . ."

"*Mr. Mayer?* Please. Louis. I'll call you Lilly. You'll call me Louis. And I'll feel young again. It's your comfort I want, dear."

"Comfort." She listened to the word as though it were in a foreign tongue. She bit her lips. "Comfort. *A brochel ich hab'nish*."

No one had uttered a word of Yiddish in this office for a decade. In a swift, unguarded moment, L. B. Mayer was transformed into Louie Meier, a boy who knew this tongue . . . and loved it. "*Zayt mir moykhl . . . es guyt Litvak?*"

By asking if she, like him, was a Lithuanian Jew, Mayer was not merely inquiring about the Hellman family roots but asserting a Jewish cultural superiority: Lithuanian Jews considered themselves intellectually superior to Galician Jews, whom they regarded as a bunch of superstitious, rabbi-ridden ignoramuses.

Lillian explained that she'd picked up her Yiddish, imperfect as it was, from her aunts in New Orleans, that was why her distinctly Southern accent made her Yiddish as sweet as his was harsh. "Originally, the family was from Minsk." A lie.

"My god, Minsk," Mayer exclaimed, "I was born in Minsk." Then he reined in his exuberance. "I don't broadcast it around. The world should know I'm true-blue American."

"Which of course we both are, thanks to our people's courage to leave such a place. But thank God also, we're Jews also, even if we don't broadcast it."

Meier wanted to get up and kiss her. What Mayer did instead was say, "So why won't you come to work for me? Can't you see what we could have here? This I don't understand."

"Perhaps. Soon we can arrange something. Right now, I'm too confused." She touched her temple and then her heart. "You know I was in Spain when the fighting was really terrible." He was about to speak; she stopped him with a wave of a heavy hand: "I know, I know. We don't agree on that, Mr. Mayer. That's not the point. What I saw . . . the suffering . . . and what Hitler is doing now with Jews . . . the indignities . . ."

He stood and poured her a glass of water.

She drank. "The suffering touched me deeply. I'm all the time *verklempt* . . . I can barely write at all."

"You're a wonderful writer. Wonderful."

"Once upon a time."

"Once? Everyone admires Lillian Hellman. *Leshem shmain, get veyter.* You'll come here and you'll write for me. I'll make it perfect for you."

"I wake up all the time depressed. I've seen too much suffering, Louis."

"Are you seeing someone? I have the name of . . ."

"Who's to see?" Lillian wondered in the ensuing silence, during which Louie Meier was seriously thinking about what he could do to help this woman, if she hadn't badly overplayed her role and her hand.

Meier said, "*Der oylam is a goylem.*"

"I know that—*the world is crazy*—but why should I allow it to make me crazy too? At any rate, I've really come to ask you for a favor."

"Anything, dear."

"A pretty big one, I'm afraid."

"I just said, *Anything, dear.*" Lilly knew, of course, that *anything* was only a word in the English language; in the Hollywood context it meant, *I'll consider and eventually you'll know.* Mayer assumed Lillian was going to ask for some work for Hammett, who hadn't written anything worth anything for two years, and in truth there were indeed some bones in the M-G-M cupboard that could be thrown his way. There were very good business reasons not to turn down this *maideleh*.

"If I'm suffering, Mr. Mayer, I have a good friend who is suffering even more . . ."

Mayer positioned himself to deal with the request for Hammett.

". . . I'm asking on her behalf because if I can see just a little bit of order restored in my world, see just a bit of sanity return, I'll be able to sleep tonight. You can have no idea how she has suffered. And you can end her *shamdeh*, snap, just like that with an okay."

"You haven't said who."

"Myra."

"Who?" Mayer knew, of course.

"Myra Ewbank. She will give you her very best." This next was most important: "And you have absolutely nothing to fear. I assure you. She'll do anything to work again for you, no questions asked. She'll sign anything, any waivers under any conditions. And I'll guarantee it. Make her this mitzvah. You won't be sorry." This last implied that at some future time the mitzvah would be repaid by Lillian.

"Tell me the name again, and I promise I'll look into it."

Lillian realized it was a good time to stand. She said, "*Zei mir metriach*, but not just for me but because it's right, Mr. Mayer."

"Louis."

"Of course. Louis."

"You'll come back when you want to talk projects?"

She wanted to shake hands. He wanted to embrace. Upon parting she said, "*Zeit gezunt*, Louis."

He said, "*Zol zein mit glik*."

"Who couldn't use a big dose of *glik* these days?"

Lillian had no idea if her impersonation was successful. Her inclination was to think not, too old, too shtctl, too sentimental by half. The New York critics would have had a field day ripping her performance apart.

ESSENTIAL TO ANY American Horatio Alger story—Rockefeller, Gould, Vanderbilt, Andrew Carnegie, L. B. Mayer, even Isaac Marx, you name it—was the ragamuffin beginning of the great success. Where would be the triumph, the drama, if the beginnings were not so very humble, even well below humble? After the wealth has come, the power and prestige, doesn't something of that original poor boy remain locked away somewhere? For L.B., whose factory produced American dreams of the same pattern as his life, the sentiments Lillian stirred up in his office caused him to consider the favor she asked of him. If Lillian Hellman fooled L. B. Mayer it was because Louie Meier wanted to be fooled.

As he sat comfortably looking out over his back lot, Mayer thought about the last time he'd heard Yiddish spoken. With his father? No, with his grandmother, his *Bubbe*, who spoke no English, to whom he was, even as a young American man, *Boychik* and *Bubbeleh*. His grandfather, an educated man, insisted the boy learn English even though he himself spoke it poorly. Mayer recalled how this old language filled the house with its melody, its pauses, its unexpected inflections and rhythms that made everything sound like a question to be pondered and parried with another question. Phrases he was certain he'd forgotten came back with context: his grandfather saying real business can only be done *oyg oyf oyg* (eye to eye), and if things went badly with the landlord, cursing him with A *choleryeh shtif der* (He should only get cholera).

For his father, almost everyone he had to deal with back in Haverill was either a *schmuck* or a *putz*. It was an evaluation even more true for the son in Hollywood. When his grandparents passed away, so did the Yiddish, except for a phrase or two between his mother and father when they didn't want the boy to understand. Who spoke Yiddish anymore? Still, he could probably hold a conversation if he had to, as he almost had with the Hellman girl. Gone was not forgotten.

Business was business of course. Only a fool would allow himself to become vulnerable in this Ewbank situation. But look how much he paid for Clare Luce's *The Women*, budget already over a million and a half, and the damned thing still creaked like a stage play. The Ewbank girl could make it feel like a movie in a week. Maybe a grateful Lillian Hellman would be good business all around. Before he called Elise,

Mayer said aloud, just to feel the pleasure of it, "A *mentsh tracht und Gott locht*" (A man plans and God laughs). Then he said, "A *zeit gezunt*" to the ceiling just in case God was listening.

IN HER SWELTERING CAR Lillian immediately rolled down the front windows and pulled off the foolish hat and that damned sweater. She threw her glasses on the front seat and opened her blouse to bra level. She ran her comb through stiff hair. Then she closed her eyes and simply breathed. There was only one review of her performance that mattered.

Before she started the car, Lilly thought back to New Orleans, to the aunts' rooming house, to the last time she'd heard real Yiddish spoken. It wasn't used often, usually when Hannah and Jenny didn't want the help, the *Schwartzeh*, to know what they were saying, which was precisely why she was drawn to the language.

Her family story wasn't, after all, so very different from the junkman's. She imagined Isaac Marx trudging through rural Alabama on his horse cart, if it really *was* a horse cart—probably he owned an ass—decades before the American Civil War. This lone, itinerant Jew from Chemnitz, wandering the back roads, landing finally in godforsaken Demopolis. It was a mule cart, she recalled now with something close to certainty. Why didn't she know these important things about her remarkable progenitor? Why in the world hadn't she taken a greater interest in Isaac? It wasn't the old man's fault his children and his grandchildren coveted his wealth, took his power, and then erased him.

She remembered seeing a tintype of a little old man sitting rigidly under a willow tree, dressed in stiff clothes a size too large. Bearded, yes, definitely bearded. And wearing a skullcap. This was Isaac Marx at the end, a boy who came with nothing and amassed a fortune, who came speaking Yiddish and left a family that was ashamed of Yiddish, ashamed to have their "Newhouse" Julia married to an itinerant Yid like Max Hellman.

How the hell did that little man converse with those salt-of-the-earth Bible belters? With numbers, of course. How, almost one hundred years ago now, did he even find his way around Alabama safely? Find places to stay? How much English could he have had? He must have been brilliant. How in the world did he defend himself in that dangerous place? With a gun, of course. My god, he must have been brave. This was a genius of a little man. Lillian had never before given Isaac Marx this much continuous thought or the consideration he had earned and deserved. She spoke to him then: "You must have been charming as hell, too, little Isaac." Did she look like him? Where was that photograph now?

The great Victorian house in Demopolis was still there. Cousins lived in it now. She should go visit, she really should, with Hammett next time they went back East. While sitting there in her car envisioning the Demopolis house, she allowed in the generation of Newhouses and Marxes she grew up with, remembered anew how hateful they were, how selfish and cold and how, apparently unlike Mayer, at least today, without sentiment.

Lillian pulled her notebook out of her bag. She wrote the description that would become, with few changes, the stage setting for her next play: *The living room of the (family name needed) home, in a small town in the Deep South, the spring of 1900. Upstage is a staircase leading to the second floor. Upstage, right, are double doors to the dining room. Upstage, left, an entrance hall with a coatrack and umbrella stand.* She stopped and saw it clearly as she wrote. *There are large lace-curtained windows on the left wall. The room is lit by a center gas chandelier and painted china oil lamps on the tables. Against the wall is a large piano.*

That was indeed how the room was furnished; but it was not what the room was. *The room is good-looking, the furniture expensive; but it reflects no particular taste. Everything is of the best and that is all that can be said for it.*

Lillian's decision to write a play using her mother's family did not come only because of her meeting with Mayer. Hammett's accumulation of family stories had already got her thinking about those Marx and Newhouse lives. What had activated the process today was her discovery that the family's rejection of Yiddish Isaac and his language were the first family betrayals that made all subsequent betrayals possible and probably inevitable. Since Mayer had become such a demonstrably patriotic American, such a prominent and public Republican, Lillian doubted there could still be much of a connection back to the immigrant junkman days. Her hope rested on the dramatic insight that not every betrayer was willing to betray that last true part of himself. And by so doing betray the memory of his father and mother and grandparents. The second generation of Marxes did precisely that in the blink of an eye.

That day Lillian had her setting for *The Little Foxes*. She had her characters—her grandmother Sophie and her two older brothers. She had the situation—an actual business deal she recalled as a child: the acquisition of vast cotton fields partially through marriage and partially through political manipulation and bribery. The construction of the necessary cotton mill and the purchase of mill equipment were done with money borrowed on nonexistent collateral. This is what the Marxes talked about openly in little Lilly's presence. When her mother, Julia, indicated these were not matters a girl of eight ought to be exposed to, Grandma Sophie said, "Don't be silly. You're never too young to learn how the world really works."

Part of the play's drama would be the appalled fascination of the audience watching betrayers at work for whom no betrayal was beyond consideration and execution. Multiple betrayals would be like mounting bets in a no-limits poker game. There was continual drama in that. None of the Marxes, to her certain knowledge at least, had ever murdered for personal gain. Lillian decided her drama would explore even that possibility of "how the world really works."

Hammett's interest in the Song of Solomon eventually brought her to the verse that gave her a larger idea into which she could grow her drama: *Take us the foxes, the little foxes, that spoil the vines. For our vines have tender grapes* . . . The process may have started before that moment in the M-G-M parking lot; that day it became the first words put to paper.

When Lillian returned to their Santa Monica house from her meeting with Mayer, she was excited that something good and important had begun. She told Hammett about how suddenly and unexpectedly the echoes of the Yiddish exchange with Mayer called up the theme and much of the structure of a new project. "There I am, sitting, dressed like a yenta, begging the man for a personal favor, and it all comes together for me. It was completely impossible."

"That's why it happened." Hammett wreathed himself in cigar smoke.

"I said *impossible*."

"I've lived with you long enough to know *impossible* is your SOP." She tipped her head. "A military term, dearie: Standard Operating Procedure." Hammett had been writing a Secret Agent X-9 radio script he thought was going pretty well until Lillian burst in with her "impossible" news. The National Broadcasting Company was interested in bringing X-9 to the airwaves, although Hammett could not for the life of him imagine why.

A few years earlier Hammett had been contacted by Sol Gewirtz of King Features, who told him they'd like Hammett to write a comic strip about spies. King had already hired the artist Alex Gordon, who had also just begun *Flash Gordon* with great success. Gewirtz told Hammett he only needed the new strip's concept and story line.

"Only that? Imagine."

"You're who we want, Mr. Hammett."

"Then I must be your first call?"

"Absolutely. We went right for the top."

"Mr. Gewirtz, I have to tell you the *liar* signal on my phone is blinking."

"Mr. Hammett, I can assure you . . ."

"Let's do this. Call me sometime tomorrow and I'll have an idea of what I'd like to do. If you like it, maybe we can do business. If we don't do business, you'll steal the idea and say it's your own."

Sol Gewirtz got it, laughed, and said, "Tomorrow."

When finally they connected Hammett offered his idea. "Secret Agent X-9. An operative so secret he doesn't even have a name. Working for an agency so clandestine it doesn't exist officially. X-9 has the authority to track down and liquidate anyone who wants to do dirt to the United States of America." This structure, or lack thereof, would make X-9 a truly free agent and allow him to do anything Hammett could possibly imagine for him.

Gewirtz said, "Secret Agent X-9, I like it. Where'd you come up with that?"

"That's secret too."

"Sounds good. Daily strip. No weekends to start with. Six panels. Interested?"

"That's why we're talking, Sol."

"We pay by the word." There was just the suggestion of tentativeness in his voice.

"You are saying, I assume, you *usually* pay by the word."

"Actually *always.*"

"Sol, I'm sorry but my pay-by-the-word days are over. Flat rate or I'll have to pass."

"Fifty dollars."

"A panel?"

"My god, no. A strip. Daily."

Hammett had calculated a bit. One hundred dollars a day would bring him about twenty-five thousand a year. That became his bottom number. "Let's say two hundred a strip, Sol."

"Mr. Hammett, we don't pay anyone anything like that."

"*Anyone* hasn't writ *anything* like Spade or the Op. You know what the Hammett name on the strip would mean."

The silence was charged and extended. "We can offer perhaps seventy-five."

Since Gewirtz had upped his offer, Hammett knew there was no *we* at the other end. Gewirtz alone had the authority. "I'm afraid nothing less than one fifty will win my heart."

"We can perhaps see one hundred. Tops."

"Sir. Let's split the difference. One twenty-five and we have a deal."

"Mr. Hammett, I'm going to have to go over the numbers. See if this can work at our end."

"Understood, Sol. I do hope it works out. Sounds like something I'd very much enjoy doing."

And Hammett did enjoy doing it the first year. The strip was story-driven. Hammett mailed Alex Gordon what was essentially a segment of a chapter—the equivalent of a movie scene. That scene became the day's script. When Hammett knew what would appear in each panel, he gave Gordon the specific dialogue over the phone. He was trying and almost succeeding in recapturing the sheer fun and adventure of the old *Black Mask* days. Except back then his tongue was not so completely in his cheek as with X-9.

So there, in a sample day's story, is X-9, looking dapper in a dark suit, casually stretched on a chair in Mrs. Powers's boudoir. Mrs. Powers, an enemy superspy, is a very dangerous woman indeed, but not nearly as dangerous as Mr. Big, her boss, the operative Secret Agent X-9 is ultimately after. In the second panel Mrs. Powers is perched on his knee; they are on the bed—a position they would never be permitted in films. Hammett has her say, "Listen to me, you are an attractive man—strong and violent . . . and I'm an attractive strong and violent woman, so why shouldn't we . . . ?"

Jump to a bemused X-9 in the next panel: "What is this, a proposal of marriage?"

The strip was not a success. Hammett wrote it for two years, during which time most of his movie work was gone. The comic strip required little work or thought because, as was his tendency, Hammett simply repackaged old stories and crime gimmicks for a new commercial market. His original magazine stories had become his novels; the novels became movie scripts; and those same stories—and much of the original dialogue—found their way into the comic strip.

Now that radio had developed a huge audience, it too demanded storytellers, and the program directors found Hammett. One night he told Lillian, "As long as they keep inventing new bottles for old wine, I can keep my name on the label." It surprised him that no one seemed to notice he was always using the same stories and essential characters, or if they did, no one seemed to mind very much. He knew, of course, that Lillian did.

Lillian asked to read the new X-9 radio script. Hammett said sure, but managed never to give it to her, and she knew never to ask for it again. Like Sol Gewirtz, however, she did want to know how he came up with the name X-9.

He refused to tell her: "Secret agent . . . secret name."

"Why X-9? It could have been B-12."

"That's a vitamin."

"You know what I mean."

"Our secret? Swear?"

"Our secret. Swear."

"Look in your bra."

"What do you mean, 'Look in my bra'? You didn't call him 32-C."

"Not the size. The model. There's a tag on the strap. X-9."

"Do you sniff my underwear too?"

"Only when I'm very lonely." They touched glasses.

Reba was TWO YEARS OLDER than I was, so when she was fourteen, I was not yet twelve. The chronology does not quite capture the difference. She was already a young woman, easily as beautiful as my mother but in a softer, more welcoming way. Boys were always hanging out near the house just for the chance to see her, I believe. They carried her books home from school, they went on walks with her down to the lake. They even followed her to the movies on Saturday afternoon. Robby Burnett appeared to be her favorite; I saw her kiss him more than once in the woods.

Reba was flirtatious in ways I could not then understand. She made herself madly desirable by being impossibly distant and inaccessible. She had a way of turning down boys and still leaving the impression they had an excellent chance at her affection next

time around. Reba could smile in such a way that a
boy could . . .

Hammett stopped cold. Everything was off. Voice and
tone and intention. Worst of all, it wasn't Reba at all. He was
writing fearfully again, a problem cropping up more often in
his "Tales." At least he recognized the symptoms and knew
to stop. He poured himself a drink, not the red wine. The
gin. He watched the sunset beyond Santa Monica for a long
while with pleasure. The light from the room behind him
touched his page and he began again.

Reba was an unusually beautiful girl. A painting.
Raphael in a rare sensual moment. I simply knew
that back then without knowing what sensual meant
or who Raphael was. She was just my older sister so
I didn't bother to think very much about her at all. I
didn't really think much about any of the members of
my family as people in their own right, only as Hammetts, which is to say I thought about them only as
their lives affected mine. Doesn't everyone, I wonder,
really think of family members in that way? Deep
down, I think so.
    Rebecca's beauty was different from Mama's.
Already tall and shapely, she was precisely what
Hollywood would eventually search for, a distinc-
tive American beauty with just the slightest touch of

something unfathomable. She was the blond girl you saw on the billboards, a combination of purity and promise. The boys who buzzed around her weren't interested in Barbasol or Lifebuoy; it was the presence of true beauty in our distinctly unbeautiful world that drew them. Of course, I had no idea back then of the aesthetic state of Hopewell, Maryland. I barely noticed that my sister attracted so much attention; to me, she was my sister and not the town's most beautiful young woman.

I was gangly and introverted, neither sensual nor sexual, a boy who did not yet know the first thing about procreation in any life form higher than a house fly. And because I associated sex with house flies, I considered them both pretty awful.

It is only now that I have come to realize that Reba's particular beauty triggered more love than lust in the local boys. Though I did notice something different in the way the men looked at her when I happened to go to town with her on market days, and even when she was in church with me and Mama and Richard. On the street their narrowed eyes stole glances. There was something sly and mean in the way men went about looking at Reba. I saw in it hunger and desperation. In church, where her beauty darkened a little, men, at least those who weren't frightened of her aura, treated her like a child; they patted her head, talked about little-girl things while they sweated profusely. Father Boylan, Mama's "Priest Charming," never allowed himself to be alone with my sister. He always called her Little Halo Girl.

All the behavior I noticed without noticing falls under the broad category of desire, which is easy for me to discern now. Back then I understood it, because of my own youthful limitations, as popularity. My sister was pretty and popular.

Dumb and sexless as I was, I nevertheless knew that Reba's attraction was not that of Hopewell's two well-known "bad girls," Nola Harrison, who dropped out of school and worked at the truck stop on Route 7, and Audrey Huff, who worked at the diner across the highway. I didn't care to know what made them so bad. I knew it wasn't robbery or murder. It was something darker that couldn't be talked about. Even my forgiving mother thought their souls were already lost.

Then my mother discovered that there were some people in town, led by Mrs. Laxalt and Miz Quintin, who spread rumors about Reba also being one of the bad girls. So one Monday morning she marched us all up to Miz Quintin's vegetable stall right next to the town fountain, pointed straight at the deformed old lady and announced loudly, "This woman does the Devil's work!" The entire market quieted and turned to take notice. "Yes, indeed, this woman does the Devil's work." I slipped behind the fountain. "She spreads malicious talk about good girls. She is the Devil's defamer." Mama stretched out her arms in a public embrace. "We all know in our hearts it is a sin to steal someone's good name. This girl . . . ," holding an embarrassed Reba by the shoulders, Mama showed her daughter to the town. "This is a good girl. You know her, a pure child. Do not take her young goodness from her."

Then, more quietly to Miz Quintin, a threat: "If you do not stop maligning this child, you will put your soul in peril." It was the only threat I ever heard from my mother's lips, and it evoked a breathless sigh from the crowd.

I looked mostly at Reba the whole time. Her face was pink and utterly impassive. There was then a prolonged silence. Her purpose at the marketplace done, Mama gathered us up and we set off on the road home.

Hammett knew when he began where this memory of Reba was going. He also knew he had the option of writing two distinct Rebecca Hammett tales. He drained his gin and poured himself another.

Being as bookish as I was made me seem even more the lonely boy. Miss Gaffer, the librarian, chose my

books based on the solid nineteenth-century belief that
a boy's character could be shaped by the biographies
of great men. She gave me Eli Whitney, Ben Frank-
lin, Lord Nelson, Napoleon Bonaparte, Commodore
Vanderbilt, Abraham Lincoln. When it looked like I
would tear through every biography in the library, she
said, "Don't you worry, Sam, I'll make sure you run out
of time before I run out of books for you."

All my reading made me seem silly in Reba's eyes.
She teased me about reading such foolishness. She
wanted me to read adventure stories and then tell her
about faraway places in the world.

I liked Reba well enough, I guess. I think I might
have liked her more if she hadn't teased me so much.
If I had perceived her teasing as a form of affection,
which I now believe it was, it might have changed
things a bit between us.

One midsummer night and very warm, I was
reading *The Life and Times of Young Andrew Carnegie* at the kitchen table beneath the old oil lamp.
My mother set a time limit on my reading at table in
order to save oil money. Young Carnegie himself was
sitting in semidarkness at a kitchen table studying
Morse code so he could apply for a job as a telegra-
pher on the Baltimore and Ohio Railroad. My mama
called out to me to finish up and go to bed.

"Five minutes, please, Mama."

Reba said, "I'll make sure of it, Mama." Shortly thereafter she damped the wick and I was in darkness. No point in complaining, I closed my book. Reba whispered to me, "Sam, I need you for something." She put her finger to her lips for silence. "Follow."

She tiptoed out of the house into the yard. I followed. There was only a sliver of moon. I couldn't exactly find her. "Sammy," she called. I traced her voice. She was sitting on Papa's woodpile at the edge of the trees. Reba wanted me to sit on the chopping block opposite her.

"I like you, Sammy." I knew Reba wanted me to say I liked her back. I couldn't because she wanted me to. "Do you ever wonder what will happen to us all?"

The truth was that I didn't because my books gave me a sense of a personal destiny that I had to shape and follow; in so doing it was clear I would have a good and eventful life. That took a lot of the guesswork out of an entire existence spent passing between home and school in Hopewell. It never occurred to me that because she was a girl, Reba did not have a destiny as fortunate as my own. I said, "I think I'll invent something and become famous."

"No one here ever becomes famous."

Hammett put down his pen and rubbed his eyes. Did he want to finish this story now? Did he want to finish it ever?

He decided it had to be written, perhaps not shown to anyone but certainly written.

Reba reached out with both hands and touched my cheeks. "I'm so proud of you, Sammy. You're different from any one else I know in the whole world. And you're my own brother." My sister had never touched me like that before, deliberately and with affection. Her hands were cool and stayed on my cheeks. "Promise to think about me when you are gone away from here." I said nothing. "Sam. Promise."

"Promise."

We sat quietly. I would have gotten up but my sister began to hum and sing "After the Ball Is Over." I forgot to mention that Reba had the sweetest voice I've ever heard. And so we stayed there. Quietly. I had never shared such a moment with another person. Reba sang low there in the dark. She whispered, "Sam, scratch my back, please." And then she sang some more.

She was wearing a dress Mama made. Mama made most of our clothing on a sewing machine her family had got her. My father disparaged her sewing as well as her machine.

Reba's summer dress was pale yellow. It had no arms and wide straps over her shoulders.

"Don't be afraid to touch me, Sam. Nothing bad will happen." As she said this, she reached behind her back and opened the top and second buttons. It turned out as I put my fingertips to her back that there was something to be afraid of. I didn't know what it was but the tightness in my stomach and chest, the near paralysis in my arms and fingers was as close to fearfulness as I'd experienced since I saw Mr. Freeman hanging from the tree beyond the lake. Reba's hair was down and smelled clean and felt soft when I bent my cheek to it.

"Scratch in circles, Sam. Slower. That's right. Oh."

I did only what Reba said to do, but the combination of my fingertips on her cool skin, the smell of her, her cooing and humming voice was so dizzying I closed my eyes and allowed a strange mixture of pleasure and fear to take me away. I became dizzy and then excited in a way that worried me.

"That feels so good. Don't stop please."

Reba leaned forward and pulled the straps of her dress off her shoulders. She rocked slightly backward so that my hands edged toward her sides. When she leaned back toward me finally, I had her breasts, soft flesh I had no right ever to touch, one breast in each hand. This was thrilling beyond imagining. And sinful without my knowing sin. My chest was on her back, my cheek and lips upon her neck.

Mama called out to Reba from the house.

"Yes, Mama. Be right there."

Reba leaned back slowly and buttoned her dress. She said, "Thank you, Sam," without looking back at me.

It was the first great confusion of my life and it never went away completely.

End

· 13 ·

The Walk

WHEN WE SPEND THIS MUCH TIME TOGETHER, we even begin to sound alike. Thank God for personal pronouns.

He can date things better than I. In this case—I guess I'm talking about our blowup—the nearest I can come is the blitzkrieg of Rotterdam, which would make it, what, early spring 1940? The bombing, similar to Guernica but on a much, much larger scale and far better organized, happened two or three days earlier. Hundreds of bombers, three hundred, according to the papers.

When we were in California the depressing impact of the war news did not hit me as it did back here in New York. Out there, it was as though we were in one surreal world reading about what was happening in another surreal world, like Martians trying to be concerned about what was happening out on Venus. I can't say Rotterdam broke my heart. Spain had already done that.

The *Journal American* showed Rotterdam leveled to dust and rubble, faint grids where streets and avenues had once intersected. Only one building, the great cathedral, was left standing, untouched as though the surrounding punishment was God's will, when it was Hitler's. No people, not a one, to be seen, even with a magnifying glass, which is what I was using when Hammett came into the kitchen. The Hearst caption read, "Rotterdam, Holland, in the aftermath of aerial military action," as though there were neither murderers nor their victims, only "action." The bastard.

Hammett picked up the morning's *Times* and read the latest reports. "Looks like they'll be going after London next. They're collecting air bases across the Channel. Can't believe how fast they're moving."

"I hope I don't hear the hint of some bullshit, he-man admiration in your voice."

"You may hear it, but it is not there. I'm only saying this will be a war of wills, and until our will matches theirs, they'll just roll on."

The mood of the day was set by that early exchange over coffee. I resented his acknowledging any superiority whatsoever to the scum . . . and for much of the day could not completely shake my resentment.

Hammett had agreed to walk to the lawyer's office with me that day and cosign a contract to purchase a farm upstate. In Westchester. Pleasantville. The world was living in

Shitsville and there we would be, tucked away safe in Pleasantville. Still, I have to say I was not guilt-ridden. Living in the country was the answer for us. You know, give old Voltaire a try, "Cultivate your garden" and all that. One hundred and forty acres on which to make things grow, nourish your soul, get food to market, grow strong, try to look away from the rest of the world for a while. Dash was always a country boy at heart and other than a few radio plays those days, he certainly wasn't growing anything in the city.

For us, the simplest exchanges in those days always had angry undertones. Blame it on the Nazis. Blame it on the weaklings who gave them the run of the house. Since blame always seeks the nearest target, blame Hammett and then blame me. He was edgy too, but I didn't think it mattered very much. Everything about buying the farm had been discussed fully, all had been agreed to. I thought.

We would become co-owners of Hardscrabble Farm, and all would become right in our small universe. He got to name the place after many long and enjoyable discussions over the dinners we prepared together. I'd say, "What about Tightwad Acres?"

"Good but not true. There's nothing cheap about either one of us. How 'bout Rewrite Farm?"

"Self-aggrandizing. What about Cornucopia?"

"You're kidding."

Hardscrabble came late in the game. Hammett offered it after doing a crossword in which the clue was "Scratch or paw the earth," eight letters. S-c-r-a-b-b-l-e. Hardscrabble was what the sharecroppers back in Hopewell called their infertile land.

I said, "That's as far from Cornucopia as you can get. But Hardscrabble it is."

I knew the property needed lots of work. The farmhouse needed everything—rewiring, a new well, a roof, a screened-in porch, new kitchen, complete paint job . . . The farm itself needed a tractor, maybe two. An irrigation system. The barn walls needed shoring up. Much of the stock had to be replaced . . . Listen to me, I'm speaking like Farmer Lill.

Money was at no time an issue, at least where I was concerned. *The Little Foxes* was going to Warners even before it closed on Broadway. *Watch on the Rhine* was on its way to town with at least three studios already bidding significant money for film rights. I knew the play would cause a stir. No one else was writing about the raw political brutality cloaked by the elegance, good breeding, and superficiality of European aristocrats and the wealthy American upper classes. In the play, a German-born engineer and his wife and three children visit his wife's very rich and apolitical mother in Washington. Kurt, the engineer, is prominent in the anti-fascist underground in Germany. Another aristocratic house-guest discovers this and is about to expose him and some of his colleagues when Kurt kills him. And there is the great moral dilemma of the play. When exactly do we take up arms against the Rats? Is killing ever justified? These are questions easily answered for me. I thought it was about time audiences had to face them too.

As far as Hardscrabble was concerned, it didn't matter a tittle to me that Hammett was cash poor at the time. Perhaps it should have, but it didn't. He could pay his way when things got better for him. Or not. I didn't care. It wasn't important.

As I said, mid-May, a glorious morning in New York. It was my idea to walk rather than ride to Sherman's office to sign the Hardscrabble papers. The walk over to Broadway, across the park, and then to Madison would set the day apart, make it feel special. It was something I thought we needed to set against the backdrop of the despicable bombing in Holland, an entr'acte, contentment stolen in a crappy world.

I knew he didn't like the financial arrangement for Hardscrabble. But was there any doubt that if the situation were reversed, he'd do everything possible for me to share the farm with him? When I said that, it turned a tense situation into an angry tense situation. He said I'd get my money soon and with interest. Instead of saying, *Fine*, and being done with it, or better, saying nothing at all, I made a joke: "First of the month, small bills, brown envelope, my agent's office." When our eyes met, I could see he didn't love me. If anyone knew that money was never about money, it was me. And unless Dash had another good novel in him or got some film work, radio plays were simply not going to cut it. As it was, half the money he did make went to his family—yes, he was still married, thank you very much—no telling precisely where the other half went. We walked on in the civil chill of a very fine day like a typical married couple.

Did I mention that he had dressed for the occasion? A haircut—not a drinker's apology, a stylish trim—and his best gray suit and tie. Just the week previous he had wandered over to Broadway and bought a Homburg. He saw Ribbentrop in the *Times* shaking hands with Molotov and said, "Dignity, thy name is Homburg." I said, "Rats in fancy hats is still Rats." But he bought the hat and looked handsome and prosperous and particularly well turned out as we crossed Columbus Avenue, where I slipped my wrist over his arm. I had to help get him through this difficult day.

When we entered the park at Eighty-sixth, I told him about a talk I'd had with Jack Warner about the rights for *Watch*. I didn't bother to tell him I'd talked with Goldwyn and Mayer as well. No deal had actually been cut with anyone yet, one certainly would be, but nothing was firm. I needed to know about scheduling and casting and, naturally, about the money. It was going to have to be substantial now that Hardscrabble was about to become a reality. Even though I owed L.B. a favor for Myra, the movie was too important to throw away with Mayer. Here was my chance to show the American public who the Rats were, why they were Rats, and how Rats invariably behaved. *Watch on the Rhine* did that. Hammett had been, as always, helpful with each draft. No, that's patronizing; more than helpful, inspiring. He knew the damned story inside out and backward.

I told Hammett I wanted to collaborate on the screenplay with him, to get it released soon enough for it to have the greatest political impact. We still weren't in the war. No reason why he couldn't get started on the writing himself until I got free of the my stage obligations. I intended the news to encourage. I didn't realize . . .

At any rate; he said, "And now I'm supposed to thank you for the payday. That's not what we are, Lill." I said nothing while we walked on.

I always pushed to get my Broadway people in the films of my plays. This one was different. Stars would give the political message a hell of a lot more bite. When Jack Warner mentioned Bette Davis and Charles Boyer, I knew we could do something important with the film. Of course I knew you never ended up with all the teaser names. Davis would be enough for me.

Warner was very reluctant to agree to Hammett writing the screenplay. "He's not drinking, Jack."

"He's not writing much either." Then he said he needed assurances for what he called "my people." Jack Warner had no "people." What kind of assurances? The best kind, he said. Warner wanted my word that if the Hammett screenplay was unsatisfactory for any reason, I would submit a final version at no additional cost. It was an insult Hammett would never have to hear. I knew Dash could produce a marvel. He wasn't drinking very much at all. No more than I was. I agreed, provided Davis played the lead. Warner said we had the outline of a deal.

"You are *not* supposed to thank me for a payday. What you *are* supposed to do is get to work on the script tomorrow morning and give my dingy, one-room political talkfest some fucking life . . . let the outside world shine its light on—"

"What are they paying for hackwork at Warners these days for someone who can't get any work on his own?"

"Dash, don't ruin the day."

WE'D ALWAYS FOUGHT, always, always broken up—well, separated at least—and then come back together after a while, a cooling off, or sometimes a heating up. Not always out of need, either. Ultimately it was a seeking that brought us back. Where'd I leave that arm of mine anyway? Or as in my case, where the hell was my heart, where'd I leave my courage? I had them just a little while ago. So it is fair to say Lillian Hellman completed me. The only problem was that sometimes a man like me doesn't want to be completed. Women in love don't ever really get that. Even amazing Lillian, brilliant Lillian, didn't get it. The Hammett she admired was not a Hammett who ever was. It was the Hammett who someday might be . . . the maybe, maybe Hammett. That's no way for a man to live.

Let me take the day from breakfast on. Very nice morning as I recall. Unusually nice, except that all the war news was particularly terrible. I mentioned at table that sometimes military conditions can deteriorate to the point where things were irreversible. Lillian said, "Are we there yet?" She was at the stove making French toast.

"Just about."

"What'll we do?"

"Us or the country?"

"The country. We're fine." Said with emphasis. "We're off to Pleasantville. Hah, Pleasantville. Bucolic life of dumb contentment."

We let ourselves be appropriately ashamed of our personal good fortune. I said, "Our side isn't going to do anything smart or brave for a while. Let's hope Herr Hitler does something monumentally stupid."

"And will he?"

That's when I saw a small note on the theater page about *Watch on the Rhine* coming to Broadway. No one outworks Shumlin's flacks. The piece said the play was going through changes to keep it as fresh as the latest news from Europe. This line struck me: "Miss Hellman—a modern-day Kassandra—has warned us all repeatedly for years of a dire future unless we act to defend our democratic way of life. Alas, Kassandra's legendary warnings went unheeded, but she was not so brilliant a playwright."

I read her the blurb. "I'm breakfasting with an effing goddess."

Her tone turned shitty, a reminder of the fight we had the night before about Roosevelt. What is it about that man that prompts such passionate defenses? When I called him a cagey bastard who played everyone against everyone, she bit my goddamned head off. Didn't I realize the Republicans had him cornered on the war? Of course, he'd act decisively as soon as he could. What the hell was wrong with me? She didn't just support or admire him, she loved the cunning devil. They all did. She abruptly clicked off the light and rolled over. End of political discussion. End of everything.

Lilly knew the myth, obviously. What she wanted to talk about was what I thought it meant . . . and then what the meaning meant. Myths are like that, Russian dolls. It pleased me to be her brains in this way. But when the ideas came back after passing through the Hellman filter, they were a fine new vintage in beautiful bottles. I also loved displaying what I knew when she was the student.

Kassandra was desired by a god. What beautiful mortal wasn't back then? The culprit deity was generally believed to be Apollo. His enticement to seduction was the gift of prophecy, which beats a Swiss watch or an ermine by a mile . . .

"I'd have taken the ermine. Which reminds me, you haven't bought me anything for aeons."

Kassandra would not return his love, don't ask me why. Since he could not take back his ermine, he made it so that her prophecies always fell on deaf ears. Kassandra could see the truth and the future. No one would believe her truth or her future. She saw it all coming, and they didn't believe. Lilly knew all this of course. Whenever she became impatient with me, she said, "Yes, yes, yes." She said, "Yes, yes, yes."

The essential element in Greek tragedy, I thought, was not the Fates turning on a decent person, it was a tortuous knot of conflicting desires that eventually strangled the best of intentions. Mortals always turn on themselves, we always undo ourselves.

Lilly looked up from the stove and said, "Breakfast, Professor."

She put the French toast and butter on the table and asked me to pour the coffee and read the blurb again. I did. She remembered that Kassandra told everyone the great wooden horse was a trick, like "Peace in our time." They didn't listen, and *pffft*, there went Troy up in smoke. But Kassandra also should have known they wouldn't listen, so fuck 'em. Lillian lit a cigarette and said, "If she had Hardscrabble and a guy like you, old Kassandra would be with us still, happily milking the horses."

We walked to the lawyer's office even though I was coming down with something chesty. Lillian said walking would make the day memorable. It did in a way. It was a good day in spite of the prospect of living out the rest of our years with a fascist Europe across the Atlantic.

I praised her good breakfast. She said it would be even better when we used our own homegrown milk and butter.

Last night's Roosevelt fight was declared over then, not even entered in the record book as a TKO.

As we ambled, we talked about how I was to pay for my share of the farm. I was strapped for cash just then so the down payment would have to be hers exclusively. Lilly said we could make my repayment an informal arrangement just between us. I needed it to be contractual, something the lawyer could put on paper that day. She said, "Certainly, dear," in just that way of hers no one could possibly bear. I told her I was serious and would walk out if it wasn't contractual. "Of course. I understand that."

What Lillian never understood, still doesn't for that matter, is how hard it is for me not to be her. She was everything she attributed to me that I knew I wasn't. She transformed stories into larger, more dramatic truths, and made them even more human in the transforming. She wore her politics wherever she went and in whatever she wrote. And she made a fortune doing it. I didn't just want to share her life, I wanted to share her. Part of me even wanted to be her. That was the part that let the envy in, but it was just a part, not the whole story. There was always far more admiration than envy, more than enough affection. And as much devotion as I was capable of. I realize it isn't like me, these admissions. But how could Kassandra know so much about the world and so goddamned little about me?

We were in the park. Everything was still holding together well enough when we came upon Shumlin; rather, he came upon us. It was a little awkward all around. He explained he was walking downtown to the theater and that he needed the time to think about working out some of the problems at the end of the first act of *Watch,* when it's revealed that Kurt Muller, the hero, had already killed a Nazi back in Germany. Even though we needed the news as foreshadowing, it had to be softened, made acceptable to an audience that did not understand yet the political context and might be uncomfortable with a hero who was already a murderer. Maybe Lillian could rewrite a line or two, at least come down and see how the scene stood now. She said she would. Later. Maybe Dash would take a look as well. Not on your life, Herman, it's Lilly's baby.

Shumlin was not my favorite person. Everything about him was right. Right liberal politics. Right connections. Right attitude about Lilly's work. Right Broadway instincts. Wrong for Lillian because artistically speaking Shumlin was not a first-rater. I'd often told her how much better off she'd be directing her own material. Problem, she said, was she didn't really have the time. Herman Shumlin made a career on Lilly's back and didn't acknowledge the fact sufficiently for my satisfaction.

Shumlin mentioned the blurb in the paper and extended a hand to me. I told him he had the wrong Kassandra. No, he was congratulating me on the movie deal and how good it must feel to have a real screenplay to write. "I'm sure you'll do wonders with her material." I think it was the *her material* that turned the day for me.

I told him the whole thing was more wonderful than he could possibly imagine. I'd thought about nothing else since I heard the news.

When he left I said, "You know, you're really something. I'm standing here with my fly wide open and you tell everyone about it but me."

"I was going to tell you as soon as I was sure it was firm."

We walked a little farther. All along the way she explained her motives in cutting a screenplay deal for me with Warner without telling me. I didn't hear what she said. I didn't want to hear what she said. I just wanted her to stop talking. She would not stop talking. I said something like, "We've got thirty feet to the curb. If you say another word, I'm turning around." She did. And I did.

THE DAY LILLIAN HELLMAN SIGNED THE CONTRACT for Hardscrabble Farm in Pleasantville, New York, did in fact occur shortly after the complete destruction of Rotterdam by German bombs. That day in mid-May was very fine in New York, sunny and in the low seventies.

They did walk crosstown together to the lawyer's office, but Hammett never arrived at the destination and therefore never signed the purchase contract. Hellman was always the sole owner of Hardscrabble Farm.

During the morning and the walk crosstown the conversation did indeed cover the subject of Kassandra as well as the war, President Roosevelt, and related current events. Yes, they also talked about writing projects and finances, but most of their talk was, naturally enough, about their expectations for life on the farm. That is not exactly what they each appear to have remembered.

They did run into Herman Shumlin in Central Park, although Lillian failed to recall the meeting. Both conveniently forgot their parting words that day: "I hate you." "I hate you too."

The two remained friends and intermittent lovers, spending more time apart than either would have wished during the war, but given the intense decade they had already spent together, nothing particularly dramatic appeared to have changed between them. There had always been fights, many far more bitter than this one. This time, however, it was as though a shadow had passed over them on that beautiful day in Manhattan and changed the climate of their lives as Lilly and Dash. That walk crosstown was not the end of them, but it was a marked diminishing.

What we remember reflects who we were when we remember it. Even the gods have imperfect memories.

.14.

Long Shots

HAMMETT REALLY KNEW HORSE RACING and he never missed the Santa Anita Handicap when he was in California. Hammett was as good at analyzing and betting on a horse race as he was at doing a crossword, even though it was a far more speculative enterprise, which was its main attraction. You could be right for all the wrong reasons, and vice versa, but those rare moments when he was right for the right reasons gave him incomparable pleasure. He believed he could make his living as a horse player if he had to, but the effort required far exceeded the return. During his infrequent visits to Santa Anita, Hammett did not lose very often. Getting to the track on time today would prove the hardest thing he had to do.

On the morning of the big race the scene at their apartment would have appalled Lillian, who was ensconced at Hardscrabble trying to get things off the ground. It might even have upset a conscious Hammett, but there was no conscious Hammett. He was unconscious—not merely asleep, unconscious—in his and Hellman's Santa Monica apartment. He had passed out on the bed around three a.m. with an open tequila bottle cradled in his arms.

There was a second body. Doris Lesser, a woman he had known from his San Francisco days, lay out cold on the sofa. She wore a red bra and torn panties. Doris was slightly battered, the result of sexual roughhousing at the hands of the man she was paid well to call "Daddy." And wouldn't he be appropriately contrite and generous when they again revived themselves as normal human beings?

There were two others present in the apartment. Kai Mindao, who took care of the place when Hammett and Lilly were back East and who drove them around and cooked a bit when they weren't, was in a stupor on the carpet by the bathroom. He wore his chauffeur's cap but nothing else. When last night's guests began to peel off their clothes, Kai decided to take part in the activities until someone stopped him. No one did. Ling Huang lay curled between Kai and Doris. Hammett couldn't keep his hands off Ling but always spared her his violent tendencies. These were women he had known before he met Lillian.

The night had been debauched, but there was nothing new or excessive by Hammett standards, which is to say that he humiliated himself almost as badly as anyone else. When the police arrived a little after midnight, they accepted his apologies for the noise and his promise that things would quiet down immediately. And they did.

Somehow Hammett awakened himself a little after midday and then everyone else enough to get his guests washed up, dressed, fed, and off to the track by the fourth race. Kai understood that last night's liberties were a notable exception to his normal duties, so he deposited his boss and the two women at the clubhouse gate and knew to wait patiently for their return at the end of the day.

A clubhouse sign demanded APPROPRIATE DRESS. Hammett in a Panama hat, an East Coast seersucker suit, and a rep tie qualified. Doris and Ling in last night's gowns were inappropriately appropriate. Hammett, particularly pleased with their manner of dress, insisted each take an arm as they made their way through the crowd to a shaded part of the stands. Just glimpsing Pat O'Brien and Jean Arthur, and then having Hammett introduce her to Ray Milland and Franchot Tone, completely restored Doris's vigor. She moved differently now, as though she belonged here. It was always impossible to tell what Ling was feeling.

Hammett had not come to Santa Anita merely to see and be seen. He was there quite deliberately to make money, a lot of it, on today's Big 'Cap. He saw the possibility for a killing shaping up days earlier, and now with the morning rain and the track drying out before the handicap, he sensed things very much breaking his way. He gave each of the women fifty dollars to bet. They asked what horses looked good. He didn't know. He wasn't betting at all, he said, until the big race, the seventh. Ling put the money in her purse. Doris went off to the betting windows.

While a preliminary race was being run, Hammett studied the *Racing Form*, carefully circling and underlining numbers with a pencil. He walked down to the railing to take a close look at the texture of the track after the rain. Doris tapped his shoulder to help him acknowledge someone calling his name. Even when he saw the woman, she didn't register for a moment. Elise Weiss, L.B.'s secretary. "Mr. Mayer," she said, touching his hand, "would very much like you to join him in his box." It didn't feel like a request.

Hammett indicated his friends. "I have my guests to consider."

"They're welcome, of course."

It took a while for them to move through the crowd to Mayer's box, where Hammett introduced Doris as "My assistant, Miss Jameson," and Ling as "Madame Tsing-Tzu." Mayer did not shake hands; he bowed from the waist, as did his wife Margaret. He did introduce the governor of California, a nonentity named Culbert Olson, and his wife to Hammett and his "assistants." The governor presented the winning trophy annually. If Olson hadn't shown up, Judge Hardy could have played the role. The governor said he had always been a big fan of Hammett's mysteries. Hammett said so that Mayer could hear, "As long as I'm not an employee, it's easy to like my stuff. Thank you, Governor."

Mayer and Jack Warner had adjoining boxes. Their rivalries in business and at the poker table paled compared to their competition at Santa Anita to beat one another with their thoroughbreds. On the day of the 1941 Santa Anita Handicap, Louis B. Mayer owned over two hundred thoroughbreds, most of them based at his ranch in Perris, California, some of them already of championship quality. Of course, once Mayer committed to racing in such a big way, nothing could keep Jack Warner away. He owned half as many horses but in recent years was doing well against Mayer in head-to-head competition. For that afternoon's race it was Warner who owned the heavy morning-line favorite, Box Office. Mayer was represented by Bindlestiff, good at the distance, a mile and a quarter. On a wet surface, Bindlestiff moved up a notch. Mayer was hoping for more rain at post time.

The two men owned large adjoining boxes right on the finish line. They were always at the track for big Saturday races, but for the handicap each year they alternated as hosts to a crowd of movie stars and politicians. Neither of the moguls had to actually win the race to have a successful day at the races, since there was a standing fifty-thousand-dollar bet between them on whichever of their horses beat the other to the wire. Their jockeys were told even if they couldn't win the race to ride their horses hard all the way to the finish line. In past years two very good Mayer horses had broken down while being pushed so desperately.

Mayer indicated the rest of the throng in his box and said to Hammett, "I'm sure you know everyone." He did indeed. Jack Warner and Selznick, of course, but they were in deep conversation and neither acknowledged Hammett. But there was also William Powell and his friend, the breathtaking Lana Turner, looking demure in a powder-blue suit and large straw hat, dressed more for Churchill Downs than Santa Anita. Mickey Rooney, Mayer's favorite performer, nuzzled a tall redhead almost twice his size.

Hammett did shake hands with J. Edgar Hoover, the nation's "Number One Cop," who also claimed to be a fan of his stories. It wasn't clear if the head of the FBI was there with the governor or was Mayer's personal guest. In the rear of the box were Phil Edmunds and Vincent Spinetti. Hammett couldn't prove it, of course, but he always assumed Spinetti—an ex–LAPD cop and now chief of security at Warners—had masterminded the Waxman killing. He was with his wife, Angel Chung, who Hammett always supposed was the call girl known as "Angel" on the Waxman police report. All in all quite a group of racing fans.

Phil Edmunds sat with Mayer's secretary Elise Weiss and at least had the modesty to look embarrassed when Hammett tipped his hat. Ling gravitated naturally to a seat alongside Angel; the two acted a bit like old friends, maybe they even knew one another from their street days. Hammett would have to ask. Doris grabbed an empty seat alongside Hoover and was speaking more intently than Hammett could have imagined. He noticed that she already had a hand on his knee.

Hammett had assumed that Mayer wanted to talk some business or at least set up such a talk. Why else invite him and his unlikely "assistants" to his private box? Most likely it was Hellman business he was interested in. It never occurred to Hammett that Mayer was showing him off to the governor and Hoover, who really did admire his work. Mayer hadn't intended Hammett's group to remain but when he asked what Hammett thought about the race, he realized that Hammett was far more than a casual bettor.

"If you're asking me if you are going to take Warner's money"—everyone in Hollywood knew about their huge side bet—"I'd say, Where can I get a piece of it?"

"Jack, Jack, come hear. Hammett wants some of your money too."

Warner turned and the three men, bent from the waist, formed a knot. Hammett said, "I know Box Office is 7 to 5, but if you don't mind taking back some of your own money, Jack, I've got ten thousand that says Mr. Mayer's horse beats you out." The "own money" reference was to the draft script he wrote for *Watch on the Rhine* and which he now knew would be touched up by Lillian. He heard Lilly's voice hectoring: It's ten thousand! What the fuck are you doing? He heard his own voice answering: I know this race. I've seen it already.

Warner had no choice but to agree or else appear somehow minimized by one of his own employees.

Hammett, expressing a careless bravado, said, "I really don't believe your horse will even finish in the money."

They bet an additional five thousand on that very unlikely possibility. Now Lillian said, Jesus Christ, that's Hardscrabble money.

Mayer touched Hammett's shoulder: "Glad you have so much confidence in my horse." Bindlestiff was now the third choice at 4 to 1.

"Don't get your hopes up, Mr. Mayer. I think he'll beat Box Office but he won't—forgive the allusion to *trayf*—take home the bacon either."

"How do you figure?"

Hammett leaned forward, program open on his knee and proceeded to show Mayer exactly how he figured, and what he foresaw. "It's a classic situation, if you follow, L.B. First, the track condition. They've upgraded it to 'fast,' but it hasn't dried out completely. Jack's horse has run over such a track twice." He indicated those races on his *Racing Form*. "Look, a fifth and a seventh. He won't like the footing today either."

Mayer leaned in attentively and smiled. "And my horse?"

"He'll like the footing. He'll run well, but I'm betting Bay View today."

Mayer looked at his program. Bay View, number one on the program, was 20 to 1 on the morning line and now 30 to 1 on the tote board. Mayer said, "Thirty to one, not possible."

"Very possible."

"How?"

"Elemental, my dear Louis." My god, how Hammett was enjoying himself. He whispered, "Let me share my secret. The one post, the rail, has the best, cleanest footing on this track. Nick Wall is the best jockey in this race. Any doubts? Who was the last jock to beat Sea Biscuit? Answer, Nick Wall. How did he get it done? Wall put his horse in the lead from the one post, controlled the pace, and even the great Sea Biscuit couldn't catch him at the wire. Wall will do the same thing today, even easier, because (a) he is the only true front-runner in the race, and (b) Sea Biscuit is retired. And (c) just take a look at the weights. Your horse is 125. Warner's is 128 . . ." He let Mayer check his program to find Bay View at 108. Mayer looked at the tote board. Bay View was now 40 to 1.

The sun, which had been out brightly for two hours, now seemed to burn with a pulse that matched the trumpeter's call to the post. As the horses moved in single file onto the track, Jack Warner's Box Office was the heavy favorite. Mayer's Bindlestiff was now 9 to 2. Bay View was 50 to 1, the longest odds the automatic tote board could register.

If Hammett had any more cash, he'd have bet it all on Nick Wall and Bay View, but four hundred dollars was what he had left from last night's romp. As he left the box to make his bet, he noticed that the girls were doing just fine. Ling and Angel Chung were gabbing away. Doris, even though her hand had been removed from Hoover's knee, was trying on his fedora. Hammett bet all four hundred on number one to win.

Sam Toperoff

After placing his bet, Hammett did not return to Mayer's box. If he lost his bets with Jack Warner, he'd put a call in to Lillian and send a check over by messenger. If Bay View did not win the race outright—and given what other bettors thought as reflected in his odds, that was likely—Hammett would just drift away, find Kai in the parking lot, head back to the apartment, and drink himself to sleep. His lady friends were taking very good care of themselves.

If Bay View, in flaming red silks, broke out of the gate very well and got to the lead quickly, he would be easy to spot. If he is to win this race, he must get the lead quickly and stay there till the homestretch. If other colors blocked that red-bloused jockey, Bay View and Hammett were cooked.

Nick Wall had his horse out of the gate a stride before the rest of the field. As planned. Entering the first turn, Bay View was in control of the pace as the field settled in tightly behind him, each horse and rider content to make his run much later. Hammett would learn a lot about the pace when the time for the first quarter-mile was posted on the infield tote board; however, the pace seemed very comfortable to Hammett's trained eye. Then it went up—25.1 seconds—inordinately slow for horses of this quality. Hammett allowed himself some excitement; he began to whisper to the jockey: Hold him, Nickie, hold him tight. Which is what Nickie did. Amazingly, no other horse attempted to challenge so slow a pace.

Warner's horse Box Office sat in second, content to stalk the leader. Bindlestiff sat on the rail in fourth.

As the field entered the backstretch, Hammett noticed a bit more daylight open between Bay View and Box Office. The second quarter-mile was even slower than the first. Hammett began to edge closer to the rail: Keep him there, Nickie, right there, right there.

The field ran down the backstretch without any change in order. The challenges from the late runners would begin on the far turn. That's where he saw Box Office begin to pick up his pace and close some ground on Bay View. No, no, not yet, Nick, n-n-n-not yet. Hammett now was calling instructions aloud to his jockey. Midway into the turn he saw Box Office begin to falter, or perhaps it was just Nick Wall letting Bay View out a notch to hold him off.

Now, coming into the head of the stretch, every horse who had any run left was running all out. Jockeys were whipping and bringing their mounts out to the middle of the track, looking for a clear path to the wire. Box Office gave up first: Hammett's big bet with Warner started looking very good. He would win the ten thousand. But Hammett wanted the artistic pleasure of seeing an unlikely scenario come true exactly as prewritten. Indeed, it was asking far too much from the gods, but one time, just one time, why not one time . . . ? He began to say in cadence as Wall whipped Bay View past him down the stretch: One time . . . one time . . . one time . . .

It was exactly as he had foreseen. The path along the rail was the most firm. The brilliant front-running, pace-controlling ride by a jockey with "a stopwatch in his head," lightest-weight in a top-heavy field—these things easily carried Bay View home by three lengths. Bindlestiff, Mayer's horse, finished second. Box Office was last.

The churning in his stomach forced Hammett to find a place to sit down. He breathed deeply. His hands shook in his lap.

What Dashiell Hammett did today in predicting—no, more than predicting, seeing—the unfolding and the outcome of the 1941 Santa Anita Handicap, was almost beyond reasonable explanation, beyond the compass of logic. He had discerned cosmic design—or was it intent?—and it had been perfectly and profitably perceived. It rivaled his imagining *The Maltese Falcon* before actually writing it. Something he knew he would never be able to do again. Even Kassandra never hit a 50-to-1 shot. He went to get a drink.

When the race became official, L. B. Mayer wasn't gloating over winning his big bet with Warner; he was telling everyone who would listen of Hammett's uncanny prerace analysis and how perfectly jockey and horse executed the race plan. He waved the fifty-dollar ticket on Bay View he had Elise buy for him. Bay View paid $118.80 for a two-dollar bet, making Mayer's ticket worth almost three thousand dollars. It gave him more pleasure than the fifty-thousand-dollar check Jack Warner would have to send him in the morning.

Hammett's payoff on Bay View was more than $23,000, which with his Warner winnings was more than enough to finally make his down payment on Hardscrabble Farm. Hammett considered returning to Mayer's box for a curtain call. He really hadn't had his moment with either Edmunds or Spinetti, and there was much he wanted to say. Better, he thought, to leave in mystery and plant a racing myth in California.

The check issued by the Santa Anita Racing Association folded neatly away in his breast pocket, Hammett walked out of the clubhouse gate into a golden California evening. He stood at the curb and waved. Kai spotted him and came along with the car immediately. Kai said, "What about the girls?"

"I think they're occupied. Let's go home."

Kai assumed his boss was leaving early and alone because he had lost all his money.

"Good morning, Mr. Childs. My name is Lillian Hellman. I just bought the farm down the road."

"Yes, I saw that. Good luck with it."

"Thank you. I'm calling because I heard you had a tractor for sale and they tell me I'm very much in need of one."

Childs drove his tractor, a 1938 Series-B John Deere Whirlwind, over to Lillian's place that afternoon. His farm was less than half a mile away. Both tractor and farmer were spiffed up, Childs in a suit and tie, the green-and-yellow machine polished and greased to perfection. Lillian, of course, did not know how to evaluate the condition of the tractor other than to be impressed with its immaculate appearance. She took a slow tour around the Whirlwind, touched its oversized wheels, its perforated radiator grill, its motor housing, and finally the springs below the elevated seat. Childs showed her where to place her foot in order to climb up to that seat, but Lillian needed his help to actually get aboard. Childs, a well-built older man, didn't quite know where to touch her and wasn't sure her hip was in play until she placed his hand there.

Lillian said, "If I use it, do I have to buy it?"

"Hell, no."

Childs stood behind Lillian on the tractor and released the brake. He explained that driving a tractor was exactly like her Town and Country stick shift. Clutch down, drop into first gear, give her some gas, let the clutch out, and off you go. Second and third gear came after that, and there you are, driving a tractor. At least in theory. When Lillian released the clutch, the tractor shuddered and the motor stalled. Childs laughed.

Lillian poured her neighbor and herself a beer as the two sat at her kitchen table looking out at the gleaming machine standing out in front of her barn. There was no doubt she intended to buy the tractor, but she wanted a narrative to go with it. Cedric Childs supplied that.

He'd made his money—a considerable amount—selling restaurant supplies in Manhattan until a day arrived when he could not stand the sight of another double boiler or a deep fryer and found the selling of water pitchers slightly demeaning. He wanted to grow things. He'd always wanted to grow things. He walked away from the restaurant supply business and bought his farm in Pleasantville six months before the Crash in '29.

Lillian asked, "Smart or just dumb luck?"

"Neither." Lillian expected elaboration. There was none, just "Neither." It was something Hammett might have said.

Childs had never heard of Lillian Hellman and did not resent her purchase of the land. Other neighbors, he told her, were not so generous of spirit. That information merely confirmed the feelings she had when she shopped at the local market or stopped for gas. All the better: If Hardscrabble was going to be an island socially as well as emotionally, wasn't that what she was looking for all along? She told Childs as she poured a second beer she didn't give a shit about what her neighbors thought of her. All she really wanted to do was learn how to operate his damn tractor and learn to farm. When Childs tapped her beer glass with his and said, "Then you've come to the right guy," the two had begun a working friendship.

There wasn't time to waste. If she wanted to get her corn in, the time was now. He proposed to leave his tractor right where it was and walk her land on his way home. Farming lessons would begin first thing in the morning. He said, "Just please, please, don't wear fashionable overalls." Lillian knew that once again she had gotten lucky with a man.

Cedric Childs arrived in a Ford pickup loaded with tools and tall stakes just after seven. They had coffee, toast, and talked a bit. Then Lillian climbed the tractor by herself and Childs took his place behind her seat, his hands resting lightly on her shoulders. Lillian was pleased by his touch. When he touched her right arm, she knew to release the hand brake, put the machine in first gear, and then ease up on the clutch. The tractor rolled forward. Childs said, "Good." Another soft tap meant second gear, and another third. "Excellent. All right, brake and throw it in neutral." She did and didn't remember ever feeling so pleased with herself.

Childs thought that if they worked hard, they could get in ten acres of sweet corn in two weeks. There wasn't much standing groundwater so the time was now. Normally he didn't believe in plowing deep for corn—it brought up the weeds and killed the worms—but the land had been fallow, the nutrients had sunk. He drained his coffee and stood: "I'll be back early afternoon with the plow attached and you can get to real farming."

"What the hell have we been doing?"

"That's prefarming."

When Childs returned that afternoon, two tillers were attached to the tractor. Their mass intimidated Lillian. Childs said, "Don't give the equipment any thought. Drive the tractor like you did straight out to the field." His hands were more comforting than his words and she did exactly as he said.

With Childs's help Lillian raised her plows at the end of a row, turned the tractor, and dropped them for the return trip. "Overlap about half a foot or so and try to go a little faster." And she did. The sun, which had been hidden all morning, came through brightly. After two more runs, his hands came off her shoulders. Lillian assumed he had turned the work over to her. She turned back. Childs was not there. He was in fact nowhere to be seen. This was her field now.

The day warmed even more. Lillian opened her blouse and took off her bandana. She looked up momentarily as the tractor rolled forward to see high clouds drawing toward one another and there, off to the west, a flock of Canada geese flying in V formation toward the lake. She was now part of this great mystery.

Lillian looked behind her at the dark earth she had turned—perhaps less than ten percent of her field—with enough satisfaction finally to call it a first day. She wasn't yet thinking like a farmer; in fact she wasn't thinking at all: instead of driving the tractor back to the barn shed, she shut it down and started walking back to the house, leaving it out there exposed to the elements, a possible rainstorm. Her body still vibrated as she walked. She was thinking only of a hot bath, a glass of wine, and some caviar. Life did not get better than this.

Cedric Childs was a little older than Hammett, shorter, but better built, rawboned, in fact stronger, more desirable. Lovemaking between farmer and neighbor was inevitable. It would come in its own time. Like the sweet corn.

Whenever Hammett called with Hollywood news and events, Lillian told him of her progress at Hardscrabble. Yes, a crew of men came in and weeded her field—he picked up the *her*. But she had graded and limed the entire field herself, hooked up and loaded the planter herself. Indeed, she laid in ten acres of sweet corn pretty much by herself. She spoke excitedly about choosing a four-inch depth and two-and-a-half-foot rows. "It rained today, isn't it great?"

"You know, Lilly, they got you all wrong. You're not Kassandra the oracle. You're Demeter the harvest goddess."

Being apart suited them both. Hammett was drinking, screwing, and pissing away his money. Hellman was farming, starting to write again, and getting ready to invite Cedric to stay the night. Lillian never mentioned Childs to Hammett. Hammett simply imagined there was someone like Childs.

Hellman's father and aunts didn't like the idea of her living alone in the country, so Hannah recommended a niece of Sophronia, her New Orleans nursemaid, a reliable young woman named Zenia Jackson who lived in New York and was looking for work. Lillian met her and liked her immediately. Zenia moved in with her boy Gilbert.

When the time came Lillian discovered that Cedric Childs was a surprisingly good lover, certainly as compared to Hammett. He was strong but gentle, thoughtful and insistent, pleasant and durable, and, important for Lillian, very well endowed. They made love in bed, on the floor, against the wall, on the stairs, and in front of the fireplace. After Childs left in the morning, Lillian slept until early afternoon.

Pleasant and satisfying as their liaisons were for each of them, Childs's stayovers never became expectations or demands for either of them. Their nights together came easily and naturally. There seemed to be an unspoken rightness about them.

In late spring the orchard's apple trees got trimmed and sprayed. During the summer the corn came in fully. Lillian found she had time to write most days and entirely on Sunday. One dramatic idea—perhaps better called commercial—attracted her strongly because of the pleasure she would have in writing it. A generational continuation of *The Little Foxes*. It had been great fun to recount and invent all those betrayals, even more fun to root them in her own family history; and very satisfying to collect the royalties that followed. Perhaps it was a little too soon for a sequel, but Lilly began to develop the idea in pencil on a steno pad near her bed.

Hammett called late one night while she was in bed scribbling away. He didn't sound too drunk; in fact, he seemed intently curious about Lillian's well-being, so she decided to get his opinion on the timing of a *Foxes* sequel. Previously when she went to Hammett for advice it had been from a position of an uncertain child asking for permission. This was no longer the case. After all, she was about to bring in ten acres of sweet corn for which she already had a buyer.

She told him her idea with tight lips. He made the sound of a cash register.

WHEN HAMMETT ARRIVED in November, all the farmwork—or most of it—had been done. Zenia Jackson and her eight-year-old were well established in a small apartment Lillian had restored downstairs. Lillian used to say proudly that she integrated the Pleasantville educational system since a yellow public school bus picked up Gilbert at Hardscrabble Farm each morning and brought him to Harding Elementary.

Lillian allowed it to become clear to Hammett that Childs was more than a neighbor, a friend, a farm mentor, so when she got around to telling him of her plan to build Hammett a cottage on the rise behind the farmhouse, there was no way for it not to sound—sincere as the offer was—like a gold watch offered to a valued retiree. He could not possibly accept. The two weeks he stayed at Hardscrabble were awkward in the extreme.

Hammett actually had some work. Sam Spade was becoming a weekly radio star. The format for the show wasn't so different really from writing a comic strip. Three panels, seven minutes each: the setup in Sam's office—a desperate client enters and tells Sam and his secretary, Effie Perrine, the reason for her—it was usually a her—desperation clarified with flashbacks, Sam takes case, client leaves, Sam and Effie banter, organ music, commercial for Wildroot Cream Oil. Panel Two: Sam goes to scene of the crime, tracks down and questions suspects, usually three of them, occasionally four if the show is short, next commercial. Panel Three: Sam lays a trap to catch the murderer and said murderer is indeed trapped and confesses or has to be shot, a drink back at the office and some light sexual banter with Effie. Last commercial and hook for next week's show. Then, regularly each week, a check from his agent for two hundred and a quarter.

By then Hammett was living in nearby Katonah, New York, cranking out his "Spades," drinking, reading, sometimes adding to his collection of "Tales." Once a week and soon after once a month, Hammett took the train to Pleasantville where Lillian met him at the station in the Town and Country. They embraced like an old married couple separated too long. When she didn't see him too often, Lillian felt very comfortable in his arms. Hammett felt less incomplete in hers. These conjugal visits suited them well; they continued into early spring, a new planting season, when Cedric Childs was often in Lillian's bed. Hammett knew this. He bit his lip and turned away.

DURING AN EXTENDED VISIT to Hardscrabble in early '42 with the newly declared war going very badly, talk in the kitchen turned to finances. He was doing fine, he said. Not much income, less expenses, more time.

Lillian said, "Fewer."

"What?"

"Not less, fewer."

"Of course it's *fewer*. I chose to say *less*. Have we gotten so out of touch?"

Lillian said she had plenty of money saved and offered some to Hammett. He scowled. Other than her royalties, she wasn't making any; and that troubled her a little.

"The *Foxes* sequel, how's that going?"

"Stop and go. I worry it's still too soon."

"It's a sequel, for Christ's sake. You strike while the iron—"

"Look at the fucking world. Doesn't a play have to mean something?"

"It will mean something. It will mean money coming in." He dropped onions in a hot buttered pan and produced a sizzle for emphasis.

Lillian said she'd really rather do something about the war, something inspiring. He groaned. She asked him how he thought the war would go. "Fortunately the bastards are overplaying their hand. They can't handle both Russia and us. Finally, a good thing for our side. Your man— the cynical bastard—would have temporized till the cows came home doing the goose step." The cynical bastard was FDR.

"His hands were tied."

"Funny, they weren't tied when he stepped in and saved the banking system for the very thieves who brought it all down."

"In order to save the American people."

"And saving Jews in Germany?"

"What about saving Jews . . . ?" She turned to him, ready to fight.

There was a metallic edge to their voices now.

At the heart of the Roosevelt conflict was their judgment about America itself. For Lillian America always meant hope—struggle, of course, but a winning struggle. At the heart of her hopefulness was the country's willingness—albeit reluctant—to make Americans out of not-Americans—her own family story of Marxes and Hellmans, the *others* overcoming all obstacles and becoming the *us* faster than you might imagine. She had traveled far more of the world than Hammett and knew there was no such comparable place. Most important, materialistic and infantile as Americans were, they weren't fascists. FDR wouldn't allow them to become that. For her America was the Americans.

For Hammett, America was its culture, or its significant lack thereof. No one's fault, he always pointed out, just bad timing and bad luck. There simply hadn't been time for a nourishing culture to take root. America became a country while Indians were being killed, plantations were slave-driven, and industry was gearing up to outproduce and outprofit the rest of the world. There was no quiet, growing-up time. Too much hubbub; too much moving about; too much polyglot babble.

To drop all this confusion into the richest land on the face of the earth and then allow capitalists to be completely in charge was the recipe for disaster—or hilarity. Hammett called America the Greatest Show on Earth. For him FDR was the latest, most seductive ringmaster.

They were both Marxists, but Hammett was a Communist—the real thing. Hellman was not. Hammett knew there was absolutely no chance for a revolution being ignited on these shores. There were no revolutions at the circus.

He picked up the argument by mocking her statement. "'In order to save the American people'? Are you delirious? What I don't understand is how you have seen through every bullshitter who has come along ever since I met you, but not him. Does your new farmer friend think he's the savior too?"

"We don't talk politics. We talk sweet corn. So how will it go now?"

"The Rooshkies will save our asses, but what a gigantic effort it will have to be for everyone. And at what a cost."

"How long?"

"Five years, maybe six or seven." But Hammett wasn't done with Roosevelt: "I've got a particular ring of hell reserved just for him. What he's done to the Japanese in California, I suppose that's all right with you too."

"It's temporary."

"Tem-por-ary?" He touched her shoulder. Probably he shouldn't have touched her. "They've got them living in the stables at Santa Anita."

"It's terrible. It really is. But it's an emergency . . . They bombed—"

Of course his anger had been mounting ever since he stepped off the train, ever since he saw her washing her tractor. Hammett swung the back of his hand up from the frying pan into Lillian's face. His father's abrupt motion at the Bog Hill. He felt her nose push into her cheek. She gasped. Blood spurted everywhere until Lillian buried her face in a dish towel, which muffled her voice: "You fucking bastard . . . you spineless prick . . . you . . ."

He reached to help her. She smacked his hands away. "Get out . . . just get out . . ."

Still he tried to help her.

"Get the fuck out. Go! Go!"

Hammett took his coat off the rack and prepared to walk to the train station without his valise.

Lillian shouted from the open doorway, "Get as far away from me as you can, you . . . Anywhere . . ." She was sobbing now and said but did not shout, "Wherever it is, make believe you're still a writer . . ."

.15.

Americans

THREE WEEKS AFTER HIS ASSAULT on Hellman, Hammett wrote this:

Lillian:

no, not Lilly or My Dear Lillushka or even Lilly Anna, none of these, simply Lillian:

> *It occurs to me that I have never written you a letter that I actually had the courage to send through the U.S. Postal Service. Our old drinking buddy, James A. Farley, that political hack whose payoff for delivering NY to Delano was to become Head Mailman of the United States of America, is sure to see this gets to you through rain or snow or dark of night . . .*
>
> *I'm putting it in writing because that is the only way I can even consider approaching you after what I have*

done. You certainly didn't deserve such treatment, but when you're dealing with Southern white trash, deserve has nothing to do with what you get. I doubt Dr. Freud his own self could help me understand whence such cruelty, such wanton betrayal of friendship.

Jealousy. That is the only thing I have been able to come up with in these weeks of self-examination. But I've always been jealous of you—of your marvelous gifts, of the people you allow into your life, and most of all of your supreme sense of who are and are not. (I've only affected the latter; on me it runs no deeper than a skin graft.) So, yes, it's jealousy. It's always been jealousy. In the past, though, it caused me to get out of town, to get the hell as far away from you as fast as I could. Why, this time, would I want to damage you? (I did not "want" to; nevertheless, I did exactly that. And done with such vehemence. Calling Dr. Freud.)

To never see you again is a fate I deserve, a fitting punishment for my offense. Still, I can't imagine living out my life—our lives—and never again spending the evening with you in silence, reading by the fireplace, cooking together, or editing the first draft of a play which will eventually alter the course of American drama. To never see you again would be impossible for me. So how and when becomes the issue, and those are entirely up to you. I'll wait but not forever.

There is also in my hateful behavior a thorny theological problem, which I have considered at length, one as old *as the Testaments. If I were a Jew—yet another source of my personal jealousy—I would willingly want you to haul off and smite me with true Old Testament fury: "A nose for a nose" requires that harsh, demanding God of your put-upon people. This would be true Jewish justice.*

But I am, alas, not a bearded Jew but just a po' li'l Catholic boy who has to turn the other cheek to have any chance of attaining the Kingdom of Heaven. We mackerel-snappers have a very specific way of climbing the ladder to Paradise. When we have sinned, as I certainly have, there is a prescribed ritual—isn't there always?—to help expiate our sinful behavior. You might find it laughable, Dr. Freud would not, because after remorse and contrition, which in my case, dear, are very real and acute, comes confession and then most importantly good deeds. Protestants, you see, can bullshit their way onto the Heaven Train, Catholics have to pay for their ticket . . .

Where the fuck, Lillian wondered, where was this crazy religious hogwash going? She went back to the top of page two and reread until she caught up.

. . . I have suffered remorse every day, every hour, since I harmed you. That is step one. This letter is my confession. That's step two. I'm going to earn my way to forgiveness by enlisting in the U.S. Army immediately

*and helping the Angels win this war against Old Scratch
hisself. Salvation for me is there.*

*I wish very much to get to Heaven now because I
think I know at last what Heaven is. It's Hollywood in
the early thirties. It's you and me working well and drinking just enough, and making love, just enough, and being
smart and funny and prosperous. That's my Heaven,
Lilly.*

*What I have done to you is unforgivable. How
dare I, to you of all people, my better in every way. I
should not ever be forgiven. Yet I hope and beg for your
forgiveness.*

Dash

Even while reading the letter, Lillian did not feel it apologetic enough. When she scanned it afterward, she confirmed
the fact that it did not contain the word *sorry* or the word
please. Nowhere did she find the word *love*, but she already
knew it would not be there. He does say he is "apologetic"
and "remorseful," even "contrite," but those are descriptions
once removed from feeling and as such as unsatisfying as the
confessional he claimed the letter to be.

That wasn't the real problem. The real problem was that
this was a crazy letter. Hammett had never been this crazy
before.

It was still Hammett all right, a man with holes in his
heart so large love blew right through them. Still, a rare man,

a man unlike any she'd ever known, a man she had loved for a long time, a man who worked ceaselessly at making himself unlovable. Lillian read the letter again slowly while seated at the kitchen table. She touched the bridge of her nose, which he had not broken but was now almost pleasantly sore. The eyes he had blackened with his blow were still discolored.

The next time through his letter she found the tone, which he acknowledged to be a problem, his problem, to be truly offensive. She said to the pages, "It's all about you, for Christ's sake. What fucking gall. Break my nose and it's your problem."

Now, there was nothing in his apology that did not offend and worry her further. And that goddamned theology lesson . . . that patronizing your put-upon people bullshit . . . the lie about harsh Jewish justice being superior to God's love . . . especially when he can't even come to use the word himself. And then trying to turn me into his all-forgiving confessor . . . Sister Lillian of the Broken Nose. Nothing but bullshit piled on more bullshit. This wasn't even the Hammett she loved to hate.

Two things he wrote required her attention. He was correct: she could never, never, not see him again. She did not have to be with him. But of course she must see him again.

Then there was that army nutiness. *Can't believe the melodramatic bastard is trying to impress me by threatening to join the army. Brave knight going off to slay the dragon to prove worthy. He's what? Forty-seven, forty-eight? Jesus. Delusional, absolutely delusional.*

Lillian had not the least inclination to forgive Hammett;
even less than least. She did, however, feel obliged to take
care of him. Before he hit her she sent Zenia and her son
over to Katonah every Saturday morning to do the week's
cooking and cleaning. Since the attack, she kept Zenia
back in Pleasantville. Now seemed the time to send them
again; it would be exactly the message she intended—*I can't
allow you to live in filth, or to starve, but that's the extent of my
concern.*

Hammett was surprised and pleased to see Miss Jackson
and Gilbert at his door the following Saturday morning. He
asked if there was any message from Miss Hellman, a letter,
any word. No, there was not.

Zenia looked around the place and said, "Where you been
keeping the pigs?" She put her smock on and started throwing things in the trash. She refused to let her son touch any
of the whiskey, beer, or gin bottles. In fact, she told Gilbert
to open all the windows wide and then to pick up as many
rugs as he could and take them outside. The boy somehow
managed to get them on a clothesline and began beating
them fiercely. For the first and only time since Zenia and her
son started coming over, Hammett helped with the cleaning.

When Zenia saw how inept he was, she gave him simple
and specific tasks: dust all the light shades; move the couch
and chairs to the center of the room; fill two large pots with
very hot water; shake the dust rags outside—busywork essentially, but things he couldn't mess up. Zenia could not

imagine how a man could grow so old and not have sense enough to do for himself what her own nine-year-old had already done for years. Good thing she didn't know what a Marxist was or she'd have disliked him for being a hypocrite instead of only pitying him as an incompetent.

THIS WAS HIS FOURTH VISIT to the enlistment center on Whitehall Street, the day he expected a final decision. Hammett would be forty-eight in three weeks.

When he had been in California it seemed as though a glamour route to military service might be open to him. The War Department deemed Hollywood propaganda so essential to the war effort that many of the people who made movies were offered military commissions. The heads of all the major studios received significant army commissions. Warner and Mayer became U.S. Army colonels and were issued braided uniforms with epaulets and an honorary ribbon or two. Studio tailors then made the fit stylish. They were assigned to help the war effort in any way they could, which meant making some of the political movies Lillian had been asking them to make for years. Most of the time they remained in civilian garb, but for public events, which meant whenever photographers were present, they were U.S. Army colonels.

Hammett only got to see L.B. in uniform once, in a Movietone newsreel announcing the mobilization of the Hollywood film industry. There he was looking spiffy in his costume amidst a phalanx of Hollywood stars in their uniforms—Jimmy Stewart, Robert Montgomery, Clark Gable, Tyrone Power, Wayne Morris—actual patriots who had signed up for a real war. Hammett smiled at the sight and the thought that the junkman from Minsk had finally become the American of his dreams, Lieutenant Colonel Louis B. Mayer.

The army needed training and morale films of its own, and lots of them. It recruited and commissioned film directors, most notably Frank Capra, Howard Hawkes, George Stevens, and Lillian's good friend William Wyler, among many others. Hammett contacted each of them, Wyler repeatedly, asking how he could be hired on. They all encouraged him to wait a bit and then wait just a bit more. While waiting he realized he'd prefer to lead the life of an enlisted man, rather do some actual fighting than supply the motivation for it. As preposterous as the idea was, he took himself down to the Whitehall Street recruitment station in New York and attempted to sign up.

It was unheard of, yes, but Hammett discovered that if the examining doctor attested that the candidate was in excellent health and would be a material asset to the service so named, it was possible for such a man to be accepted. Since he was much too old to be drafted, Hammett's task was to convince that doctor, in this case Major Marvin Gold, he was precisely such a rare specimen. A man with previous military training from the First World War who had unique communication skills the U.S. Army Signal Corps required. A selling job was necessary.

Major Gold met Hammett on his first visit. After filling out a very long enlistment form, Hammett waited on a bench near a large window overlooking Bowling Green. The Statue of Liberty was visible in the gloom of the harbor, faintly green and indistinct; it was not her best day. Ships' foghorns sounded unhappily. Hammett finished three crosswords while he waited for the interview. He jotted down an idea for a Spade radio script on the margin of his newspaper:

Army general in charge of secret weapon research found dead in his study. Top Secret papers missing— anything but a bombsight! Assumption that enemy agents are responsible. General's daughter—beautiful redhead, why not! Sheila something—comes to Spade because govt investigation is focused on finding the papers not murderer of father . . . Can't take case. Got no authority; government deal. They can break me if they choose. Sheila: But he was killed at home. Palo Alto. Couldn't you please take a look? Spade's questions—How? When? Where? She begs . . . great legs. Okay, he'll take a look. Stepmother not bad either,

not much older than Sheila. An adjutant, Colonel
Webb, a Korean gardener, general's wounded brother
in a wheelchair . . . Need one more suspect? . . . trouble with army investigators.

Hammett had been waiting for an hour and a half. No
one had called his name. No one had come to talk to him.
This was the army he remembered. Hammett realized at this
point that he could actually begin to write the complete epi-
sode rather than merely sketch it. He approached the grizzled
master sergeant at the desk and asked for a piece of typing
paper. The sergeant, no spring chicken himself, said, "Help
yourself, Gramps."

Hammett wrote:

Telephone rings twice.

EFFIE: Samuel Spade, Private Investigations. Mr.
Spade isn't in at the moment. May I take a
message?

TELEPHONE VOICE, BREATHLESS, DESPERATE: This
is Miss Carver, Sheila Carver. I must see Mr.
Spade as soon as possible.

EFFIE: Try to be calm, Miss Carver. Just tell me what the
problem is. I'm sure Mr. Spade will be able to help.

SHEILA, TEARFULLY: It's my father. They say he
    killed himself. He never would have . . . he
    couldn't have. I'm sure he was murd—

"Hammett, Samuel." It sounded exactly like roll call. The
master sergeant pointed to the first office door: "Major'll see
you now."

On that first visit Major Gold never looked up from the
old man's application. All his words were discouraging: age,
of course, rigors of basic, not the same army as twenty-five
years ago, problem fitting in with the kids. Hammett said
he had the legal right to a physical exam and didn't plan to
leave until he received one. Dr. Gold took his blood pressure,
listened to his heart, looked down his throat and in his ears,
tapped his patella, grabbed his nuts, and had him cough and
then cough again. A passable forty-eight-year-old man. But
barely. Chest problems?

"Heavy smoker."

"Pneumonia maybe?"

"Long ago. A touch."

Hammett said, "I don't want to seem pushy here, Doc,
but don't the country owe me a little consideration for my
first service?"

Major Gold did look at him then and said he would need
to see some new lung X-rays and offered to make an appointment for him at Fort Hamilton Veterans Hospital. Come

back in three weeks and we'll look at the pictures. Gold was sure he'd seen the last of Samuel Hammett.

Hammett was back with his X-rays one week later. Dr. Marvin Gold came out of his office as soon as he heard Hammett speaking to the master sergeant. Gold said, "Why didn't you tell me who you were? It hit me soon as I saw the middle name." He led the celebrity to his office.

Hammett said, "I'm the same old codger I was last week. Only a week older."

"You know what I mean. Please. Sit."

Gold was a movie buff and had seen every *Thin Man* twice. He wanted to know what Myrna Loy was really like. As sweet and funny as she seemed? And Powell, what kind of guy? How long did it take Hammett to write one of those scripts? And Asta, how did they get him to do all those things; was it trick photography?

Hammett not only answered all his questions, he expanded his answers with anecdotes, lots of them, a few of which were true. By the time they finally got around to discussing his enlistment, Major Gold was inclined to be an ally. There were still some significant bureaucratic obstacles—Gold said he had to clear these sorts of cases with superiors—but he himself was favorably inclined. Somewhat less so when he put Hammett's X-rays up on the scope. They called it consumption back in '19 when he first succumbed. Then tuberculosis. It was TB to the world now. It had left indelible scars on Hammett's left lung that were going to be a very hard sell to the doctor's colonel, but Gold would see what he could do. Come back in two weeks . . . and more important, did Hammett actually know any of the stars personally as friends? Who, for example? Marlene Dietrich, did he know her to talk to?

"Extremely well," Hammett said. He'd met her twice briefly.

"Was there any chance he could get her to . . . ?"

"You'll have it next time I see you. Do you want it *To Major Gold* or *Dear Marvin?*"

"*Marvin* would drive my wife crazy."

"*Marvin* it'll be."

Hammett bought a posed glossy photo of Dietrich in *Morocco* from Steuben's Stationery on Broadway. He had a choice and opted for the still with the brightest background. Von Sternberg, the director, was so in love with Dietrich he always highlighted her brilliantly with surrounding darkness. In the *Morocco* glossy she wears the signature top hat and tails. A cigarette holder is clenched in her teeth. There is at least enough light in the upper right-hand corner for an inscription. Hammett wrote, *To my dear Marvin—There's something about a soldier! Fondly, Marlene.*

He slipped the photo in an oversized envelope in which he had received a returned screenplay from Paramount. Perfect fit.

Major Gold was speechless when he held the photo before him, lip-reading *To my dear Marvin* . . . But even before he handed Gold the promised bribe, Hammett felt something had gone wrong. There was a problem with his enlistment.

"I feel terrible," Gold said. "They overruled."

"The problem?"

"Lungs."

"So I'll go get some better-looking X-rays. Was it an order?"

"What do you mean?"

"Did they order you to reject?"

"It's not like that. They returned the file with a finding. See, it's on the folder, here—'We find the candidate unqualified at this time for . . .'"

"Marvin. Surely you still have some discretion in the matter. It isn't an order. You've got that 'at this time' to play with . . ."

"I've never done anything like—"

"Let me ask you this. If you were to accept my enlistment, where would that file go?"

"It would follow you to assignment. I'd recommend Signal Corps. Fort Monmouth."

"Then it wouldn't go back upstairs. They'd never know—or even care—what happened to Hammett with the lungs."

Gold shook his head. And then sat silently. He was mulling. Hammett knew to remain silent. Gold reached into his desk and pulled out an official form. He began to print. "Okay," he said to Hammett, "I'll let you into this war. But I hope you understand this is absolutely the last time."

LILLIAN WAS AT THE TABLE when the phone rang, looking approvingly at her arms and the backs of her strong hands in the sunlight. Her habit of anticipating her caller and determining whether or not to pick up caused her to signal Zenia to let it ring. It could be Hammett, whom she did not want to speak with. Or Childs, whom she did. She picked up warily. The voice was its own identification. Early in the day as it was, his voice was already tuned like a cello. Even before she heard "This is the president," it was indeed the president.

What she remembered of the conversation was a string of compliments about the quality of her work, especially *The Spanish Earth*, her courage and patriotism, and the country's need for an even more pressing political film. When the president left pauses, Lillian filled with, "Yes, Mr. President," "Of course, sir," "Thank you, Mr. President."

Would she be willing to create—that was his word, *create*—a film that introduced the Soviet Union favorably to the American public?

"More than willing, Mr. President."

"Object, you see, is to transform a former adversary into an admired ally. Quickly. No mean feat. Up to it?"

"Please, Mr. President." This was as close as she came to being her truest self with the caller.

Did she know Mr. Goldwyn well? He pronounced the name *Goldwine*.

"Extremely well, sir."

Goldwyn's studio would produce and distribute the film. If Miss Hellman was "on board," she would hear later today from the president's son James, who was organizing things in Hollywood. The pause pertained to *if* and *on board*.

"They'll have to throw me off the train, sir."

"Questions?"

"Only the time frame, sir."

"Surely you know the answer to that, Miss Hellman."

Afterward she sat quietly at the table smiling and looking out over Hardscrabble. Zenia was at the sink shaking her head and clucking. The President Roosevelt himself, *cluck, cluck, cluck,* my, my, my.

Lillian's personal pleasure gave way to the pleasure of the challenge—adversary to ally. No, not the *why* of it, *only what it could mean to us . . . the lives saved. Getting even with the Rats. Spain had not gone well, maybe this time . . .*

She was taken out of her thoughts by a tapping on the back window. Cedric Childs, right on time.

"Coffee, Zenia." That meant Lilly wanted to talk. Childs sat down.

She asked him to guess who had just called. He refused. "The president. I just hung up. Right, Zenia?"

"Yes, Mr. Childs." She placed a cup of coffee in front of him.

"He had an assignment for me, which I accepted. I'm afraid it's going to screw up our plans for the planting royally." Lillian explained in general and said she'd know more of the details after she spoke with the president's son, maybe as early as later today.

"Which means?"

"Which means, I think, our planting season has gone to war."

"And why exactly is that?"

"The president wants the movie made right away. I've got to start writing immediately. I'll be working on it all the time, probably traveling out to the coast for it. Much as I love farming this place . . ."

"How long do you anticipate . . ."

"I'll know better after I talk to . . ."

Zenia said, "If you won't be needing me, I'll just . . ." She left the room.

"It would break my heart to see this place go fallow again. I would never have asked you to. I'm not even asking you to now."

"The farm's asking, isn't it?"

She squeezed his hand. "You're remarkable." Lillian stood and kissed Cedric Childs on an unshaved cheek.

JAMES ROOSEVELT CALLED that evening. If the father's was a cello, James's voice was a viola. The speech patterns, the intonations, the accent and pronunciations were the same. The son, however, pronounced Goldwyn correctly.

This is what Lillian learned: the project had been presented to colonels Warner, Mayer, and Goldwyn. Only Goldwyn accepted. Production costs would be carried by the government and repaid out of profits, if any. The film would be a commercial release, so Lillian would have to make arrangements with Goldwyn for a fee, a surprise because Lillian hadn't expected to be paid for her contribution. Some very fine and well-known actors had already committed, Roosevelt said. Which ones? Not yet at liberty to say, which meant that the project was still at the throwing-names-around stage.

Did Lillian have any story ideas?

She did indeed. Her basic Spanish Earth idea, which had really been discarded by Hemingway and Ivens—only now it will be a farming village in the Ukraine that comes under attack. Bombed by the Luftwaffe, taken by the Wehrmacht. The peasants organize and resist. This plot idea came straight off daily news reports as the German army rolled eastward across the wheat fields of the Soviet Union. "The important thing here, Mr. Roosevelt . . ."

"Please call me Jimmy, Miss Hellman."

"I'm Lilly, Jimmy."

"Fine."

"The important thing is to start the story earlier and show how much like us these people are . . . or were . . . before they were attacked. Same hardworking people as us. Same aspirations for our children. Same taste for freedom. That essential similarity is the key for me dramatically and psychologically, and it's what we have in common and what we both risk losing to these bastards." Lillian knew she had something good to build on and certainly had Roosevelt's attention. "So the Nazis take over the village. The young men take to the hills to form partisan defense groups. This all has to be worked out—I only heard about the project a few hours ago, but . . ."

"I'm enthused, Lillian . . ."

". . . but I can assure you everything will be a drama, not a tract. There must be young lovers, the village mayor, the doctor, the teacher, a class of children. Do you have any idea who will direct?"

"Goldwyn tells me Milestone."

"Lewis would be ideal."

Lewis Milestone already had two Academy Awards and two other nominations. For this project his *All Quiet on the Western Front* was credential enough. *Milestone* was an American invention: Lev Milstein was born in Russia, another obvious advantage.

"It's clear this project needed you. Thank you for coming on board."

"I hate *on board*. I'm simply glad to have the chance to work on this."

"Stand corrected. Tell me, when do you think we can see a story outline? No matter how rough."

"Give me two weeks."

"If not sooner. They tell me you're fast."

"I beg your pardon?"

"Anyway, I'll see what progress I can make out here. Would it be okay to have Mr. Milestone call you?"

"Fine."

"And Mr. Goldwyn?"

"Less fine, but fine."

"Well, Miss Hel—, Lilly, I have to say I'm very encouraged having spoken with you. I've had my doubts this project would ever happen or be successful. Now, I'm quite sure of both."

"Thanks, Jimmy."

A STORY IN TWO WEEKS, something like that required talks with Hammett. She knew she'd have to call him, because she had always called him, but she decided to see how well she could do on her own first.

Lillian knew next to nothing about the Ukraine, at least not about the non-Jewish Ukraine, or village life therein. Nothing about wheat farming. And, other than the headlines, very little about the German advance into Russia strategically or tactically. Hammett. Damn him. Who else?

When Zenia arrived in Katonah, she had a message for Hammett from Lillian: "I have a surprise. Please call." He did. After the house cleaning Lillian picked them all up and drove them back to Pleasantville. As awkward as it was for

Zenia, Lillian insisted she sit in the front with her; Hammett was in the back with Gilbert.

"So what's your big surprise?"

"Tell you after you've got a fire going and we have drinks in hand."

"Sounds like a surprise I'm going to like."

Gilbert played with a toy soldier, a British "Tommy" Hammett had given him. Except for some machine gun sounds the boy made, they drove the darkening back roads in silence.

Hammett started a fire and made drinks. Zenia began dinner. Lillian changed from a sweater and slacks into another sweater and slacks. She joined him on the sofa that faced the fire. The wood crackled while they watched. Hammett raised his glass first.

"So?"

Lillian traced what she knew about the project from the president's phone call to the present moment.

Hammett thought while fingering his mustache, his lips, his chin. All his first questions dealt with the specifics of production. Commercial release? Goldwyn's role? Director? Cast? Locations? Time frame? Censorship? Basically all the questions Lillian had asked and was still waiting to have clarified. Had she signed anything? Would she be paid? How much? Was it only script work?

They spoke slowly and with care about all these things before they advanced to the more challenging matter of how to make a movie that could change an American's attitude about Communist Russia.

Zenia called, "Dinner."

As they walked into the kitchen, Hammett said, "I've got your title." He explained over T-bones, green beans, and baked potatoes that the most successful farm collective in the Ukraine was called "The North Star." Hellman liked the title.

This was what Lillian loved—talking about projects—his and hers—discovering facts, finding connections, developing strategies. Hammett was especially good at this. What he said rarely translated directly into what she did with an idea, but what he said usually set her off on a Hellman riff that produced music he could never make himself. If collaboration of this quality was a form of love, Hellman and Hammett were very much in love again on this night.

His most important suggestion Lillian had already come up with on her own: set the piece in a time before the Germans arrive so we see the contrast between people working hard and raising families well and those same people later fighting for their lives. Americans are just starting to learn these same lessons for themselves. Remind the audience of that dramatic contrast—normal life poisoned by a war they did not start.

She let him speak on and on. Costumes authentic, yes. Tractors, hay wagons, wheat fields, all location stuff really. But no phony Russian accents. Make them all sound like Americans. Give the Germans the accents. As the Nazis advance, the people are required to burn their crops, or they will be used to nourish the enemy—in one scene the villagers argue among themselves about Russia's "scorched earth" policy. Imagine! Farmers having to destroy what they grow. Farmers! And then having to destroy every other damn thing the Germans might find useful. Homes, barns, farm equipment, everything. The dramatic possibilities were powerful.

It wasn't yet midnight. Lillian said, "Wait." She picked up the phone and asked for the long distance operator. "I'm sorry to call this late . . . You're kind. I have a working title I wanted to share with you. I find it so much easier to work when I have a title. It tells me where I'm going . . . *The North Star* . . . Yes, I do too . . . Thank you, Jimmy. Remember, *The North Star.* Tell the others. Of course . . . It's going well . . . Talk to you soon."

Hammett said, "He's single . . . and they say he's Jewish too."

"Very funny."

Which brought him to Lewis Milestone né Lev Milstein. Regardless of reputation and awards, Lillian knew that no director she worked with could ever be good enough for her in Hammett's eyes. So when he warned her against caving in to Milestone's authority, dramatic authority he meant, Lillian said, "But he's a Russian, for Christ's sake."

"No. He's a Jew from Bessarabia. Here's what that means. The Ukrainians in the story are not Jews. If truth be told, they hate Jews. Milstein left before the Revolution. Nicholas was tsar. I'd wager he never saw a wheat field in his life. So don't assume—"

"I won't, dear."

It wasn't enough, he went on, to make it a war story, even an antiwar story, certainly not another *All Quiet*. It must be a morality play. Evil attempts to destroy good. Good fights back bravely. Will it triumph? Can't be sure . . . that's why we fight. The problem, the writing challenge, is how to create and dramatize the evil. In Spain it was bombing civilians and no one gave a shit. They do it now every night in London, and that gets our attention, but we still don't see it as a morality play.

"So how?"

"Real evil has a certain defining quality. It's perverse and we often see it better in small things. The smile on a villain's face, even in a bad movie. The look in his eyes. The unnecessary gesture he makes with his knife. The threat of a punch that doesn't get thrown. Intimidation is evil's calling card. The German officer who takes command of your village has to have this quality—civilized but evil. Von Ströheim, even when he smiles—especially when he smiles—is the most frightening man in the world. He takes his white gloves off slowly one finger at a time and you can tell he's a fiend."

Hammett told Lillian of reports he had read about medical experiments in concentration camps that had scared the hell out of him. Disgusted him. Their real evil came out in their crazy scientific theories of racial purity. Hammett couldn't see how she could work any of it into *North Star*, but for him it was at the heart of the Nazi darkness.

Lillian had lots of new questions. That's how the process always worked: ideas strewn on the floor like pickup sticks. Some left. Some discarded. Some picked up, examined, questioned, put aside or onto the save-for-later pile. Some became "must use," others "must use but how."

Zenia had cleaned up long before and gone to sleep. Hellman and Hammett spoke late into the night, now in more general terms about the war and eventually about what they were reading, what he was writing, about the texture and details of their lives, and about old times. Was his racetrack story really true? And did Warner ever pay up? Yes and yes. And did she really make money with last year's sweet corn crop? And did she really run a farm stand down at the road? Yes and yes.

They spoke more slowly and quietly the later it got. The cigarette smoke in the room began to settle. The whiskey had not quite run out. Just before bed Hammett said, "Oh, I almost forgot. I've got a little surprise of my own."

"CAP'N, HOW THE HELL ARE YOU?"

Hammett pointed to the stripes on his arm. "Just a corporal, Jimmy, just a corporal."

"You're a captain to me, Dash."

When the doorman first opened the door of the cab and saw Lillian he was genuinely pleased—"Miss H.! We've missed you." Hammett in uniform produced a second excitement. Jimmy could not resist the instinct to embrace Hammett, uniform or no uniform. He kept saying, "Pleasure, real pleasure." In fact, he made such a fuss that many in the crowd waiting to enter "21"—almost all the men were officers in uniform—turned to look at the corporal and his lady.

Lillian said to the crowd, "Forgive them, folks, they fought together at Gettysburg."

Jimmy took their arms and escorted them past the waiting crowd, talking all the while: "How'd you pull it off, Mr. H.? Where they got you stationed? Jeez, it's good to see you both again." He guided them through the door and past the hat check, right up to the maître d's stand. Lillian loved the murmurs of discontent from women hanging on the arms of big brass over the privileged treatment of an old corporal and his woman.

Jimmy turned the couple over to Tomaso, who gave Hammett a crisp salute and Lillian a polite kiss and then led them to the corner table they had always considered theirs. As they passed through the room, eyes followed. Someone called out, "Bravo." Three or four others applauded briefly. Neither of them acknowledged. There would be time when they were seated to look around for old friends.

Their waiter was Martin. Like old times. It was hard for him to keep his smile in its professional range, but he did reach out impetuously and shake their hands. He said it was a pleasure to have them back, an honor to serve them.

"Menus?"

"Not really, Martin."

"Does Madame have an idea?"

"Something Russian, I think, Martin."

"The Beluga to start?"

"Perfect."

"Lamb, kabob-style perhaps."

"Oh, yes."

Lillian took out a cigarette and offered one to Hammett. He refused. Martin lit hers. "And for Mr. Hammett?"

"The regular, please." *My god*, he thought, *I'm really going to miss this place.*

"And to drink, sir?"

"Champagne, Martin. We're celebrating. Mumm's. You pick the year."

The restaurant was full of braided and medaled officer uniforms of all the services, of gilded and spangled women, few of whom were very young, and some older members of the smart New York set for whom the war was still something of an abstraction, but less so than before.

The theater crowd was there as well, almost no actors—most couldn't afford this place—but she recognized George Abbott and the Shubert brothers with their wives. Lillian saw Jimmy Walker, the old mayor, drinking alone at a corner table. Tallulah was there with her young man of the evening, so Lillian prepared for a terrible scene. Tallulah held Lillian personally responsible for giving Bette Davis her role in the *Little Foxes* movie. David Sarnoff was there. So was Paley. And, oh shit, there was Winchell, who was certain to come by.

Hammett's surveillance of the room stopped abruptly when he saw Alfred Knopf and his wife, Blanche. He had taken a Knopf advance and written nothing. Fortunately that's when Martin arrived with their champagne, which Hammett always insisted on opening himself. The pressure of the cork in his hand was not only pleasurable but gave him a sense of the bottle's quality.

"Look, there's Blanche and Alfred. Why not go over and say goodbye? Maybe he'll want an army memoir."

"I'm a soldier, not a writer."

"My hero. Go on over."

Hammett poured the champagne slowly and expertly. "Maybe later. Here's to crime."

"To crime." Lillian paused before touching glasses. "I think I'm going to miss you terribly."

"*Now* you tell me." *Clink.*

When Hammett looked up again, Alfred and Blanche were at the table. Alfred leaned down to kiss Lillian. He said, "How did you manage it, old man?"

"That's the British *old man*, I take it. Not *old man* as in 'OLD' man."

"I think I meant both. And it's awfully good to see you two . . . together."

Lillian: "It's good to be you two . . . together."

Dash said, "Unfortunately not for long. I'll be shipping out next week."

Blanche Knopf observed that this news was startling to Lillian. She asked, "To where?"

"Top Secret, I'm afraid. Slip of the lip may sink a ship . . ."

"You take care, both of you."

"We will." Said in unison as they watched the Knopfs walk away.

"So why the hell didn't you tell me? Made me look like a fool with them."

"Just found out. Didn't want to ruin our evening."

"That's a nice way not to ruin an evening." She glared at him. "So where? Or is it Top Secret even to me?"

"West Coast is all I know. Honestly."

"Wonderful. I'm going to be in L.A. a good deal with *North Star*. Maybe our paths will cross."

As their meal ended and more well-wishers came by, Lilly's pique softened. Lilly and Dash felt appreciated, a feeling they usually shared only with one another, and certainly not all the time. That others also valued them came as surprising good news.

Hammett popped the cork on a second bottle of Mumm's before dessert was done. He poured. "To crime," he said.

"To the man who knows nothing whatsoever about love."

He stopped before the clink: "Oh, how I hate you."

"Oh, how I hate you more."

Clink.

.16.

At War

SAM GOLDWYN CAME THROUGH on the *North Star* project as Lillian could never have imagined. She always had a strong ally in Jimmy Roosevelt, but he had given up being a costumed lieutenant colonel in Hollywood and become a captain in the Marines. He was on active and dangerous duty fighting a real war in the Pacific. But he had kept an office in Washington that expeditiously forwarded Lillian's messages. Through that office he kept a distant eye on *North Star*.

The talents assembled for the project were remarkable for any studio film, unprecedented for a propaganda piece about the Soviet Union. Besides Milestone and the excellent cinematographer James Wong Howe, the film featured some of Hollywood's finest actors, most of whom believed in its wartime importance as much as Lillian. The Russian villagers were Anne Baxter, Dana Andrews, Walter Huston, Farley Granger, Walter Brennan, Dean Jagger, Jane Withers, Ann Harding, and every homey-looking character actor on the M-G-M lot. The Nazi villain was indeed von Stroheim, whom Hammett called the absolute best of the absolute worst. Aaron Copland signed on for the Russian-sounding music score; and none other than Ira Gershwin wrote the patriotic lyrics . . . in English of course.

Lillian did not count herself among the luminaries who had hired on. All the others did, however.

The moral and dramatic conflict at the heart of her script is the tension between two doctors—one a Russian civilian, Dr. Pavel Kurin, the other a German officer—over the issue of blood transfusions for wounded German troops. The soldiers are dying of wounds they received from the Russian defenders of the village in which the story is set. The German commandant orders transfusions for his men with blood taken from healthy Russians, including the village children. For Lillian this was the dramatic heart of the conflict, and more importantly the most elemental metaphor she could create.

Goldwyn and Milestone thought this bloody plot device too gruesome for an American audience. Lillian was adamant that the transfusions stay in. She told Goldwyn, "Squeamish about blood, are you? What do they think the war is all about? It's a fucking bloodbath, for Christ's sake." And then she issued an ultimatum: remove the transfusions and she would remove herself. And she would make sure the president heard about it.

The blood transfusions stayed in.

At the plot's climax, a dangerous transfusion is performed by Dr. von Harden, played by von Stroheim with frightening civility. The German officer lives but the Russian boy dies. The Russian Dr. Kurin, the avuncular Walter Huston, confronts von Harden. In the doctor-to-doctor confrontation, Lillian delivers her political message:

PAVEL KURIN: You knew he would die.

VON HARDEN: They took too much blood. I'm sorry for that.

KURIN: I've heard about you . . . civilized men who are sorry . . . men who do the work of Fascists while they pretend to themselves that they are better than the beasts for whom they work . . . men who do murder while they laugh at those who order them to do it. It is men like you who have sold their people to men like them!

[*Kurin takes out a gun and shoots von Harden at point blank range.*]

KURIN: You see, Doctor von Harden, you were wrong about me. I AM a man who kills.

Given the cultural climate created by the war, it was almost impossible for most movie critics to evaluate *The North Star* harshly or as other than what it was, an effective propaganda film. The Hearst movie critics, however, wanted no part of Rooshkie propaganda. Don McConnell in the *Journal American* ended his review with a warning, one Lillian dismissed without a second thought:

> Lillian Hellman's latest film project, *The North Star*, has been of great benefit to our newly discovered Soviet buddies. It depicts them as peace-loving, noble, and innocent victims tormented by a ruthless aggressor. But wait just a minute here, weren't those roles reversed just a couple of years ago when it was the Soviet Armies that rolled ruthlessly over innocent civilians in Finland and eastern Poland? And did said Miss Hellman come to the defense of those peaceful peasants then? Not for a moment.
>
> If Miss Hellman were a more scrupulous student of recent history, she would know that yesterday's Enemy turned today's Ally is likely to become tomorrow's Enemy once again. Comrade Hellman would be wise to sing "The Internationale" a bit more softly, if at all, when that tomorrow comes.

CORPORAL HAMMETT'S BUNK was at the far end of a Quonset hut, near the latrines, and he composed his letter on military V-mail paper in the dark with the help of his field flashlight:

> *Dear Lillushka—(Is it still safe to call you by your Soviet diminutive?)*
>
> *I'm well, after a very rugged journey, but I am, alas, forbidden to reveal its destination. I won't do that because correspondence to and from this destination will be censored severely. However, if you read "The Widow's Peak," you will remember how interesting the correspondence was. Did you read it?*

In that early Hammett story, conspirators send each other coded letters. Every time a question is asked it meant the very next sentence contained a clue to some important piece of information. Lillian remembered and could now discover where in the world Hammett was.

The sentence after the question read:

> *Dear, I miss your cooking most of all, especially the delicious stuffed derma you always made for the Holidays.*

There it was. Lillian had never made stuffed derma in her life and knew immediately that was the clue. To go from *derma* to *kishka*, its Yiddish equivalent, might take a while for some people, but not for Lillian. From *kishka* to the Aleutian island of Kiska was not a difficult step. Finally, Lillian knew where in this secret military world Hammett was.

She went to the great atlas in the room where Hammett had usually stayed and found a map with commentary. Her finger touched Kiska and she imagined the Hammett she had seen off at Grand Central months before. There was much she wanted to tell him tonight about herself. There was much she wanted to know about him. Helplessness always made her angry. The atlas commentary called the chain of islands part of the Pacific Ring of Fire, an allusion to its volcanic creation, not the ironical fact that the temperature was a maximum of fifty degrees in midsummer and sub-zero most other times. She would begin to knit him a pair of wool socks in the morning. Maybe have Zenia start a pair as well.

It's a difficult, hopeful time for both of us. We'll see this through. I like the kids I'm with. They call me Pops—it smacks of an old Blues Man—which of course is what I am: Pops Hammett crooning "Daddy's Got a Spankin' Heart"! These kids are mostly about half my age. They see me as a complete enigma, part uncle, part scoutmaster, part priest, part teacher, part fossil. Forty-eight to them makes me one of our country's Founding Fathers. Since the army hasn't changed a whit since my last time around, my advice is often sought. I'm going to be important here. It's a role I sort of like. Maybe when you see me again, you'll call me Pops too.

He was writing in a very tight script because the V-mail form was so small. Since he was running out of space, he began to write even smaller. Lillian would need a magnifying glass to decipher it.

A confession. When this show is finally over in a few years I will allow myself to be lauded as a self-sacrificing, patriotic American. (I'll do my best to see that it is not done posthumously, only because I won't be able to hear what they say about me.) Patriotism in the Grand Old Flag sense has nothing to do with it. I joined up because it was by far the best option open to me. My writing was crap. The family stories started to dry up. Movie scripts were not going to happen again. A radio script a night, what sort of challenge was that! (I'm telling you what you already know and doing it in the tiniest words possible.) The army could save me from myself: it would insure me, clothe me, house me, feed me, force me to drink 3.2 beer. It would put me back into a world of men, where I've always managed well, and allow me to kill Rats indirectly and hopefully directly as well. And the only cost to me is my enforced absence from you. We have been apart before, separated mostly for foolish personal reasons. This separation is completely different, achingly and sorrowfully so, but it must be endured.

Oh, by the way, I've become the company barber. I'm good at it too. Man with the clippers. You'll be pleased to know I demand payment for my services.

Well, gal, tell me how things are going in the Ukraine.
Oh, I just remembered, I'm going to need, really need,
lots of reading material. Send me subscriptions to all the
good mags real soon.
I miss your face. I miss your brains. I miss you. I
have always missed you.

Pops

The last few words barely got on the page.

Alaska Command required a newspaper to help indoctrinate, inform, and entertain the thousands of troops gathering for a likely attack on imperial Japan. Sergeant Hammett—the promotion matched his new assignment—became the editor in chief of *The Adakian*, an eight-sheet publication of fifty thousand copies.

Hammett put together a staff of young men, city kids for the most part with some experience on college newspapers, and quickly went about the task of organizing assignments and setting deadlines, opening production and distribution channels, and above all establishing the standards, the tone, and the point of view of the paper. He edited everything that went to print and wrote about half the paper himself. He even began doing some of the political cartoons, drawing an American eagle that managed to look like FDR, a Stalin-like Kodiak bear, a Hitler rat, and an evil Japanese face on the setting sun. He worked very long hours and was profoundly tired and quietly happy.

Each week after the paper had been put to bed, he drank piss beer with his staff. They begged him to tell Hollywood stories, which he occasionally did only because they wanted them so badly. He told them true and unvarnished; the young soldiers were left open-mouthed and speechless by the debaucheries he described. Hammett never told any stories about himself. Although they were curious, none of his staff ever asked.

The editor of *The Adakian* was often relieved of his military assignments. Some but not all. Hammett was required to qualify on the rifle range every three months. This meant a two-mile march to the rifle range with his Headquarters Company in full gear, then lying prone and hitting the target from as far away as five hundred yards. Most times, either Pops Hammett or a kid from Alabama had the highest score.

Also every three months the company was required to make a four-mile forced march at double time. It became an ordeal for Hammett over the last mile and a half—his lungs betrayed him—but even though he fell behind he always finished, and he was never among the worst stragglers. He did need two days at least to recapture what was left of his strength.

THE COMMANDER OF SIGNAL BATTALION, Alaskan Department, was Colonel Orville Avery, an engineering graduate of West Point, whose specialty was telegraphic communications. The battalion's main mission was the construction of telegraph lines on all the islands on which the army had deployed troops. And to set up wireless radio stations at all outposts to monitor the Jap Morse communications, which were usually encoded. As a result most of the U.S. troops stationed in the Aleutians dug holes, poured cement, set poles, strung wires, and trained in case of a possible Jap attack to be able to defend their featureless terrain. Hammett had met Colonel Avery on two occasions—once when Avery toured the *Adakian* office and then when Hammett was promoted to tech sergeant. Hammett never heard from his commanding officer about the newspaper, which meant that he either had no complaints or was no longer aware of its existence. Either way, Hammett was satisfied.

It came as a surprise, then, when his company commander had a jeep sent to his Quonset with orders to take Hammett to battalion headquarters for a meeting with Colonel Avery, Colonel's orders. Hammett was given no sense of the colonel's intention. He assumed the worst, problems with his left-leaning editorials, drawn from information gleaned from *Commonweal* and *The Nation*, two of the periodicals Lillian had sent. He did not want to lose his newspaper. That's how he had come to think of it—*his* newspaper.

Avery—glasses, crew cut, red cherubic face—was sitting behind his desk when Sergeant Hammett entered, reported, saluted, and held his salute as Colonel Avery muttered, "At ease, Sergeant." Five copies of recent *Adakian*s were on his desk.

"These cartoons of yours, Hammett. What in the world were you thinking?"

"Sir?"

"A newspaper is supposed to boost morale, for Christ's sake."

"I believe the men think they're moderately funny, sir."

"This one, funny? Captain leads his company up a volcano and says, 'Keep going, men, at least we'll be able to get warm.' Can't you see?"

"Excuse me, see what, sir?"

"It makes the officer look stupid. So do these others. A major talking to a walrus, 'Seen any Japs come ashore?' Two generals arguing about how to spell *archipelago*. An officer with a compass asking an Eskimo which way is north. You make us all look like a bunch of prize morons."

"The men like to think they can laugh at their officers, sir. It's really a form of equality that denotes respect, sir."

"Bullshit, Hammett. If it doesn't stop immediately, I'll ship your sorry old ass the hell out of here."

"Understood, sir. Anything else, sir?"

"Otherwise, good paper. Dismissed."

Older man and younger man exchanged salutes.

LILLIAN AT HARDSCRABBLE was healthy and strong, very strong.

For her the last moments of wakefulness in her large bed at night were the sweetest of her long day; she was conscious of how vital she was, intellectually and physically. Farmwork pleased her enormously. She loved feeling the tautness of her stomach muscles, the strength in her thighs, the muscularity of her arms and back. She wrote Hammett, "My ass muscles would make Rodin drool."

Lillian thought of Hammett in a somewhat new fashion. Her attraction had always, from the very beginning, been based on admiration. They always differed over how deserved it was. Now, really for the first time, envy was present. Even when they had been separated in the past, she knew part of him belonged to her. She no longer felt that way. The world of men he inhabited now gave her the sense that Hammett no longer needed her. His letters were mostly about that masculine world, and, yes, they did evoke her jealousy.

James Roosevelt's office called again from Washington with a request that she heard as an opportunity. No, not another propaganda film. This time something much more active, participatory, perhaps even somewhat dangerous. The tide of the war on the Russian front had turned dramatically after Stalingrad and the Red Army was now sweeping westward through Poland and toward Germany. Did Lillian wish to accompany that army and write about its advance? The Russians had actually requested her presence and participation.

Lillian wanted very much to see the war. At least that envy of Hammett would be dealt with. And she wanted to see the war won. Wasn't this, after all, the reversal of the misfortunes she had witnessed in Spain years before, the just conclusion she had hoped for then?

The trip to Moscow tested her physically and emotionally. Thirty-six hours in a variety of transport planes with stops in Anchorage—Hammett could not have been too far away—and Irkutsk, Ulan-Ude, Novgorod—she'd heard of that city, at least—and stopovers in places that had no names.

After three days in Moscow being wined and dined and fussed over, and after seeing a lifeless performance of *The Little Foxes* that offered more Chekhovian ennui than Hellman rage, and another good evening talking about film with Sergei Eisenstein, Lillian was more anxious than ever to see the war. And especially to see it being won.

A small military transport finally took her and a young captain who spoke passable English to Warsaw and then on a second hop to within a hundred miles of Prague, from where Lillian and her interpreter joined a truck supply route to the Second Armored Division, which had fought at Stalingrad and was now pushing inexorably toward Germany itself. She was perhaps a day or two from the siege of Prague. She wrote in her notebook:

Fighting and war are two very different matters.
I have seen war, and war is destruction, destruction
of lives, of what has been carefully built, of plans,
of the very spirit that underlies all these things, the

spark that allows what is human in us to ignite in the first place. War is the snuffing of that flame. War is civilization's funeral. War is the face of a very beautiful dead woman in Madrid.

Fighting is a different creature entirely. It is energy and force of will. It is vengeance and sinew brought to fever pitch. It thrives and flames in its own time, self-contained, unmindful, and, of course, unaware of what future fighting it will bring. It feeds on itself. And while it lives it is more alive than anything else men do. More alive than laughter, more alive, if you can believe it, than the exhilaration and expectation of sex.

Kurin not only kills von Harden . . . a part of him enjoys doing it. To my shame, I anticipate sharing his enjoyment.

Lillian joined the Second Armored Division on the eastern shore of the Vltava as it bombarded the Germans and Czech fascists who defended the city with heavy cannon fire and multiple rocket launchers continually. Lillian wadded cotton in her ears and pulled her beret down over them. Russian planes bombed and strafed the city during daylight hours.

German artillery returned fire from the heights across the river. Their firepower remained substantial no matter how much damage the Russians believed they had caused. Much

of the old city would have to be destroyed before any attempt
could be made to cross the river. It puzzled Lillian: The situation was hopeless. Why won't the bastards surrender?

She wrote:

> The Russians have set up headquarters in an old
> Customs House on the eastern quay of the Vltava.
> From here I see the great Gothic city above us to the
> west on the other side of the rushing river, almost
> invulnerable to direct attack since none of her many
> bridges remained intact. There is no telling how
> long the bombardment from artillery and air attack
> must continue. Pieces of Prague crumble daily before
> my very eyes.
>
> Our command post has been hit repeatedly by
> German artillery. Still, we are safe in its basement.
> Most days I watch the effect of the artillery assault
> on the old city. I had been in Prague briefly years
> ago during my honeymoon and remember standing
> on the rampart of Praha Castle at night and look-
> ing down over the glittering town, the black Vltava
> reflecting the stars. Now I look through field glasses
> and see those same ramparts, still intact because it,
> the great cathedral, and the monastery beyond have
> been spared until this point. I spend hours scanning
> the city; it is impossible for me to turn away from
> any civilian activity—the attempt to clear debris, a

delivery of food, a family moving to a safer place—all that I can see through my glasses.

Here is what I saw not more than one hour ago. From just below the piling of the Charles Bridge my eye caught a fleck of white and then another. Slowly, from behind the stone wall of the boathouse three figures emerged, a woman, a man, a child. The child, a girl, was waving a white scarf. The woman waved a white hat. The man, short and wide, carried what appeared to be a wooden platform. When he placed it at water's edge, it was clear he had been carrying a small raft.

This was most likely a family, and they were trying to escape the bombardment by crossing the river and joining the Russians. The three lay flat on the raft, parents atop the child; they drifted out into the river. The father had a short paddle. The mother never stopped waving her daughter's white scarf.

The raft was about a quarter of the way across the Vltava when shots at them from the other side of the river began to pelt the waters around them. When the father was hit, his knees came up suddenly and then he slipped into the river, his wife and daughter held him briefly before he tumbled off the raft. The raft tipped over, plunging the woman and child into the water. The mother clung to the raft while the current started to pull the girl away. She reached for her child

too late and after a terrible moment began swimming after her daughter.

She and then the daughter were overwhelmed by the current at midriver. I saw the white hat and the white scarf touch, entangle, and get carried downstream.

.17.

Shock, Aftershock

ZENIA HEARD FIRST and simply went to pieces. When I got to the kitchen, she was on her knees sobbing, "No, oh no, oh no." Her son was standing soldier-straight against the wall. He looked frightened. Zenia said, "He's dead. The president. He's dead." I went to my knees and we held each other, sobbing, both sobbing.

She had heard the news on the radio. Now we sat with coffee and listened while more complete information came. It was late afternoon, a Thursday. Cerebral hemorrhage. He complained of a terrible headache, terrible, slumped over unconscious. It all happened so fast.

The sun was low.

I noticed that Gilbert did not understand our extreme grief, so I explained to him that his mother and I loved President Roosevelt very much and that we were taken by surprise that he had died. Gilbert wanted to know how old he was. "Sixty-four, sixty-five," I thought.

"Ain't that plenty old enough to die, Mama?"

Zenia looked at me to respond. "You miss someone however old he is, Gilbert. And the president is a very important someone to us. The war, we need him to win the war."

"Are we going to lose the war now?"

"No, Gilbert, we're going to win the war, but he won't be there to see it, and that's really sad."

Max didn't allow me to cry as a child. I learned to cry after I met Hammett, but I pretty much got over that. The war, its destruction, its victims, rarely brought me to tears. But I was weeping now. The cello voice I loved silenced. I don't know why, but I asked Zenia if I could hold Gilbert. He looked over at her to see if he ought to step into my arms. Zenia said, "Go on."

The boy's hair roughed my cheek. My tears flowed onto him. His strong body was wire-stiff. He smelled like a newborn. I said, "You always have to remember this day, Gilbert. Always. It is the day a very great man died." It was a speech out of a scene I'd never write.

When the phone rang I didn't answer. It couldn't have been Hammett. Seven time zones away, he may not even have gotten the news. Goddamned war.

We listened to the radio in the kitchen all evening. We cooked a little. Ate some egg sandwiches. Excerpts from many of his recent speeches filled the kitchen. How clear they were. How strong. How smart. How comforting. Even now. It was exactly the voice I heard when he telephoned me about the *North Star* project. That voice was presidential but sweeter, more charming. He wanted something from me that day.

The radio told of preliminary plans being made for the funeral. FDR's casket would be transported slowly northward by train along the eastern shore. Mourners could pay respects as the funeral train made its way toward Washington. It would slow for the mourners. After resting in state at the capitol, the president would be carried home to Hyde Park, New York, which is only about half an hour away from here. I'll drive over in a month or so.

It bothered me again that Hammett wouldn't allow himself to see his greatness. Our fight, the worst we'd ever had, wasn't about drinking or lying or fucking around, it was about FDR, about what he meant. It was hard to trust Hammett's judgment about anything political after that.

After Zenia saw Gilbert to sleep, we sat and listened to the radio. Zenia, who didn't drink, had a glass of sherry with me. When she started to cry, I started to cry again. She said she was crying because *her people lost a friend.* Then she said she was crying for Mrs. Roosevelt.

That's when I thought of James and wondered how I would get in touch to offer my condolences.

The radio voice told us in glowing terms about the new president. Praise was heaped upon this little-known and little-accomplished man. The radio text dutifully reminded us how remarkable our democracy was, since a new president had already replaced the old and this process had taken place swiftly and peacefully. "We can thank our lucky stars—or rather our wise and benevolent Founding Fathers—that we are the world's leading constitutional democracy, a nation of laws and not of men, whereas in many other parts of the world . . ."

Why do they have to spoil things with crap like that?

I KNEW SOMETHING WAS UP when Colonel Avery made *The Adakian* a biweekly and put us all on an active training schedule. Full-time training *and* the paper made our once sweet lives a hell on Kiska. That was about three months ago.

If that didn't make it abundantly clear that an attack on the Jap mainland was imminent, the nature of our new training assured it. Have you ever scrambled over the side of a troop ship at three in the morning, climbed down a rope ladder that tore your hands apart, crammed yourself into an LST in open sea with a hundred other guys? And doing it all under full field pack? Twice a day? Every day? Toughest thing I ever did. Even when I was young. Still, I managed to keep up. 'Nuff said.

An army doesn't travel on its stomach. It travels on rumors. In our Aleutian army all rumors pointed to a Hokkaido attack in the summer. I clearly remember looking around the barracks or the mess hall, especially in the LST, looking into the faces of the kids and realizing they could not all survive the attack. I caught myself looking around and trying to imagine which ones would be killed. I blacked out faces arbitrarily—*He doesn't make it. He does. This one, no. This one, yes. No, yes, yes, yes, no, no, yes, no.* That is how it will be, just that arbitrary, only it will be a capricious god who pushes the blackout button.

Mornings were freezing cold. It was May. I had gotten to the point where I was coming to welcome the goddamned invasion. If I get blacked out, so be it, just as long as I didn't have to climb down that effing ladder with bleeding hands. We trained vigorously until summer, and then as quickly as it began, training ended.

Russo, who wrote sports for the paper, ran into the Quonset breathless with the news: "Over, it's almost over." He gasped and pointed to the shortwave. Boudine found some American news from Anchorage. A superbomb is what they were calling it. An explosion to end all explosions. Not like anything in human history, they said. At 8:15 a.m. Broad daylight. The entire city of Hiroshima destroyed, completely leveled by a single bomb. Most of the population killed instantly. Government officials were calling the weapon an atomic bomb, reported to have the destructive power of one thousand of the biggest bombs in our arsenal. A single bomb. Reports are that the entire horizon was lighted like a second sunrise before a great mushroom cloud filled the sky.

The announcer did not mention specific casualties or the population of Hiroshima, which I knew to be just short of half a million. It was not easy to see them as human beings in the same way I saw the boys gathered around the shortwave. I cared not a whit about them, so it didn't matter at that moment to me that for the people of Hiroshima there were no individual *yeses* and *nos*; no lottery for them, they were all blacked out in an instant.

I knew it was possible, theoretically possible, but not now, so suddenly, like this. Used on civilians? This Truman. His decision to make, and the little man made it. I wondered if the great man would have made it. To the little man it was Save American lives and the devil be damned. Of course Churchill had a major hand in this thing. A message loud and clear to Uncle Joe.

When all's said and done, terrible as this thing is, and the dubious ethics of war aside, this may have been the best way after all. That landing at Hokkaido would have been a fight to the death, far worse for us than Guadalcanal and Saipan and Okinawa combined. It would have been a ring of hell. Russo, Boudine, all the kids on *The Adakian*, even old man Hammett his own self, I wouldn't have wanted to see a single one of us blacked out. I'll pass on judgment for now since . . .

.18.

Comm-a-nists

OTHER THAN GOING to "21," Lilly and Dash liked to celebrate during the after-war healing and adjustment at Café
Society, the club down on Sheridan Square in the Village,
especially when the pianist Hazel Scott was playing there.
Hammett was absolutely wild about her. For him no one rivaled her technique, her brio; only Art Tatum and Bud Powell came close. And some singer too.

Café Society was classy and intimate and chic, the flavor
of a Paris bistro with a touch of Viennese elegance. Anyone
who was anyone in New York—or aspired to be anyone—
tried very hard to be seen here. Lilly and Dash were regulars.
So were Ed Murrow, Martha Graham, Ezio Pinza, Leopold
Stokowski, Gypsy Rose Lee, Cole Porter, Dorothy Parker,
Noël Coward, and Fiorello La Guardia and his wife Marie.
Such was the clientele of Café Society.

This evening wasn't really a celebration, although Lillian,
after doing her patriotic duty acting as goodwill ambassador

to the Soviet Union, finally did have another play running uptown—*Another Part of the Forest*, that family sequel to *The Little Foxes*—and it was doing good business. Since Hammett had been back in New York for well over a year already, this wasn't in any way a welcome home party, but once again his writing caught the breeze of a new development in the storytelling industry. The shortage of paper during the war led to the creation of paperback books. His novels and short stories were being released again in the new form for a new generation of readers. There wasn't much money in it for him, but he didn't need much money these days. He was being appreciated once again and that warranted this small celebration.

He had been despondent during much of his time back from the war. He spent most of it alone at the cottage in Katonah, where he said he was writing a bit. He was drinking a lot. He also spent more time at Hardscrabble talking with Lilly about new projects—hers. She contemplated another movie for Goldwyn—she liked to call him Goldwine now, in honor of FDR—and a play set in a New Orleans boardinghouse. She thought this idea for a drama too small; Hammett reminded her the world was nothing but a big boardinghouse that badly needed the two Hellman aunts to keep things going.

Almost everything Lillian wrote in those postwar days had a dispirited, melancholy quality she just couldn't shake. When she had been Kassandra warning about danger, there was energy. When she was herself part of the war or encouraging others to be brave and unselfish, she was passionate. But somehow after the great victory celebration, exhaustion set in. It lingered still, unshakable.

Hammett was not himself either, at least not his old self. His last three army years, time spent almost exclusively in the world of young men, writing editorials and drawing amateurish cartoons on deadline, even the physical training, had suited him so perfectly that he was lost when thrust back into civilian life. There was an absent quality, a distractedness about him he could no more break out of than Lillian could lose her world-weariness.

But Café Society, especially when Hazel Scott or Pearl Bailey or Billie Holiday, the club regulars, performed, brought out the best in each and both of them for an evening. Toward the end of an evening, after she played a late set, Hazel Scott usually joined them to talk politics and have a drink. Hazel was a civil rights activist before there were civil rights activists. When she went to Hollywood to make some movies, she made it quite clear from the get-go she would never play a maid or even wear an apron.

So she was mostly featured doing a specialty number at the piano in a nightclub while the stars entered and were being shown to their seats. The camera stayed on Hazel for a while and then followed the likes of Don Ameche and Janet Blair or Robert Alda and Joan Leslie to their table. Sometimes Hazel finished up her song, took her applause, and approached the stars to deliver a line or two before moving off camera.

Scott could never be the headliner in Hollywood that she was here in Manhattan. Hollywood wanted to showcase a light-skinned Negro woman with a virtuoso talent in very small doses to make white America sit up and take notice while giving the liberal producers a sense of personal satisfaction. That is how the world saw Hazel Scott until she started organizing other Negro studio performers. She was immediately labeled uppity and was soon after unwelcome in Hollywood. She had just returned to New York.

She finished "Mean to Me," and the lights came up to appreciative applause.

Hammett stood when Hazel approached. He intended to kiss her cheek. "You folks got a minute?" It was said mostly to Lillian. She pulled out a chair before Lilly could respond. It was early in the evening; she had just finished the second of four sets.

Hammett said, "Jesus, you're in some form tonight, young lady." It was true. She had played a Fats Waller medley at top speed with perfect classical piano technique.

"I always play great when I'm furious."

"Hollywood does that to a girl," Lillian said to her glass. She was drinking good Scotch. Hammett ordered one for Hazel.

"That's history, dearie. When RKO told me I'd never work there as long as I lived, I didn't believe them. I do now. I can't get a sniff from anyone."

Lillian: "So, that's the *furious*?"

"No, now the *furious* is that damn Committee they set up about who's a real American. I got subpoenaed again."

Of course they had read about it and thought a Congressional committee investigating who and what was un-American was pretty silly, political posturing, a facial blemish on democracy that would pass soon enough. Hazel Scott had been one of the first performers called to testify. Paul Robeson was another. "You've got to see these guys. They're the same Crackers my mama had to deal with when she toured the South with her band. Scum of the earth, let me tell you, I mean *scum* of the earth." Except for its chairman, the Committee was overwhelmingly and deeply Southern.

"Wanted to know if I was a Comm-a-nist—they say the word the way they say *Nig-ra*. If any of the people I worked with or any of my friends was Comm-a-nist. Don't laugh. These are scary men and they got themselves some real power now in this country. This thing has already cost me a small fortune."

It was 1948 and already HUAC, the House Un-American Activities Committee, chaired by J. Parnell Thomas, a successful stockbroker and Jersey City Republican, had begun calling movie actors, writers, and directors to testify and affirm their loyalty to America under oath. Hollywood was where the publicity was and the Committee stoked up plenty of it. Only Thomas chose to say *Communist* and *Negro* correctly.

"I thought you were all done with Hollywood before this who's American stuff."

"Apparently Hollywood wasn't all done with me. It's payback time. And like I said, it's already cost me real bucks." Scott shook her head, angry and bewildered. "You need to get a good lawyer and you need him for a while. That's not cheap. Then, three weeks after I testified, I get this bill from whatever you call those guys claiming I owe taxes since '39. My accountant tells me I can fight them but in the long run it's better to pay up and make them go away. The Committee's only the front door. Taxes is the back door. So they got you coming and going. We don't really stand much of a chance against them."

"We?" Said in harmony.

"Of course *we*. You don't think they're going to stop with a little colored girl who plays piano and sings in a dump like this, do you? They just start with us."

Lillian said, "But at least you've got New York. You can work here till your teeth fall out."

"That's what I'm trying to tell you. There ain't no *forever* work anywhere with these guys. Soon lots of people who are working ain't going to be working no more. I looked into their faces and it scared the hell out of me. I didn't show it, but they got to me."

Hammett said, "What are you going to do?"

"I got to testify again next month. Paul too. Their letter says they want to ask me extensively about my associates. 'My associates,' what the hell does that mean? Fortunately, I hear Paris is lovely this time of year."

Hammett said, "Careful about that. Talk to your lawyer first."

"Can't put him in jeopardy. He's a friend."

"He's your *lawyer*. He's protected."

"Glad you think so."

Lillian wanted to know how it felt to testify.

"Dirty. They're the scum and I felt dirty. They kept throwing the word *subversive* around, so I asked if they were going to investigate the Ku Klux Klan as 'subversive.' This Cracker jumps in and tells me, 'Young lady, the Klan is a venable—*venable*—American institution.' I said my family could vouch for how *venable* it was. He said right now the threat to this country was the Comm-a-nists, not the Klan, and did I know any of them. These guys want names and believe me, they're going to get names one way or another."

There was nothing, Hammett thought, they could do to him; rather, nothing they could do to him that would touch him. His concern was for Lillian. He was right about that. And wrong about their doing nothing to hurt him.

Hazel went back to the piano and announced as the lights dimmed, "Here's a ballad, ladies and gentlemen, that's been on my mind a great deal lately. Bing Crosby got himself some credit writing lyrics on this one. I hope he forgives my taking some liberties with the words."

She gave herself some tempo with her left hand and after exploring a number of possibilities with her right, she drifted into the refrain of "I Don't Stand a Ghost of a Chance with You." Hazel sang:

They need our love so madly
Or they'll behave quite badly . . .
No, we don't stand a ghost of a chance with them.
The man from Carolina
Thinks there's nothing finer
Than the Klan coming around for you . . .
So please look around for Commies,
Even if they're your mommies
Cause we don't stand a ghost of chance with them.

After a second chorus, she only played the melody. Beautifully.

The term *cold war* had already been minted and was in wide circulation on the nightly news. The homegrown Rats were free to come out and roam. It was the Weasels, as she dubbed them, those in service to the Rats, Lillian despised most. Weasels testified before the Committee, offered up names, made its work run smoother as it rolled over more and more lives, gathering tremendous momentum and no moss. The Weasels offered up Hammett's name far more often than Lillian's. She hated them doubly for that.

The Committee was legally authorized—the legality was particularly ironic given what was learned about Nazi legalities at the Nuremberg Trials—"under mandate of Public Law 601" to pursue Communists or Communist sympathizers for the public good. The punishment it meted out was supported by the Smith Act of 1940, which made it a crime to advocate the overthrow of the U.S. government and punishable by up to twenty years in federal prison.

Hazel Scott had been deemed uncooperative; she named no one. She was now performing in Paris. Others testified freely and the Committee publicly applauded their cooperation. These were the more widely acknowledged Weasels. Hammett kept the distinction between victim and Weasel very clear; he always had sympathy for human weakness. To Lillian anyone who gave a name for any reason whatsoever was pure Weasel.

All of this is old hat now, relegated to a brief, unfortunate period of American history by most historians, but certainly not by the Committee's victims. The damage done was far more widespread than history records; it devastated many thousands of un-American American lives. Hammett addressed the situation in a speech he gave at Cooper Union on "The Cop and the Criminal," ostensibly a talk about his approach to the detective story, but in fact a public defiance of what the Committee was doing to America. Hammett was no longer an effective public speaker.

Lillian made herself inconspicuous at the fringe of the audience. A cold sober Hammett began:

Let's get this straight from the start. The cop is paid by the state. The state gives him his badge, his gun, his billy club, and permission to use them, his uniform, and, if he's lucky, a police car to drive around in. His job is to protect the law-abiding public from criminals. So far, so good. There are times, however, when the crooks and the cops and the state are indistinguishable from one another, when they are all mixed together and aligned against the interests and guaranteed rights of those same law-abiding citizens.

We are in one of those times now. Those of you who may have had the ill fortune to have stumbled upon my *Red Harvest* or even *The Glass Key* probably know that I have dealt with just this sort of corrupt situation before in fiction. In both cases—I must tell you *Red Harvest* was based on a real miners' strike in Montana in which the company, the cops, and the government ganged up on the miners—in both cases my lone detective character is successful in combating the corrupt cops and turning the tide. Remember, though, that's just what happens in novels. In Montana, the bums mopped up the miners.

Lillian noticed Hammett's hand begin to tremble. He needed a drink. No way for her to get him one. He sipped some water.

> In America today the cops and the crooks and, of course, the judges and the pols are all in cahoots again. It happens periodically, usually around union busting time, which for them is all the time. They like to send very dramatic, unmistakable messages. What else is this preposterous Committee deciding who is American and who is not, but a shot across the bow? Sometimes the legal criminality even reaches the level of political murder.

For a moment Lillian thought he might talk about Jerry Waxman. She held her breath.

> What else was Vanzetti and Sacco if not precisely that? These new thugs dressed up as Congressional cops are surely nothing new. They crawl out of the woodwork whenever they have the chance. But every time they appear, we must each become detectives and reveal that they are really the crooks and not the cops.

Lillian scanned the crowd and picked out four men at least she was sure were government agents. Two were taking notes. She also recognized a legit guy from the *Times*, a gal from the *Trib*.

 If I was trying to turn this current mess into a detective story, I'd see it as an old-fashioned protec-tion racket. I'd set it in Mom and Pop's grocery store. Gunsels come in and want fifty bucks a week to keep trouble away. Pop tells them he's never had any trouble. They smash his front window. That'll be fifty bucks. Pop goes to the police. They'll watch his store when the thugs return, but they can't promise anything more. Next week the gunsels return for their fifty; a cop watches from across the street while the thugs break the other front window. The cop across the street smiles.
 So what's to be done? And who is there to do it? Certainly not the likes of Nick Charles. He's too tipsy for the task. He and Nora hobnob in the wrong social circles. A society murder is one thing. The protection racket is a very dirty, roll-up-your-sleeves business. Sam Spade? I don't think so. There are no beautiful dames involved and no big money to be made in a Mom and Pop grocery. No, the guy I need—the guy we need—is the Op. He's far tougher than either one of the others and breaking up this protection racket's going to take a bear of a man, a courageous brute. That's the Op. He's also a working stiff, and for me that counts for an awful lot when it comes to a matter of integrity.

As Hammett continued, his quiver became more pronounced. Lillian wanted to hold him, steady his hand. Hammett was never at his best in front of an audience, but he accepted this engagement as a necessary first skirmish in what he knew was now to be a long, difficult battle with the U.S. government. During the question period after his talk he really began to come apart, but he knew to keep his answers brief and somewhat cryptic. He needed a drink badly now, something the cops in the crowd could not miss. Hellman loved her Hammett very much at that moment.

In the cab uptown she took his hand and offered him a flask. He accepted it gratefully with a growl and a slow smile. Traffic was heavy. They didn't talk. He continued to shake, so she held his arm hard with both hands and tried to absorb his tremor.

They were almost at Columbus Circle when he said, "I could have done it better. But I had to take the first shot. I want them to know I'm ready."

"*We're* ready."

"My guess is they'll do me first. You're the bigger fish to fry."

"I beg your pardon." She made a pronounced huffy face and then smiled. "I hope that's not how they see it. But I'm ready for them too."

"You haven't been reading your Solomon."

"Uh-oh."

"The time to get and the time to lose deal. Sweetheart, this looks like our time to lose. Let's know that and see what we can hold on to."

"And let's see how many of those pricks we can take down with us."

"Jesus, you are something."

"Jesus had nothing to do with it." She passed the flask back to Hammett.

THE BRIGHTEST LIGHTS were placed behind the Committee, backlighting the Congressmen, making them more silhouettes from the witnesses' position than recognizable individuals. Somehow it seemed appropriate to Hammett that the inquisitors should be indistinguishable from one another. The lighting had been arranged for the movie and new television cameras shooting down from a platform behind the Committee. Smaller lights and cameras were set up before the panel to capture their questioning. The witness was the story.

When John S. Wood, the Committee's new chairman, a Democrat from Georgia—the Committee's dirty work was truly bipartisan—rapped for order, the large hearing room in Manhattan's Federal Building remained abuzz with conversation. He rapped again and the chamber, thronged to standing room with the curious, the politically engaged, the friends and enemies of the Committee, prospective witnesses, members of the press, radio, and television, still did not fall to silence. The chairman rapped twice more for order. In fact, as Mr. Wood gave the required Congressional justification for the Committee's investigative hearings on un-American activity, namely the subversion of the country's political and social system by Comm-a-nists, fellow travelers, and bedfellows, he could still barely be heard. Hammett and his lawyer were already seated at the witness table ready to be legally uncooperative. Finally the room quieted. The chairman turned up his microphone and said, "Please state your full name, address, and occupation."

Victor Rabinowitz, Hammett's attorney, interrupted. "Mr. Chairman." He covered his eyes in a salute. "The lights behind you, Mr. Chairman, are quite blinding and cause great discomfort when we have to look—"

"Nothing can be done 'bout that now, Mr. Rab-nowitz. Maybe we can correct that after the morning session."

Rabinowitz said, "I really must object, Mr. Chairman. These conditions are impossible and unfair to the witness, sir."

"Overruled. Please state your full name and—"

"Samuel Dashiell Hammett. Katonah, New York. I am a writer." Few people in the room had ever heard his voice, sweet and Southern and, today, strong.

"Mr. Hammett, are you now or have you ever been a member of the Comm-a-nist Party?"

"If, Mr. Chairman, your question is intended to determine if I am totally loyal to the United States of America, I welcome it because it allows me to speak of my proven participation. Even though the lighting does not permit me to see you all with absolute clarity, I can see that almost every member of the Committee is wearing a small American flag pin on the lapel of his jacket. It is a way, I assume, of professing the type of Americanism you would like to see on everyone who comes before you . . ."

"Mr. Hammett, you can speechify after you answer my question. Are you now or have you ever been a member of the Comm·a·nist Party?"

"Mr. Chairman, believe me, my speechifying days are long over. I was simply trying to assure you of how pure my Americanism is."

"Are you now or have you ever been—"

"Mr. Wood, I can assure you I will respond if you simply let me finish what I intended to say about our lapels. On yours I see our flag. If you"—here he addressed the cameramen—"shine your light on my lapel, you'll see four ribbons." He pointed them out. "Honorable discharge from the U.S. Army, World War I, and honorable discharge, World War II, Pacific Theater ribbon, and Sharpshooter's medal." He fingered the latter. "I'm particularly proud of this one. I was almost fifty years old when I qualified . . ." He paused while the room murmured. "I've taken the liberty to ascertain the military service of the Committee members." The murmur became a buzz again. "You, Mr. Chairman, did not serve at all. As is true of five of your eight colleagues. Two members did serve, one in the Procurement

Office of the War Department in Washington, the other in a Coast Guard recruitment office in his hometown. So my question to you, Mr. Chairman, is how do you determine someone's patriotism? Is it by a lapel flag or is it by actual military service to that flag?"

There was some applause followed by a very firm series of raps from Mr. Wood's gavel.

Hammett testified for two and a half hours before the chairman announced a lunch break. When the hearing resumed, the lights had not been moved. Questioning continued until almost five o'clock, when the Committee huddled to decide whether to ask Hammett to return tomorrow. There was more, it turned out, they wished to ask him, even though he had already invoked the Fifth Amendment forty-one times. Most witnesses who did not recognize the Committee's constitutional authority invoked the Fifth as follows: "I refuse to answer on the grounds that my answer might tend to incriminate me." Hammett's lawyer preferred he answer this way: "Mr. Chairman, I choose to decline to respond to your question because I do not believe you have the legal standing to question me and because any answer I give may tend to incriminate me." Hammett had to answer in precisely that manner after a brief discussion with Rabinowitz. Every time. This process took a very long while.

Although Hammett the Pinkerton man knew his way around a courtroom—he had testified at dozens of trials—he had never been a defendant before, nor were the rules of testimony here as fair. So when he was asked by the Committee lawyers if he knew or had ever met Charles Chaplin, that prompted a long discussion with his lawyer, who advised him to invoke the Fifth. Same with Walter Huston, Hazel Scott, Paul Muni, Sylvia Sidney, Paul Robeson, Lew Ayres, Dalton Trumbo, and dozens of others. Hammett knew that many of those people had already been blacklisted in Hollywood. He took the Fifth because admitting even to knowing them opened the way to questions about conversations he had with them, political and personal, which if he then refused to answer could open him to a charge of "contempt of Congress." Better to shut off the line of questioning early. Late with these guys meant "too late," especially when you didn't know what they knew or what other witnesses were likely to say about you.

By the end of the second day Hammett's Fifth Amendment total was well over seventy, prompting Chairman Wood to call him "the least cooperative witness ever to have come before me, sir."

"Did you ever consider the fact that your unconstitutional bullying might be the problem?"

"Is this how you have decided to show your so-called patriotism for this country?"

"Mr. Wood, I choose to decline to answer that question because my answer would bewilder a Yahoo like yourself . . ."

LILLIAN'S TRIAL BY INNUENDO occurred months later. Same place, same general cast of characters. Hammett had already heard from the Internal Revenue Service, the Committee's and the FBI's backdoor muscle. Starting back in 1937, Hammett's accountant, now deceased, claimed writing losses and expenses against profits of about $5,000 a year. Now, with interest and penalties, the IRS claimed Hammett owed $106,000. He could, of course, contest. Lillian's accountant told him he could never win—maybe settle for a bit less, but never win. Her accountant, in fact, was more concerned about what the IRS was going to try to get from Lillian. The IRS took possession of all rights to Hammett's work, past, present, and future. The government had kidnapped Spade, Nick Charles, and the Op. Hammett could not make a penny as a writer again.

Hammett was correct: Hellman was a far bigger deal, at least in New York, where *Another Part of the Forest* was still running on Broadway. Most observers were positive she would give up no one, but would she take them on directly and risk contempt? Would she denounce the Committee? Denounce the Weasels who had in their testimony already denounced her? Play it safe and take the Fifth? Or some combination of each? Drama was expected at the Foley Square courthouse.

Her lawyer, Joseph Rauh, had been in negotiations with Committee lawyers for weeks hoping to get a private hearing or at least some line on their approach to questioning. He told them his client was not now and never had been a member of the Communist Party but that she could not in good conscience so testify because she believed all political beliefs were protected by the First Amendment to the Constitution. Rauh came away from the meeting with a sense that Committee members intended to rough up Lillian Hellman, or to try.

She wore her hair short that day, permanent-waved with golden highlights, a small rust-colored beret sat rakishly on her head. She wore an elegantly tailored tan suit and carried a brown purse and a legal pad. Costume, she knew, was always important. She stopped and talked to no one, she smiled at no one. She was here for a fight. Although she was a frightened woman, there was no indication that she was a frightened woman.

Lillian had met privately before entering the hearing room—Rauh encouraged the meeting—with one of the Committee lawyers, Eric Weissen, in a witness room in the bowels of the building. Weissen told her how much he admired her work. "I studied you in college."

"Oh, God, son, you've got to do better than that."

"No, no, that's not what I mean. Actually, I took my parents to see *The Little Foxes* for their wedding anniversary. They were big fans too, admirers actually, so I wondered if you could . . ." Young Weissen produced a slim volume of *Foxes*.

Lillian stood. "Did you enjoy the play, Mr. Weissner, young as you must have been?"

"It's Weissen. Yes, very much."

"And you say you studied it. So does this ring a bell? 'There are people who eat the earth and all the people on it like in the Bible with the locusts. And other people who stand around and watch them . . .'"

Weissen said, "That's Uncle Horace. Act two, I think."

"Close. Alexandra at the end of the play. Sweet as you appear to be, dear boy, I think you're one of the locusts. And I won't stand around and watch. We are not playing a game here. You want to send me to prison for something I think. You want to take away my livelihood for something I believe. And not just me but so many of my friends. So for Christ's sake, kid, stop trying to schmooze me."

The young man put her book to his chest as though thoroughly offended. She had, he said, a completely wrong understanding of his position. The Committee already knew she had not been a member of the Party. Her political zeal was for the most part far more antifascist than it was pro-Communist and he planned to establish that in his questioning. But there were, he said, members of the Committee who simply believed her antifascist zeal to have been premature.

"How the—" Lillian caught herself before she said *fuck*. "How in the world do you determine just when is the perfect moment to begin to fight fascism, the most appropriate moment to act? After ten Jews are incinerated? Or is the proper number five hundred? Ten thousand? Three million? *Premature?* Think what you're saying, Weissner. It's insane. Call me overzealous, call me a rabid dog on the subject, but since everything I warned about since '35 has come true—and cost the lives of so many millions—call me *premature* publicly at your own peril. Shame on you and on your family if you believe that. And I can only conjecture you must have had family in Europe."

Invoking a sense of shame was a tactic that would have had no effect on any of the Congressmen on the Committee. They had parted with shame years ago. It might have had a slight effect on Weissen, but probably not. *Have you no shame?* was a question that always ought to be asked again and again in public of shameless men.

After swearing her in and having her state her full name, address, and occupation, the chairman asked the leading question. Lillian said, "Mr. Chairman, at the request of a member of this Committee I have composed in one of the Committee offices just a short while ago a statement in which I try to set straight my political history and clarify my position on testifying before this Committee."

"Does it respond to my question?"

"Directly, sir. I gave it to Mr. Weissner to be read aloud."

"Do you have this letter, Mr. Weissner?"

"Yes, sir, I do." Weissen began reading from the top. The chairman was distracted by a photographer who approached Lillian after all photos had been ordered terminated. Weissen read on in monotone. It was he who read into the record what might be the most enduring lines Lillian Hellman would ever write: "To hurt innocent people whom I knew many years ago in order to save myself is, to me, inhuman and indecent and dishonorable. I cannot and will not cut my conscience to fit this year's fashions, even though I long ago came to the conclusion that I was not a political person and could have no comfortable place in any political group."

Once her statement had been completely read into the record, Joe Rauh had two young assistants begin to distribute copies of it to the press and to other members of the Committee. Congressman Wood rapped for order. "No Comm-a-nist is going to give out their propaganda at my hearings." *Bam. Bam. Bam.* "Take your seats. De-sist!"

They did not de-sist. Rauh was on the microphone: "Mr. Chairman, Mr. Chairman, once my client's statement was read aloud by the Committee's own counsel, it became part of the public record and as such can be publicly distributed. We are well within our rights here to—"

Bam. Bam. Bam. "Sergeant at arms. Sergeant at arms." But no sergeant at arms appeared. Lillian's statement was papering the room. Wood said to the absent sergeant at arms, "I want these people removed from my hearing room."

Rauh turned quickly to Lillian: "That's it. They just screwed themselves. Let's get the hell out of here, *tout de suite.*"

They didn't quite run. But they weren't walking either. They didn't stop until they ordered drinks at the Mayflower Hotel bar.

THE AFTERMATH OF THEIR HEARINGS was dreadful, but dreadful in very different ways.

Lillian's IRS punishment was a major one, over $160,000 for back taxes and fines. There was no way she could even begin to pay it without losing Hardscrabble. She sold the farm for $67,000, a ridiculously low price for 140 acres in Pleasantville, New York, but all potential buyers knew of her need. It was the best she could do. In essence she was selling her farm to the government at bargain prices. She might have stayed in Katonah or on the Upper West Side with Hammett, if Hammett had been a free man.

Dashiell Hammett had been a member of the board of the American Civil Rights Bail Fund, a very left-wing organization that raised bail money for political activists—primarily union organizers—convicted of Smith Act violations. Four such men jumped bail and the government hauled Hammett into federal court to testify as to their whereabouts, which he did not know, and also to give the names of the contributors to the bail fund, which he refused to do. His sentence for contempt of court, of which he possessed a great deal, was six months in the federal penitentiary at Morgantown, West Virginia.

He wouldn't be doing hard time, Hammett assured Lillian, because he knew Morgantown, and it wasn't that sort of place. The only difficult thing would be not being able to help Lilly. Unlike the three war years, this absence wasn't of his choosing, and she had been badly damaged herself and could have used his help. The world still saw a surprisingly strong woman, a fierce battler for her beliefs. He saw her pride and confidence undermined by public insult and more so by the theft of her wealth. Money was about much more than money; and she had lost much more than money.

Hardscrabble was the symbol of everything she had made of herself—her plays and movies, her political commitments, her material and psychological freedom, her stature in the world. All was taken away, and this strong woman punished like a child, unfairly she thought, and sent off to bed without any supper. Her sweet corn nevermore to be sold down by the road. How stupid not to have known something like this could happen. She was forty-six years old.

Hammett had been wounded less and in those painful days helped her as much as he could. He was fifty-eight and looked seventy. His best advice, counsel he could not take himself, was for her to write her way out of this. But how the hell could she?

Lillian found good work for Zenia with friends of the Knopfs. Zenia's son Gilbert joined the U.S. Marines. She could not believe he was no longer a boy. Although Cedric Childs felt uncomfortable with the idea, Lillian talked him into making a legal claim for her farm equipment, charging it was his and that she had never paid him for it. "Think of it

this way," she said. "You'll be storing it for me. Yes, it's stealing, but it's stealing from thieves, you goddamned dope." She
shipped three tractors, a reaper, a dump truck, and a pickup
loaded with seed and fertilizer to Childs's farm. The cheat
gave her a measure of satisfaction.

One night in the New York apartment just before the
government was to ship Hammett off to prison, the two, each
looking particularly haggard, totaled up their recent losses. It
was clear to them Lillian was the big loser, because prison for
Hammett would be another escape, a refuge. It was a vodka
night and they were in their pajamas sitting on opposite ends
of a new sofa Hellman hadn't paid for yet.

"If they had to lock me up, I'm glad it's with crooks and
not cops."

"To crime." Lillian leaned across and tapped his glass.

"Morgantown is full of my kind of guys—bank robbers,
forgers, Ponzi schemers, kidnappers. Guys you can turn your
back on, guys you can trust."

"Didn't Raymond Chandler once do time there?"

"That daisy? Come on. Hammett will be running the
place in two weeks." The joke fell flat. If they were lucky,
it would be six months before there could be another night
like this.

"At least you'll come out sober."

"Violently so, as if that matters."

"Does to me. I want you to live forever."

"Hah."

They listened to boat horns for a while. Hammett said, "Go to Europe. They've shamed you here."

"No, they haven't. They've shamed themselves."

"Both things are true." After a while he said, "There was an empress of China, Tin Tang, a very wise and beautiful woman . . ."

"A lot like me, I'll bet."

"Very much so, but with slant eyes. She wrote remarkable poetry . . ."

"Not true. She wasn't beautiful."

"She was. Very. Her jealous uncle created a scandal about her that the people believed. They said her poetry was not remarkable poetry but poor poetry. So many people said her poetry was poor that she was ashamed to have written it . . ."

"But it was still good poetry."

"Not if her uncle and his falsehoods and the people who believed the falsehoods made her think about them and not about her poetry."

"So what did she do, this wise, beautiful Chinese empress?"

"She went to where her uncle and these unworthy people were not. She went to England."

"England?"

"They know you there, Lilly. They respect you there, Lilly. They love theater and they find you honorable. And they still speak a sort of English."

They each wanted to make love one last time. Each was too tired, too used.

The U.S. government shipped Samuel Dashiell Hammett to the Federal Correctional Facility at Morgantown, West Virginia. Soon after, Lillian Florence Hellman put herself on the *Queen Mary* bound for Southampton.

Dear Lillushka—

I've opted not to take the mysterious kishka approach. If the censor doesn't like what I say, let him pick up his scissors and earn his money.

I can do six months here standing on my head, holding my breath, juggling with my feet. I would not have said that three weeks ago. I craved a drink so badly I was biting my tongue, pounding my now-collapsed chest, and imagining my tears tasted like Beefeaters. My craving subsided because it had to, which is about the same as saying I willed it to. These months will be a good thing for me—if not for us.

I may have found my true calling. I clean toilets. By choice, since I had these options—laundry, kitchen, commissary, storage (hell, it's all storage here). All those other things required being part of a team. Toilets you do alone, and you can imagine how that suited me. But wait, there's more. I approach each toilet as an art restorer would a Vermeer: a soiled masterpiece to be brought back to its original glory. I pride myself on knowing what the glory once was.

I clean the warden's toilet, an honor bestowed only on a master craftsman, which I am already recognized as being. His is a deluxe model—"The Lady with Pitcher" of toilets, you might say. It is a massive thing, tall and wide and beautifully sculpted. Equipped with brush, rags, sponge, and cleanser, I scrub and cleanse it once a week. Not content merely with hygienic cleansing, I polish his throne to a high luster. You will never guess why, dear girl. To see my face. I achieve mirror brightness only in order to look at myself in its curved surface. I lie on the floor and look into the convex whiteness and see me as I was, or think I was, not as I know I am, full-cheeked, wide-browed, bright and hardy, instead of the skeletal bone-bag I've become. My toilet image, not the one I observe while shaving, is who I hope to resemble when my West Virginia days are done. I'm beginning to feel healthy.

Oh, in addition to my calling I have an occupation. A job that pays me in cigarettes. Some guys here take extension courses through the university. I write their papers for three packs of Camels. (No one here ever heard of Fatimas.) I got a B-plus on a five-pager on the League of Nations and a B on Melville's South Pacific novels. We've got some hard graders down here in the Alleghenies.

I also supplement life as a plagiarist by using the tonsorial skills I mastered up in Alaska. I'll change my name to Guido and open a small shop off Riverside when I get back.

I'm going to close with what should have been my open, call it burying the lead.

I miss you enormously. Enormously. But I mustn't allow myself to miss you at all. That creates some interesting tensions I can only release late at night in the privacy of my private room. I'm without a roommate, a boon given because I think I'm seen and treated as something of a celebrity. Most of the guards and many of the crooks know my work. Some find it admirable. In that sense I'm with my people and right where I belong.

Bisous, Lilly Marlene, or should I say Ta-ta?

Fondly, Pops

P.S. As I write this, I'm sure I'll live to regret doing it. It'll probably end up in a memoir about you—of which there are sure to be scores; or in some scholarly tome on "The Blacklist Casualties" before America moves on to its next diversion. Still, I want to say it, formally, at least once: I'd give my life, yes, my life, for what I think democracy is, but I will never let cops and judges ever, ever tell me what I think democracy is. My mind is my Upper House, my supreme Supreme Court.

Dash

.19.

Lost and Found

WHEN THEY LOOKED UP Dash and Lillian realized they'd lost the better part of a decade. It didn't matter particularly if that time had been stolen or misplaced. Lost was what mattered. They had spent much more time apart than together. Each in separate ways came to the same realization: time together eventually drove them apart. Apart for long periods was precisely what it took to stoke the desire each had for the other, or if not desire, at least mutual need.

Hammett got out of prison in early November 1953 after serving five months, one month off for good behavior. He said it was the warden's way of thanking the man who made his ass sparkle.

He was driven to the bus stop on the road to Morgantown by a guard getting off shift. No one was there to meet him. The guard would have driven Hammett into town but he lived in the other direction and his wife needed the car.

Hammett waited for the bus chilled to the bone because he was wearing the summer suit he went in with. Tall old man, stooped, suit collar up against the wind, holding a small valise. It was midafternoon; cloud cover gave the green hills a chalky look. He could as easily have been standing on Route 7 back in Hopewell, but he was glad his failed life was on display here rather than back there. People around Hopewell would all know Richard Hammett's smart-alecky kid, even as an old man.

A car pulled up to the bus stop. The driver rolled down the window. It was the guard who had dropped him off. "Get on in. I can't leave you out here."

"I thought you had to—"

"I did. Get in."

Most of the way back to town, the guard—his name was Paul Chase—apologized. *Don't know what I was thinkin'* got repeated a few times. "Man like you."

"Man like me, what?"

"Man serves his time and I dump him right like that. What was I thinkin'?"

"Thinkin' your wife needed the car."

"She does. I'll have to make it up to her some way. You got enough cash to get home with?"

The word hit Hammett unexpectedly. *Home.* It must mean something important; why else did it make him think he was one of those rare humans who had no need for it. The only home he had ever known was Lillian, a place that always scared the hell out of him. "Uh-huh. They gave me fare."

"Bus or train station?"

"I don't know. Which is best for New York?"

"Six of one. Bus is cheaper."

"Bus it is."

At the Greyhound Station Hammett offered to pay Chase for the ride. "Buy the wife some flowers." Chase refused to take money. They shook hands. Hammett dropped ten dollars on the floor of the passenger side.

The bus was full of *Bus-is-cheaper* people. College kids, Negro women with children, out-of-work guys, an ex-con— an Eisenhower-era "Bus of Fools" he had an urge to write about, and then a stronger impulse came, reminding him that he wasn't up to the task. Only Lillian was. And Lillian was in England. Unhappily ensconced in Belgravia, as it turned out.

He thought of a young Lillian with pleasure. What a piece of work was she. He thought all the way back to that despairing girl all but crushed by the reviews of *Days to Come*, but who as a woman had outbraved him, outwritten him, and who would certainly outlive him; in fact, had already out*lived* him. The thought of what she was pleased him. He could not love, simply wasn't capable of it. But he loved her. Only he did not love her all the time.

America's wasteland rolled past his window. Bus routes in Pennsylvania were rarely scenic. Decaying factories, towns half closed, car lots, junkyards, railroad sidings, loading docks, cement and dirt and ashes. During moments when the sun broke through nothing was absolutely hideous, leading Hammett to remember Billy Wilder saying to Lillian, "No such thing as ugly, darling, there is only bad lighting."

The bus stopped in every town that had three churches and five bars. Forty minutes was the longest time between stops. The same people got off and on. At every stopover, no matter how brief, Hammett walked across the street to a bus-stop bar and threw down a shot and a beer. In Scranton he had a second whiskey before he left. He didn't pay much attention to his money.

Back on the bus for the last leg of the trip, he looked at his knobby-boned fingers. In their time these hands had held a pickax and shovel, loaded freight cars, tapped telegraph keys, formed a fist that struck bone, moved across a typewriter, hoisted drinks; these were fingers he only noticed during the flush times when he got a manicure. They often prompted compliments from a manicurist and on more than one occasion led to an erotic encounter, manicured fingers unbuttoning, unhooking, petting, fondling. A man was his hands, Hammett realized just now that he saw his own as pale and skeletal. As he was now. He even managed to shave these days without seeing himself in the mirror. He felt more spirit than substance, already a ghost, not invisible quite but eerily translucent, milky white. Faint and frail. Hammett was not particularly ill or terribly old.

During a twenty-minute stop in Newark, he called the West Side apartment, not expecting anyone. He let the phone ring many times. He was disappointed at not being disappointed. He had hoped against hope she'd be there. She wasn't waiting for him at the gate when he was released. So at least when he got to New York . . . He assumed there were practical, perhaps even legal reasons for her absence. He'd been wounded, hors de combat. Lillian remained an important political target. Hammett decided to go straight to Katonah when the bus got to midtown. He had to borrow a dollar from a stranger.

THE ENGLISH DIDN'T HAVE their own Joan of Arc. For a year and a half, in liberal political circles at least, Lillian Hellman played the role. Her treatment as an expatriate heroine had its benefits—writing income, a few loyal friends, and one memorable evening with Charlie Chaplin, who had left the States for the London premiere of *Limelight* and found his reentry permit revoked. In the expanding world of what and who was un-American, Joe McCarthy and J. Edgar Hoover had become powerful deciders. McCarthy's Senate subcommittee and Hoover's FBI also controlled the IRS and, as in Chaplin's case, the U.S. Immigration Service—in other words, controlled money and movement—and God only knows what else they could manipulate.

Chaplin, insulted and angry, had announced to the world that he'd never attempt to return to America again. It was in no way a defeated man who sat to Lillian's left in Noël Coward's dining room. Lillian immediately told him of being passed off as his sister on her trip to Madrid in 1937. Chaplin loved it but turned the subject back to the madness infecting America. Lillian said it would pass eventually and that they'd be able to continue on with their careers soon enough. He looked at her in disbelief. "Such profound optimism always astonishes me. Pleases me too."

"I'm just more American than you, *n'est-ce pas?*"

"True, true. Our situations are quite different, my dear." Lillian hated being called *my dear*; this time she allowed it. "I'm just a music hall urchin from the alleyways of East London, so in a sense I've been sent home. You are an important literary personage . . ." He let the word sound French. ". . . a child of the Deep South—Georgia is it?"

"Alabama. New Orleans."

"—and you've been sent away. You're being punished, naughty girl, whereas I'm just picking up my life where I left it off years ago." Chaplin dropped his head, scowled, and lowered his voice: "But tell me, as one political criminal to another, what'd they get you for?"

Lillian matched him perfectly in hugger-mugger style: "Premature antifascism."

Chaplin's guffaw stopped all conversation at the table. He announced, "I'm crushed. They exile this girl on a charge of 'premature antifascism' and they only get me as a 'Communist sympathizer.' I'm desolated." He turned to his wife Oona: "Have you ever known anyone more premature than I?"

"Only Humphrey Bogart and Cary Grant and Jimmy Stew—" There was laughter, which Chaplin quieted.

"Thirty-five. I started writing *The Great Dictator* back in '35. What was more antifascist than that? Nineteen thirty-five, for heaven's sake. If that's not pre-premature, what is? I'm going to write that Charlie McCarthy a very strong letter."

The personal advice Chaplin tried to leave with Lillian was to renew herself with her work. "You know we are only our work, my dear. They . . ." He waved his hand. "They will pass. If the work is good and true, it will live on. And you will live on with it. Live in time, not in a country. I give my address as Posterity Street. Why don't you move into my neighborhood?"

"Because I'm not Chaplin."

The statement created a pause. So Lillian added, "You are surer of your work than I. Your reputation gives you an enormous margin for error. You are Charlot everywhere in the world. Charlot can appear inadvertently to trip the rich villain with his cane and have him fall ass-first into the cake batter. You can do that anywhere in the world and get a laugh with it."

"Yes, of course, but no longer in the United—"

"Remember Hammett?"

"I do, yes."

"Well, he once had something of the reputation you talk about. Not internationally perhaps, but certainly back there. He lived on Posterity Street, but they are taking even that address away from him. There is this constant drumbeat of criticism of all his work, a so-called reevaluation of his entire career—all part of the political indecency—and frankly it's killing him."

"So why then aren't you with him now?"

They looked into one another's eyes until Lillian looked away.

The benefits of London aside, Lillian did not like the city, disliked it in fact. The weather displeased her. The strong remnants of class and its palpable anti-Semitism sickened her. She felt the constant scrutiny of the house guest. The hypocrisy of liberals who talked strong and acted weak disgusted her. Still, it was too soon to return. All reports from home indicated that things were getting worse with a befuddled Eisenhower in the White House and Nixon, plucked right off the House Un-American Activities Committee, at his right hand. And in London at least there were cashable checks for writing scripts and articles.

She called the apartment often—Hammett had been left a key—hoping he'd pick up. She also called Katonah and Santa Monica without success.

Very late one night or early on a dark morning she called Katonah and he did pick up. "Thank God," she said.

"You're welcome, I'm sure."

"How long have you been there?"

"Five weeks, six. Can't be sure. I'm waiting for the electricity."

"No electricity. It's cold. Are you eating?"

"Apples."

"Apples?"

"Apples mostly. And sourdough rolls."

"Do you have a pencil and some paper?"

"Paper. No pencil."

"For Christ's sake, find one." She waited.

"Okay."

"Write this down. It's Cedric's number. Call him and have him come over."

"Okay."

"Promise?"

"Cross my heart."

"Promise."

"Absolutely."

"I miss you." Hammett said nothing.

When she hung up, Lillian realized that of course he couldn't be trusted. She called Childs herself and asked him to please go over and "make things right for Hammett." Hammett, of course, never did call Childs.

There was a great deal to be "made right for Hammett." Childs continued his visits so that things became reasonably right—heat, a supply of food. Thereafter whenever Lillian called and Hammett answered, the conversation was rational at the very least. Childs confirmed that Hammett had begun taking better care of himself. He was keeping himself cleaner. He did a bit of cooking now. Kept the cottage in a semblance of order. Childs paid the electric bills.

Childs had wood delivered to Hammett for winter. He left money at the market and the gas station that Hammett could draw against but which was never used fully. The cottage was full of books, and Childs had no idea how they got there or who paid for them. He did see postal wrapping paper around the place and assumed someone else was subsidizing Hammett's intellectual life.

Lillian asked if Childs thought Hammett was writing.

"Hard to tell. There's a different piece of paper in the machine each week. I don't stay very long. I'm sure I make him uncomfortable."

"It's not you, it's me he's upset with. How about the drinking?"

"It might be pretty bad sometimes. Lots of bottles to get rid of. Don't know how he gets it either. But I have a feeling he's been a lot worse."

"Is he a danger?"

"To himself, you mean?"

"Yes, to himself."

"No, I don't think so. You talk to him too. What do you think?"

"He doesn't always answer when I call. When he does, he's more and more like his old self."

"So you've answered your own question."

"But you *see* him. Is he old-looking? Is he broken down?"

"Old maybe, but not broken."

The sun came out and Lillian decided to walk to Harrods to buy a scarf. The air was chill but the sun on her face felt marvelous.

The store was crowded but not jam-packed. Still, it bothered her that she was jostled near the handbag counter. Crowded in London was different from crowded in New York; space normally remained much more respected here. Lillian glared after the woman who had bumped her sideways and disappeared.

Lillian stopped to look at leather bags. The bags were wonderful, from Florence and staggeringly expensive, but wonderful. A large brown shoulder bag, soft and light, suited her perfectly. She saw herself traveling with it comfortably; it would, in fact, encourage her to travel. She switched shoulders and took a few steps with it. It felt just right and it lifted her spirits. Lillian asked the saleswoman the price. Forty-five pounds, around two hundred dollars. An extravagance she thought she could afford.

The saleswoman wondered if she'd like to see some other Italian leather goods. Gloves, wallets, sewing boxes?

Perhaps a wallet for Hammett. She hadn't bought him anything for a very long while . . . since . . . forever.

In the showcase alongside the wallets were leather-bound notebooks. This was her immediate inclination, a notebook for a writer, until she realized that Hammett would see it not as a gift but as an obligation. So a wallet it was. Not the long leather fold that slipped into a jacket pocket—Hammett wasn't wearing many suit jackets these days—but a thin, stylishly black billfold for a pants pocket. Nineteen pounds.

Lillian's check was accepted by the saleswoman, who needed a manager to sign the slip and initial the check. He asked for identification; she produced her passport. Everything was fine.

Rather than have the handbag wrapped, Lillian said she wished to carry it home on her shoulder. Might she transfer the contents of her old bag and have that one wrapped instead? Of course, madam. And the wallet, she'd like that gift wrapped as well. Why certainly. And here is your receipt. Thank you for your patronage.

Lillian felt fine, reinvigorated in fact, as she stepped out onto the Brompton Road. The chill in the air made her decide to take a cab home. A large red-faced man in a black coat and a black bowler suddenly blocked her path. "Excuse me, madam. I must ask you to return to the shop with me. There has been a discrepancy."

"—the hell out of my way. I'm getting a cab." Lillian was sidestepping the man when a smaller man put his hand on her shoulder. She smacked it away.

The large man said, "Not here, madam. It's better in the privacy of—"

"Privacy, my ass. Get the hell out of my way." Now they had her pretty well wedged between them.

"You have a receipt for your purchases?"

"Who the hell are you anyway?"

"Your receipt, please."

"Get your goddamned hands—"

"Don't let's allow this to be a public situation. Just show me your receipt and you'll be on your way. Nothing untoward."

The *untoward* got to her. "There's nothing fucking *untoward*. Two items, I purchased two items. This bag. This wallet. Here." The receipt was in the bag with the wallet. She fished it out. The man looked at it carefully, nodding the whole while. Lillian expected an apology.

The man said, "The item in your coat pocket, madam, I don't believe is quite covered by this receipt."

Lillian put her hand in the pocket indicated and touched something that did not belong there. A pen of some sort. Her surprise quickly replaced by comprehension, Lillian put out her arms and said, "Okay, you got me. Put me in cuffs."

"Please let's go back to the privacy of the shop."

Why the fuck does he call it a shop! *It's the most famous fucking store in the world.*

Lillian walked between the men back into the *shop*. In the elevator she said, "Just for the hell of it, why don't you show me your identification."

They did. Store detectives. Hammett once held such a job, briefly. He quit. He identified too closely with the shoplifters.

In an upstairs office, she sat before a desk with the detectives standing behind her by the door, hats in hand, apparently waiting for someone important. The store manager entered, a Mr. Kittle, and offered to shake her hand. He was accompanied by another man in a tan raincoat who remained nameless.

Mr. Kittle asked to see *the item*. Lillian handed him a beautiful silver pen, an *item* she might have bought had she seen it in the showcase.

Kittle dismissed the two cops and said, "Since you possess no receipt for this item, Mrs. Hellman, I must assume it to be confiscated." He paused for a response. She offered none.

"We would never wish to accuse publicly someone of your renown of—"

"Who he?" Lillian threw a thumb back over her shoulder without turning.

"... the theft of an item from Harrods."

"I said, 'Who he?'"

"I'm not important. I'm only here to witness the proceedings and make sure there is justice done in case . . ."

"In case what?"

"In case things begin to spin out of control. We wouldn't want a mere misunderstanding to grow into some mad cause célèbre by misjudgment or mischance."

"I'm sure *we* wouldn't. By the way, you're not the little *putz* who put this thing in my pocket downstairs? No, you wouldn't be. You'd have used a woman for that, wouldn't you?"

The man behind her said calmly, "Please consider your practical options, Miss Hellman."

She said, cutely, "It looks like this poor little un-American Jew-girl doesn't seem to have a great many options against big, strong British gentlemen like yourselves. Still, I'm inclined to go the *Please-call-my-lawyer* route."

"Be very, very sure about that decision," the voice said. "Harrods also has a very big stake in the situation. When I entered the store I was stopped by a reporter from the *Telegraph* who wondered what I was doing here. In terms of public opinion, the press trumps the law in England, I'm afraid."

Lillian realized then that un-Americans like her not only had to fight Congressional committees, the FBI, the Internal Revenue Service, various other governmental agencies, and professional reputation spoilers, the blight had spread to foreign governments as well. Word had gone forth from some office in Washington to another office in Whitehall—*Get her!* And on the first floor in crowded Harrods on a busy shopping day, they did just that. Hammett's *Crooks and Cops* were of course one and the same, only now internationally so. Amazing. Disgusting. Yet impressive in its way.

Since she had nothing to do that afternoon, Lillian opted to stay silent, curious to see what would ensue. Evening came. The mystery man said, "Fifteen minutes more, I'm afraid, Miss Hellman. We can place you under arrest formally. I can then call my friend at the *Telegraph*."

"Or, of course," said Mr. Kittle, "you may offer to repurchase the item."

"As a souvenir of my memorable visit to Harrods?"

The voice behind said, "Of your visit to the United Kingdom, I believe." A threat.

Lillian recalled Chaplin's comment: *So why then aren't you with him now?*

FINALLY, DASHIELL HAMMETT was Lillian's United States of America.

She returned to him after an enforced absence of sixteen months. Foolishly, she chose to surprise him at the cottage in Katonah. The visit was not impetuous. She called Childs first to get an idea of what shape Hammett was in then. Childs said, "He's skinny and he's drinking. It's not really awful, but what he needs more than anything is a good home-cooked meal and some conversation."

Lillian called Katonah from her New York apartment. She simply wanted to be sure he was there. They had talked a bit about their lost years over the phone, not in any great detail and not where they could see what they were saying. She intended to tell him her Harrods story at length and in depth.

They needed hours and hours across a table, across a sofa and even a bed, to be Lilly and Dash again, if that were ever possible. She doubted it could happen quickly.

He doubted it could happen at all. Perhaps something new could be created.

His voice on the phone was deep, resonant, without slur or interruption. He had just started the day's drinking. Lillian said, "Before we were so rudely interrupted," and immediately wished she hadn't.

"Where in the world are you?"

"The city."

"I'll bet you miss London more than I miss London."

"I'll take that bet and raise you ten. Tell me, young man, how's your health?"

"My health is fine. I just don't know where I put it."

"Yuk, yuk, yuk."

"Actually, it's my gun shoulder, it's sore as hell."

"What've you been shooting?"

"Haven't been. That's the problem."

"How bad?"

"More than annoying."

"See a doctor?"

"Only doctor I know is a Commie, so how can I trust him?"

"I know a reliable true-American doctor. Interested?"

"It'll pass. Rheumatic condition, I think."

Lillian asked with unconvincing casualness, "So what're you doing up there all alone, as if I didn't know." She hoped he was writing a Spade script at least, or a family memoir at best.

He said, "Reading."

"Marx or Lenin?"

"Mao Tse-tung."

"Who?"

"Actually, Lao-tzu."

Lillian had already planned the home-cooked meal—fried chicken, potato salad, coleslaw, chocolate mousse—and a trip to Katonah even before she said, "You interested in coming down here? We can play a game of rescue-one-another like in the old days."

"That's the best offer I had since Mayer bought *The Thin Man*."

"We could dress up like Nick and Nora, thirties-style, and do the town. Sound good?"

"Only if you let me pick up girls."

"Let you? I'll solicit."

"I'm on the next train."

"No. You stay right where you are."

Lillian hadn't worn an apron for well over a year, hadn't done any real cooking in all that time, and certainly had not been this happy while not doing it. She was humming quietly as she mixed the batter for fried chicken that she had learned in her aunts' kitchen from Sophronia as a girl in New Orleans. Surprisingly, Zenia didn't know it, so Lillian taught it to her at Hardscrabble. Oh, Hardscrabble. The loss still throbbed.

She cut up the chicken expertly, dipped each piece, and deep-fried them in cooking oil. She watched them turn golden in the oil as she rolled them with a long fork. Not so quietly she began to sing. *"I've got a crush on you, Sweetie Pie . . ."*

The chicken cooled on a plate as she prepared the potato salad he loved. Dill was her secret there. For the coleslaw she whipped up her own mayonnaise; she squeezed a lemon flat to give it the bite that pleased Hammett. Her happiness, rare as it was, began to feel comfortable again.

She packed the dinner in a picnic basket even though it was too cold and too late for a picnic. She took two bottles of champagne out of the closet but put one back before she left. Where were the car keys?

As she drove upstate via the Triborough, the sunset to her left begged attention; orange clouds piled on flaming coals. The world became beautiful again, at least for this evening. The aroma of the fried chicken, her fried chicken, *their* fried chicken, created just the right amount of expectation.

Katonah was almost dark as she drove through cautiously—the town was a well-known speed trap; she'd been ticketed there once. Lillian welcomed expectation's last obstacle. She remembered the turnoff to his cottage, which she used to miss as often as not. His place was at the end of the road.

All the lights were on in the cottage, a welcoming sign. The front door was open wide. That made her smile. She carried the dinner inside, expecting some sort of surprise.

The front room was a mess, wherever she looked disorder. He did not jump out and shout *Surprise.* He did not walk up behind her and tap her on one shoulder and duck the other way for an embrace. Lillian said, "Okay, where are you? Let's clean up this place." She cleared some used plates from the table and put down her basket.

Hammett wasn't there. The back door was also wide open and Lillian's long shadow led her outside to look toward the woods that encroached. She saw a something, a looming shadow, or thought she did. She heard a something, a barking, or thought she did. The moon had risen. The night was clear.

"Hammett. Don't fool around. I'm serious."

She saw movement now, in the trees, out beyond the trees. "Damn you, Hammett, don't ruin this." As Lillian stepped out toward the first stand of trees she almost tripped over something. It was a pair of pants. She instinctively picked them up and began folding. Then a pair of white shorts. Those she left.

She stopped abruptly and caught her breath, striking a pose she'd have thought silly in one of her actresses, one hand on her chest, mouth agape, the other hand to her forehead.

Hammett was naked in the moonlight, a long gray man bent backward like a birch. He was holding a bottle low at his side. He dropped his head and raised it up to the moon and howled, a sound so mournful, so unhuman, so wolflike. It was Lillian, not Hammett, who fell to her knees and closed her eyes.

Lillian heard the howling continue and realized she had to go toward him, help him come back to something. She suspected it would be dangerous. He would flail at her touch.

She came up behind him saying his name, calling him *Samuel*, loudly yet comfortingly. Howl still followed howl. A man, a drunken, broken man, a man she loved, baying at the moon. She sensed that only her touch could make him stop.

Lillian wrapped her arms strongly around his waist—my god he was thin—and continued to call his name. Hammett tried to throw her off at first; his efforts flagged but he ended his howling. He tried to pull away from her and stumbled; she hung on dearly and they fell in a tangle on wet grass. His attempt to howl when he was grounded produced only gutturals and then coughs. At no point did he attempt to attack or even repel her. Still she clung to him. It almost became an embrace. She was stronger, finally, than he.

Hammett quieted in time.

"Think I can get you up?"

"Not. Yet."

"You tell me when." The ground was very cold and very wet; still they remained.

"Now?"

"Okay."

Lillian Hellman helped Dashiell Hammett off the ground, to his feet. She offered him his pants. He required help putting them on.

They were near the back door when he said, "D.T.'s. All ruined. D.T.'s."

He was shivering.

She gave him a long hot shower—at least until the hot water gave out—dried and dressed him, and put on the tea water. He remained cold and silent for a very long while.

Hammett sat wrapped in Lillian's arms, a quilt covering him from his neck to the floor. She patted his head with a towel as though he were a child. For some reason she said, "You're not supposed to know you're having the D.T.'s when you're having the D.T.'s."

"If I can say it, it means I'm away from them."

"So say it to me again."

"I don't have to now. I'm back. Thank you."

"So say *thank you* again."

"Sorry, only one per customer."

.20.

Ends

SHE SOBERED HIM UP at the end.

She got some color back in his cheeks; in fact, she even managed to give him those cheeks by putting some weight on him. She had the cottage neatened up by a cleaning service and retaught a sober Hammett how to live in it. She visited once a week whenever possible. Even more often, he stayed with her in Manhattan.

Little by little her career returned. Money—not big money but steady money—was finding its way to her bank account and through her to him. She brought her interpretation of Jean Anouilh's *L'Alouette*—*The Lark*—to Broadway. It was about Joan of Arc. In this version of the tale, Joan lives. As Hammett had been urging for years, she directed the play herself and realized she was good at it.

Leonard Bernstein, her political fellow traveler, did some incidental music for the play and afterward Lillian asked him to consider a musical version of Voltaire's *Candide*.

She told Lenny at one of his lavish East Side soirees, "Look around. If this isn't the best of all possible worlds, what the fuck is?"

No one saw through American naïveté in 1956 more clearly than Lillian Hellman. Richard Milhous Nixon was a heartbeat away from the presidency, and what could be more dangerously or darkly comic than that? If America needed anything right now, Lillian decided, it was a strong dose of someone like Voltaire. But America did not have a Voltaire; it only had Hellman and Bernstein to invite him over.

The night Hammett was to accompany her to the Broadway Theatre for the premiere of *Candide*, the sudden pain in that gun shoulder almost doubled him over in the limo. She told the driver to return to the apartment. Hammett insisted they go on. "I'm a selfish bastard, there's no doubt, but I don't upstage a coronation. I'm fine. I'll be fine."

"Good. Because I was just about to call Sigmund and tell him I've discovered the first confirmed case of unambiguous vagina envy."

Throughout the performance she couldn't help notice him wincing or biting his lip. He could not applaud but instead blew kisses to her. Lillian held his left hand throughout. When they got back to the apartment, he took two more painkillers and went to bed.

Lillian Hellman had indeed come all the way back. For her, New York really had become the best of all possible worlds. Briefly.

Hammett's ailing gun shoulder perplexed two highly regarded Park Avenue doctors, and since they were perplexed they settled on a particularly painful "rheumatoid arthritic condition," a diagnosis as vague as a wish but certainly nothing life-threatening. It was a diagnosis a stoical Hammett was glad to try to soldier his way through. He called it his "shootin'" pain.

Lilly and Dash did not socialize a great deal thereafter. He did some of the cooking when he could; she most other times. A relative of Zenia, a cousin she said, stayed over on weekends, and then more often, to take care of Hammett's increasing needs and later to cook and clean full-time.

Hammett read books on Asian art and philosophy mostly but also the works of the English Romantic poets. When he found one he admired, Coleridge for example, he read the autobiography and then collections of his correspondence as follow-ups. As far as Lillian was concerned Hammett was living well and thoughtfully through other writers' lives.

In the evening they spoke about her work. Lillian said she wanted to write another family drama and direct it herself. She had been dreaming a great deal about her father Max and his two sisters, all now deceased. An incident she observed as a girl in the rooming house had begun to emerge more and more clearly as she drifted off and then woke from sleep. Max had come down the back stairs looking strangely confused and upset; Hannah followed, her arms forward, either beseeching or accusing, Lillian then couldn't be sure, but something had occurred on the stairs. Whatever it might have been struck Lillian now as extremely important. The stuff of drama.

Just as they had done all those years ago with the Drumsheugh story, so now they began to suppose dramatic relationships among the Hellmans, as they had among the Marxes.

"Sexual?" Lillian wondered.

"Ever see them kiss?"

"I can't honestly remember. Why?"

"Just fomenting."

THE DOCTOR WHO FINALLY conjectured accurately about the gun shoulder had a practice in Katonah, not on Park Avenue. His name was Feldman. The nature of the pain, Dr. Feldman believed, indicated that it was referred, probably from the chest area.

Lung X-rays at Lenox Hill Hospital revealed cancer. Advanced. Inoperable.

They would share the time left as they had since Lillian's return from England. A hospital bed was installed in the West Side apartment. Hammett avoided it by making very bad old vaudeville jokes: "Oy, Doctor, Doctor, do you know I've got a bed cough? So get out of bed. No, no, it's not a bed cough, it's a bed cough . . . a very bed cough."

Lillian invited him back into her bed. He couldn't do very much, but he felt as though he had come home.

Lillian hired a nurse to take care of him, mostly to administer his pain medication. She stayed in the guest room.

One day after Hammett found it necessary finally to take to the hospital bed for reading comfort, Lillian entered the room and saw that he had his hand on the nurse's ass. The young woman was turned away from him preparing his medication. His hand on her ass meant absolutely nothing to her. It seemed to mean the world to Hammett, which the nurse apparently understood. Lillian smiled. Hammett was being Hammett in a world that no longer minded a great deal.

Lillian was willing to carry him to the very end even though that might take many months.

She thought the end had come when his breathing became so shallow, so labored he lay on his bed like a bird fallen to the pavement. The doctor ordered an ambulance that brought him again to Lenox Hill. Lillian waited patiently in the hallway. This was the very end. She imagined the situation reversed and wondered what she would want Hammett to do for her. Only to have him tell her he loved her. Only that.

She then realized the reverse gift—her declaration of love past and future—was something he already had. She further realized that dying was so fucking hard to do it didn't really matter what anyone else thought about it.

But dying wasn't only for the dying. It was as much for who got left behind. The perfect gift for him came to her then. A priest. She'd give him a priest.

The hospital provided Lillian with a name and a parish. She sent a cab to St. Stephen's. It took the old man an hour to come down from the Bronx. Father Gerrity it was, who told Lillian with a brogue that there was no such thing as a lapsed Catholic, only comatose ones. Lillian was in the room as Gerrity administered last rites. She believed Hammett rolled his eyes in her direction. *Oy, Doctor, Doctor.*

The next morning his breathing deepened. His face took on a weak expression, an almost smile, a faint thoughtfulness, faint disapproval. The doctor was hopeful. Hammett was beginning to come back and Lillian welcomed the reprieve. She still wanted a Hammett, any Hammett, in her life. It looked as though she would have him. But no.

DASHIELL HAMMETT ALWAYS ASSUMED he'd be buried at the Arlington National Cemetery. It fell to Lillian to see to an interment befitting the man who had been a U.S. Army sergeant in two world wars.

There was a concerted campaign by Hammett's implacable political enemies to deny him such a burial. A sample editorial in the *Journal American* ended as follows: "A soldier, yes, certainly. An honorable American, not by a long stretch. Mr. Hammett was an enemy of the United States as we know and love it, a man convicted of traitorous un-American principles and activities. To allow him to lie in such hallowed ground, next to true American heroes, would be an affront and an insult to the service of loyal and true Americans."

There were many such pieces in many such places.

Lillian prevailed in the legal and public battle to have Sergeant Samuel Dashiell Hammett buried with full military honors at Arlington. Afterward, on the Dick Cavett television show, Lillian said, "You know, it's beautiful in Washington this time of year. Cherry blossoms fill the air. You can come and read the Constitution for yourself—not some tortured Supreme Court interpretation. In the evening you might want to take in a new play, *Toys in the Attic.* It's by some bright young thing, named Lillian, who . . ." The APPLAUSE sign flashed on. ". . . and . . . and I'd strongly recommend you take a cab ride across the Potomac to Arlington National Cemetery. Standing there you will have some sense of how much our freedom actually costs . . ." She swallowed. "I have a friend buried there. Dashiell Hammett. The writer. He is in section 12, site 508." She repeated the site for emphasis. "I really don't want him to be alone for too long. So please stop by and introduce yourself. He's a good listener."

HALF AN HOUR before Dashiell Hammett became that forever silent good listener, he began his tumble toward and through oblivion. Lillian was called away from a party.

Hammett was alive, still alive when she got to him. He was being allowed to die by the doctor. Hammett signaled her closer with his eyes. She thought he said, "I may not live to see you again, Miss Amanda . . ."

Lillian flushed, put a hand to her chest, batted her lashes, and said, "My word, Captain Beauregard, you have declared your love for little ole me so sweetly and so often, I'm having the devil's own time not pulling off my beautiful undergarments and lying down with you right here in this gazebo." She slid toward him on the bed.

Hammett's eyes smiled and beckoned her very close. His voice was scratches in air coming from parched lips to her shelled ear. Not words, only scratches.

Author's Note

All lives are mysterious. What we do not know about ourselves is only exceeded by what we cannot know about others, which is why novelists try to live so intimately with the characters they create. Fiction writers may think they've gotten to the heart of the mystery if they create characters out of whole cloth. I've never believed that. Mystery is as inherent in the human condition as our contradictory emotions, our need to love and be loved, and our impulse to create and destroy.

When I first encountered Lillian and Dash in their own words and in biographies written by others, I knew it would have been foolish—and unnecessary—to re-create them as characters in a novel with different names. The *who, what, when,* and *where* of their lives were all pretty well established by the biographies and autobiographies. The mysterious *why*—the mystery, the fiction writer's domain—was not. So I embarked.

For me interwoven fact and fiction—the hybrid "fictional biography"—is the best path to satisfying novelistic truth. In *Aspects of the Novel*, E. M. Forster writes, "A memoir is history, it is based on evidence. A novel is based on evidence + or − *x*, the unknown quantity being the temperament of the novelist, and the unknown quantity always modifies the effect of the evidence . . ." To remain faithful to the facts—the "evidence"—and still arrive at the "truth" I hope for in a good novel has been my goal in *Lillian & Dash*.

So in essence what remains factual in this novel are all those things a reader would encounter in a good Hellman or Hammett biography—and there are many. Chronology is by and large untouched, as are their family backgrounds and literary output, their travels, their personal interests, their politics, and well-documented anecdotes about their public behavior and misbehavior.

What we cannot know about them—Forster's mysterious *x* factor—is where the novelist's temperament, intelligence, and inspiration can transform evidence into compelling fiction. The nature of their lovemaking, their private conversations as well as those with friends, rivals, and colleagues, events that have gone unrecorded, their inner lives and memories, in short, everything we cannot know about another human being—these are the elements of this novel that are no different from those in any other fiction.

Of course there is always that undifferentiated middle ground between evidence and imagination where incident and character and dialogue must be invented to carry the characters and the plot forward in a meaningful way. Where it is necessary to invent as a true novelist does, I've not been shy. In these instances, readers will have to determine the degree of truthfulness for themselves. That's the fun of the fictional biography—actually, I prefer to call it the novel of conjecture—both in the making and in the reading.

My "evidence" has been gathered assiduously from the same sources a scholarly biographer would have explored. I have read and seen all the novels, plays and screenplays, memoirs, radio scripts, letters, newspaper pieces and cartoons, and interviews with both Hammett and Hellman. In short, it's fair to say I've been a fan of both from an early age. When the idea of writing about their relationship occurred to me, I read as many biographies of each as I could acquire. The most helpful were: William Wright, *Lillian Hellman: The Image, the Woman*; Joan Mellen, *Two Invented Lives: Hellman and Hammett*; and Richard Layman, *Shadow Man: The Life of Dashiell Hammett*. I particularly loved reading *Dashiell Hammett: Selected Letters*, edited by Richard Layman with Julie M. Rivett. Martin Grams Jr., *The Radio Adventures of Sam Spade*, gave me back my childhood.

After *Lillian & Dash* was finished and sent off to the publisher, I happened to see Wim Wenders's 1982 film, *Dashiell Hammett*, in which he imagines Hammett holed up in his San Francisco apartment writing *The Maltese Falcon* while at the same time trying to solve the murder of a local prostitute and drinking himself nightly into oblivion. Good movie, and good to know that Wenders and I shared the same appreciation.

I promised myself in this note not to make a two-column list of facts and fictions, of true and false. But I very much want the reader to know that Dashiell Hammett really is buried in Arlington National Cemetery in section 12, site 508. Like Lillian, I too loved and admired him in spite of himself, and would very much like you to visit the site when you're in the neighborhood.

After a long writing career I've come to discover that what satisfies me most is simply a good story well told. Around a dinner table someone taking liberties with the facts in order to tell an interesting and instructive tale always has my attention and admiration. I like it most when I'm the teller.

—Sam Toperoff
May 6, 2012
Champ Clavel, France

SAM TOPEROFF has published twelve books of fiction and nonfiction, including *Jimmy Dean Prepares* (Granta) and *Queen of Desire* (Harper Collins). His stories and articles have appeared in the *Atlantic Monthly, Harper's, Granta, New York Times Magazine, Town & Country,* and *Sports Illustrated.* He was awarded an Emmy for his documentary work at PBS. He lives in France, in a house he built.